In and Out of Time

Jini Liljeqvist

A catalogue record for this book is available from the National Library of Australia

For my beautiful boys,
Simon and Sam

"In Einstein's equation, time is a river. It speeds up, meanders, and slows down. The new wrinkle is that it can have whirlpools and fork into two rivers. So, if the river of time can be bent into a pretzel, create whirlpools and fork into two rivers, then time travel cannot be ruled out."

Michio Kaku

Chapter 1

8.45 p.m., Tuesday, 14 January, 1992

If anyone had been looking into the shadows at that precise moment, if they'd been able to discern dark mass from empty dimness, they might have seen her transition. As it was, no one was looking – when she edged to the boundaries of the shadow cast by the unlit building and craned her neck to carefully scan the street, she faced an empty intersection.

Letting out a short, sharp breath, she flexed her shoulders to shift the tension.

Further down the street opposite, lights from the Chinese restaurant spilled warmly over the footpath. She could hear the muffled buzz of celebration – but here it was quiet. Here, there was only the eerie emptiness that fills commercial thoroughfares at night. All shadows. Some possibly occupied, as hers was.

Slowly her fingers tensed around the sledgehammer. Her heart thudded a steady collaboration – preceding her – preparing her – flooding her body with adrenaline and beating away second thoughts like a battle drum.

Her window of opportunity was closing.

Launching herself into the light, she bounded across the street in long, hard strides, a lioness to the attack. By the time she reached her target she was hot with rage. She didn't hesitate. She raised the hammer and smashed with all her strength, again and again and again in a frenzy of determined desecration.

Further up the street to the left, a man startled. He stood transfixed, unable to look away, as she shattered the automatic teller machine into oblivion.

* * *

8.52 p.m., Tuesday, 14 January, 1992

Mike and Gillian were savouring the last few mouthfuls of their desserts in their favourite restaurant; at least Gillian was – savouring the last few mouthfuls of Mike's dessert. Well, she *was* eating for two, and Ming Cha's deep fried ice cream was her ultimate treat – hot crunch through to icy cold, dribbled over with sticky spiced syrup and decorated with delicate raspberry slivers – unbeatable!

Once both bowls were scraped clean, and after an appropriate sigh of appreciation, Gillian picked up the conversation as though there'd been no interruption.

Mike beamed happily as she chattered away, his heart full. The meal had exceeded his expectations and his wife's eyes were dancing with pleasure. *He'd* done that. This anniversary dinner was definitely a ten-pointer. He smiled as he thought of the aftermath that awaited them when they got home. And she looked stunning tonight. Her rich, olive complexion, soft and flawless, was glowing in the candlelight and her curves were lush with the fullness of late pregnancy.

Gillian basked in his approval. She was enjoying their 'alone' time, happy to let the conversation meander frivolously through un-child-related topics, uninterrupted for once by their vivacious toddler. She barely allowed Mike to get a word in, but he didn't care. He was tired of speaking anyway and knew that eventually Gillian would reach the end of her words and then be ready for some unspoken communication. He grinned in anticipation and Gillian, recognising the twinkle of love and lust in his eyes, loved him for it – and kept on talking.

All too soon it was time to go. Gillian's mother would be wanting to hand back responsibility for her grandchild and go to bed.

Stretching, Gillian laid down her spoon and smiled.

'I—'

'—need to go to the toilet,' Mike finished for her, and she laughed.

'How did you guess?'

'Well, it has been at least fifteen minutes.'

'Oooh, a new record,' she cooed smugly as she hauled herself up.

Mike stood as well. 'I'll go pay. Meet you up front.'

He'd seen the host eyeing their table. Even though it was a Tuesday night, the Ming Cha was still packing them in. Again, he congratulated himself on his choice of venue and made his way to the counter.

But payment didn't go as expected.

The restaurant's credit card imprinter was having problems, transactions were cash only, and Mike didn't have enough. The cashier could only offer apologies and directions to the nearest ATM. At least it was only up the street.

'If it no good, there's another one, one street over,' the cashier promised. 'George Street. Plenty up on George Street.'

'OK, thanks. I'll just tell my wife.'

Gillian was wearing high heels in honour of the occasion and he knew she wouldn't appreciate the extra walk. He'd tell her to wait for him.

'She won't be a moment.'

'No problem,' the cashier accepted graciously and turned his attention to the next customer.

* * *

9.12 p.m., Tuesday, 14 January, 1992

It's surprising how quick and how simple it is to end a human life. Just a small slip of steel, thrust accurately. It only takes seconds.

Mike never saw them coming. Absorbed in his trans-action, he didn't notice them until it was too late and once they had surrounded him there was no escape, no way to avoid the confrontation. If it had been only the money, he would have given it to them: what's money, after all? He knew the standard security advice ... don't resist … give them what they want … keep your life. But it wasn't just the money.

They were high, salivating for a fight. They threw insults; jabbed at his chest. And when he tried to defend himself – a knife flashed.

He barely had time to register what had happened, or to worry one last time for the care of his family, before his life slipped out and seeped away between the cracks in the paving.

* * *

Saturday 10 July, 2010

Beth's eyes flashed as she slammed the printout down on the table. 'He went around the corner, to *another* ATM!'

Allan let out a deep sigh. 'I told you it wouldn't work. You can't go messing with this stuff. We agreed—'

'No. *We* didn't agree. *You* agreed! *I* didn't agree.'

She was beyond reason. Her body was as taut as the stretched string of a bow, her jaw clenched tight against any disagreement. 'It's *my* choice, not yours. *I* have to make it, not *you*. And maybe I was always supposed to? Maybe *that's* what this whole thing is about? *Me*, making *this* choice!'

Allan's shoulders sank. 'Beth … it's not working.'

'It is! I just have to figure out *how*. There's got to be a way!'

'There's not. It's time to stop. This is dangerous.'

'It's a gamble,' she countered. 'But anything worth having comes with a risk.'

'And a price.' Allan slumped back into the couch, his expression sour but no longer combative. There was no point.

Beth hesitated, but then nodded. 'And a price.'

Grabbing her bag, she left. A few seconds later Allan heard the gate open and then slam shut.

Chapter 2

7.50 a.m., Tuesday morning, January 14, 1992

Sun streamed in the windows. It was almost too intense, in spite of the Venetian blinds. Gillian was wearing sunglasses at the breakfast table as she perused the property section of the local paper.

'There's one up at Balgowlah: two bedrooms, three hundred and fifty thousand,' she said. 'It looks OK. Wanna check it out?'

Mike joined her with two cups of tea and glanced at the listing: a post-war cottage, perched precariously on a steep incline and touted optimistically as a 'first home-buyer opportunity!'

'Not bad ...' he agreed cautiously. 'I think we should wait, though.'

'But it would be *so* nice to have a *real* home. We'll be tripping over ourselves once the baby comes, and Lili needs a garden.'

Lili was playing happily with her breakfast in her highchair. She was the image of her mother with the same thick, dark curls, large brown eyes and olive complexion, but she had her father's delicate features and slim frame.

Mike agreed they needed more space. Their home was the glassed-in verandah and front room of a 1920s beach cottage that had been converted into a separate flat by closing off the connecting door and adding cooking and bathroom facilities. Cramped was a generous description. But it was cheap. And across the road was Manly Beach!

'Lili's happy with the park for now,' said Mike. 'And I'd rather get a little more saved up.'

'But Dad said he'd help with the deposit.'

'Yes, but we'd still need to handle the repayments. That'd be a stretch until I finish my training. And what if they send us to the country?'

Mike was a probationary ambulance officer with the New South Wales Ambulance Service. After training he'd be assigned a permanent position wherever the service needed him to be and that could be anywhere in the state.

But Gillian's hormones were at full pre-birth strength.

'You won't get a position for another six months. And if we're sent away we could rent the house out. It could help pay off the mortgage.'

'Honey, even if we bought a house tomorrow it would be six weeks before settlement. You'd be fresh out of hospital, trying to move house with a newborn.'

Gillian's disappointment was clear, but she didn't argue it further. It wasn't a practical plan and she knew it.

Lili splashed her hand into her bowl of porridge and shook a spray of soggy oats at the window with a joyful little giggle.

'Lili, no! That's naughty!' corrected Gillian patiently as she picked up the purpose-ready cloth. Mike moved the porridge bowl out of the way and leant back in his chair.

'How'd you like to go to the Ming Cha tonight?'

She halted mid-wipe. '*Really?*'

'It's all arranged.' He laughed. 'Your mum will babysit. Happy anniversary!'

'Oh honey, thank you! *Thank* you!' she cried, housing woes instantly forgotten. They'd agreed to play it simple this year, with the baby coming and all, and she'd accepted that – but it had been *so* long since they'd had a proper night out. She was thrilled. She bounced up and down in his arms, squealing happily, and Lili, always keen to join in with any kind of kerfuffle, banged her spoon enthusiastically against the chipped laminate tabletop in a joyous accompaniment.

* * *

September, 1996

The first time it happened, Beth was only six. She'd been staring at the photograph of an autumn landscape in West Virginia. It was bursting with colour and took up an entire page in her grandmother's enormous coffee-table book.

Beth had never seen a deciduous tree in full autumn glory before; all the local flora were evergreen. She was fascinated by the vibrant reds and yellows of the trees in Nonna's book and couldn't draw her eyes away.

When she told her mother the picture had moved, the words didn't even register and the momentous event went unnoticed.

* * *

8.56 a.m., Tuesday, 14 January, 1992

When Mike wasn't working and the weather was good, spending time at the park was a default choice. This morning the weather was off-the-charts gorgeous. They filled a thermos, packed a few essentials for Lili and crossed the road to the beachside promenade. It was already crowded; residents and visitors were making the best of the morning before the sun got too intense. Cafes were overflowing, shops were open for business, bright umbrellas staked territorial claims along the sand, and surfers jostled on the waves for the best positions.

Slathered with sunscreen, Lili lounged in her stroller, taking in the sights as her parents wheeled her along the promenade. She seemed in no hurry to escape but as soon as they passed under the old sandstone bridge that spanned the estuary and led to the park, she began to writhe and pull at her harness.

'Nearly there,' soothed Gillian, but Lili refused to be placated. She set up a squall of escalating cries for release until Gillian finally gave in and undid her restraints. Clambering free, Lili tottered happily to the lagoon with Gillian following close behind. The two of them then spent several minutes tossing pebbles and watching the ripples scatter. Mike stayed with the stroller and extricated his camera. Photography was his one indulgence. He'd been hooked ever since buying a little instamatic to record his European travels and now he had a Ricoh A-100 and his interest had broadened to special lenses and experimenting with different lighting conditions. His 'girls' were his favourite subjects and moments like this couldn't be missed. He'd bought a new roll of film to capture the last weeks of Gillian's pregnancy.

When the pebbles lost their fascination, Lili scampered up to the sandpit and Mike and Gillian found a nearby bench in the shade of a massive Norfolk pine and pulled out the thermos to enjoy some coffee while Lili threw her enthusiasm into building a sand fortress. Within seconds the sand was flying and walls began to rise.

'She's going to be unstoppable when she grows up,' Gillian laughed, stretching back against the wooden slats. 'She takes everything so seriously. You'd think she was setting out to save the world by the look on her face, and heaven help anyone who gets in her way.'

As if on cue, a small boy ran through Lili's construction, obliterating it, and she screamed an enraged protest and began to attack the child with her plastic spade.

He ran off, unperturbed, but Lili was devastated. Turning a teary face to her parents, she howled for justice; Gillian put down her coffee and went to her aid. Squatting awkwardly in the sand, she murmured comforts and initiated a reconstruction project. Soon the tears were dry and the fortress began to re-emerge from the ruins.

Definitely another photo opportunity, thought Mike.

He retrieved his camera and, adopting a look of concentration that matched his daughter's, peered through the viewfinder to choose the perfect pose. The girls were almost nose-to-nose, laughing in the sunlight, lost in the fun of the moment. Depressing the shutter, he smiled. 'Nice one!'

Beth watched from the shade of another nearby tree.

Her eyes were wide – hungry – intense. They followed Mike, scrutinising his calm, methodical movements as he worked the camera back into the case. She took in every detail: the gentleness of his fingers; their precision; the intelligence behind his eyes. She watched as his face softened, caught up in some private contemplative pleasure, and hers did too, mirroring his. She wondered what he was thinking, what had triggered that smile. Was it her? It pleased her to think it might be.

Mike put the camera in the bag at the back of the stroller, and then looked up at his family once more. In the dappled light his eyes were a vibrant china-blue.

Beth's heart clenched.

'Beautiful, darling!' he said. 'That's an excellent castle!'

Beth's attention followed his – to the sandpit – but at that same moment, Gillian looked up – and their eyes *met*.

Panic jolted through Beth. She leapt back behind the tree, scrambling for balance as she almost toppled over a group of boys who were playing there, and searched for a better place to hide. Seeing none, she sprinted instead for the nearest exit from the park.

'Stop!' yelled Gillian. '*Stop!*'

A few eyes turned but no one moved to intervene as Beth bolted down a side street towards the beach.

Mike hurried to Gillian, who gripped his arm to haul herself up. 'It was her,' she puffed. 'Over there, by the tree. The girl in the red coat! Only, she didn't have the coat on.'

Mike looked around, confused.

Gillian huffed in frustration and pointed. 'She went that way. Towards the beach. *Hurry!*'

He set off in the direction he'd been sent, but Beth was long gone. By the time he reached the beach she was nowhere to be seen. Scratching his head, he scanned the busy street. He wasn't even sure what he should be looking for. A girl *not* in a red coat?

Inside the public toilets, Beth pushed past an elderly lady and claimed the last vacant stall. Ignoring the muttered condemnations, she locked the door and vomited violently into the bowl.

Chapter 3

June, 1998

Beth was eight before she again caught the attention of adults.

She kicked at her schoolbag as she sat miserably on the little wooden bench outside her classroom where she'd been told to wait while her mother spoke with her teacher, Miss Mellander. She didn't understand the point of waiting outside. She could hear everything that was being said.

'No,' said Miss Mellander, 'her work is fine, and she's never disruptive in class. Quite the opposite. This is most unlike her.'

'Then I really don't see—'

'She punched Julia Crothers in the face,' Miss Mellander pronounced with all the serious import her training and experience had entrenched in her. 'We can't have that kind of behaviour at school.'

Beth felt sick. Humiliation burned as she picked up her schoolbag and ran all the way home. She considered running away – she certainly never wanted to go to school again and she knew her mother would be furious she'd run off without permission – but she was too old for that. Anyway, there was nowhere to run. Instead, she let herself in the back door, retreated to her bedroom and climbed into the dark safety of the top shelf of her wardrobe. She was still small enough to fit. There, she wriggled in among the boxed-up Christmas decorations, abandoned toys and hoarded baby clothes and squashed herself into a tight knot, her knees mushed up against her chest. With the door slid across, the only light came through a narrow slit where the frame didn't quite meet. Too small to see in through, and even if someone tried she'd be indistinguishable from the darkened clutter. As long as she stayed still.

The tight confines offered solace, holding her together like an artificial exoskeleton, providing boundaries to keep the pain inside her from blowing her apart. She wished she could stay there forever, but she knew discovery was inevitable. Retribution was unavoidable. Her sentence had been passed and execution approached. She could do nothing but wait for the axe to fall.

But her dire expectations were never met. When her mother returned, instead of crashing down in anger, she tapped on the wardrobe door and coaxed her out with her favourite food. She said nothing about what had happened – not the violence in the playground or her running off. Instead she was extra attentive, extra kind. She even read her an extra chapter of her favourite bedtime story. There was something vaguely disquieting about not receiving justly deserved punishment, but Beth was grateful for reprieve and happy to play along.

The strangeness continued the next day at school. Beth cringed when Julia Crothers turned up with a black eye, and her face scorched as the stares burned into her, but Miss Mellander said nothing. She even intervened when the boys tried to tease her, though mostly the other children gave her a wide berth – which was understandable considering the blackness of Julia's eye – and that was fine by Beth. She preferred to be left alone and she'd learnt her lesson. She wouldn't confide again.

When her mother drove her to a city office to speak with a scrawny, frog-like man with thick glasses, she had no idea the visit was related to the incident at school. Dr Martin talked to her in a disconcertingly invasive way that reeked of judgement. He asked her to draw pictures for him, and when she asked what of, he told her – anything she liked. But this licence was deceptive. His eyes glinted as he inspected her work and she knew she'd sealed something by her choices.

He gave her the same look when he asked her about the photographs. Even at eight years of age she could tell he had no understanding at all – just like her classmates, just like her teacher, just like her mother. Just like everyone.

'Your teacher says you hit Julia because she called you a liar,' said the toad-like doctor. 'Is that so?'

Beth chose a blue crayon and began to fill in the sky on her drawing.

The doctor tried again.

'Did Julia call you a liar?'

'Yes,' she mumbled.

'Why did she call you a liar?'

''Cause she's stupid.'

Dr Martin tried a different tack. 'Miss Mellander says you told Julia you could "go into" photographs.'

'Miss Mellander doesn't know anything.'

Dr Martin leant back in his chair and peered at her over the tops of his fingertips. 'It seems a lot of people around you don't know anything.'

Beth shrugged her shoulders and pressed harder with her blue crayon.

'Did you?' he asked. 'Did you tell your friend you could go into photographs?'

'She's not my friend.'

'Did you tell her you can go into a photograph?'

For this, he got another shrug.

'What did you mean by that?' he persisted, his eyes bulging with insistence behind the thick lenses, but Beth ignored him.

Sniffing dismissively, the doctor crossed his legs.

'Do you know how a photograph is made, Lilibeth?' he asked smoothly.

Beth looked up at him as though he were the one under scrutiny and not she. 'Yes,' she answered tartly. 'You use a lens in a camera to focus light from something onto light sensitive material. Then you use chemicals to develop it.'

'Very good,' said Dr Martin, impressed in spite of himself. 'Did they teach you that in school?'

'No.'

'Did you see it on the television?'

She ignored him.

Shifting position, the doctor leant in, resting his arms on the table between them and coming level with her face.

'And what is a photograph?'

Edging back, Beth peered at him suspiciously. 'A picture on paper. A picture of something real.'

A smirk snuck to the doctor's thin lips.

'Just a picture,' he echoed.

Beth treated that with the disdain she felt it deserved by returning her attention to colouring, starting this time on the sun.

Dr Martin leant in further.

'That's a lovely picture you're making there, Lilibeth.'

She finished the sun and selected a green crayon for the grass.

'Can you go into that picture?'

Beth glared back up at him. 'Of course not. That's silly. This isn't real. It's a drawing.'

'Oh.' He nodded. 'I see.'

She gave him a disgusted look and went back to her grass.

'But you think it's possible to go into a photograph?'

Beth paused in her colouring. It was several moments before she replied. 'No,' she said slowly. 'It's not possible.'

The doctor smiled. 'Not possible,' he repeated.

Beth remained still, staring down at her picture as the doctor waited for her response, but she gave none, so after a few more moments he continued. 'It's a lovely story though, isn't it?' he said. 'Imagination is a wonderful thing. It would make you very special if you could really step into a photograph and go exploring.'

'I didn't say I went exploring,' she snapped. 'I just look. I just look at what's in the picture, that's all.'

Immediately she regretted saying it. Shaking with frustration, shaking at the betrayal of her own intentions, she gripped her crayon even tighter and continued ferociously with the grass.

'Of course you do,' soothed Dr Martin. 'Pictures can be very interesting and very beautiful to look at. It's easy to get lost in a picture, to feel like you're really there. Just like we can get involved in a story when it's being read to us, or a piece of music when we hear it. Art is a very powerful thing. It has the power to transport us, to transform us, to … carry us away.' He paused and allowed himself a knowing smile. 'But of course, we don't really go anywhere. You know that when the teacher reads you a story, don't you, Lilibeth? It's not really happening, is it?'

'No,' she admitted reluctantly. 'But sometimes it *did* happen. Before. Some stories are about real things.'

'Yes. That's true,' agreed the doctor, unsure if he hadn't lost ground on that one. 'Some stories are about things that really happened, and photographs are *pictures* of real things and places, but they are *not* real places, are they? They are just images on pieces of paper. Flat. Two dimensional.'

Beth stared at him blankly, and Dr Martin was reminded that she was, after all, only eight years old.

'That's a lovely picture you've drawn, Lilibeth,' he said sweetly. 'You're very good at drawing. You have an artist's eye. You can see the detail. I can see you are a very creative child.'

Carefully, Beth pushed the drawing and crayons

away, as though he'd somehow defiled them with his comment, but Dr Martin was not perturbed. He smiled with calm satisfaction.

'That's enough for today, Lilibeth. I think we've made good progress.'

Regular visits followed, along with lots of annoying tests. Pills became a daily ritual, making her feel sluggish and damp in her head. But eventually she learnt what answers were required to stop the questions and what behaviour would keep her out of trouble at school. After a while the pills were abandoned and the visits to Dr Martin ceased. She was careful not to draw attention to herself to keep it that way.

* * *

July 10, 2010

Allan stepped gingerly into their bathroom. The acrid smell lingered. He flushed the toilet, knowing it would make little difference, and added some toilet cleaner to the bowl to at least mask the smell.

Worry slithered down his back and wrapped around him like a lead coat.

He thought of the album, wedged under their bed.

Maybe he should burn it? Perhaps that would—

No. She'd never forgive him.

Irritated, he turned on the bathroom fan and shut the door. He hated that album. He'd known it was trouble from the moment Beth received it, but she'd been so delighted with it. And wasn't it normal to want a few pictures of your mother?

Normal.

Yes, it was normal, but Beth wasn't.

Pulling out his phone, he tried again to reach her. Again it diverted to the message bank.

Ignoring that, he sent another SMS.

'*Call me.*'

Chapter 4

December, 2000

Beth's paternal grandmother lived in a tumbledown shack on a large property on the other side of the Great Dividing Range northwest of Sydney.

Of Irish heritage, Elizabeth O'Malley had a face like a dried apple with ageless, bright blue eyes that were sharp with cunning. Wiry and strong, she was a woman used to managing on her own, hardened from sixty-seven years of warring with an unyielding environment under a harsh, baking sun. The jut of her chin, at once defensive and combative, was as clear a 'keep-away' signal as the stripe on a redback spider. The locals whispered she was a witch. And she could be said to look like one, especially when her long grey hair whipped loose in the wind. This was an impression she did nothing to dispel. She enjoyed the apprehensive respect she got when she went into town. It amused her and left her in peace.

Beth was a little afraid of Nanna as well, at least at first, perhaps because she sensed her mother was uncomfortable with her, but also because she didn't really know her. For the first ten years of her life, Nanna O'Malley was little more than Christmas and birthday cards, unlike her mother's mother, Nonna, who'd been a constant presence until she'd died shortly before Richard came into their lives. Since then, it had been only the three of them: her mother, herself … and Richard. There were aunts and uncles and several cousins on her mother's side, and she'd got to know most of them from various family get-togethers, but they all lived in Perth. She'd met Nanna as well, visited her in hospital once, and then there was Uncle Jack's funeral, but both were awkward and stressed occasions. In the hospital she'd been ordered to sit in the corner and stay out of the way, and at the funeral Nanna O'Malley was swathed in black and Beth hadn't even seen her face. They'd never had a proper conversation. So she was not happy when her mother told her she'd be spending the summer with her grandmother while she and Richard went on a trip to Europe.

'What if she turns me into a pumpkin, or puts a curse on me?'

'Don't be silly, Lili,' said her mother as she checked the contents of her daughter's suitcase one last time.

'I'm not being silly. You said she's a witch.'

'I did not.'

'Yes, you did. I heard you telling Richard.'

Gillian sighed and zipped the suitcase shut.

'Why can't I come with you?' Beth whined.

'Because it's our honeymoon, Lili. Brides and grooms go off on honeymoons *alone*. No one goes with them.'

'But—'

'Lili, that's enough. We'll only be gone six weeks. You'll have a lovely holiday at Kimberlee. There're horses, and chickens, and sheep. You can go riding. And it will give you a chance to spend time with your grandmother. She's been asking if you could come and stay.'

'But—'

'And I *didn't* say she was a witch, I said the *locals* said she was a witch. That's completely different. That's just gossip. You mustn't—'

'But, you said—'

'Lilibeth!' Gillian had reached her limit. 'I wouldn't send you to stay with her if she was a witch, now would I? She's your grandmother. She won't turn you into a pumpkin, but *I* might if you don't get dressed quickly. We're leaving in ten minutes!'

When it came down to it, Beth didn't want to go with her mother and Richard either. He wasn't a bad person and he'd been making an effort to win her over – but she just plain didn't like him, and she resented his intrusion between her mother and herself. Not that things had been great before he arrived, and he did bring a new kind of smile to her mother's face that almost banished the sadness from her eyes, but that in itself was kind of scary. It was as though something quintessentially 'Mum' left with the sadness. Worst though, when Richard was there: she felt like she was in the way.

So no, she didn't want to go with them. And even *she* could see that her grandmother was her best option – the downside of having no friends – so grudgingly she allowed herself to be bundled onto the train to Lithgow.

She was met at the other end by her grandmother and got in her old ute for the two-hour drive to Kimberlee. Beth was tired and grumpy and her grandmother seemed to have even less desire to chat than she did, so it was a very quiet journey. Beth stared out the window, watching the miles of parched, empty countryside slip by, taking her further and further away from civilisation. How was she going to survive six weeks out here? She'd heard her grandmother didn't even have a television!

Nanna's house was at the end of a long dirt road, sectioned by several dilapidated wooden gates. Each gate needed to be opened and carefully shut after them. This became Beth's job. She counted four gates before they reached the house. She wasn't sure whether the gates were to keep something out, or to keep something in – and in her present mood she wasn't disposed to ask – but there were no locks on any of them so they'd hardly keep anything out, and, as the paddocks were empty, containing things didn't seem an option either.

The property looked even more desolate than the countryside they'd driven through to get there, but when they climbed the last hill and came around the last bend, Beth was surprised. A lush oasis awaited. Surrounding an old weatherboard house was a wild mass of vegetation. Shading the front, like the protective wings of a giant bird, were two massive gnarled figs, and at the back, a mess of willows, lily pillies, spindly palms and impossibly out of place frangipani and hibiscus tangled together in a shock of tropical vibrancy. It was as though all the life of the entire property had been sucked into one concentrated spot.

Beth's interest rose. But as they pulled up, first appraisals confirmed the house was in even worse condition than she'd anticipated. Her grandfather had died nearly twenty years ago and Nanna stayed on with her eldest son, Jack, to work the property. They'd scraped out a living, but since Jack's death Nanna kept going only because of the pension. The house and property had been steadily decaying around her. Still, she'd refused to sell up and move into town. She'd lived on Kimberlee all her life and intended to die there.

Beth's eyes narrowed in distaste as she mounted the rotting steps. The boards of the wide front verandah had fallen through in places and the peeling paint on the walls gave an equally neglected impression. She drew in her arms as she stepped into the dark entry hall, as though contact with the house might contaminate her.

'That's your room in there,' said Nanna gruffly, indicating the first doorway on the left.

Beth peered in at a large, sunlit and surprisingly fresh-smelling room, dominated by a huge, cast-iron bed with a bright pink quilt. Delicately patterned floral curtains fluttered gently at the window and brightly coloured crocheted rugs warmed the worn floorboards. A massive oak wardrobe with a matching dressing table waited for the contents of her overstuffed suitcase, which she hauled into the room and deposited with a thud. The bright colours cheered her. She was relieved that at least the inside of the house was comfortable and walked over to feel the thickness of the quilt.

'Gets cold here at night,' said her grandmother.

Beth turned to respond, but the room behind her was empty. She heard Nanna clumping down the hall towards the back of the house.

Definitely a witch, thought Beth.

After putting her things away, she went to find her grandmother. It wasn't hard to do. The house had a simple plan with two bedrooms at the front on either side of a central hall, a bathroom and a third bedroom in the middle and a kitchen and living room out the back, overlooking a fenced-in garden. The third bedroom was reached by a door from the living room. This was Nanna's bedroom.

Nanna was in the kitchen beginning on dinner. She didn't look up when Beth parted the dangly bead curtain that separated the living rooms from the hall and front bedrooms.

'Toilet's out the back,' she said, 'near the gate. I hope you like sausages?'

Fortunately, she did.

'Dinner will be ready in half an hour. Why don't you have a look at the garden and then come in and set the table. See if you can find some eggs while you're at it.'

The back garden was planted so thickly Beth couldn't see through to the other side. In its depths, she could barely see the sky. Lacing through, leading to hidden water features and rockeries, were dark tunnels of foliage with twisting gravelled paths. They crunched underfoot, sending little unseen creatures scattering – the permanent residents of the garden. They were too quick for Beth to spot, but she suspected lizards or small marsupials. She hoped, not snakes. Peeping out from under bushes or perched in unexpected nooks were dozens of miniature guardians: little china elves, chubby gnomes and cheeky-faced goblins. And suspended from low-lying branches a multitude of translucent fairies glistened in the last of the afternoon sun. The space was thick with life, seen and unseen, rich and lush.

Breathing in the cool, damp air, she couldn't decide which path to explore first. There were so many. All enticingly dim. The garden seemed to go on forever. In reality though, it was roughly the same size as the house, enclosed on three sides by a simple fence. Its size was deceptive, but its boundaries were clear. All hints of green ended at the fence. Beyond lay the Wild West: a derelict barn in a bowl of dust; two enormous water tanks, raised on shaky wooden platforms and nibbled by rust; and an ocean of brown paddocks leading to distant blue hills. Fairyland transplanted into the Wild West. And these two radically contrasting worlds, thrust incongruously together, created an excitement all their own. Beth's spirits brightened.

Trailing back through the garden, she found the chicken coop near the house. It was empty, but the chickens could be heard clucking contentedly somewhere under the shrubbery.

It took a few moments to figure out how to unlatch the nesting box, but once she did, Beth was rewarded with three large brown eggs, which she carried proudly to her grandmother. The looming weeks didn't seem quite so daunting, and they proved not to be. There was lots to learn and lots to do. Apart from the chickens, Nanna had three cows, a calf and a horse. The sheep were no longer resident. Beth soon learnt how to care for the animals and was given responsibility for feeding the chickens, collecting the eggs and cleaning out the coop. She also helped milk the cows and learnt how to ride the horse – a white stallion named Blue. He was a gentle creature, easy to ride but with some spirit. He liked to get out in the back paddocks and run, racing the kangaroos and leaping over fallen trees. All Beth had to do was hang on. When she and Blue had had enough, she just gave the horse free rein and he found the way home.

And as for Nanna, Beth found her company comfortable. Though quiet, and definitely a little strange, she never pushed or demanded anything. Her instruction was patient and encouraging, with never a hint of stress. While she seemed to rely on nuance and subtle physical clues more than actual words for communication, Beth had no difficulty understanding her. It was as though they were separate planets, orbiting each other with a connecting gravitational pull, intrinsically linked yet respectfully separate.

It was an idyllic summer for Beth and an important one. It was the summer she learnt she was not alone. About three weeks into her stay, when she was putting some washing away in Nanna's room, she noticed an old photograph on the wall. It featured a much younger Nanna with what looked like a family group, posed in front of the house. She thought she could identify her father in one of the young boys and guessed the other boy was her uncle Jack and the man her grandfather. Nanna was easy to recognise. She looked much the same except her skin had only just begun to leather and her thick grey hair was raven-black. It made the blue of her eyes even more astounding.

* * *

March, 1965

'One more,' yelled her grandfather. 'Just in case.'

'Oh, Cecil, that's enough,' said young Nanna irritably. 'I have to get that cake out of the oven.'

The boys were poking each other, losing patience with the forced inactivity. Bursting into a scrap, they raced off around the side of the house.

'Thank you, Edie,' said Nanna curtly. 'That'll do. Come on in for tea.'

She turned and headed into the house.

Grandfather shrugged apologetically and smiled at the photographer, Edie, who laughed good-naturedly and walked past Beth to link arms with him.

She was a beautiful woman; petite with golden curls and a radiant smile – the polar opposite of Nanna who was robust and dark. Edie's was a fragile beauty, polished and dainty, and she was dressed to accentuate her charms in tight-fitting pants and a bright tailored blouse with matching sandals.

Her bottom wiggled as she mounted the stairs.

Grandfather was a good-looking man as well – tall and lanky with a good-humoured tilt to his mouth and soft, wavy auburn hair. He moved with an easy grace. Opening the door, he ushered Edie inside with a smooth flourish that seemed out of step with Nanna's tight, self-contained ways.

The screen door banged shut behind them.

Left alone, Beth took in the verandah. It was new, sound and freshly painted. The corrugated iron roof was free from rust.

From somewhere out back she could hear the boys

fighting.

* * *

December, 2000

'Lili?'

Beth gasped as she came back in a rush of senses. Nanna was standing beside her, a worried look creasing her dried-apple face even further. 'What were you doing?' Nanna asked.

Beth blushed beet red.

'I—' she tried, but reared back. This was a pit too deep. She ran from the room and out into the garden, where she sought out her favourite rock and shrank back under an overhanging branch.

It was a few minutes before Nanna joined her. Saying nothing, the old woman eased herself down on an exposed jut of the rockery and placed an iron key on the rock between them. It was as long as Beth's hand, as thick as her middle finger and red with rust.

'Did you think I'd rouse on you for being in my room?' Nanna asked softly.

Beth peered out from under the foliage. 'I was just putting away your washing. Then I saw the picture.'

Nanna nodded. 'That was taken back in '65. With your grandfather and the boys. Your father was the little one.'

Beth avoided her eyes and looked instead at the rusty key.

'But you weren't just looking, were you?' asked Nanna.

It wasn't really a question.

Beth's breath caught in her chest.

'Pick it up,' said Nanna gently.

Beth knew what she was referring to. The key was lying there. Taunting her.

'Go on. I'm here,' the old woman encouraged.

Years later, Beth would long to hear those words again, with Nanna's clear, calm reassurance. *'I'm here.'* How unfair to lose such a treasured security before she ever understood its value. At that moment though, she registered only a chance to escape further interrogation – and a challenge. And she had no fear of the key. Stubbornly, she took hold of it and met Nanna's searching eyes.

The birds seemed to hush, and even the blow flies stopped pestering, as though waiting on a verdict.

Beth refused to look away, and it was eventually Nanna who broke the stalemate.

'Nothing?' she asked.

Beth heard the taint of disappointment. 'It's just a key,' she said, filling with a disturbing sense she'd somehow missed something.

'Ah yes,' said her grandmother, 'but it holds a secret. When *I* hold it, and concentrate very hard, I see my grandfather's hand locking an old oak door.'

* * *

A whole new world opened for Beth that summer. She learnt she wasn't the only one who 'saw' things. Nanna could be transported to strange places as well, but she did it through her fingers rather than through her eyes. She needed to *touch* things rather than *look* at them – and she wasn't limited to photographs. Touching any object could send her hurtling into a new world.

Like Beth, the places Nanna visited were real and in the past, but her experience was more like a misty dream than a crisp reality. She was transported through a memory associated with the object she touched and saw only scraps that were often obscured by emotion.

Beth was transported to an actual place; an intruder; an invisible observer.

'Can you shut it out?' Beth asked one morning. She was helping Nanna bake a cake. They'd spent hours sharing experiences. Nanna was no longer scary or distant – she was the font of all wisdom, the only one who *understood*.

'Mostly,' Nanna answered. 'Sometimes, though, things leap out and bite me like a black snake.'

Beth giggled. Nanna looked around at the comfortable clutter of her kitchen. 'It's easier here. Nothing I haven't touched. No surprises. But yes, mostly I have to determine to see. A bit like you and pictures.'

Beth's thoughts returned to the photograph in Nanna's bedroom. 'Who's Edie?'

In all their talk, Edie hadn't been mentioned. Nanna hadn't asked for details of what Beth had seen inside her photograph and didn't seem interested, but at the mention of Edie's name the muscles around her mouth tensed. It took a moment before she answered.

'Edie was my sister.'

Beth could sense the heaviness surrounding this topic.

'Is she dead?'

'No,' Nanna answered brusquely. 'Mind you get all the lumps out there.'

Clearly this was forbidden territory, but that only made it more tantalising. 'She was very pretty,' she offered, hoping that would get her more, but Nanna just set to fishing out a cake tin with far more clatter than required.

'Why don't you have any pictures of her?' Beth persisted.

In fact, there were few photographs of anyone in the house – Nanna said she didn't care for them. But there was at least one image of every family member – except Edie. It seemed odd there were none of her.

Nanna dropped the chosen cake tin in front of Beth and handed her the wrapper from a stick of butter to grease it. 'Because we had a falling out. She went to New Zealand and I haven't heard from her since.'

Nanna obviously wanted to close the subject. This time Beth honoured that. They finished the cake in companionable silence, but once it was placed in the oven and they were sitting out on the back verandah eating lunch, Nanna seemed to shift a little. Finishing her sandwich, she selected another and inspected it with apparent deep interest before asking quietly, 'You saw her?'

Beth looked up, taking a moment to find the thread. 'Edie?'

'Yes. Did you see her, when you …?' She let her voice trail off.

Beth swallowed the mouthful of sandwich she'd been working on. 'Yes. She was taking the picture. And then she walked past me to Grandfather—' Nanna's eyes speared into her and her mouth went dry. 'And then …

they went inside,' she faltered, wondering what she'd said to hurt Nanna. 'Sorry.'

Nanna looked away and her face softened. 'It was a long time ago,' she said. 'Nothing to worry about now.' She gave Beth her tired smile by way of a peace offering.

Beth tried another topic. 'Did my father have it too?'

'What?'

'Could he *see* things?'

'No. Not your father, or your uncle either. Just me.' Her face broke into a smile. 'And now you.'

Beth wasn't so sure it was something to be pleased about. Or whether her father would have been pleased she had it either.

'Did he know?' she asked. 'About you?'

'Oh yes. The children used to think it was fun, when they were young. But it got embarrassing when they were older. Not fun to have a witch for a mother when you're at school.'

'So … you *are* a witch?' whispered Beth. 'Am *I*?'

Nanna laughed. 'No, no. I'm not a witch. That's something you choose. I didn't choose this. I was born with it. And so were you. Though I'm sure they've burnt women for it in the past.' Beth's eyes widened in horror. Nanna took on a more level tone. 'Some say it's passed down through the generations, through the women. You and I aren't the only women in our family. I've heard of others. Not my mother, but my mother's mother. And there was a great-aunt. Probably others too, but I never met any of them. My grandmother died before I was born. Some people call it being psychic or having second sight. I call it a "gift".'

Beth thought about it a moment.

'I'm not sure I want it.'

Nanna's eyes sparkled. 'That's because you know it can do good ... but it can also cause trouble. You can see things other people can't ... but some things are better left *un*seen.'

Chapter 5

1.30 p.m., Tuesday afternoon, January 14, 1992

'She wasn't wearing the red coat!'

Gillian was huddled in a beanbag, nursing a cup of tea. Lili was finally down for her nap and lunch had been cleared away. They'd spent most of the morning discussing this.

'It was *her!* I'd know her anywhere – but why wasn't she wearing her coat?'

'It *is* summer,' said Mike. He was slouched into the other beanbag, the twin of Gillian's that completed their 'lounge suite'.

'She was wearing it at the mall! It was hotter then than today. And she wore it to the wedding!'

'Gilly, honey—'

Gillian thrust the photo album across the floor towards him. It was their wedding album, open at pictures of the reception in the garden of a hotel in the Blue Mountains. Standing on the hotel verandah, almost shielded from sight, was a slim, dark-haired girl in a long red winter coat.

'It's her,' said Gillian fiercely. 'That's the same girl.'

'Honey, how could it be the same girl? That doesn't make sense.'

'But, it *was* her!'

'It may have *looked* like her, but lots of people look like someone else. It's just coincidence,' said Mike.

'Then what was she doing in the mall, and at the park? And what about the *other* times?'

Mike shook his head. 'That was a long time ago. You were only a little girl. Maybe whoever it was was wearing red and you've just mixed the two together.'

'*Eight*. If that's the case, I'm mixing *eight* times together, not *two*. I've seen her at least eight times!'

'Honey—'

'I have! At *least* eight times: twice at the beach, all those school photos, our wedding, the mall, this morning – and that's just the ones I've *noticed*. How many times was she there and I *didn't* notice her?'

'Gilly, be reasonable. It can't be the same person.'

'I'm not insane. And I'm not mixing things up. It was *her!*'

Mike raked his hands back through his hair. 'Yeah, well, if you see her again, we'll just have to be quicker.'

That wasn't in any way a satisfactory course of action for Gillian – 'There must be a way to identify her,' she said. 'There's got to be some way to find out who she is and why she's doing this. Maybe I could go to the police? Maybe they have records. I mean, she might be doing this to someone else.'

Mike had had enough. 'Maybe she's a ghost?' he offered. 'Maybe we should go to Ghostbusters?'

Gillian tossed him an irritated glare, but then she stopped to think.

Was that possible?

Seeing the thoughts flit through his wife's mind, Mike burst into a peal of laughter. 'Oh, honey, come on.'

'No. I'm serious. This is seriously strange.'

'And so am I. Serious, that is. Honey, this isn't good. The doctor said you should take it easy. You don't need this now, all this stress. It's not good for you, or the baby.'

'I'm not stressed!'

'Yes, you are. Look at you. You're in manic mode.'

He was right.

'I guess,' she sighed. 'But it *is* weird, isn't it? You've got to admit that. Even if it is a coincidence, even if the only other place I've seen her was last Wednesday and at the wedding and the others just happened to have the same red coat, why did she run in the park?'

'Well, you did yell at her,' Mike pointed out. 'And the whole park turned to look at her, like she'd just stolen a kid.'

'They did not.' Gillian giggled, realising he had a point. 'Oh well, I guess you're right. If it *was* just some weird, random coincidence, I guess I might have looked a bit scary …'

'You can be very frightening, honey,' agreed Mike.

'She did look just like her though … I'd swear they were all the same girl.'

'Well, I don't think she's going to hurt us, whoever she is. And however many times you've seen her, or her doppelganger, we've got other things to worry about right now.' He reached over to gently stroke her tummy. 'This is what's important now.'

Gillian placed her hands over his, and as she did, the life inside her rolled, as though it were attempting to add its opinion to the discussion. The smile danced back into her eyes.

Relieved, Mike crawled over and kissed her on the top of her head and she relaxed into his embrace. This was much better, but still, he'd feel a lot easier once the baby was born.

* * *

July 10, 2010

Beth pulled her coat close and pushed back against the cool plastic. She hitched her feet up on the seat in front of her and stared out the window of the train as it crawled out of the station and rocked down the suburban line. The winter sun was already hanging low in the sky even though it was only late afternoon and the carriage was noisy with students on their way home from private schools. But none of them sat next to her. Alone at the front of the carriage with her sunglasses on she felt almost invisible, which was just the way she wanted it. Trains were the perfect place to think – and she needed space to think, *because it hadn't worked*. Twice now she'd tried, and twice she'd failed.

Should she go back and destroy all the ATMs in the area? She could. If she was quick. She'd have at least an hour. She could look up the location of every machine

– say within a street in all directions – and take them all out. But would that stop him? Wouldn't he be just as vulnerable wandering around looking for another ATM?

She knew he would be.

Her thoughts went round and round, picking at her problem like jackals at carrion, as the stations slipped past and the city lights began to poke out of the gathering gloom.

She removed her sunglasses and returned them to her bag. Traffic was thickening. Streams of red and yellow lights nudged through the bottlenecks, inching towards escape into the back streets. They, at least, had clear destinations, thought Beth. Where was hers?

As her train reached the end of the line and the doors wheezed open for the last time, lethargy engulfed her. She made no move to exit as the students jostled out and remained seated as a seemingly endless procession of business commuters shuffled by. She even waited for the few remaining elderly passengers to wobble out onto the platform before dropping her feet to the floor.

Once out, she glanced at the Arrivals and Departures board and crossed the platform to wait for a return transit. The evening chill was numbing. Shivering, she turned her collar up and eyed the group waiting with her for the next train. Not as many as those disembarking from the out-bound trains but still substantial. Already she felt invaded. When a sharp-featured lady in a Dior suit began loudly dissecting an associate's health problems on her mobile phone, Beth moved off down the platform. But the interaction made her conscience itch over Allan's ignored SMS.

He didn't deserve that.

Chastened, she fished out her phone and sent a reply: '*Sorry. C U after work.*'

She clicked send just as the train arrived.

Chapter 6

November, 2001

Nanna O'Malley slipped from this world and into the next on the day Beth graduated from primary school. For Beth, this had the pang of pure tragedy. Her mother had arranged for her to spend the summer holidays at Kimberlee – riding wild on Blue, rummaging in the garden, taking care of the animals and spending time with the only person on the planet who understood her – and it had been ripped away from her, at the last moment, without warning: without even a chance to say goodbye.

How could such an outrage have been allowed to happen?

There were so many questions she'd been storing up for her visit.

So many things unsaid.

The funeral was a dismal affair. The only attendees

were the three of them and an ancient neighbour of Nanna's with his slack-faced daughter. It was a dry, dour service. Beth was sure Nanna would have hated it. The only relief was the graveyard itself. Nanna was buried in the same plot as her husband and elder son, in a tenderly nurtured garden adjoining the country church where the funeral was held. Beth felt sure she would have liked that. Placing a rose gently on the grave marker, she at least had a chance to say her own private goodbye while the adults gathered to thank the priest. It wasn't enough though. It didn't feel like a proper goodbye when the person she was talking to couldn't talk back.

Beth's heart ached as the little party drove out to Nanna's house to make final decisions about property. Edie had sent word from New Zealand that she didn't want any of her sister's things and there were no other relatives, so it was all up to them. Her mother had arranged for an agent to come in and handle disposal and sale, but first she wanted one last inspection.

The house held a strange sense of fullness and emptiness at the same time. Its private spaces, crowded with the hastily abandoned remnants of its owner, seemed to resist them. But Nanna was gone. The animals had all been taken away, the garden was already showing signs of neglect and the houseplants were pining.

It seemed so *wrong*.

How could something so vital, so vibrant, so intertwined with this little patch of earth, be so completely … *gone*?

A rush of panic attacked her, and she immediately set about watering everything as Gillian and Richard began a cursory tour of the house. She hauled Nanna's watering can from pot to pot, silently consoling each withered occupant as she ministered to its needs. Then she went to the back garden. Her eyes filled at the knowledge that no one would care for the plants after she'd gone. They would never survive. They'd be taken by the bush – unnatural extraordinary would revert to natural ordinary – and there was nothing she could do to prevent it.

With a heavy heart Beth climbed the back stairs to find her mother and Richard having a cup of tea at Nanna's kitchen table.

'I like the tea set,' her mother was saying to Richard. 'I think Beth and Cecil got that for their wedding, but she didn't use it much. I remember Mike telling me that the china cabinet was strictly off limits. She wanted to keep a good set, for guests, but I don't think she ever had guests good enough for the tea set. Oh, hello, darling.' Her mother smiled. 'Would you like a cup of tea? It's just made. And there are biscuits too. We might as well eat those.'

The casual invitation grated. It didn't feel right that her mother should offer something that wasn't hers – but she knew that whatever food they left behind was destined for the bin. Perhaps that was an even greater violation? Nanna hated waste.

Ignoring the offered precious bone-china teacup, Beth retrieved her Nanna's favourite everyday mug and poured herself tea.

Gillian smiled kindly. 'You can take that if you like. Was it special to you?'

'It was Nanna's mug.' Beth shrugged.

'If there's anything you'd like, just say. It'll only be

thrown away otherwise.'

Gillian meant it as a kindness, but Beth bristled with resentment. How could they think of throwing away anything of Nanna's? She looked around the room, cluttered with so many of Nanna's possessions, each of them holding a piece of her.

If only she was able to reach people through their things the way Nanna had.

Her face settled into a scowl as the hurt bubbled in her chest, but then she saw the rusted key on the kitchen sideboard. 'I want that key,' she blurted, and Gillian's eyebrows rose in surprise. 'And the geranium,' Beth added, pointing to a potted plant on the kitchen windowsill. 'It was Nanna's favourite.'

'OK, Lili. That's no problem. Let us know if you want anything else. There're a few pieces of jewellery in the bedroom, nothing valuable, except perhaps her wedding ring. Oh, and we're going to take that quilt in the front room and a few of the rugs. And what about that sheet set, Richard?'

'No, I draw the line at used bedding.'

'But she had some nice—'

'I don't want Beth's old sheets!'

It seemed strange hearing Nanna being called 'Beth', as though she was something other than 'Nanna', but of course she had a christened name as well: Elizabeth. Beth filled with pride at the thought of having been named after her. She would have preferred Elizabeth to Lilibeth, but at least they shared the 'Beth' bit.

'Oh, Lili, I nearly forgot. Nanna left something specially for you.'

Her mother went to Nanna's room and came out

with the framed photograph of the house.

'When I spoke to her on the telephone a couple of weeks ago to organise your coming here, Nanna said that when she died she wanted you to have this.' Gillian handed Beth the photograph. 'I didn't ask her why. I mean it seemed a strange thing to be talking about – and then I just forgot about it.' She hesitated at the flick of devastation on her daughter's face. 'Sorry, love,' she said, reaching a tender hand to her shoulder. 'She was very fond of you.'

Beth's fingers shook as she stared down at the yellowing image. Nanna *knew*, she realised. She *knew* she was going to die, *and she wanted her to have a way of seeing her again.* Tears stung into her eyes, and Richard gave an embarrassed little cough.

'Well, we'd better get started if we want to get back to the hotel by dinner time.'

He scraped his chair against the wooden floor as he stood.

Gillian finished off her tea and put the cups near the sink.

'Take your time, honey,' she said, before following her husband into her mother-in-law's bedroom.

Two hours later the little group drove back down the dirt road. Although Richard insisted there was no need, Beth shut each of the gates carefully behind them. It seemed disrespectful not to. Gillian was happy to support her in that. It was such a little thing, but she knew little things could be important in times like these and it did seem to lighten Beth's mood.

Once the final gate was secured, Beth relaxed a little. The car was full of treasures, including a collection of elves, fairies and gnomes and two other houseplants. She was pleased she'd rescued these at least. Even if she couldn't reach her Nanna through them, they'd hold her memory. She'd treasure them and keep them close. But the most important thing she'd brought away with her, besides Nanna's picture, was a decision.

'I want to be called Beth from now on,' she declared.

Gillian started in surprise. She turned around to see the serious intent on her little girl's face.

'You want to be called *Beth?*'

'Yes.'

'Well, we can talk about ...'

But Beth was not seeking permission. She looked back out the window; as far as she was concerned the conversation was over.

Gillian stole a glance at Richard, who shrugged, not overly concerned one way or the other, but it was harder for Gillian to accept. Lili had always been Lili to her, Lili to her Gilly. It seemed like a rejection of her personally, not just of the name she'd chosen – but she saw Lili was determined. And perhaps it was just a passing, and certainly touching, nod to her grandmother? Lili might change her mind in a few days' time. So, she let it go.

But Beth remained solid in her intention. She crossed out the name Lili in all her books and wrote in 'Beth'; labelled her new high school uniforms with a 'B' instead of an 'L'; and patiently corrected her mother whenever she 'slipped'.

Beth had come to stay, and soon *Lili* was forgotten.

* * *

6.00 p.m., Tuesday evening, January 14, 1992

Twilight brought a magical calm to the beach opposite Gillian and Mike's house. Locals and tourists alike had retreated to prepare their evening meals, and only a few joggers and dog walkers still trailed along the promenade. The dusky light, softening the detail and muting the colours, intensified the warm orange of the sinking sun, creating an awe-inspiring panorama.

Mike couldn't resist. The play of the light on the waves was amazing. He grabbed his camera to take one last photograph while Gillian prepared Lilibeth for Nonna's. He walked out to the kerb in front of their house, focused his camera and waited for a clean shot between the cars.

'Got it!' he cried, happy with the shot even though he suspected it might be a shade too dark. It would be beautiful if it *did* work. Flushed with pleasure, he lingered, revelling in the deepening colours.

On the other side of the road, Beth stood watching him.

She was in his direct line of sight, but he did not see her.

When he headed back to the house, she waited until he reached his front door and then followed. She darted across the road and slipped into their tiny bricked-in yard. The wall was only a little higher than her knees and the yard no wider than three swift steps. A narrow path led from the gate to the front door, but Beth avoided this and walked straight to the window. Through the venetian blinds she could see her mother filling a large squashy bag with baby necessities. For her younger self, presumably. She looked so beautiful, dressed in a soft green gown that lit her complexion and flattered the curves of her full belly. Her face glowed with happiness.

So young and full of life.

Full of her un-born, never to be born, child …

Beth's chest began to tighten.

She was so close. If the window hadn't been there, she could've reached out and touched her … but an un-crossable abyss seared between them now, not just a window.

'I'm so sorry, Mum,' she whispered, her throat aching with regret, and pulled back out of the photograph.

Chapter 7

June, 2003

'But you could find out. Once and for all.'

Allan's eyes glowed a rich, deep green. Sometimes they were blue or even amber, depending on the light. He said they were hazel, but Beth didn't think they could be limited to just one colour. They were *all* colours. Right now though, she was oblivious to their charms, annoyed at being pushed.

'What makes you think I'd see anything that hasn't already been seen? There were hundreds of people watching that day.'

'But they didn't know where to look! Aw, please, Beth. Come on. Don't you want to know too?'

'What difference is it gunna make?'

'It's the mystery of the century – and we'd know what happened!

'But it won't change anything.'

'Well … not that. No … but, we might be able to prove—'

'No!' The ferocity of her rebuke stopped him mid-sentence. 'No, I don't want to *prove* it to anyone. I don't want anyone else digging into my life.'

Allan slumped back against the brick wall of the school toilet block and stared up at the sky. 'Then, it'd just be for us,' he grumbled. 'It'd still be good to *know* …'

Beth's lips thinned, pinching her face into a dark scowl – but she couldn't stay mad at him for long. Letting go of her annoyance, she reached over and slipped her hand into his – and he surrendered his tension as well and gave her fingers a reassuring squeeze. He loved those fingers. They were so fine and delicate compared to his own. All of her was fine and delicate. Like a butterfly. But she could hold her own. She was really more like a wasp than a butterfly. And the prettiness of her face was tempered by the wildness of her hair; thick and almost black, it tumbled defiantly about her determined shoulders.

The first time Allan looked into those eyes was when they were herded into the assembly hall, nervous year sevens, almost a year and a half ago. In an instant he was smitten. But Beth rebuffed him at every approach, seeming not to hear him when he tried to talk to her and looking at him with dull disinterest if he did get her attention. At least she wasn't interested in anybody else – but it hurt that she cared nothing for him. He certainly cared for her. He couldn't shake it. Thoughts of her consumed him. It took all his discipline to keep his eyes from searching for her and his face from blushing in her presence. Having her so close yet so unreachable filled his first year of high school with awkwardness and swamping insecurity, but then his luck suddenly changed. They were paired on a class project – mainly because no one else wanted them, at least that's how Allan figured it – but regardless, it gave them time together and, though she greeted him with a withering glare when he first moved his books to her desk, she slowly thawed. In spite of their bumpy start, they worked well together. Allan was careful, plodding and pedantic, and Beth provided erratic but often inspirational direction. They balanced each other.

Allan was in heaven. Beth enjoyed the arrangement as well, happy just to have someone who'd work with her ideas and turn them into classroom-acceptable material without invading her space – but their conversation was always project-focused and never personal. Beth paid Allan no attention at all unless they were working together. And that didn't look like changing – until Beth used Richard's credit card to buy tickets to see Raven, a hot American boy band touring Australia.

She hadn't planned it. She didn't even like Raven. And if she had, she could have gone to a concert through a photograph instead of a ticket – she'd been practising and was now able to stay 'in world' for up to an hour; plenty of time for a concert; she'd visited hundreds – but collecting experiences she could never share was a lonely obsession. She felt cut off from those around her, as though she were looking at them through a window, an invisible observer as she was in photographs, a *half-there* person. Her classmates ignored her, excluding her from the gossip, the jokes and the fun, and even the teachers didn't seem to notice if she was there or not.

She told herself she didn't care, but the lie was becoming harder to believe. A deep longing to become part of a group of friends gnawed at her, any kind of friends, appreciated and accepted, one of the pack. So when three of the cooler girls in her class – Stacey Adams, Rebecca Sweet and Ambrosia Mackleray – drooled over Raven's lead singer, Beth found herself blurting out that she could get tickets to the group's concert.

It was a pity, she'd reflected later, that she wasn't able to go back and change things in the past, instead of just observing them. Her rash statement earned her immediate popularity, but also the need to come up with tickets. And what other way was there to do that than with Richard's credit card? It wasn't hard to get. Richard always left his wallet on the key table near the door with his sunglasses. It needed no planning; and it left no time for second thoughts.

Stupid. It had been stupid. The concert was a let-down: Stacey, Rebecca and Ambrosia ignored her from the moment they gained entry to the venue and the next day at school she was back to being invisible. All she'd achieved were the consequences of the credit card theft – and these couldn't be avoided. Richard opened the statement at the breakfast table two weeks after the concert and her actions were exposed. Richard was furious; her mother was horrified, and worse – disappointed.

Beth could offer no explanation.

Fortunately, she was late for school and, as no one had time to take her if she missed the bus, she was able to escape immediate confrontation and storm from the house with nothing more than dark threats of 'sorting this out tonight' ringing in her ears.

She was in the foulest mood when she arrived at school. Her classmates gave her an even wider berth than usual, and she spent lunch in detention for back-chatting a teacher.

Allan was at a loss. They'd arranged to spend lunch together to work on their project and when she didn't show up he went looking for her and learnt about her detention. He wasn't sure what to do next. He tried to talk to her after class but she hurried off. It wasn't as though they *needed* to get together to work on the project – they were well ahead of schedule – so in the end he thought it best not to push it. At the core, he decided, he was a coward. So, after school he went straight to the library, but as he got to work, a stormy-faced Beth thumped her schoolbag down on the desk beside him. With no preliminaries, she pulled up a chair and began to pour out her heart. Promoted in a moment from study-partner to confidant, Allan was exhilarated. He proved a good listener, nodding with sympathy as she told him of the disaster she'd brought upon herself and showing no reproach. He remained calm and level in the storm of her distress. And she *was* distressed. She saw her situation as completely hopeless.

'Couldn't you just … offer to pay it back?' Allan suggested cautiously.

She looked at him in outraged disbelief. 'That won't make any difference. Richard will never forget this. He'll never forgive me. He's like an elephant. He never forgets *anything.* He's still mad at me for losing my excursion money once in year six! That's nothing compared to this.'

'Well, maybe not … but if you just say you're sorry,

and pay the money—'

She shook her head angrily. 'He won't care. He's never gunna trust me again. He'll want to ground me for the rest of high school!'

'What about your mum?'

'She won't go against Richard.' Despairing, she stared down at the table. Allan reached over and laid his hand on hers in awkward reassurance. To his relief, she didn't pull away. Instead, she let out a deep sigh. 'I guess all I can do is run away.'

Allan blanched. 'No. No, you can't do that,' he blurted, a little stronger than he meant to, and then blushed. 'I mean … that's not … I mean, you can't … it's just not a good idea.' She stared at him, confused, and he was forced to find better words to hide behind. 'It's just no good,' he stumbled, 'being on your own … out there … trying to survive by yourself with no help. I mean, where would you go?'

Beth's expression took on a defensive edge. 'I'd be all right. I can take care of myself.'

'Well, I know that, but … I … I just meant … that it's not a …' but he saw he was not getting through to her. 'And your parents. They'll get over it. It's probably not as bad as you think.'

Her countenance chilled. 'It *is* that bad. They don't want me there anyway. Richard doesn't want me. He's just waiting for me to grow up so he can kick me out. And I'm grown-up enough already.'

'But … but, what about school?'

She was momentarily thrown, but then with equal swiftness she brightened. 'Could I come to your place?'

Allan's heart froze in his chest.

'Just for tonight,' she said, seeing his obvious resistance but gaining enthusiasm anyway. 'I could stay in your garage. You don't need to tell your parents. I'll be quiet. They won't know I'm there.'

Allan's mouth dropped open, but he wasn't able to force out any comprehensible words.

'It'll give me time to figure out what to do,' she pleaded. 'I can't go home. *Please*, Allan.'

'I ... It's not ... right, Beth,' he said weakly. 'It's not—'

And he saw his newfound relationship shredding to pieces.

'Never mind,' she snapped, tears forming in her eyes as she grabbed her bag and almost sprinted for the door.

Allan was hurled into desperate action. He picked up his bag and raced after her, catching up with her in the car park.

'Beth, wait!'

She stopped and turned to face him, her eyes hard.

No help there.

'I didn't mean you *couldn't* stay,' he said. 'It's just that I ... my home ... my parents ...'

He just couldn't get the words out. They were way too big.

Beth huffed. 'You don't have to explain,' she said. 'I'll be all right. You don't need to worry.'

'No ... Beth—'

'Forget it, Allan!'

Again, she spun away. Allan had no choice. He dropped all his safety nets and threw himself into the abyss.

'No,' he said, with a strength of command that surprised even himself, and when she paused, he ran to her side and gruffly took hold of her hand. 'Come on.'

Giving her no time to object, he steered her across the car park to a block of flats opposite. The lobby was dark, but a light flickered on when he pushed the heavy glass door open. It stayed on as they climbed a grimy set of stairs to the second floor where Allan thumped another light switch and continued up, pushing other light switches as they progressed all the way to the sixth floor. There, he fished out a key and opened a door at the end of the passage.

The flat inside was dark, but Allan didn't turn on the light. Instead, he worked his way down the darkened hall towards the kitchen, where he struck a match and lit a spirit lamp.

'What's wrong with the lights?' Beth asked.

'No power.'

'No power? Why not?'

'I didn't pay the bill, and it got cut off.' He watched Beth's face as she sought to make sense of that.

'But ... why don't ... your parents ...'

'Don't have parents. Never had a dad, and my mum's dead.'

Beth's eyes widened in surprise.

'Want something to eat?' he asked. 'I've got bread, peanut butter, margarine, jam, chips?'

Beth looked around at the lamp-lit room. It was tidy and clean.

'I've got cereal,' he said brightly, 'but it's too hot to keep the milk. I could buy some though. Or I can heat up some baked beans. I've got a camp cooker.'

His grin was infectious and Beth burst out in a giggle

– but quickly sobered as the implications of his revelations sank in. 'You mean you live here by yourself? Isn't there anyone who can take care of you? Wouldn't the government—?'

'They'd stick me in a foster home.' The lines of his young face hardened in the flickering light.

'But … but … how …?'

'Peanut butter sandwich?' he offered.

At a loss, Beth nodded, and Allan set about making them sandwiches, chatting calmly as he worked.

'It's not so hard. Mum died last year. It happened down in Melbourne. Her friend called me. Drug overdose. She'd been down there nearly a year anyway, so I knew how to take care of myself. I do OK.'

'But, if she's dead … why didn't Centrelink—?'

'I didn't tell them, did I? They still think she's alive. She used another name in Melbourne, and we had it set up here so they'd leave me alone. I can forge her signature. It's easy to play them.'

Beth watched the proud curve of the back of his neck as he worked on their supper, her surprised respect for him soaring him into super-hero status.

'I'll need more kero soon,' he said conversationally.

Beth looked over at the lamp. 'How do you pay for stuff? Where do you get money, for everything?'

'This is public housing – the rent comes out of Mum's account once her pension and stuff goes in. I pay bills at the post office. She left me her bank card too.'

He put the sandwiches on two little plates, handed one to Beth, grabbed the lantern and led the way into the living room. It, too, was clean and tidy and looked comfortable in the glow of the lamp, even though the furniture was old and mismatched.

'Looks better in daylight,' he said cheerfully, 'but I just go to bed when it's dark, and I don't come home until the library shuts.'

He plopped down into a pile of pillows that padded out an old chair, offering her the obviously nicer and only other seating option: an old leather recliner.

'The lever works,' he informed. 'Just pull and the footstool comes out.'

She did, and it did. She wriggled back into the squashy softness, laughing.

'Nice!' she approved, and Allan smiled proudly.

After a few moments of companionable silence, while they wolfed down their sandwiches, Beth glanced at Allan curiously. 'Don't you get lonely?'

'Nah. I'm at school all day, and then the library. And I work on Saturdays.'

'You're too young!'

'They think I'm fifteen.' He leant back cockily in his chair. 'I look it, don't you think?'

She had to admit he did. Not physically – he was skinny to the point of scrawny and not much taller than she was. In his school uniform he actually looked younger than most of the other boys his age, his slender body still waiting for its growth spurt – but his eyes were old. Much older than his years. And the confident tilt of his chin gave an assurance of maturity.

Yes, she could understand how he got away with it.

'What about school?' she asked. 'Parent nights, and stuff.'

'Mum gets sick. A *lot*.' He grinned. 'When she's not working, that is. Her signature's no problem, and I even got away with imitating her voice once. As long as my marks are OK and I don't cause any trouble they don't care about seeing her.'

'Wow.'

Beth was awed. Allan's ability to keep a secret out-stripped hers, and he did it so well, so calmly and so competently.

'Look,' Allan took on a more serious tone. 'I don't have much, but I get by, and you can stay here, if you want. I never meant you couldn't. I can take care of me, and I can take care of you too … it's just that—' his confidence slipped a little '—you'd probably be better off with your parents.' Inadequacy flickered around the corners of his mouth. 'No hot water, no TV.' Suddenly he looked many years younger. 'And I'm not sure if your parents would let you stay here. They'd come get you for sure. You'd have to hide.'

Beth had no difficulty seeing where this would lead. 'And if they found me here, *you'd* be in trouble. People would find out about … all this,' she finished the sentence for him.

'I didn't mean that,' Allan rushed to object. 'I don't care—'

'*They* would though, and I *do* care. I'm not going to ruin this for you.'

'Beth—'

'No. It's OK.' She smiled. 'You're right. I can go home and sort this out, and that's what I *should* do. It was dumb of me to have taken the money in the first place, and I deserve to get into trouble. But you don't. And I couldn't stand it if you got found out because of me and they took you away.'

She pushed herself up out of the deep chair and stood, facing him. 'I'd better go home. They'll be calling the police soon if I don't show up.'

'I'll come with you.'

She didn't object. She was as reluctant as he was to break the new, but oddly comfortable, intimacy that had woven between them. Instead of taking the bus they walked the five kilometres to her house, just to give them a little extra time together, and as Allan talked, sharing his secrets and survival strategies in his calm quiet voice, her difficulties with Richard shrank into proportion. His strength seemed to infuse into her. And quite without her expecting it, the thought of ever losing his friendship became something painful.

'Maybe, in a couple of years' time, when it's no longer illegal, I can come back and stay with you,' she suggested shyly as they stood in the shadows of the carport at her house.

Allan smiled.

'I'd like that.'

'And, if they let me out of the house tomorrow,' she said, 'I'll bring an extra sandwich for you for lunch.'

He grinned; and that began a collaboration that lasted for the rest of their school years. Beth supplied him with home-packed lunches and a multitude of other smuggled necessities and he provided her with a social life. She became the trusted keeper of his secret, his one and only confidant – and after another six months, he became the keeper of hers.

Chapter 8

January, 1961

The steamy heat of the day had not yet abated but the mosquitoes were already out in force. The adults swatted at them, laughing together over pre-dinner drinks as they got the evening meal under way.

Gillian's dad, Uncle Bill and her cousin Robert hovered over the barbeque, poking and prodding at the fire as they argued with good-natured gusto over fire-starting techniques. Smoke billowed up in their faces as Robert puffed enthusiastically on the embers – he was the eldest of the cousins and proud to be allowed to help. He blew with all his might as his father and uncle coughed and wiped their watering eyes.

Gillian's grandfather chuckled from his folding camp chair. Lean and leathered with patchy tufts of white hair, his broad shoulders had collapsed under the weight of

the years and his muddy blue eyes didn't always sparkle, but his wide gentle mouth revealed good humour.
His wife was the mirror opposite. Plump, with hydran-
gea-blue permed hair and over-rouged cheeks, she was
by nature dyspeptic. Clearly not in the camping spirit,
she sat sourly under an unnecessary rug.

'Smile,' called Gillian's mother, her camera aimed at
the men.

In her early thirties, Gina was in her prime. Curva-
ceous, with dark Mediterranean colouring, she was an
exotic beauty. The men cooperated without complaint,
proudly holding up barely singed sausages on their long
forks.

'Thank you,' said Gina, rewarding them with a smile.
Her voice was like warm honey, the foreign intonation
increasing its seductive quality. The men glowed in her
approval, even Robert. Gina laughed and turned to take
a snap of her sisters-in-law who were fussing with salads
and buttering bread.

'Isn't it getting too dark for that?' criticised Gillian's
grandmother.

'Nothing lost if it doesn't turn out,' said Gina sweetly.

'Except the film,' returned the old woman tartly.

Gina swallowed her retort and carried the camera
back to one of the canvas tents.

'I want a copy if they turn out, Gina,' called out
Auntie Barbara, a leggy red-head who sat cross-legged
on a tartan blanket buttering bread. An in-law like Gina,
Barbara had a fiery temper and delighted in siding with
her sister-in-law against their autocratically English
mother-in-law.

'No problem,' called Gina from the tent.

'Do you think that's enough? Or should I put in another tomato?' asked the youngest of the women, Auntie Margaret, who was mixing the salad on the blanket next to Barbara. She was the image of her brothers in female form, slender and pale with broad, good-natured features.

'Definitely. At least one more, possibly two,' cut in Barbara before her mother-in-law could interject. It was a game they played, manoeuvring for control; and often Margaret was in the middle. She reached for another tomato as Gina re-joined the group with the makings for potato salad.

'Gaby, you're getting it all over the sausages!' yelled Gillian's father.

Gillian's elder sister, Gabrielle, had control of the Aerogard and clouds of insecticide misted the air as she sprayed everything that moved.

'That's enough, Gaby!' ordered Gina. 'You're killing Grandpa.' The old man was indeed turning a nasty shade of puce as he tried to fight the engulfing fumes. 'Go and help your cousins get more kindling.'

Puffing out her bottom lip in protest, Gaby tossed the Aerogard onto the picnic blanket and left to join her cousins in the surrounding trees. The boys were attacking a large dead branch, smashing it into smaller pieces for the younger ones to gather into a pile. Gaby felt a little above that, but soon found satisfaction in ordering them about.

Gillian wasn't interested in sticks. She was gathering shells on the beach. It was only a small beach compared to the vast Sydney ones, but away from the city clamour and shared with only a few other holidaying families, it seemed spacious. Gillian had already collected half a bucket of shells: round smooth yellow ones; stripy, swirly cone-shaped ones; pink fan-shaped ones and lots of little bumpy turban-shaped ones. Beautiful shells. Each unique in shape or colour. Some still had remnants of their inhabitants in them and would be discarded as they began to smell, and others would be replaced by even more beautiful ones when they were found, but most would be brought home with her after their holiday. The best ones would be fixed in putty to decorate jars or threaded on string to make necklaces for birthday and Christmas presents. Gillian was pleased with her haul. As the sun retreated, it was becoming difficult to find good ones, but she didn't mind. The sand was warm and pleasant between her toes. She wriggled her bottom, forming a little seat for herself, and sifted the sand onto her legs, humming happily.

'What about this one?'

The soft voice startled Gillian. She turned to see a woman squatting beside her, wearing a long, bright red coat. She had short black hair, all mussed up, and in her outstretched hand was an exquisite piece of mother-of-pearl, the largest and most brilliant that Gillian had ever seen.

She hesitated only a moment before reaching for it.

'Pretty isn't it?' The woman smiled.

Gillian moved the shell to catch the remaining light, fracturing its iridescent beauty into a lustrous rainbow.

'Wow!'

'It's all yours, if you want it.'

'Really?'

The woman nodded solemnly. 'Absolutely.'

'Gillian?' Gina was calling from the campsite. Her view of the beach was obscured by a grassy mound and she couldn't see her daughter. 'Gillian!' she called again, her voice taking on an edge of threatened consequence should this second summons be ignored and Gillian bounced up over the mound.

'Here I am!'

Hands on hips, Gina relaxed. 'You shouldn't wander off like that. I thought you were with your cousins.'

Gillian held up her pail. 'I got some more shells!'

'Oh, well that's nice. But come up here and help me set the table now.'

'There isn't a table.'

'Don't be so smart! The blanket then. Come on.'

Gillian looked back at her new friend, who was still squatting behind the mound. The lady smiled and waved her away, so Gillian raced back to her mother.

'Look what the lady gave me,' she bubbled, holding up her new treasure.

'Ooh, that's beautiful, darling,' said Gina, stooping to see. 'Just look at those colours! It will make a lovely ashtray.'

'It was a present.' Gillian beamed, and Gina, finally registering, gave her a confused look.

'What lady?'

'The lady on the beach.'

They looked to the beach, but it was deserted. Gillian ran back to the mound, but the lady was definitely gone. 'Aw, she went away.'

'Well, she can't have gone far,' said Gina. 'You can find her tomorrow, but right now we need to get dinner ready.'

Obediently, Gillian slipped the shell into the pocket of her shift and trudged back over the dune.

* * *

April, 2003

Allan and Beth were in the school library, huddled together at their favourite table, hidden behind the biology section. Beth was struggling with her maths homework while Allan was working on an assignment about UFOs; he was absorbed in a photograph of a supposed UFO taken by a farmer in Ohio. His part of the desk was piled high with a cluttering of books and magazines he'd foraged from the library shelves.

They were firm friends now. Six months had passed since Beth learnt Allan's secret and they spent most of their free time together. The library was their favourite haunt. It offered privacy and peace. The only problem was the 'no food' rule, but that was easily handled. Checking no one was watching, Beth popped a grape into her mouth and then passed one under the table to Allan. Taking it absently, his eyes narrowed in dissatisfaction as he peered at his photograph.

'I bet it's a fake,' he said, chomping down on the grape. 'It looks real enough, but the guy is sus, and no one else saw it.'

Beth leant over. It was impressive, showing a shiny disc ringed by glowing lights, high in a night sky. 'Are you going to put it in your assignment?'

'It's a good photo … but this other one here is better authenticated. Lots of people saw that.'

Beth considered the other photo. 'Would you like to know if they're fake?'

'Course I would. Wouldn't you? I would've loved to have been there!'

'Mind if I have a closer look?'

'Sure, go ahead. I'm just going to photocopy this.'

He handed her the book and joined the line-up for the photocopier. There was quite a queue waiting. When he returned, Beth was back to working on her sums.

'It's fake,' she said, without looking up. 'The one you thought was sus. It's just a little model hung up against a black screen with lots of lights.'

Allan stopped in his tracks.

'But the other one could be real,' she continued. 'There was something there at least, up in the sky. I just couldn't tell what it was.'

Shyly, she glanced at him. She could see he had no idea what she was talking about, and her heart began to pound.

'I took a look,' she said softly. 'You said … you wanted to know.'

There was no way back now. Swallowing to clear the lump in her throat, she prayed he'd understand. 'I … have a kind of … gift. I can … see… things. Things from the past. I wanted to tell you, but … I … It's not easy. Most people don't understand. And it's got me into trouble before, at my last school, so I just decided to keep it a secret. But … I wanted to tell you. I was just waiting for the right moment.'

She wasn't sure if the scowl on his face was anger or hurt or just plain straight disbelief, but it didn't look encouraging.

'Are you kidding me?' he asked finally, with a wariness she'd only heard him use in classroom debates.

Her throat squeezed tight. 'No. It's the truth. I can see into the past.'

'The past? How ... how can ...?'

'I don't know. It just ... happens. When I look at a photograph, I ... kind of ... fall in. I go to where the photograph was taken, at the moment it was taken.' She trailed off, her face blazing pink. Allan's incredulous expression didn't help.

'You went into *this* photograph,' he asked slowly, 'and saw it was a *fake?*'

'You asked ...'

'You can do *time travel?*'

'I guess ...'

'Seriously?'

Beth shrugged.

Allan looked down at the photograph, and then back up at her. 'You went *there?* Really *went* there ... to when that picture was taken?'

Beth nodded, embarrassment sizzling across her cheeks, but Allan burst into a grin. 'No shit! Why didn't you tell me? This is incredible!'

'I ... thought you'd think I was a ... freak.'

'Shit, no way. This is just ... *no way!*' He was almost bouncing in his seat.

Beth hung her head, unsure of how he was re-forming her in his mind.

'Anyone else know about this?' he asked eagerly. 'How come you're not on the news? Why aren't you famous? Are you in some kind of secret program?'

The questions were tumbling out at a terrifying

speed and Beth reached out her hand to shut him up, afraid they'd attract attention. 'No. Nobody else *really* knows,' she whispered. 'I told Mum once, and some girls at my old school, but they didn't believe me. Mum took me to a shrink and he thought I was just imagining it … so I played along. It's easier that way. I can't prove it, and anyway, what good is it to anyone else? It's not so special. I just see what's in the picture, and everyone can see that.'

'But you can see *more!* You can see what's *outside* the picture as well, can't you? You saw the screen! You just exposed a scam!' His enthusiasm was unstoppable. 'That's amazing! You could expose *all* the scams.'

'No one would believe me.'

'There'd be a way to prove it. There must be. This is incredible!'

'No, it's not. It's a nightmare. It makes me a *freak*, and if you tell anyone they'll just pump me full of drugs again.'

'Beth—'

'So don't,' she begged. 'Please don't. You've got *your* secret, and I'm keeping that, so you keep *mine!*'

The ferocity of her plea deflated him, like she'd slammed a door in his face – but he could see she meant it, and that she wasn't going to be pushed. And secrecy was probably a good thing; all superheroes had to keep their powers secret … didn't they?

But he was *desperate* to know more.

'Please, Allan,' she pleaded as the bell rang. 'Don't say anything – to anyone. *Promise me!*'

'Sure … Of course.' He swallowed his frustration and tried to look understanding as she crammed her things into her bag and hurried for the door but the afternoon was shot for him. It was impossible to turn his thoughts away from this fantastic revelation.

Beth's afternoon was equally unproductive. English and history passed in a blur: her concentration was shredded. *Had she done the right thing? Would Allan betray her?*

She didn't think he would – but she knew she was asking a lot to expect him to understand. No one had ever understood – except Nanna. And even if he did, would he still want to be friends? … with a freak like her?

Frozen with apprehension, she dawdled after her last class, afraid to step out of the classroom in case he wasn't there – nervous about what to say if he was …

He *was* there.

When she appeared, he gave her his usual half-anxious smile and raised his hand in an awkward wave.

She felt immediately relieved and walked down to meet him.

'I thought of something,' he said, jumping over preliminaries and placing a small, worn photograph in her hand. It was of a woman in her late thirties, thin and drawn, but still pretty. She was at a backyard party, surrounded by other partygoers, and it was night. Her eyes and mouth were unmistakeably Allan's.

Beth looked up slowly. 'Your mother?'

He nodded, excitement dancing in his eyes. 'Who took the photograph?'

That threw her. She stared back at him stupidly, and Allan was suddenly unsure. 'You can do that, can't you? You can see who the photographer is when you …' He shrugged '… You know?'

'Yes, I can. But—'

'Then go on. Do it, and then tell me who took the photograph.' He grinned, triumphant. 'Only *I* know who did that. It's not in the picture, is it? So, if you can tell me who took the photograph it proves you went there. You see?'

'I guess,' said Beth, looking around at the mob of students still jostling for the buses. 'But, not here. Not in public.'

Allan's eyes grew large. 'Why? Are you going to disappear or something?'

That caused a sudden flush to rush to her cheeks. 'No. But I … I don't know what it … *looks* like, when I … I've never done it with anyone watching.'

Allan felt chastened by his presumption. 'Oh. Well, we could go somewhere else. Somewhere private,' he suggested gently. 'Would that be OK?'

Beth bit anxiously into her bottom lip.

'I'll make sure no one else sees,' he reassured her.

'*You'll* see though. What if I go all … weird?'

Allan reached out and swept a stray lock of hair away from her eyes. 'You'll never be weird to me, even if you grow two heads and turn green.'

That made her giggle.

She looked around for a possible place. They chose the no-man's-land behind the school toilet block. It couldn't be seen from the road or the school. Allan brushed the spiders off an abandoned milk crate that had been considerately left by the lunch-break-smokers and offered it to Beth who accepted it and sat. Holding the photograph in her lap, she relaxed and allowed it to pull her in.

* * *

December, 2000

The clamour of the party smashed into her as the bright afternoon sunlight was ripped away and replaced with sudden night. For a few seconds she was blinded. Her skin puckered into goosebumps and her ears rang with the thump of the music.

But soon these sensations eased; her pupils dilated and she adjusted to the loud noise and cooler temperature. All around her, the partygoers came into focus. They were dancing in the patchy light, drinking, laughing, smoking sickly sweet cigarettes and straining to yell scraps of conversation at each other. Large speakers, balanced in the open windows, belted out '80s hits.

They were packed into the backyard. Fortunately, Beth was in a relatively clear space, probably to allow the photographer a clear shot of Allan's mother, who was directly in front of her. She was dressed in low-cut jeans and a singlet and was dancing with her friends. As laughter lit her face, she was even more beautiful than she was in the photograph – but at the same time frailer. Especially when she tottered slightly as she tried to keep time to the beat of the music.

'Take one of us!' screeched a grating voice, way too close to Beth's ear. It pierced through her like a fire alarm. The owner was an overweight middle-aged woman in a bright purple caftan. She was wresting a gaunt younger man into what was left of the clear space next to Beth. 'Go on. Quick! Take the bloody picture,' she shouted –

and Beth turned to see who she was talking to.

It was Allan. Younger, but otherwise much the same. His face was a little fuller, a little rounder, and he wasn't quite as tall as he was now, but it was him. Obediently, he aimed his camera and blinded everyone with the flash.

'Oh for God's sake, enough of that damn camera, Allan!' chided his mother with an amused, drunken slur. Allan opened his mouth to reply, but Beth couldn't understand what he said. The words echoed strangely in her ears, and suddenly the darkness fled. With a chaotic rush the blinding light returned.

* * *

April, 2003

Gasping, she opened her eyes to look directly into Allan's.

'Well?' he prodded.

'Gimme a minute!' she said crossly, and Allan was instantly contrite.

'Are you OK?'

'Yes. I'm fine. It's just a bit of a jolt, coming back. I need a second to get my breath.'

'Really?'

He was all set to grill her about that, but she circumvented his questions by handing him back his photograph.

'It was you. You were the photographer. You were a couple of years younger than you are now … maybe ten? Or eleven? Your hair was longer, and you were wearing a dark coloured hoodie and jeans.'

'Hah! I'd forgotten that.'

Beth leant back against the brick wall of the toilet block.

'Wow, this is awesome!' he enthused. 'Fully sick! You really did it, Beth. You're a *time traveller! Awesome!*'

But Beth couldn't quite share his excitement. She felt instead suddenly sad. 'Your mum was really pretty,' she said, shutting her eyes against a wave of exhaustion.

'Sick!' whispered Allan, unable to think of a more appropriate a comment. His tummy began to churn with painful thoughts of his mother and exhilaration at Beth's powers all mixed together. 'Sick,' he repeated, and looked back at Beth. Her skin had taken on a yellowish pallor. 'You sure you're OK?'

'Yeah, it's just tiring.' She rolled her head to smile at him. 'So, you don't think I'm a freak?'

'No way. No *damn* way.' He beamed up at the sky.

Impulsively, he jumped up and launched into a funny little dance. Beth couldn't help laughing.

Perhaps her gift wasn't *all* bad.

* * *

July, 2010

Allan shuddered at the dark emptiness that greeted him when he opened the door to their flat.

She wasn't home.

The sickly sweet residue of unvented toilet cleaner stung his nose as he hung his keys on the hook by the door and switched on the light.

At first he missed her. He didn't see her hunched on

the floor in the far corner of the room, her knees clasped to her chest, her eyes fixed sadly on him. When he saw her, his heart leapt in relief.

'Sorry,' said Beth softly, and Allan didn't hesitate. He went to her and wrapped his arms around her, pulling her close. She curled unresisting into his chest as a tear slid down her cheek.

'It's OK, Beth, it's going to be OK.' She was so cold. Her fingers were white. The soft foresty fragrance of her hair wafted over him, making him ache. 'Some things you just can't change,' he said, 'and that's life. We have to accept it. We all have to do that, Beth. It's just part of being human.'

A little sob muffled into his chest and he held her tighter, rocking her tenderly as she fought her tears and lost. They broke through in cramping spasms, convulsing through her slender frame – and there was nothing he could do but hold her, nothing he could give her but his warmth. Silently, he prayed it would be enough … and eventually she calmed and her body stilled.

Stroking her back gently, he waited – and after a few minutes, sniffing deeply, she wiped her face against her sleeve and reached her small hand up to his.

'It's different when you can change things though,' she said, her voice still a little gluggy from the tears. 'And I can.'

Allan felt the ice gush into his stomach as she pushed herself from his chest to face him. Her eyes were puffy and red, but in their depths was a steady resolve.

'It's different if you don't have a choice, because then all you've got is acceptance. There isn't any other way. But I do have a choice. I can change things. I can change things that other people can't.'

'But you shouldn't.'

'But I *can*,' she said, 'and that changes the rules.'

'No. No, Beth. Life ends. It has to.'

She shook her head. 'It didn't have to end *then*.'

'Didn't it?'

'No. No, it didn't. It didn't have to end then, and there's a way to change that. I just have to find it. I'm *supposed* to find it. And I *will*.'

She pulled away and headed for the bathroom.

Allan stood, but didn't follow.

'Beth, *please*.'

'I can't.' She turned to him, her eyes filling again. 'I can't, Allan. I'm sorry.'

And suddenly he realised what her initial sorry had meant.

She wasn't giving in.

She was telling him she couldn't.

Chapter 9

April, 2003

'I can't go to the moon,' Beth said flatly. 'I wouldn't be able to breathe.'

She and Allan were picnicking on McDonald's burgers under the cosy flicker of the spirit lamp on Allan's living room floor. It was the day after Beth had shared her secret with him. Her mother had been extraordinarily accommodating with requests to visit friends since the incident with the credit card – one benefit of her having been a social pariah for so long Beth guessed, her mother was so relieved at the appearance of 'a friend' she hadn't even asked about gender. Beth thought it best to keep her uninformed. Officially, she was having dinner with the friend's family and staying on afterwards to study. Which was kind of the truth. Except for the 'family' part. But Allan also had other ideas than studying. After wolfing down two burgers, he'd scuttered into his bedroom and returned with a large glossy book that he opened and placed in her lap. Dominating the opened page was an iconic shot of Neil Armstrong on the moon, standing next to a raised American flag.

Beth stared at his eager face. 'There's no air on the moon.'

Allan was astonished. 'You need air?'

'Of course I need air. Don't you?'

'Well, yes, but, don't you just … *see* things? Like, in your head? I mean, you don't actually *go* anywhere do you? Your body stayed right where it was when you did it yesterday.'

'Something of me goes,' she said, 'and not just a mental bit. It's more than that. It's not just in my head. I'm *there*. I'm invisible, but I can hear things, and smell things, and *feel* things. I can feel the wind, and if it's cold or hot … and I have to breathe. So part of me *has* to be there.'

'You can *feel* things?' Allan flopped back onto his bottom and stared up at her in envious awe.

'And taste them. I've tasted salt in the air near the sea.'

Allan let out a low, appreciative whistle.

'It wasn't always like that. When I was little it was more like looking at a television set, kind of separate. The photographs just … moved, and I thought they moved for everyone. But, as I got older, it … changed. First it got more like looking out a window instead of at a television set. I could get closer somehow, and I could see things that weren't in the photograph, like off to the sides and stuff like that … and then ...' Her eyes wandered over to the window and the inky night sky beyond '... It was like I could sort of … *open* the window. I could hear things, and smell them.' She met his eyes again. 'And now, it's more like I can … step through.'

'Into the photograph?'

She nodded.

Allan screwed up his face as he tried to make sense of it. 'But, your body stays here, and they can't see you there?'

Beth had no explanation.

'Maybe you have two bodies … kind of,' said Allan. 'One that stays here … and one that can go places?' He grinned. 'Or maybe one and a half bodies, since your other body is invisible.'

'Well, I don't know about that.'

'Can they feel you?' he asked. 'I mean, what if they walk into you, or you land on someone when you, you know, arrive or whatever you call it?'

'I don't "land" on anyone, 'cause I can see if there is anything close in front of the lens before I go in, and I don't go if there isn't any room, but, I have been walked into a few times. I just zap out if that happens. I don't know what it's like for them, but it's so quick they probably think they just tripped on something.'

Allan's eyes went huge. 'You "zap" out?'

'It's more like I'm kind of *thrown* out.'

'Like yesterday?'

'Well, sort of. I don't know what happened yesterday. I can't always tell if something's bumped me, especially if it's come from behind. It happens so quick. And it can happen even if nobody bumps me. I have to concentrate to stay there, and if I get distracted or something I can let go, and … fall out.'

Allan stared at her, goggle-eyed, and Beth blushed, remembering his worry from the day before. 'It doesn't hurt,' she shrugged. 'It's just a bit jarring. And I'm getting better at hanging on. I used to only be able to stay a few seconds … but now my record is fifty-five minutes!'

For a moment, her insecurity disappeared beneath a jaunty pride and Allan, suitably impressed, wriggled to his knees. 'So, it's about concentration? If you just concentrate hard enough, you can stay as long as you want?'

'Mostly, but concentration doesn't help if I get bumped. I don't know why … but I think maybe it's 'cause we can't both be in that same spot, at the same time. You know? Like, it just *can't* happen … so it doesn't.'

Allan's face went blank. 'Why don't you just move?'

'I can't move. I can't move anywhere. I just stay where I came in, even if the photographer moves.'

'You can't *move?*'

She shook her head. 'It's kind of like being paralysed. I can't get my body to move. Well, except for my upper body. I can move my head and shoulders a bit, and my arms. I can breathe and stuff like that – but I can't move my legs. Not to walk anywhere at least.'

'So, if something bumps into you, instead of getting knocked over, you get knocked right out of the picture?'

She shrugged. 'Seems like that.'

'So you need to pick a photo where you've got lots of space to land, where nothing's going to bump into you.' His mind was buzzing with all the possibilities and challenges. 'What about if the photographer was at the edge of a cliff or something? What about if you land in mid-air?'

'I can't float. I can't do anything inside a photograph that I can't do here … except be invisible of course.'

'—so if you stayed in the photo, you'd fall?'

She nodded.

'But you can come back when you want to, so that's not a problem.' Suddenly his face lit up. 'Are you *sure* you need air?'

She looked at him suspiciously. 'Yes, I'm sure. I told you, it's the same as being here.'

'But, if it doesn't hurt you if there is no air to breathe, and you can just pop back—'

'I don't want to go to the moon!' she said crossly. 'What about the pressure? Isn't it a vacuum on the moon? I could get crushed! And it's cold. What if I get snap frozen, or if I pass out?'

'Wouldn't you just zap back?'

'Well, how would I know? I've never tried it. What if I can't if I'm frozen solid, or if I'm unconscious? I haven't tried that before.'

'Oh,' he said, clearly disappointed. 'Well, OK, but I don't think it will matter anyway. Look at this.' He wriggled in close and pointed at the flag in the picture. 'See how the flag is flapping?' He stared up at her, his enthusiasm refired. 'How could it flap if there's no air?'

Beth examined the photo, unsure of what he wanted. It was true, the little red, white and blue flag did appear to be flapping in the wind.

'And here,' he said. 'There's no crater.' If the capsule had really landed on the moon, there should have been a crater. There isn't.' Giving her no time to respond, he flipped the page over. 'And this one. See how the shadows are going in different directions? There should have only been one light source. The sun. How can you have shadows going in different directions? There must have been more than *one* light source. Like you can have in a film studio.'

Beth was now totally confused.

'A lot of people think these photos are fake,' he explained patiently. 'They say the whole moon landing was a hoax and these photos were taken in a film studio.' His eyes were shining. 'You could find that out for certain if you went there, couldn't you? You could *see* if it was a hoax.'

'And if it's not a hoax, and it really *was* taken on the moon, I'd be dead!' She glared at him. 'It's not a game, Allan. I'm not going to risk my life to prove a photo is a fake.'

'But—'

'*No.* I'm not going to the moon!'

Allan's face fell. 'But it's most likely *not* the moon. These photos—'

'Allan, no. I said *no*. I'm *not* going to do it!'

Allan huffed and collapsed back onto his bottom and Beth began to feel bad about letting him down. It was fun seeing him so excited … but going to the moon without a spacesuit was out of the question.

'Isn't there any other picture I could try?' she offered. 'On Earth, I mean?'

'We're not going to be able to prove the moon landing was a fake unless we can prove those pictures are fake,' he said petulantly. But when he saw her hurt he couldn't stay mad. 'Well … maybe something else then.'

He shuffled back to her side, picked up the book

and leafed slowly through the pages. After a while, he stopped at a picture of the Apollo 11 launch.

'Could you go there?'

Flames were pouring out the bottom of the spaceship as it fired into the sky.

'It seems quite close,' she said dubiously. 'Where was this photograph taken? Was it safe? I mean for the people taking the pictures? Couldn't you burn up being that close?'

Allan peered at it. 'Oh, yeah, I guess,' he conceded. But then he regrouped. 'Hang on.' He flicked a few pages over to a shot that was taken from much further away. 'How's this?'

Beth studied the selected photograph. 'What would you like to know? I'd only see what you can see in the photograph, and there isn't any doubt the rocket took off, is there?'

'Well, not really. But of course, it could have taken off empty – though I guess you couldn't tell that from there.'

'No. I don't think so,' Beth agreed.

'But it would be cool to see it.' He grinned. 'Don't you think? And you could tell me what it felt like; *actually* being there.'

His unquenchable enthusiasm was infectious.

'Oh, all right,' she surrendered with a smile, 'but then I should go home. It's getting late.'

Allan readily agreed and Beth prepared herself. She drew in a steadying breath, pulled the book closer and stared into its depths.

* * *

9.31a.m., Wednesday morning, July 16, 1969, Cape Canaveral, Florida

'Eleven,' boomed a sombre male voice over a loud-speaker somewhere behind her.

She was standing on grass in full sunlight, in front of a group of men, pressing in close, almost touching her, staring collectively in silent focus directly ahead. Off in the distance, across an expanse of grass, stood the rocket, ready to launch.

'Ten.'

It looked so tiny.

'Nine.'

Hot breath tickled the back of her neck and she turned to see the photographer who had captured her entry to this place. He was directly behind her, tall and thin with oiled, combed-back hair. He seemed hypnotised by the scene in front of him.

Behind him was a set of bleachers filled with important-looking people, most of them wearing suits and sunglasses or thick-rimmed regular glasses. Their faces were all frozen in awe. The eerie silence of the crowd gave the impression she'd stepped into a still frame, except for the row of coloured flags that fluttered behind them on tall white poles.

'Ignition sequence starts.'

Beth turned back to the rocket, her heart pounding.

'Six.'

'Five.'

'Four.'

The crowd held their breath as a speck of light ignited at the base of the rocket. Beth, like all those around her, couldn't drag her eyes away.

'Three.'

'Two.'

'One.'

'Zero.'

The speck of light flared into a huge yellow-orange fireball. Smoke and flame shot out to the sides, and slowly, soundlessly, the rocket began to rise.

'Lift off, we have a lift off,' confirmed the voice from the loudspeaker.

The crowd erupted in an enormous cheer. Beth, grinning from ear to ear, yelled along with them, screaming out her enthusiasm as loud as she could as the rocket dragged up past the launch tower. Only then did the thunderous crash of the engines reach them. It thudded into Beth's body, shaking the ground beneath her feet, instantly silencing her and those around her. She covered her ears and watched, spellbound, as the delicate, flaming needle clawed its way into the clouds, aware of nothing else until all she could see was a speck of orange in the blue sky.

Finally, she gasped in a breath.

Was it the first she'd taken since the take off? She couldn't remember.

Excited voices began to flutter around her.

Had they been silent all that time, like her? Or had she been deaf? The whole situation was surreal.

Suddenly, a heavy weight crashed into her and she flew violently back.

* * *

April, 2003

Allan bounced with excitement, barely containing his impatience as he waited for Beth to collect herself.

'Did you see it? Did you see the launch?'

She was as excited as he was. Her eyes were huge, glowing.

'Yes! Everything! I saw *everything.*' Her face was luminous with thrill. 'The countdown, the rocket going up ... and all the people, *thousands* of them. It was *awesome!*'

Allan whooped in delight.

'Definitely not a fake. It went up. *All* the way up. And all the people ... they were all so quiet – and then they all cheered, thousands of them, all at once, so *loud.* And I did too!' She stopped suddenly as a new thought hit. 'Did you hear me? I was screaming. We were all cheering ... and I was *yelling.*'

Allan's blank expression indicated he hadn't.

'You didn't hear me? I wasn't yelling here?'

'No. No yelling going on here,' he said. 'You were just kind of sitting there.'

'Really?'

Allan nodded.

'Wow,' she said thoughtfully, and then dissolved into another all-consuming smile. 'You should have felt it! It kind of crashed into me, like a wave. I could *feel* it, in my *chest! Literally* feel it. Hitting me in the chest!' Her eyes sparkled and she giggled. 'Oh, it was *awesome.*' She reached for his hand, her face full of longing. 'Oh, I wish I could take you too!'

So did Allan, but second-hand was almost as exciting – especially if it inspired her to hold his hand … He smiled stupidly as she babbled on, watching her eyes dance in the light of the spirit lamp, enraptured by the sight of her face so bright with joy and he could have sat there all night, just listening to her – but he didn't want to risk her getting grounded. Finally he had to insist on walking her home.

She chatted all the way, and was still buzzing as they sheltered in the shadows of her carport, stretching the seconds before parting. Again, Allan had to take the initiative.

'I guess … I'd better go,' he said – it almost physically hurt to say it, but he knew he should, and 'shoulds' were important. When ignored, they brought unwanted consequences.

'I guess,' she agreed, clinging to his fingers.

Her warmth stole into him. It seeped down to his loins and set off a disturbing quiver. His heart began to pulse in heady expectation, and he was grateful for the cover of darkness, nervous his excitement would be exposed – but when her eyes looked into his … so warm, and brown, and deep … his control snapped. Before rationale could intervene, his lips were on hers. Quick and awkward and trembling and tender.

The effect was shattering.

His body leapt in response, frightening and powerful – and there was only one thing to do. Mumbling good night, his face scarlet in the dark, he pulled his hand away and ran into the night.

He'd only had just enough time to register her open-mouthed astonishment – it chased him all the way home and shamed him into scurrying for cover under his quilt – but, as he lay in the dark, reliving the moment for the thousandth time, he dared to hope that, behind the astonishment, he'd seen a smile in her eyes.

Chapter 10

July, 2010

It was an anonymous, uncaring place. But it was safe. Nobody would intrude. She'd paid in advance and hung up the "Do Not Disturb" sign. She could die in this room and they wouldn't break in before her payments ran out.

Allan would never find her here.

She had no fresh clothes, no toiletries. She hadn't even thought to grab a fresh pair of knickers – but then she didn't plan to be here too long.

She surveyed the suite with a grim satisfaction. There were only two rooms: a bedroom and an ensuite. The walls were painted a tired beige and the carpet was long overdue replacement but at least it was a dark colour and you couldn't see the stains. In any case, the bed filled most of the room.

Almost as though the room had taken offence at her

judgement, the light in the ensuite began an annoying flicker.

She reached out and switched it off.

How had it come to this?

A deep sadness pressed into Beth's heart. She hadn't meant to hurt Allan, hadn't wanted to. She hoped he would forgive her. The memory of his delight when she'd first told him about her ability ached like a lost love. Would he have run then, if he'd known what he knew now? Would she have run ... to spare him? Was the only way to love through denying who you were and becoming someone else?

That was unfair, and she knew it. He was only trying to protect her. She knew that too – but still, he didn't understand, couldn't *ever* fully understand. She was alone. No one could walk this journey with her and she was a fool to even let herself *want* that.

And cruel to expect it of anyone else.

No. In this, she had to answer to herself. *She* had to decide and *she* had to pay the consequences.

And there *would* be consequences ...

Beth dropped her coat and bag on the bed and crossed to the window. The night was alive with neon, sparkling like Christmas. Somewhere far below an ambulance wailed.

Poor Allan.

Had he discovered she was gone yet?

She turned back to the room. Slowly she walked to the bed and reached for her coat. Even in this dismal setting, the rich red of the wool was vibrant. It would draw attention. It would be remembered, and its classic style wouldn't be too out of place. It was perfect. A smile curved her lips. This would work! She could sense it, see it. It *would* work – and then she could let it go.

In an almost ritualistic acceptance of mission, she slipped her arms into the coat and buttoned it up to her neck.

* * *

5.45 p.m., Tuesday evening, January 14, 1992

Gillian smoothed her dress out on the towel on the floor as the iron heated up. With no ironing board, the floor was the next best place to iron clothes. Their table was way too cluttered.

The dress was a beautiful shade of green and the fabric was soft and flowy. Better still, she'd snapped it up at a garage sale for three dollars. A bargain! She loved bargains. And such a pretty colour!

'Have you packed Lili's bag?' asked Mike, entering naked and dripping from the shower with Lili in his arms swaddled in a towel.

'Not yet. Do you need anything ironed?'

'My blue shirt. Thanks.'

He carried Lili over to their bed and went to retrieve a nappy. Gillian followed and leant down to give Lili a kiss. 'How's my beautiful girl?' she cooed. 'Did you have a nice shower with Daddy?'

Lili giggled as Gillian began to dry her off.

'You going to rub me down too?' asked Mike, returning with the nappy, the baby powder and a cheeky smile.

'You're making puddles on the floor,' she moaned, rolling her eyes at the gathering wet patch around his feet.

'Thought it was better than Lili making puddles on our bed.'

Lili kicked enthusiastically at the air and Mike leant in to wrestle her into her nappy – with Lili, this process was always a wrestle, but Mike enjoyed the challenge.

'When did you tell your mum we'd be there?' he asked, sprinkling on the powder.

'A quarter past six. I'd better get our clothes ironed!' Slapping Mike on his raised, naked bum, she grabbed his shirt from the clotheshorse and waltzed back into the front room before he could retaliate. A few minutes later, Mike, dry and dressed for the evening – minus his shirt – joined her with Lili. She was now snug in her pyjamas and chewing happily on a rusk.

'Nearly done,' said Gillian. She finished off the collar and handed it to him. 'Goes so nice with your eyes, that blue.'

'Thank you. I suppose I should get your mother to buy all my shirts then.'

He draped the shirt over a chair, put Lili in her high-chair and helped Gillian up from the floor – not an easy task with all the extra weight she was carrying.

'She does have impeccable taste,' grunted Gillian, rising like a whale from the depths. 'It's the Italian in her genes. I think she channels Zampatti.'

'Well, it's a good thing you inherited the fashion bit, but forget about the channelling.'

She smiled and tossed her dress over her head. It slithered down over her curves, swathing her in rich emerald green.

'You know, we should get an ironing board,' said

Mike, turning back to Lili. 'You can't keep on ironing stuff on the floor like that.'

'When we get the new house,' countered Gillian. 'Where would we put it now?'

'We'll just have to find a place. You'll soon have your hands full with the new baby, and we can't have Lili crawling around with hot irons on the floor.'

'Hmmm, I guess you're right.'

It grated a little. There really was nowhere to squeeze anything else in. It would be a challenge to find places for the new baby things – but she couldn't stay irritated for long, not with a night out in front of her. She went to find Lili's baby bag, lightened by anticipation. When she returned, Mike had opened the venetian blinds and was buttoning up his shirt, admiring the view. The sky was streaked orange and rose.

'Red sky at night, sailor's delight,' she chanted. 'Gunna be another perfect day tomorrow.'

'It's stunning out there right now. I should take a picture!'

'You're not going to have any film left for the birth if you keep that up.'

'Then we'll get another roll!' He grabbed the camera from the table. 'Won't be a moment.'

'Better not be. We need to leave in five.'

He was already out on the footpath, focusing his camera on the sunset and missed her last fussing, but Gillian didn't care. She smiled at the sway of his slender back as he stood, arms raised with camera poised. She loved his wiry slimness. There was something so *strong* in it, so ready for action, with nothing to hold him back.

'Got it!' he called, and she smiled and turned back to

Lili's baby bag. Lili didn't need much, Gillian's mother had most things at her place, but she did need more nappies and a change of clothes, just in case.

'That'll be amazing if it wasn't too dark,' puffed Mike as he bustled in. 'I'll just put this away. Won't be a sec.'

Gillian reached for Lili's favourite teddy. It was a ragged blue thing, with one eye missing and an almost maniacal smirk on its face. Mike's mother had given it to Lili as a christening present. Lili wouldn't be separated from it.

'Ded, Ded,' she cried gleefully when she saw it, and reached out her arms. Gillian handed it over, but as she did, a sudden movement caught her attention. On the other side of the window, right up close to the glass, *in their own yard*, was the girl in the red coat!

For a second, Gillian could only stare – and Beth stared back – her pupils dilated unnaturally large and her lips parted as though about to speak.

A scream caught in Gillian's throat – and when Beth slowly reached out her hand and placed it flat against the glass – she released it.

Chapter 11

June, 2003

Allan and Beth had fun in the weeks that followed her experience at the moon launch. She visited the set of the latest Harry Potter film, attended several concerts in America and even went to Woodstock. She got to stand on stage with Jimi Hendricks! Allan's mother had been a fan of Jimi and Allan wanted to know what all the fuss was about, but Beth wasn't overly impressed. Still, she thought it was interesting to experience it: photographs just didn't capture the smells, the depth or the vivid immediacy of *really* being there. So many people!

Historical shots were Allan's favourites. Beth preferred nature scenes or famous buildings. The two of them spent hours searching for interesting photographs. When they found something, Beth would explore and then relate what she'd seen to Allan.

'What about this one?' Allan asked, his eyes shining.

They were sitting in the shade behind the toilet block – the year nines who normally claimed this prime position during lunch break were away on a school excursion. Allan presented her with a book he'd smuggled out of the school library, opened at a glossy image of a dark blue presidential limousine driving along a Dallas street.

Beth's shoulders slumped as she stared at the iconic photograph of President Kennedy waving at a crowd of cheering supporters, moments before his assassination.

'I don't want to see that.'

'You'd be safe,' said Allan, surprised at her lack of enthusiasm. 'Nothing happened to Zapruder or his secretary. No bullets went flying that way, and they had the perfect viewpoint.'

'Who's Zapruder?'

'He's the one who took that photo. It's a still from the film he shot. He was a businessman who was there taking home movies of the president's visit, and his secretary was helping him. She was up on the wall with him, keeping him steady while he was filming. Look. That's them.' He pointed to another picture, a black and white, showing a blurry image of two people standing on a low white concrete wall.

Beth peered down at the photograph. 'It's very blurry.'

'Doesn't matter. This is just to show you where they were – where you'll be standing. You'll be going in through Zapruder's photograph.'

He opened the book to a map of Dealey Plaza. 'See, they were up here on the wall, there. The grassy knoll was here, right next to them, and the president's car came down the road here, right in front of them. That's where he was shot.'

'Allan—'

'And that's the School Book Depository, where Oswald supposedly shot from. From where you'll be standing, it will be that way.' He gestured off towards the school assembly hall, getting more excited by the minute as he tried to orient her. 'And Kennedy's car will be right here, in front of you.'

Beth stared dubiously at the spot he indicated.

'But,' he said, 'if Oswald *had* shot him from over there, Kennedy would've been shot in the *back* of the head, 'cause Oswald was behind Kennedy. And in Zapruder's film you can see Kennedy's head gets thrown backwards, so he had to have been shot from the front! Like from where the knoll is.'

'Allan, I don't want to watch someone getting shot.'

'But – well, you don't have to look at *that*. You don't have to look at the car. Just look at the knoll. That's where they think the sniper was.' He pointed back down at the diagram of Dealey Plaza. 'See? Behind this fence here – which will be over there, from where you'll be standing.' He pointed towards the school oval and then grinned back at her. 'Just look at the knoll. Just look for the sniper.'

Beth turned her mouth down in distaste. 'I don't know ...'

'But you could find out. Once and for all.'

'What makes you think I'd see anything that hasn't already been seen? There were hundreds of people watching that day.'

'But they didn't know where to look! Aw, please,

Beth. Come on. Don't you want to know?'

'What difference is it gunna to make?'

'It's the mystery of the century – and we'd know what happened!

'But it won't change anything.'

'Well ... not that. No ... but, we might be able to prove—'

'No!' Her eyes flashed. 'No. I don't want to *prove* it to anyone. I don't want anyone else digging into my life.'

Allan sighed. 'Then, it'd just be for us,' he grumbled. 'It'd still be good to *know* ...'

For a moment, disquiet rankled between them, but then Beth reached over and slipped her hand into his – and he relented too, giving her fingers a gentle squeeze.

'OK,' he said. 'I guess it doesn't matter.' He put the book aside.

'It's just – it seems so – ghoulish.'

'It's just history ...'

'I guess ...'

'Never mind. It's OK.' He smiled sadly and pushed the book into his bag.

'Wait!' She reached for him. 'I probably wouldn't even see anything. I mean, what if it *was* Oswald, and I'm looking in the opposite direction?'

Allan's face lit with hope. 'That's OK. It'd rule out the sniper on the grassy knoll theory. That's something. I just want to know, one way or the other.'

She wasn't convinced, but still, she reached out a hand for the book.

* * *

12:29 p.m., Friday, November 22, 1963, Dallas, Texas

The first thing she saw was the car: long and low, dark blue and shiny, with two flags flying at the front.

The president was sitting in the back seat, seemingly looking straight at her, smiling, happy and free from care.

Her heart went into overdrive.

Behind her was the concrete pedestal. She could see the photographer and his secretary – perched up high – their expressions excited as the car drew nearer. Remembering her mission, she turned to look for the fence. It was just behind the white concrete wall that continued on from the colonnade she was standing in front of. There was no sign of a sniper, but there was a black man and woman near the end of the wall – leaning with their elbows on it – watching the parade and drinking Coke from glass bottles.

Suddenly, she heard a noise like a firecracker and she turned back to the motorcade.

The car was almost directly in front of her now. She could see the president and his wife clearly. The president's wife was dressed in pink with a little matching box-like hat on her head, very pretty. She was bending near to her husband who'd brought his hands up to his throat.

Before Beth could look away, another shot rang out – and the president's head exploded.

Brain matter flew across the car.

Beth raised her hands to her mouth in horror as the beautiful pink lady launched herself over the back of the car and crawled across the boot, scrambling to get away

– and someone screamed: 'They killed him, they killed him!'

Somewhere, glass smashed.

Beth felt someone running past – quite close to her. She felt the breeze of their passing – and others were running in the opposite direction – up the little hill – scrambling away from the horror just as the president's wife had done.

Zapruder's secretary was now with some men – official-looking men – down by the road.

'They killed him!' she screamed, as the presidential car slipped under the bypass. 'They *killed* him! *They killed him!*'

* * *

June, 2003

Beth was a mess.

Allan was frightened at the state of her.

He'd watched her while she was gone, her face still and vacant. He'd kept an eye out to make sure no one came round the toilet block to discover them. Nothing seemed any different to other times, and she wasn't gone long, just a few seconds – when suddenly, shatteringly, she let out an agonised scream. And she kept on screaming, and screaming, as Allan frantically tried to gather her into his arms to calm her.

But she wouldn't be calmed. She was completely hysterical.

He tried to cover her mouth, desperate to protect them from intruding eyes, but she only screamed louder and began to fight him and pound his chest, and before he could help her gain any control, a teacher arrived and hauled her out of his arms. He was left, shocked and shaking, standing alone, as the teacher directed incomprehensible orders at him and hustled Beth away through a crowd of gawking students.

Oblivious to his schoolmates' jeers, Allan numbly followed the teacher until he was separated to isolation in the deputy principal's office.

'What happened, Allan?' the head teacher demanded.

'Nothing!' said Allan, his face white.

'Don't give me that. Obviously something happened. Did you hurt her?'

'No. No, I didn't—' But he had. He *had* hurt her. She hadn't wanted to go ... Tears filled his eyes as he looked past the teacher, out through the half-closed door, trying to catch a glimpse of Beth – but he couldn't even hear her any more.

Desperately, he wanted to apologise.

'Allan? Allan!'

Dully, Allan met the head teacher's eyes. They were piercing under his unruly eyebrows, glaring in accusation.

'What happened?'

'We ... We were ...' A fierce shaking threatened to overwhelm him and he locked his muscles tight to force control and bit into his lip. How could he possibly explain this? *He* didn't even know what had happened.

The sound of an approaching ambulance siren drew his attention to the window. Thankfully, the teacher sighed, said something dismissive and left the room. A few moments later Allan saw the uniformed officers with their equipment shuffle by. He waited for what seemed like forever until they passed by again, this time pushing a trolley with Beth stretched out upon it.

He jumped up and ran to the door, but she didn't see him.

'Allan?'

The principal was now in front of him as the ambulance officers and Beth disappeared around the corner of the corridor. Mr Cavendish was a giant of a man with a physique resembling a grizzly bear. The inherent ferocity of his appearance was tempered somewhat by his thinning grey hair, but he still had no difficulty maintaining the respect of the students. Standing in front of Allan now, he filled most of the doorway.

'I've been trying to reach your mother, but I've only been able to leave a message.'

'She's ... in Melbourne,' Allan croaked, frantically trying to figure out how he was going to manage this.

'Do you have another number for her?'

'Ah ... no. She ... was going to a conference, I think. She should call me tonight.'

The principal frowned.

'I didn't hurt Beth. She's my friend. She just got upset. I ... don't know why ...'

He thought it best to let Beth decide what she wanted to tell them ... when she was able to.

Cold fear speared his belly. What if she never recovered enough to tell them? *What if this had done something really bad?*

'Can I go to the hospital?' he begged. 'Can I see her?'

In spite of his intimidating stature, the principal was a kind man. He was a believer in giving his students a fair chance, and he was smart enough to recognise the absence of threat. He knew that Beth and Allan were friends, and she had insisted that Allan hadn't done anything wrong when the ambulance officer had questioned her. She hadn't been able to get anything else out, but she'd been clear about that – but the principal was also smart enough to follow sensible policy. Allan was kept in the office until the end of the school day. Miserable and alone, he spent an agonising afternoon of recriminations and regret, and was damp with nervous sweat by the time the final bell rang. The raucous sound of departing students drew him to the window. He watched as they clamoured for the buses, and kept on watching until the last bus had driven off, but still no one came for him.

Were they going to keep him here until his mother was contacted? How was he going to organise that?

Once, he'd talked a friend of his mother's into attending a parent interview, but that was back in primary school when his mother was still alive, and he wasn't sure he could even find 'Auntie' Monica now. She also might not want to help if she wasn't only covering a temporary absence. In any case, he couldn't find her or ask her while he was shut up in this room. He felt sick. And his trepidation began to build as the minutes ticked by.

Down the hall, the school secretaries were talking, chatting as though it was just an ordinary day and nothing unusual had happened. There was no way he could sneak out past them. He'd have to wait until he was released. But, had the teachers all gone home? Had they forgotten him?

His eyes swung back to the window. It wasn't high from the ground. He could get out – he could run away

– but, Beth …

His eyes filled with tears again as he thought of her; he couldn't leave without knowing she was all right. But would they tell him? Would they even know? How could the doctors help when they had no idea what had happened – and Beth hadn't looked up to telling anyone anything when they'd taken her away. The thought of her, small and quiet on the ambulance trolley, pierced like a shard of glass into an open wound.

This was all his fault! And there was *nothing* he could do to *un*do it.

'Allan.'

It was the principal.

'We haven't heard from your mother. Who is staying with you tonight?'

'The neighbour looks in,' he lied, 'but Mum travels a lot, and I can take care of myself.'

The principal's face clouded, but Allan straightened his back and generated what, he hoped, was his most responsible look. 'She calls home most nights she's away. I can tell her to call you.'

'You're only thirteen, Allan. Your mother should have left a number. How are you to get hold of her in an emergency?'

'She usually does leave a number – it's just that she's travelling. She should call tonight.'

'What about your neighbour's number?'

'She's at work. She won't be home until after six.'

Oh, shit! He was digging this one deeper and deeper.

Mr Cavendish pulled out his mobile phone. 'What's her name, Allan?'

Allan's mouth went dry. 'Mrs Anderson. Nine nine

eight six, three five one eight.'

The principal's face relaxed as he keyed in the information. 'OK, Allan. You can go home. Get your mother to call me first thing.'

Reprieve.

'Yes, sir.'

The principal stood back to let Allan pass out of the room, but Allan hesitated. 'Sir … is Beth all right?'

'She's fine, Allan. The hospital said it was some kind of seizure, and her parents have taken her home. She should be back at school tomorrow, I should think.'

The relief on Alan's face was almost comical.

'Anything you want to tell me, Watson?' asked Mr Cavendish, his eyes searching.

'No. No, sir.'

Allan's fingers began to fidget, but he forced himself not to look away as the principal's eyes continued to search.

'Allan,' Mr Cavendish said thoughtfully, 'sometimes, girls can give you the impression they are ready for something when really they aren't.' Allan blushed beet red. 'Young Beth is a sensitive girl. She's had a few difficult things to deal with in her life.'

'I know that.' Allan stiffened in defence, but Mr Cavendish interrupted firmly.

'You should be careful with her, Allan.'

'What do you mean?'

'Just that,' he said kindly. 'You need to learn the signals. You need to learn to recognise when a girl is telling you to back off, because sometimes they can't tell you outright. Especially when they are young, like Beth.'

Allan felt sick again as a wave of regret washed over

him.

'It's all right, Allan. I can see you care about Beth, and she's not blaming you for anything. I'm sure you'll be able to sort this out once she's feeling better. But for the moment, I think you should give her a little space. OK?'

Humiliated, Allan nodded.

He walked out of the school grounds in a daze. He hoped he'd be able to make it up to Beth, prayed that he could at least apologise to her, but first he needed to think of a way out of the mess he was in or he wouldn't even be going back to school. He needed to find Auntie Monica!

Chapter 12

4.56p.m., Tuesday, January 14, 1992

Mike raced in from the bedroom.

Lilibeth was screaming in her high chair. Gillian was out at the street, standing on the footpath in her stock-inged feet looking frantically up and down the road. The front door was wide open.

Mike ran out to her, but before he could say any-thing, Gillian turned on him, red-faced and ready for war. 'She came into the courtyard! Right up to the window! She put her *hand* on it!' Her eyes were blazing. 'I came straight out, but she's gone. I don't see her anywhere. I don't know how she got away so fast. I—'

'Gilly, slow down. What are you talking about?'

'The *girl!*'

Mike shook his head uncomprehendingly.

'The girl in the red coat,' Gillian repeated impatiently. 'She came here! Right into our yard! I saw her, and she just … reached out and put her hand on the window … like this.' She imitated the action, and looked to Mike, desperate for some kind of explanation. But he could give none. 'I think she wanted to tell me something … but she didn't. And I just … screamed. And then, I … I ran out, but she got away again.' Her eyes were wide, astonished. 'Why is she doing this?'

Lilibeth was still screaming in her highchair. Her infuriated yowl finally got Gillian's attention. 'Oh, God,' she gasped and ran back inside to pick up the child.

Mike took one last look up and down the street and over at the beach. Nothing. Gillian was waiting at the door, holding a slightly mollified Lilibeth close, jiggling her up and down on her hip in an attempt to soothe her. The child continued to wail miserably, but Gillian was now immune to her protests.

'Look,' she said, pointing at a smear on the window.

Mike bent down for a closer inspection.

Against the glow of the kitchen light, the outline of a small handprint could be clearly seen.

* * *

June, 2003

Allan knocked cautiously on the battered fly screen. Someone was in there and they were awake – he could see the light through the curtains and hear the muffled beat of music. He just hoped it was Auntie Monica.

Getting no response, he bit into his lip and considered coming back another time, but he didn't have another time. Instead, he steeled his courage and knocked again, louder. At last he heard the approach of footsteps from within and the door opened up a crack. Auntie Monica peeped out. She looked a lot older than the last time he'd seen her, though it had only been a couple of years: her sun-baked skin had lost its spring and she was unhealthily thin. Glaring at him now through the crack, her wan face was pinched with suspicion, but it immediately brightened as she recognised him. 'Allan, love, is that you?' she asked, opening the door widely. 'It's been ages! Look at you! You're in high school now?'

'Yeah, I—'

'But what you doing out this late? It *is* late, isn't it?' She checked her watch. 'Shit, Allan, ten past one!'

'I know, but—'

'Never mind.' She brushed his excuses aside in a gush of warmth. 'Come on in. Come in.'

She ushered him inside and led the way into her living room, turning down the music as she passed her sound system. Swaying slightly, she sat on the couch and indicated a chair for him.

Her home was the same as ever – damp, stale and uncared for, like its owner. Allan sat and offered Auntie Monica what he hoped would come over as a polite smile. She was staring at him now with a wobbly kind of joy. He could see she'd been drinking, or was high on something – and he hoped it wouldn't impede her thinking too much.

'So, how you doing, love?' she asked kindly. 'You getting on well? Staying with a nice family?'

Allan made an appropriate affirming noise and Monica tumbled into a rapid monologue.

'Sorry I haven't been in touch,' she began. 'Lots of stuff going on – you know how it is. And I've been away a bit. But I have been thinking of you, and your mum. God I miss her … She was so beautiful, your mum. And she passed that on to you, I see. Yes she did, you're a good-looking boy, Alley. Yes, you are. You got her eyes.' She nodded with deep sincerity. 'Alley,' she said softly. 'Her little Alley Cat. That's what she called you. Did you know that? Because you could take care of yourself. You brought your own self up really, you did. Just like a cat.'

She laughed at that, and Allan did his best to look amused as well, though it didn't really strike him as funny. Memories of his mother high on drugs, calling him her cat – not really funny.

'She would've been proud, you know,' continued Auntie Monica. 'She would've been *so* proud. She loved you, you know. She did, even if she couldn't always be there for you. She wanted to, but …' She trailed off sadly. 'Dreadful that. Such a waste. But she lived her life her own way, your mum did. So sad …'

Her eyes welled and tears spilled down her face. Allan couldn't think of anything appropriate to say. Fortunately she pulled herself together fairly quickly.

'Like some tea?' she asked abruptly, wiping her tears away and forcing a smile to her face. Allan said he would. If nothing else, he hoped some kind of action might relieve the awkwardness of the moment. And it did. A few minutes later Auntie Monica returned with two steaming mugs of tea and a plate of cold Kentucky Fried Chicken.

Not having had any dinner, food was welcome, even if it did look a little iffy and had probably been in Auntie

Monica's fridge a lot longer than recommended. Wolfing it down, Allan was soon feeling much better and Monica seemed better with the help of her tea as well. Watched him eat, she entertained him happily with a few more uncomfortable reminiscences of his mother. But as Allan finished off the last few mouthfuls of the chicken, her forehead began to crinkle with concern.

'So … what's up? Strange time to be visiting your Auntie Mon. Not that I mind, of course, but what do your foster parents think about it?'

The last time he'd talked to Monica was when she called to tell him about his mother's death. She'd been in Melbourne. She offered to fly up to help him sort out his mother's things and organise care for him, but he told her he'd be all right and she didn't need to come. She wasn't sure about that, but she gave in. She told him how to contact Family Services and tried to encourage him that they'd find a good foster home for him. He promised her he'd contact them – but of course he hadn't.

'That … didn't work out, Auntie Mon,' he said quietly, 'but I'm OK. I'm doing fine by myself.'

'By *yourself?*'

Straightening his shoulders, Allan met her eyes. 'I've still got Mum's flat. I never told 'em she died. I'm living there by myself, and I'm taking care of it. I have a job, and her welfare payments, and I'm still at school. Everything's OK.'

He stuck out his chin, expecting reproof, but Monica just sat there, a little stunned, saying nothing.

Allan took a deep breath. 'But … I need some help.'

This seemed to snap her back. 'Oh, well, Allan, honey, I don't have much money—'

'I don't need money. I told you. I have a job.'

'Oh, well—'

'I need you to talk to my school. As my mum. They want to talk to her.'

Monica's eyes widened fearfully.

'Just once,' he assured her quickly. 'You don't need to turn up to all the parent nights or anything. Just this once.'

'Honey … I can't pretend to be your mother.'

'Why not?'

'Well … I … I mean … it's not legal.'

'You did it before.'

'Well, yes, but—'

'I just need you to help one more time, and no one will ever know you're not my mum. They don't care. They just need *someone* to be responsible for me, but I don't need anyone. It's better for everyone this way. If I go into the system, someone else will have to take care of me and they've got enough kids in care already.'

'Sweetheart—'

Allan could feel his lifeline slipping away. 'You said I could come to you. If I needed to. You said you promised Mum.'

'Well, yes, but—'

'Just once, Auntie Mon. All you have to do is call the school and ask to speak to Mr Cavendish. He's the principal. Then, just tell him you're in Melbourne—'

'Melbourne?'

Allan shrugged. 'I said she was at a conference.'

'Oh.'

'He'll probably want to talk to you about my behaviour, and all you have to do is listen to him, and let him know you've got it all in hand.'

Again, fear clouded her drawn features. 'What have you done?'

'Nothing,' he spat out defensively, and immediately regretted it. 'Sorry,' he mumbled, 'but I *haven't* done anything. It's just my friend, Beth, she got upset … about something she saw … and I was trying to help her … but she was … upset.' Monica clearly wasn't following. Allan sighed and tried again.

'We were out, behind the toilet blocks, and she … she …'

How could he explain this?

'She … thought she *saw* … something … and she started … screaming.'

Monica's eyebrows rose. 'Screaming?'

Allan nodded miserably.

'What did she think she saw?'

'I don't know – she was upset, she couldn't tell me, but Mr Cavendish thinks it's *my* fault, that *I* upset her – and I guess I did in a way – but not like he thinks. I didn't do what *he* thinks.'

'What does he think?'

Allan shrugged awkwardly. 'I think he thinks I was … you know … and that she didn't want to … But I *didn't*. It wasn't *that*. I swear.'

Monica shook her head slowly. 'Oh, Allan. You're a strange one.' She leant in towards him. 'Why don't you want to go to a foster family, sweetheart? Wouldn't it be easier than this? I mean, surely it's not nice being by yourself?'

Allan's back stiffened.

'I like it. I don't want to go to strangers and have

them telling me what to do, and maybe taking me away from my school, and my friends.'

'But … do your friends know about this? About you living by yourself?'

'Beth does.'

'I see.' Her gentle, sad eyes showed that she did. 'I don't know, Allan, I really shouldn't do this.' She shook her head again. 'You're just like your mum, you know. She didn't want anyone telling her what to do either. Ran away from home when she was fifteen – but see where it got her?' She looked at him in impotent appeal, and Allan dropped his defiance.

'I don't do drugs,' he said softly, 'and I won't *ever* do drugs. I'm not stupid.'

Monica winced at that. Her eyes dropped to her lap, undecided. 'OK. I'll do it,' she said, 'because I reckon your mum would've wanted me to, bloody fool that she was. But just this once. And if your principal tells me you're going wrong—'

'He won't.' Allan grinned. 'I'm an A student.'

She shook her head. 'What's his number?'

* * *

Monica called Mr Cavendish the next day and – as she was well experienced in the manipulation of those in positions of authority – she had no difficulty assuring him she'd spoken with Allan and would guide him through this difficulty without any further assistance. As Beth had returned to school and seemed to be coping well enough, that seemed to satisfy Mr Cavendish. The conversation finished with promises from Monica to attend the next parent night – if she wasn't tied up with work commitments – and assurances from Mr Cavendish to keep her informed if any further difficulties arose.

Mr Cavendish brought the year adviser up to date and asked him to keep an eye on Allan, but there were no further repercussions. Beth, however, was referred to the school counsellor.

Ms Crabshaw was a well-meaning but naïve woman, who was generally regarded by the student body as a harmless pushover. Beth considered her a waste of time. She had no intention of actually confiding in her, and she knew the right phrases to use to ensure she could move on from Ms Crabshaw's ministrations as quickly as possible. Within an hour, the counsellor had decided on a diagnosis: 'Likely just a routine incidence of teen-age angst and growing pains aggravated by difficulties at home with a stepparent.' She concluded that nothing needed to be done except to make a note of it and Beth was encouraged to come and have a chat at any time.

That suited Beth fine.

Harder to deal with were the other students. She was now a fully certified nut-job to them. Instead of being ignored, she was the brutally exposed centre of everyone's attention. Curious eyes bored into her every-where she went, conversations stopped abruptly as she approached and snickers followed as she walked away. Rebecca, Ambrosia and Stacey were the worst, taking every opportunity to poke fun at her, and the louder boys were happy to join in. The less assertive kept their distance, isolating Beth to her fate.

Allan also seemed to be keeping his distance, but at the end of their first class together he slipped her a note before hurrying off to his next class. She watched him disappear up the steps of the science block before slowly unfolding it.

'*I'm sorry,*' was all it said.

Beth was waiting for him after his last class. He saw her standing by the lone tree that dominated the court-yard in front of the maths block and approached timidly, worried by her grim expression, but as he drew near she gave him a fragile smile. 'I can't stay. Mum wants me home. She wants me to go back to that stupid doctor, so I have to prove I don't need to.'

Allan felt stung to the core. 'Are you all right? I'm so sorry. I should never—'

'It's my fault. I didn't mean …' She bit into her lip. 'It's just – it was so horrible. His head … his head just … exploded.'

Allan's face bled white. 'I'm *so* sorry.'

'You gunna make her scream again, Watson?' yelled one of their classmates as he and his friends ambled for the buses. Allan reddened, and they all burst out laughing. Another wailed in mock distress, 'Waaaa … No … NOooooo. Leave me alone …'

'Shut the *fuck* up!' spat Beth.

Allan almost choked in surprise.

'Whoa!' laughed the biggest of the boys. 'O'Malley's a psycho!' he yelled to the playground in general as they raced for the buses, laughing and shouting insults until their voices were lost in the after-school din.

Beth squared her shoulders. 'I have to go. See you tomorrow?

'Beth—'

'I'm OK. They're arseholes,' she reassured him.

'Sorry if I got you into trouble.'

'All I care about is you being all right.'

Beth gave him a quick smile and headed off for the school gate.

On the other side of the road, Gillian waited in her car. She smiled and waved as Beth reached the crossing, but quickly reverted to her thoughtful evaluation of the scrawny young boy whose eyes remained fixed on her daughter.

* * *

'Who was that boy, Beth?' asked Gillian, as Beth buckled up her seat belt.

'What boy?'

'The one you were talking with just then. Was that the boy you were with yesterday?'

Beth turned away. 'He's just a friend.'

'A *boy* friend?'

'Yes, Mum. He's a boy and he's a friend.'

'You don't need to be rude. I'm just concerned.'

'You don't need to be concerned. He's just a friend,' returned Beth. 'We're not having sex or anything.'

Gillian's jaw dropped.

Beth fixed her attention on the street in front of them, her expression rebellious, her mouth firmly shut, and Gillian, outmatched, reached for the key and started the engine. They drove in silence for the few kilometres back to the house, but when the car was in the garage and the engine turned off, Beth hesitated before getting out. 'Sorry, Mum. I didn't mean to be rude. I just had a hard day. Everyone's treating me like a psycho.'

Gillian's throat clutched. 'Well, I guess it was all pretty dramatic, with the ambulance and everything. You've provided the excitement for the week – but they'll settle down. Just ignore them.'

'I am.' She paused. 'His name is Allan. He's an A student, and he helps me with assignments. He's just a friend.'

'OK …' said Gillian, anxious to not shatter the rarely-offered intimacy. 'That's nice. I'm glad you've got a friend.'

'Better than none, eh?' Beth tried to joke.

'Yes, it certainly is. Just—' Beth waited for the lecture, but it never came. Gillian's overwrought expression melted. 'It certainly is. Come on. I'll make some hot chocolate.' She reached for her purse. 'Why don't you ask him over for dinner?'

Beth saw only a desire to please.

'Sure,' she said. 'I'll ask him.'

* * *

Beth shut the bedroom door behind her and tossed her schoolbag on her bed. For a moment she just stood there, staring at it, but then she slowly she unzipped it and pulled out the JFK book she'd smuggled out of the school library.

Her fingers trembled as she held it. Caught somewhere between opening it and thrusting it back into the bag, she wavered, uncertain, before finally sitting down on the edge of the bed and laying it on her lap, closed.

The cover featured a full-colour photograph of President Kennedy, taken from behind, as he reached out to adoring crowds. It was a good choice for a cover photograph – and *it* didn't threaten Beth – but when she opened the book and was confronted by pictures of the presidential cavalcade on that fateful day, memories of the president's exploding head immediately splashed into her head – splattering brain matter – *flying across the car in a blood-red cloud – smacking indecently into his wife – covering her – his face half gone—*

Beth slammed the book shut.

Her heart was pounding as though trying to escape her chest. She felt like *she* was about to explode – and clamped her hand over her mouth to stifle her scream—

Had they heard her?

She stilled, her hand still firmly against her mouth, listening for signs of exposure – but she heard nothing. There was no one outside her door, no steps running up the stairs. No one calling out to her.

Thank goodness.

Drawing a shaky breath, she forced herself to look back at the book– but instantly the images flew at her again, this time without her even opening it. She squeezed her eyes shut, trying to drive them away, but the harder she fought, the more they came, and unable to take it any more, she flung the book to the other end of the bed.

She couldn't do it. She had to admit it. She couldn't open that book again.

She just couldn't.

'I'm sorry, Allan,' she whispered.

She reached for the book and shoved it back in her bag.

* * *

The next day she met up with Allan in the library. She pushed the JFK book across the table towards him in a subdued gesture of defeat.

'I tried to go back again,' she said quietly, before he could say anything, 'so I could find out what you wanted to know, but I ... I just couldn't do it. I'm sorry.'

'Beth, you don't need to apologise. I—'

'I didn't see anything the first time.' She pushed on, determined to say what she'd come to say. 'I tried to look where you said, but I didn't see any snipers ... and then I heard the shot and ... and then—' her eyes threatened to mist '—I couldn't ...'

Allan tried to interrupt, but she placed her hand on his, stopping him. 'It was just so ... *horrible.*' Her voice was tiny, naked in its hurt. 'It wasn't a bit like the movies. His head—' She swallowed and looked away. 'I just ... freaked out.'

Allan knew he should say something ... something comforting ... anything – but the words wouldn't come. Thankfully, Beth seemed to draw encouragement from his silence.

'I don't think the bullet came from the fence though,' she said. 'I was right near there, and the shots sounded like they came from further away. I've thought about it, and I think they *did* come from that building, the school one. I thought I'd go back, and check – just to look at the building and nowhere else – but I didn't trust myself. And I ... I just couldn't bear to see it again.'

Allan reached for her hand and took it gently. 'I'm sorry. I shouldn't have asked you. You were right, it's not a game. I was an idiot. You shouldn't go to places like that.'

His eyes were so full of concern.

'OK …' she said, and Allan put the JFK book solemnly to the side.

It was as though a pact had been made between them.

'My grandmother told me some things were better left unseen,' she said. 'I guess she was right.'

'She knows about this?'

'Knew. She's dead, but I guess she was the one I got this from. She was psychic. When she touched things she could see stuff, like pictures, or feelings. Not quite like me, but sort of. She told me I should be careful – that people, like us, were the kind that got burnt as witches.

Allan laughed. 'Could she cast spells?'

For the first time that day, Beth smiled. 'Don't think so, and neither can I.'

'Maybe you should have gone to Hogwarts.'

'Shut *up!*'

Allan grinned. 'Well, anyway, your gran was probably right. We should be careful.'

Beth looked up at that – *we* should be careful. She smiled and nodded, her heart soaring at the use of that magical word: we. It was so good not to feel alone. She was part of a *we*.

'What about the shrink?' Allan asked. 'What's your mum said?'

'I convinced her I'm not mental.' She couldn't resist a smug smile. 'He's a jerk. I don't think she likes him either.'

Allan relaxed and Beth felt his peace flowing into her.

Yes, she thought, it was good to be part of a *we*.

Chapter 13

Thursday, November 16, 1965

'Here you go.'

The rosy-cheeked baker handed each of the children a hot, fresh bun. He was smiling as they reached greedily for his offerings.

The bakery was in a large, open, industrial building just across from the beach. It didn't sell retail but serviced most of the local shops. Half of its cavernous space was taken up by a huge kitchen; the other half served as a drive-in area where the bread was loaded into delivery vans. The last of the vans had just rolled out with the morning's orders and the bakers were cleaning up and getting ready to take a break, but the owner always had time for the local school children who stopped by. Usually there were a few left-over buns for him to hand out like a jolly-faced, real-life Santa Claus.

'Now, get on with you.' The old man chuckled. 'You'll be late for school.'

The children thanked him and trotted out, devouring their winnings as they walked the two blocks to their small community school. Simple wood-slat buildings were scattered across the grounds, separated by grass and asphalt areas with lots of shading trees, giving it a disorganised, open feel. The classrooms were light and airy, raised up on brick pedestals with broad covered verandahs and large wooden-framed windows.

With a burst of laughter, Gillian's brothers and sister ran on ahead and raced each other through the school gate, but she was in no hurry. This wasn't a *normal* school day. It was 'school photograph day'!

Excitedly, she peered up and down the street in front of the school.

No sign of her. But it was early. There was still time.

It was a beautiful summer's day. Across the street, the sun was playing on the waves. Gillian shut her eyes and raised her face to receive its warmth. It filled her like a smile as she swallowed the last of her bun.

'Gilly!'

A tall, skinny eight-year-old girl with wiry red hair was waving at her from the verandah of their classroom: Gillian's best friend, Lorraine. The girl held up a fist full of brightly coloured plastic knucklebones. 'Come on. We're waiting for you.'

Gillian skipped up to join her. She placed her little cardboard school case in its usual spot and sat with her friends in a patch of sun. Gillian was the champion at jacks. Her quick fingers tossed and grabbed better than any of her friends'. She was two rounds ahead before the bell rang for milk.

There were four girls in their gang: Gillian, Lorraine and the De Veaux twins, Annette and Babette. Much to everyone's disappointment the twins weren't identical. Annette had fine, straight white-blonde hair and Babette was a curly brunette. They couldn't play tricks by pretending to be the other, but all the same they seemed to share a personality and were inseparable. When spats occurred, the twins would always choose the same side, leaving Gillian or Lorraine temporarily ostracised. Fortunately spats were few. Today, they were all in a good mood because school photograph day was always fun. They'd be allowed out of their classrooms to line up in orderly, posed groups – and it would take *lots* of time. There'd be no proper lessons before lunch!

When the bell rang, the girls put the jacks away and scampered down into the assembly area to get their milk. Lukewarm, it sat in individual glass bottles in metal crates on the asphalt for the teachers to distribute. Gillian liked milk, so she shook the little bottle to mix the thick cream in, licking her lips in anticipation, but Lorraine hated it. Huddling under a pine, the girls hid her from view as she tipped her unwanted calcium into the mess of pine needles at their feet. Several other students had similar strategies. For the girls, this daily game added spice to the beginning of the school day, but today Gillian was distracted. Her eyes kept wandering to the boundary fence, searching.

'Is she there? Did you see her?' asked Lorraine.

'No,' said Gillian. 'She might not be coming this time.'

'She could just be late,' offered Annette. 'When'd

she come last time?'

Gillian tried to remember. 'Don't know. I just saw her after the photo.'

'Where was she?' asked Babette.

Gillian pointed to the fence near the gate. 'But when we were in third class, she was over there, next to the toilets.'

'In the school grounds?' Babette was amazed. 'Didn't the teachers see her?'

'Don't think so. She was only there for a bit. I saw her when we were going back into the classroom. And then I went to tell you,' she nodded to Lorraine, 'but by then she was gone.'

'Probably went behind the toilet block,' declared Lorraine confidently. She'd never seen the mysterious woman, but she was desperate to.

'And her coat's always red?' asked Annette.

Gillian nodded.

The girls looked around eagerly, but there was no sign of any red-coated lady.

'Maybe she's a ghost,' said Annette, wiggling with excitement.

Lorraine rolled her eyes. 'It's daytime! And what would a *ghost* want to haunt school photograph day for?'

Lorraine didn't believe in ghosts.

But Babette's enthusiasm was not in the least dampened. 'Maybe she's searching for her long-lost child. And she can't rest 'cause she misses her daughter.'

'Or maybe she went to school here, and she was *murdered*,' said Annette, 'and she's buried under the toilet block!'

That didn't sit right with Gillian at all. 'She wasn't

a kid. She was a grown-up. And she didn't look like a ghost – she just looked normal, 'cept for the coat.'

Lorraine tilted her head speculatively. 'You're not adopted, are you, Gilly? Could she be your real—'

'No! I'm not adopted. Everyone says I'm just like my mum.'

'She is like her mum,' agreed Annette and Babette in unison.

'Maybe an aunt, then?'

Gillian shook her head and Lorraine leant back against the pine tree, disgruntled.

'Well, maybe she's not even watching *you*. She could be here to see any of us. We're all in the photo, aren't we?'

This caught the twins' imagination. 'Maybe she's Sally Prior's real mum? Sally's not *anything* like her mum.'

'Or her dad,' threw in Babette. 'She's not like her dad either.'

'He works for the government.' Annette nodded conspiratorially. 'And he has a *gun*. A *big* one.'

'We *saw* it!'

'Sally said the gun was from the war. Your lady could be a *spy*!'

'Or the *ghost* of a spy, coming to get revenge!'

Neither Gillian nor Lorraine was satisfied with those explanations, but further speculation was curtailed. Their teacher, Mrs Noble – a stout, strict veteran teacher – intervened to shuffle them off to their classroom while the photographer arrived and the benches were set up. She tried to distract them with some free reading time, but Gillian couldn't concentrate in the least. Every chance she got, she wandered over to the windows to see if the lady had arrived, but there were no strangers in the school yard except for the photographer, and no lingerers at the fence.

Half an hour later Gillian's class was herded to the benches and organised according to height. Gillian and the twins were positioned on the lower bench in the middle while Lorraine was exiled to the back row with the taller boys. Ties were straightened and hair was tidied until at last Mrs Noble was satisfied. The class heaved a sigh of relief when she stood back and handed the proceedings over to the photographer.

Gillian was pleased with her appearance. Her red and white checked cotton uniform had been especially laundered and felt crisp and fresh against her skin, her shoes were polished to a deep shine, and she was particularly proud of the bright new ribbons her mother had bought her for the occasion. She smiled readily for the photographer when he instructed them all to say, 'Cheese.' In the midst of the jostling and giggles the red-coated lady was forgotten, but when it was all done and they were being ushered from the benches, she couldn't help looking around.

Still no sign of her.

Gillian began to think she must have been imagining things. After all, she'd only seen the lady twice, and if it hadn't been for the red coat she probably wouldn't have noticed her.

'She was probably with the photographer,' whispered Lorraine as they walked back to the classroom. 'It's a new photographer this year, isn't it? So that's why she's not here.'

Gillian couldn't remember whether it was a new photographer or not, but Lorraine's explanation made more sense than Annette and Babette's, even if it wasn't as much fun. Lorraine's opinions were always like that: sensible and not much fun, but she was usually right. For whatever the reason, the lady in the red coat wasn't there; so it didn't really matter. She nodded her head in agreement and followed Lorraine into the classroom.

There was still a little time before play-lunch, and Mrs Noble thought it should be well spent in some maths revision. She made them take out their maths books and began writing sums up on the board. Gillian could barely keep her eyes open; the whole thing seemed so deadly dull after the morning's excitement. She got all her sums wrong. She was considering asking to be excused to go to the toilet when a foot kicked swiftly into her backside. Lorraine was gesturing frenetically towards the window. Swivelling quickly, Gillian saw her. Behind the fence, right next to their classroom, in a gap between two large, thick bushes, was the lady in the red coat. She was just the same as the other times – a dark-haired woman with demanding brown eyes, wrapped in an unnecessary, bright red coat – only this time, unlike the other times, she smiled at Gillian and waved.

Gillian couldn't believe it. She stared back stunned, too surprised to respond.

'Gillian! Lorraine!' snapped Mrs Noble. 'Concentrate on your work, please.'

Gillian jumped as Lorraine leapt to her feet. 'But there's a lady out there spying on us,' she objected. 'She comes every year. She's spying on Gillian!'

The whole class craned and clamoured to get a look.

Mrs Noble ordered them back to their seats and went to the window to investigate, but by the time she got there, there was nothing to see. The lady in the red coat had slipped into the bushes.

'Settle down. Settle *down!*' she commanded, taking off her glasses for extra emphasis – her most threatening gesture. Even so, it was several minutes before she could regain control. She hated school photograph day. The disruption to normal routine always unsettled the children and made it impossible to accomplish anything useful for the rest of the day. Giving up, she put on a record of Mozart's *Piano Concerto no. 21* and told the children to take out their readers for free reading time while she turned her attention to marking. The room soon had the appearance of order again, but under cover of their readers Gillian and her friends wrote excited notes to each other, sharing details and developing theories.

The topic dominated their conversation for the rest of the week, with remembrances growing daily and becoming less and less recognisable, but when the mysterious woman didn't show up again – and it seemed apparent she probably wouldn't until at least the next school photograph day – the girls eventually found other matters to take their attention. The following year though, as school photograph day approached, anticipation rose again. The girls excitedly rehashed their theories and expectations and eagerly kept watch, hoping to spot the distinctive red coat in the local area.

By the time the day arrived, anticipation had reached fever pitch. The girls got to school early to prepare and plan. They searched the entire grounds for hiding places and then each claimed an area to keep a special watch on. Secret signals were developed for alerting each other if the lady was spotted. In fact, the whole school was on the lookout. Even the teachers had picked up on it and cast curious or wary glances around the yard and boundaries while the photographer was setting up and taking the photographs – but no red-coated lady was seen. Not even Gillian saw her.

It was disappointingly anti-climactic.

When the lady didn't turn up the following year either, or the year after that, the girls decided that whatever the woman was doing and whyever she was doing it, she wasn't doing it any more. With no further visitations and puberty bringing far more interesting concerns, the red-coated lady was relegated to the dusty drawer of childhood myths to be quietly forgotten.

Chapter 14

April, 2003, Peru

The air was crisp, cool and thin.

Underneath her bare feet the cobblestone path was damp.

In front of her stretched an impossible depth. At her toes the ground fell away in a mighty vertical drop of over four hundred metres to the valley floor. There was no guardrail, but a thin rope ran along the mossy rock face at her back for those too timid to navigate the narrow path without something to hang on to.

It was early, and she was alone. The hordes of tourists hadn't yet arrived and the photographer who'd taken the photograph she'd entered through had moved on. She wouldn't be interrupted for almost half an hour. Peace owned the mountain. Silence enveloped her. The only thing missing was Allan. One day, she determined, she'd bring him here. She knew he'd appreciate the power of this place. She could see him running his fingers over the ancient stones, identifying all the plants, taking pictures of the birds. It made her smile.

For now though, this lonely ledge on the outer edge of the Inca fortress was her own private sanctuary, impenetrable in these captured moments. No one could enter. No one could venture down the path on a whim. No one could, or ever would, see this exact moment in this exact place. No one except her – because no one ever had.

It was her fifteenth birthday. Machu Picchu seemed an appropriately sacred place to begin the day. Her fifteenth year had been a happy one, perhaps the happiest year of her life so far. She'd experienced no major problems at home or at school, and though she still didn't get on with Richard, they rarely locked horns. Most importantly, Allan's friendship had ended all sense of isolation. And his introduction to her parents had gone well. Her mother prepared her 'best' meal – roast chicken and vegetables with crispy potatoes – and Allan behaved with perfect charm, winning even Richard over. Gillian was disappointed Allan's mother couldn't come, but after chatting with her on the phone and being promised a future get together – 'once business craziness settled down' – she'd felt assured first contact had at least been made and parental responsibility met. Allan was awarded 'accepted friend' status and became a regular guest at the Fletcher table. The lack of reciprocation at the Watson table wasn't questioned.

Allan and Beth's friendship had deepened to an easy closeness. She couldn't imagine life without him – but not everything between them was aligned. She and Allan didn't talk about her travelling much anymore. Not that any decision had been made *not* to, but after the upset with Kennedy's assassination Allan hadn't asked her to investigate any more conspiracies and he seemed generally to think that picture-travelling was best left alone. That quashed any excitement for the topic. She hadn't lost interest, but felt it was mostly easier to keep it to herself.

Machu Picchu was her favourite destination. She'd visited it hundreds of times. The poster she entered through was a Christmas present from Richard, who of course had no idea of the sanctuary he'd provided for her, but she treasured it. She'd been to the pyramids in Egypt and dozens of other ancient sites as well, but nowhere held the same heavy fascination as Machu Picchu – except for pictures of her family. Her mother had given her an album filled with photographs of her early childhood, most of them taken by her father. It gave her an opportunity to get to know her father, to fill the void where the real memories of him should have been: how he sounded ... how he moved ... how he smiled. She visited every one of them until she'd memorised each microsecond of the scraps of life they contained. Her favourite was one of her mother and herself playing in Manly Lagoon, taken just hours before her father died of a heart attack. The joy on his face took away some of the pain; he was happy in those last hours. Another special one was of her mother walking down the sunlit aisle at their garden wedding. It allowed the perfect position to observe the wedding. She must have watched it at least a dozen times. She could play the whole event through in her head like a movie.

And of course, there was the picture she'd inherited from Nanna. It hung in pride of place above her bed. She'd absorbed every word and every movement of the short interchange that followed the taking of the picture. It didn't bring Nanna any closer, and somehow, after a while, it hurt to see her so close and not be able to call out to her or run into her arms, but still she was compelled to visit. She couldn't *not* go. These experiences were so precious – but she couldn't share them with Allan. After all, she had something he could never, *ever* have. He could never see *his* mother again. He didn't even have a name for his father, let alone a picture.

It seemed unfair to dwell on this with him. So she didn't. She kept it to herself.

But one day, she determined as she sat on the ledge at Machu Picchu, she would share this beautiful place with him in *real* time. They'd travel there together and he'd get to experience its power *exactly* as she did.

She drew the cool, damp air deep into her lungs and shut her eyes. Machu Picchu was like the ocean, always the same and yet always new. Its peace soaked into her, never ending, never depleted, as though it kept getting filled from some secret source and waited for her every time she came, waited to escape through her, from timelessness back into time.

Raising her face to catch the first drops of the misting rain, she listened through the silence for the laugh.

On cue, it sounded.

The honeymooners rounded the corner, like actors entering from the wings to play their rehearsed scene in a long-running play; and others would soon follow.

Dawdling no longer, she slipped out—

* * *

February 28, 2005

—and back into her bedroom, just in time to sit up in bed before her mother burst in singing 'Happy Birthday' with an armful of brightly wrapped presents. Beth unwrapped them in a tangle of hugs and kisses: a new jumper – one she'd admired in a shop the last time they were at the mall – a gift voucher for the music shop, the new pair of shoes they'd picked out on the weekend and a whole box of Ferrero Rochers!

Richard smiled awkwardly from the doorway. 'Happy birthday, Beth.'

On a morning such as this, Beth didn't begrudge even him a smile. She beamed as she ordered him out so she could get dressed. Richard happily complied.

Breakfast was Beth's favourite: French toast with maple syrup. There was even time for seconds because her mother promised to drive her to school as a birthday treat. She was eager to get on with her day though, knowing Allan would be waiting for her, and didn't linger once she'd finished.

She found him by the canteen and he lit up with pleasure when he saw her. His glow burnt even brighter as he presented her with his gift: a delicate silver bracelet.

Beth was delighted with it.

'It's beautiful.'

Allan flushed pink as he draped it over her wrist. 'It was Mum's. It's not expensive or anything, but I thought it was pretty.'

'It is.' Beth smiled and hugged him. 'I love it!'

The rest of the day went equally well, even though it was a Monday. Not even a maths test derailed Beth's good mood. That night, they all went out, Allan included, for a Chinese meal. The perfect end to a perfect day.

The next morning, however, everything changed.

It was such a subtle shift; just one of those small turnings in the road that you barely notice until you wind up in some place entirely unexpected. On the breakfast table, laid out as usual, was Richard's newspaper. He'd already finished with it and had left for work before Beth came down. The bold headline caught her eye:

SCHOOLGIRL MISSING

Underneath the headline was a photograph of a schoolgirl: smiling, fresh and full of hope – and Beth recognised her. It was Anna Johnston, a year twelve student at Beth's school, not a friend of hers but she'd seen her around. Her face was horribly out of place on the front page of the paper underneath this headline.

Beth pulled the paper towards her to read the accompanying story. Anna had gone out with friends to a party the previous Saturday night. Afterwards, she'd caught the train back to Chatswood by herself, arriving at about eleven pm. There, she was supposed to have transferred to a bus for the rest of the journey home, and CCTV footage confirmed she'd left the station, but she never made it to the bus. Her parents made an appeal for anyone who knew anything to come forward.

At school, the students buzzed with gossip: rumours

of a secret boyfriend and drug use at the party were the most circulated. Anna's friends cloistered in a tight knot, their faces serious. Her younger sister – a year seven student – was seen sobbing in the playground. Darker possibilities scratched at the edges of hushed conversations. When the principal requested over the loud speaker that anyone with information about Anna's disappearance come to the office, and police officers arrived to speak with the whole of year twelve in their homeroom, a hush fell over the school. By the time the last bell rang a different excitement began to bubble.

The story hit current affairs programs that night and the next morning it was in all the national newspapers. Abduction was considered a possibility, although a boyfriend was not discounted. One of Anna's girlfriends described a boy Anna was friendly with at the party – a surfer type, blond, about nineteen years old. A blurry image of someone like that was seen with Anna at Central Station, but at Chatswood Station, the CCTV camera recorded her leaving the station alone. This last photograph dominated most of the newspapers' front pages, including the one Richard subscribed to.

Beth stared at it, transfixed. The ghostly image was like a call to mission. All that could be seen was the back of a slender teen in jeans and a halter top walking down Chatswood Mall, but for Beth it offered an entry point. The photograph was taken at the beginning of the mall near the train station entrance. It didn't show any further into the mall than a few shops, but from there, if she entered the photograph, Beth would be able to look down the entire length of the mall. Since Anna never made it to the bus stop – which was just around the corner at the far end of the mall – whatever happened to her must have happened somewhere between the range of this CCTV camera and the end of the mall. All Beth needed to do was enter and look. She held the key to this mystery – and it wasn't some distant historic conspiracy where it made no difference whether she knew or not, *this one was still happening.* She had a chance to solve it – and maybe help find Anna.

Carefully, she folded the front page, making sure not to crease the picture, and slipped it into her folder.

'Do you know her?' asked Gillian.

Beth started and turned to her mother who was standing in the doorway. Her instant reaction was to be cross, she hated it when her mother snuck up on her like that, but she could see the concern creasing around her mother's eyes and her irritation eased. 'Nah. She's in year twelve.'

'Have you heard anything at school about it?'

Beth zipped up her bag.

'No. The police came, asking questions, but nothing's been said.' Beth felt suddenly guilty, though she wasn't sure why. 'I'd better go,' she said. 'I'll miss the bus.'

Gillian nodded and stepped aside to let her pass. 'Take care.'

Her cautioning words were obliterated by the bang of the front door.

Beth claimed her usual seat on the bus and slipped across to the window, her thoughts consumed by the photograph in her folder. She could hardly wait to enter it, or to see Allan's face when she told him. He'd be even more excited than she was. She knew it. He'd want to know what happened as much as she did. She grinned at the thought and tapped her foot impatiently as the bus chugged even more slowly than usual; there was a hold-up with some road works. By the time she got to school there were only five minutes before the first bell.

No time to find Allan – but she couldn't wait for recess. The importance of what she was about to do was firing inside her. She'd just have to tell him later.

With the zeal of a missionary she marched to the toilet block and, to her relief, it was empty. She didn't want witnesses. Allan told her she didn't make any noise when she travelled – but he hadn't seen her travel in a long time and things had changed over the past few months: her concentration had improved and she was staying in longer and exiting in a more controlled manner; she could also turn her upper body a little further to look around. She didn't know if these changes might mean she also did things differently in real-time, and she didn't want to take any risks.

Entering the stall furthest from the door, she locked herself in and listened for intruders. Hearing nothing, she relaxed. She fished the newspaper page from her bag and hung the bag on the hook on the door. The floor was wet from its hosing by the cleaners. Unpleasant, but wet and clean was better than dirty and smelly. Gingerly, she wiped the closed lid of the toilet with some toilet paper and sat on it, unfolding the page on her knees to reveal the photograph. It was dark and grainy – which raised a concern. She'd tried pictures in newspapers before; it was like entering a fog, with details indistinct like the photographs. There was no guarantee she'd be able to enter at all, which was a frustrating thought. Still, there was nothing to lose. If she couldn't enter, she'd just have to get a clearer photograph. That might be difficult – she wasn't even sure if CCTV photographs were ever clear, even in the original film – but she'd find a way.

Suddenly, the first bell rang.

Beth drew a deep breath and focused on the dark image.

In an instant, she was there.

* * *

11.07 p.m., February 26, 2005

She was standing in a dark, viscous place surrounded by fog. The air was thick and fibrous, hard to breathe.

A chill rushed through her.

What if she was caught here, stuck in the fibres of the paper, somewhere between the toilets and last Saturday night?

Her heart began to pound and she quickly let go.

With a jolt, she returned to the toilet seat.

* * *

March 2, 2005

Immediately, she felt foolish – but she also felt reassured. If she could get out, she could also stay in a little longer to see what could be seen.

With an impatient shrug, she tried again.

* * *

11.07 p.m., February 26, 2005

Again she was immersed in thick, sticky, darkness – but slowly it began to clear, like a misty mirror heated with a hairdryer. Through the mist the form of Anna Johnston gradually sharpened to crystal clear detail. She looked tiny and vulnerable walking by herself in the dark, wearing her tight-fitting jeans and halter top. Beth could now see it was a deep, shimmery blue. She watched, mesmerised, as Anna walked to the end of the mall, turned the corner – *and disappeared from sight!*

Gone.

The mall stretched empty in front of Beth.

Her opportunity was over.

And she hadn't seen anything at all useful!

Clearly, whatever happened to Anna had happened around the corner. Which made perfect sense, because that was where the road met the mall. If her boyfriend had picked her up in a car, there would be the most likely place. No one saw her get into a car, but then, there was no one *there* to see.

Not even her.

Disappointed, Beth was about to exit when a white van with a blaring stereo drove past the end of the mall in the same direction Anna had taken. What caught Beth's attention was that it seemed to stop just around the corner. The music wasn't getting further away.

Her boyfriend?

Without thinking, Beth hurried forwards to see if she could see more. When she heard loud voices above the music, she started to run and when she reached the corner she looked around it to see Anna talking to a man who was standing next to the white van. It didn't sound like a friendly conversation. He was clearly harassing her. Anna turned away – but as she did, a second man leapt out of the back of the van, raced up behind her, and punched her on the side of her head. A sickening thud resonated through the empty quiet of the night. Before Beth had time to process what she was seeing, the two men wrestled Anna to the van. She fought them, but her reactions were slow and she was no match for their weight. They forced her inside and jumped in after her, pulling the door shut on her desperate screams.

* * *

March 2, 2005

With a searing wrench Beth returned, reeling at what she'd seen.

Anna had been kidnapped!

There was no boyfriend. She'd been hit and forced into a van – and since she hadn't been seen since …

Beth began to shake.

Was Anna still alive? Could she save her – or was it already too late?

She had to tell the police! She had to go straight to the police station and tell them what happened, what she'd seen—

But how could she do that? How could she explain what she knew without exposing herself? And *what* could she really tell them? She hadn't even thought to get the number plate!

She'd have to go back.

She'd have to go back, get the number plate number at least, and any other details she could …

It was only then it hit her. She'd *moved!* She'd actually moved *inside* the picture. She'd *walked* all the way to the end of the mall!

How had she done that?

She'd never done it before. She'd tried a couple of times but was always flung back to the present. She'd never been able to take a step in any direction.

The realisation was dizzying – but she had no time to explore it. She had to get back to help Anna.

Flattening the photograph, she took a deep breath.

* * *

11.07 p.m., February 26, 2005

For the third time she was immersed in the murkiness, her heart beating fiercely as she waited for it to clear. When it did, and Anna became visible at the other end of the mall, Beth followed quickly after her. This time she reached the corner at the same time as the van. She watched it pull up beside Anna.

Anna was oblivious, checking her mobile phone. She didn't notice the man and was surprised when he approached, innocent to the horror that was about to engulf her.

He was tall, a head higher than Anna and heavily built, wearing jeans and a T-shirt. His head was shaved. Beth still couldn't hear the conversation because of the loud music, but she could read the number plate. A NSW plate: SMI 121.

Heart pounding, Beth watched as the argument between Anna and the man escalated. She saw the irritation build on Anna's face, saw her turn away and be caught unawares by the second man. He was smaller and chunkier, also with a shaved head, and he had tattoos down the whole length of his arms.

Beth watched in horror as the blow crashed once more into the side of Anna's head. Her hands flew to her mouth to keep from crying out. She felt so helpless, standing there, impotent, as they dragged Anna into the van – and as the door of the van was pulled shut a fierce rage filled her. She opened her mouth and screamed, screamed to stop them, screamed to get help, screamed with the desperate hope that if she could *move*, perhaps she could also be *heard*.

But if her cry was audible, it made no impact. No one came running to help.

Sobbing, Beth raced after the van as it pulled away from the curb and slammed her hands against it—

* * *

March 2, 2005

—and swung violently back to the school toilet.

With a heaving yell, she threw up all over the floor of the stall.

Chapter 15

March 2, 2005

Detective Sergeant Alexander Blaine examined the signed statement he'd been handed and then asked the young, redheaded constable: 'Are the parents here yet?'

'The mother just arrived. Gillian Fletcher.'

Blaine raised an eyebrow, and the constable shrugged. 'Second marriage. Daughter kept her father's name. They're in Room 2.'

Blaine nodded and walked down the hall, scanning the notes as he went. Four days after Anna Johnston disappeared, these notes didn't project a positive outcome for the girl.

At thirty-six, Blaine considered himself at the peak of his career. All he'd ever wanted was to be a detective involved with active fieldwork. He'd no desire to climb into higher paid administrative positions. He wanted nothing more than to stay where he was, watch his kids grow up and pay the mortgage. Lithe and slender, his threat potential was often underestimated. This, he used to his advantage. His benign persona, coupled with a warm, worn face and piercing grey eyes, had eroded many defences and earned him a reputation as one of the police service's top interviewers. This was the area in which he felt the most comfortable.

Blaine downed the last of his coffee, returned his cup to the staff kitchen and entered the interview room opposite.

The first thing he noticed was the tension in the room. The woman and girl waiting for him sat as far apart from each other as the space behind the table allowed. He could almost see the chasm between them.

Mother-daughter issues he concluded as he introduced himself and sat opposite them.

The mother appeared a decent woman to Blaine. She was well-dressed and smartly groomed in an understated, practical style. Came straight from work, he decided. Her thick, brown hair was swept up in an efficient bun and she wore quality shoes. He noted the kindness in her eyes and the concern. But there was something else there – fear.

What was she afraid of, he wondered?

The girl had a definite defensive edge. Not unusual for fifteen-year-old girls. In fact, *all* teenage girls were difficult, as far as Blaine was concerned. If they weren't, there was probably something wrong with them. But was this one out of control?

He smoothed his standard introductory remarks with a few relaxed conversational comments to put them at ease and give him a few more seconds to observe them. He liked to be prepared. His methods usually paid off, although these two didn't seem to relax any. The mother was doing her best to communicate polite attention, but she couldn't quite banish the worry from her eyes, and the daughter remained fixed in an impatient glare.

Blaine's grey eyes regarded her evenly. She was unusually pretty, even with a scowl on her face. Clear olive skin and enormous brown eyes like her mother. *Very* pretty – but in a childlike way. No make-up, or any other of the attempts to enhance beauty that most girls her age were experimenting with, and her hair hung in loose disarray. Not into fashion yet? Or just didn't care?

'So, Lilibeth,' he began.

'Beth,' the girl corrected bluntly; and the mother shifted uncomfortably in her seat.

'Beth,' Blaine acknowledged politely. 'I understand you saw Anna Johnston being pulled into a van last Saturday night at—' he referred to the statement '—just after eleven o'clock, at the Chatswood bus exchange?'

'A Ford Transit van. NSW plate, SMI 121. Yes,' she answered crisply.

Blaine's interest was further aroused. She had that down pat.

'Why didn't you contact the police at the time?'

She hesitated only a second. 'I didn't want to get into trouble. My mother didn't know I was out.'

'Why were you out?'

Beth shrugged. 'I went to a party.'

Credible, he thought. Yet it didn't quite ring true. Her answer seemed rehearsed, and the mother was distinctly uncomfortable. Was she feeling guilty because she was being exposed as an irresponsible mother with no idea what her daughter was up to? Or was it something else? What did she know? Or suspect?

'Can't you just look the plates up?' snapped Beth. 'I'm sorry I didn't come in sooner, but you might still find Anna if you get on with it.'

'It's being looked up,' Blaine assured her, 'but it has been four days …'

She flushed bright red, but said nothing. Blaine waited, giving her space to add more. In his experience, you got the most useful information by just letting people talk. If you waited and gave them space, more often than not they'd step into the noose and hang themselves. But this girl didn't. Having regained her self-control she sat there tightly, locking her secrets out of reach.

Her initial distress intrigued him though. She clearly cared, and the depth of her caring was surprising considering she'd waited so long to bring the information forwards.

Merely because of the fear of parental wrath?

He gave Mrs Fletcher another thoughtful look, but she withered under his gaze, looking anything but threatening. OK then, he thought. He'd come back to that.

'Why don't you tell me what you saw?' he asked Beth in his friendly, father-figure voice.

Beth straightened her back a little and calmly told him everything she'd seen. Her descriptions were precise, as though she were presenting a well-prepared account. Blaine didn't interrupt except to confirm details and she readily replied to every request. She didn't vary from her statement, and her alleged observations were credible, both in the likelihood and in the telling of it. She'd been there all right, decided Blaine, but her testimony had too many questions attached to it. The girl herself was a question. She didn't ring true. Blaine had learnt to trust his instincts on these sorts of things. Busying himself with his notes he added as though it was an afterthought, 'How did you get to Chatswood?'

'By train.'

'The same one as Anna's?'

Beth hesitated. She wouldn't have been on any CCTV footage. 'No. Earlier. I walked around a bit.'

'Down the mall?'

'No … I went the other way. I didn't go down the mall.'

Blaine nodded understandingly. 'I see. Which train did you arrive on?'

This time she flushed. 'I don't know. I caught it at Central, don't know the time. Look, this isn't about me: it's about Anna. I *saw* her. I saw her being *kidnapped* by three men in a white Ford Transit, SMI 121, and that's all you need. Just check that out! What does it matter where *I* was, or what *I* was doing? You're supposed to be looking for Anna! Just look up the van!'

Blaine thought it was time to brandish a little authority. 'Miss O'Malley, it's important to establish the credibility of a lead before investigating it.'

But she spat straight back. 'And what if I'd just put in an anonymous note? Wouldn't you have checked that out?'

Gillian blanched. 'Beth! Beth, don't—'

She reached out to her daughter, but Beth brushed her aside. 'I'm doing what's right! For Anna,' she snapped, and turned her fiery eyes back on Blaine. 'Just check it out. Find those men before it's too late. And if you *don't* find a white Ford Transit van owned by those pricks, *then* you can call me a liar.'

'Beth!' It was almost a wail.

'It's all right, Mrs Fletcher,' said Blaine calmly. 'Nobody's calling you a liar, Beth. Please, just take a deep breath, then we can sort this out properly.'

Beth bristled, clearly wanting other options, but finally she did as she was told. Blaine watched – impressed as she regained her calm, determined, control. He then asked again, 'Is there anything you can add to this statement, Beth?'

She shook her head with definite certainty.

'You didn't recognise any of the men?'

'No.'

'You're sure?'

'Of course I'm sure. I'd have said if I did. I've never seen any of them before.'

'Your descriptions of them are very … detailed.'

'I'm observant.'

Blaine smiled. 'That you are.'

She didn't blush. It was clear he wouldn't get anything else out of her for the moment. It frustrated him to have to content himself with the tip of an iceberg, but it was at least a potentially valuable tip. And the girl was right – Anna *was* first priority here. There would be time to unravel Beth's connection to the 'pricks' later on. Clearly there *was* a connection. All would eventually be revealed, and the possibilities of that made him a little sad. Even though he'd spent his entire professional life mucking through the bilge of humanity, kids in trouble still unsettled him. It never gave him any satisfaction to see the ruin of their young lives exposed.

With careful deliberation he closed his folder. 'All right, Miss O'Malley, thank you for your assistance.' Instantly, Beth's confidence evaporated, making her appear half her age.

'You'll find the van?'

'We'll look into it. Yes.' He held her gaze, noting her relief.

'Thank you, Detective,' said Gillian, standing stiffly.

Blaine stood and reached out to shake her hand. It was ice-cold. How interesting to be a fly on their rear vision mirror, he thought as the two walked from the room.

* * *

Gillian gripped the steering wheel, her knuckles white, as she navigated her way home; Beth stared out the window, her chin set, ready for war.

Did it matter, Gillian wondered? Was it worth the battle?

Dry-throated, she broke the silence. 'Are you in some kind of trouble, honey?'

Beth responded with an exaggerated, aggressive sigh.

'Beth … I just need to know what's going on here—'

'Nothing's going on!'

The fury of her reply made Gillian cringe. Beth, noticing, seemed to regret her sharpness and pulled her attack back a notch. 'I'm sorry you got dragged into this. I didn't know they were going to make you come in. I was just trying to help. I thought the police should know what I saw.'

'But you *didn't* see anything. You weren't there. You didn't *see* it.'

Beth froze. 'How do you know?'

Gillian tried to keep her voice calm and reasonable. 'We were watching a movie. We didn't go to bed until eleven … Beth, I know you didn't leave the house.'

Part of her hoped Beth would come out with some simple explanation; but she didn't. Instead she turned away.

'Are you … involved in something?' Gillian asked carefully. 'Did one of your friends know something abo—'

'*No!*' Beth's face flushed red. 'It wasn't one of my *friends!*'

'I wasn't suggesting—'

'It *wasn't* one of my friends! I just *know*. That's *all*.'

'But, how—'

'What difference does it make? It's still the *truth!*'

'But, *I*—'

'Just stay out of it, Mum! It's none of your business, and it's not going to come back on you, or Richard. I haven't done anything wrong. I'm not *doing* anything wrong.'

Gillian bit back on her tongue, horrified this had escalated into such a mess. Conversations with Beth could so easily become a minefield. She could see no way through. Leaden with worry she tried to focus on the road. Beth wanted to go back to school, even though it was nearly one o'clock, and she'd agreed to take her. They continued in silence. When she pulled up at the gate, Beth jumped out of the car before she'd had a chance to pull the handbrake. Gillian was left quivering.

She watched her daughter stride into the school grounds without a backwards glance.

* * *

Beth signed in at the school office saying she'd had a doctor's appointment. No fuss was made, and she went to join her class. It was double English. They were watching a video of a Shakespeare performance so Beth entered with little notice and sat undisturbed with her thoughts for the rest of the lesson. Allan was in another class. She didn't catch up with him until after school. He grinned happily when he saw her.

'I thought you were off sick today.'

'I was at the police station.' Instantly, Allan's good mood evaporated. 'Can we talk?'

They sat under a tree outside the library and Beth told him everything that had happened.

Words tumbled out, all jumbled up in emotions. She was feeling particularly bad about the fight with her mother. There was little Allan could do except listen, but eventually her words slowed and then stopped.

'Maybe you should just tell her,' suggested Allan after some quiet consideration.

'She'll send me back to the shrink!'

'You don't know that. She might listen. Your mum's not stupid, and you're not sick. You have a gift, and you could prove it if you want to—'

'She'd freak out!'

'Maybe not.'

'You don't know her. She would. And she'd tell Richard. If I tried to *prove* anything to them, he'd get me committed for sure.'

Allan looked doubtful about that.

'He would! He'd have them shoving me into a test tube to find out exactly what kind of freak I am and I'd never get out again!' She pushed back angrily against the tree and drew her knees up to her chest. 'I can't tell them.'

'Well ...' said Allan '... if that's the case, you're going to have to come up with a better story for your parents, and for the police.'

'Why? What difference does it make? The police won't care. They'll find the van, then they'll know I didn't make it up.'

'And think you were probably in on the kidnapping.'

She stared at him, confused.

'How else could you know?' Allan shrugged.

'But ... I've never met those men.'

'So, how do you know all about them?'

Beth was too stunned to speak.

'That's what they're going to ask, Beth. And, if it turns into a murder investigation, they're going to ask a *lot* of questions ... and you've set yourself up as the only witness.'

'*Murder?*'

'She'd come home if she could, wouldn't she?' said Allan reasonably. 'I'm not saying she *was* murdered. Maybe they'll find her and she'll be all right, and all of this won't matter ... but, you've got to be prepared. When you're trying to hide something, you have to come up with something that's easy to believe, that doesn't raise any questions. Telling them you *saw* it, when your mum knows you were at home, isn't going to work.'

'But Mum won't say anything. She's shit-scared I'm covering for someone else. She won't say anything because then *she'd* look bad.'

Allan shook his head. 'Even if she doesn't say anything, you're still gunna have to come up with something for the police.'

'Why?'

'Because they're gunna see through it. They're not stupid. They're not gunna leave you alone until you come up with something better; and the sooner you do, the sooner they'll stop going after you.'

'Well ... what should I tell them?'

Presented now with her open trust, his mind went blank. 'I don't know ... but we'll think of something.'

This only spiralled her into deeper fright.

'It's OK,' he soothed. 'Maybe they won't even ask. They probably won't. You told them about the van so they'll be following that up, and that might end it. Don't worry about it. I always go negative on everything.'

He tried to conjure a relaxed laugh, but Beth wasn't fooled. 'No. No, you're right. Mum'll tell Richard. I know she will, she tells him *everything*, and he'll tell the police. He's such a straight-arse—'

'It still might not matter.'

She grabbed his hands, completely frightened now. 'But, if they tell the police I was home, they're going to think—'

'If it comes to that,' said Allan seriously, 'tell them *I* told you.'

'No!'

'I'll get Monica to vouch for me.'

'But they'll find out you're on your own! They'll find

out about your mum, about everything, and they'll put you in a home!'

'So?' He shrugged. 'I'll run away.'

'No! No, I won't do that to you. I won't. It's not your fault I'm in trouble, and I won't drag you into this.'

'Beth—'

'I couldn't bear it!' Tears filled her eyes.

'It probably won't come to that,' said Allan gently, 'but if it does, that's OK. Really, it is. I can take care of myself. And who knows, it might even be a good home.'

He attempted a brave smile, but Beth burst into tears.

'I'm sorry. I'm so sorry,' she sobbed. 'I never thought this would happen. I was only trying to help Anna, and it's probably too late for her now anyway. Oh God … oh God, I'm sorry.'

Allan felt helpless. Hating to see her so upset, he reached an arm over her shoulders.

'I wanted to talk to you first,' she said miserably. 'I did. But I thought … I didn't think I should wait … I thought I had to be quick … but I should have waited to talk with you first.'

Allan wished she had too, but there was no point going there now. 'You did what you thought was right,' he said, but this seemed only to shatter her further. She buried her face in his chest and wrapped her arms tightly around him as though trying to squeeze her fear away. It certainly pushed his away. Having her in his arms was worth whatever sacrifice he'd have to make. Gently he stroked her hair and let his thoughts drift over his potentially altered future.

After a moment, she sniffed deeply and declared

with calm determination, 'If you have to run away, I'm coming with you.'

A grateful smile crept to his face. 'Well, for now, just stick with what you've said. Don't say anything more to the police and don't change anything you've said, or they'll jump on that. Maybe they'll find Anna and it'll all be over. No sense making trouble for ourselves if we don't have to.'

'OK,' she agreed and snuggled closer.

He didn't want to say it, but he knew he should: 'You should probably go home. Your mum will be waiting.'

She moaned and held on tighter.

'Go home,' he said softly. 'And be nice. And if your mum asks who you're covering for, just tell her it's a friend and you promised not to say. Say your friend's parents will kill her if they find out she snuck out. That'll make sense. You don't have to say anything about me yet.'

Reluctantly, Beth pulled away from the safety of his chest and gazed into his eyes. They were soft with caring and love for her.

'I wish I could just stay with you.'

Allan grinned. 'Yeah, that'd work.'

Giggling, her eyes regained a little of their sparkle, and Allan felt a heavy flush in his loins; it only needed one smile from her to demolish him completely. Scrambling to hide the nakedness of his feelings, he helped her up – but he was too late. She'd seen. He saw his heart reflected in her deep brown eyes, and terror gripped him – but she didn't laugh or back away. Instead, she gently kissed him, shy and hesitant. Her lips lingered only a moment, but the intimacy of it shivered through him, setting him trembling, rendering him incapable.

'Thank you,' she whispered, her breath hot against his cheek. 'Walk with me to the bus?'

Allan nodded stupidly, and they strolled off across the playground – she, smiling contentedly; he, walking with embarrassing stiffness – as she continued to cling to his hand.

All too soon, she was on the bus and he was left standing alone watching as the bus disappeared down the street.

But he wasn't alone.

Unnoticed, in an unmarked car further down on the other side of the street, Detective Sergeant Blaine was watching.

Chapter 16

March 4, 2005

Blaine picked his way through the cluttered garage. Two cars hoisted above pits were being worked on by an older mechanic and two younger ones in their late teens or twenties. A lanky kid, barely more than sixteen, with close cropped hair and pimples, was sweeping the floor. Obviously the apprentice. The older man straightened as Blaine entered, his greeting friendly enough.

'Be with you in a minute, mate.'

He gave a few instructions to the younger mechanic, wiped his greasy hands on his overalls and walked up to Blaine with a smile. 'What can I do for you?'

Short and stocky, the girth of the man's gut and redness of his nose indicated a love of beer, but the obvious strength in his massive hands and the aggressive line of his jaw left no doubt he could hold his own.

Blaine showed him his ID. 'Detective Sergeant Blaine. I'd like to speak with Mr Corelli.'

The man was instantly wary. 'That's me.'

'I understand you are the owner of a white Ford Transit van, SMI 121?'

'Yeah … What of it?'

The other mechanics had stopped work and were watching curiously.

'Can you tell me where that van was last Saturday night?' asked Blaine politely.

'Why?'

'We're just making enquiries, sir.'

The 'sir' seemed to ease Corelli a little, but it didn't dent his defensiveness. Something to hide, wondered Blaine? An abduction? Or a car re-birthing racket? Or perhaps only an understandable feeling of threat when confronted by authority of any kind?

Whatever the reason, Corelli didn't appear too open to cooperation.

'It was at home,' he grunted. 'I didn't use the van. I was at home with the wife, and she'll vouch for that.' He folded his thick arms across his chest.

Blaine kept his gaze steady. 'Any possibility the vehicle was lent to anybody else, or used without your knowledge?' His eyes wandered to the young mechanic who now regarded him with the same bold challenge as his boss. Or perhaps father? Yes. He could pass for a younger version of Corelli, thought Blaine, though with a weaker chin. He was also short and stocky, but with a cleanly shaved head. His rolled-up sleeves revealed a colourful mat of tattoos creeping up both his arms.

'What's all this about?' asked Corelli. 'Why are you

asking about my van?'

'We have a witness who claims to have seen this vehicle in Chatswood last Saturday night.'

The man appeared genuinely confused. 'Chatswood?'

Blaine nodded. He glanced back at the tattooed mechanic, but the younger man's head was now buried in the engine of the vehicle he was working on.

'I weren't in Chatswood,' said Corelli, his confusion now replaced by hard certainty. 'And I ain't lent it to no one. Your witness musta got it wrong.'

'You're sure about that?'

'You want me to sign something?' The little man's stance shifted to bullish aggression.

Blaine didn't miss a beat. 'Yes. I'd like you to come in and make an official statement at your earliest convenience,' he said, handing Corelli his card.

Corelli's ears blazed crimson. 'What's this about? Drink drivin' or something? The van weren't in no accident. Take a look at it yourself. It's out back. No damage on it.'

'Thank you,' said Blaine. 'I'd appreciate that.'

Corelli was momentarily thrown, but he walked over to the rough wooden counter and grabbed a set of keys. Behind him, on the wall, was a large poster of an abnormally buxom woman in a highly sexualised pose with a car.

'This way,' he said, and led the way out of the garage to a white van. 'See? Nothing wrong with it.'

It was an old van, covered in dings and scratches, but there was no evidence of new work.

'Can you open the back, please?'

'Why?'

'You could bring it down to the station with me now if you'd rather.'

Corelli grunted and opened the back door. He made a gesture of invitation and stepped aside to allow Blaine access.

Blaine stepped up and peered inside.

It was pretty much empty. A piece of carpet covered the base, with no obvious stains other than expected mechanical spills and leakages – still, it was impossible to know what they were without forensic testing. Two large speakers were hooked up in the back, with more in the front, lining up with the O'Malley girl's statement about loud music. There was an old plastic milk crate up against the back seats, filled with greasy rags and a few tools, but that was about it.

On the dash was a little dancing hula girl.

'You like loud music?' Blaine asked.

Corelli looked shifty. 'No, that's for … My son put that in. He likes it.'

'Your son?' Blaine asked politely. 'Is that your son in the garage? The young man with the tattoos?'

Corelli looked wary again. 'Yeah, that's my son. I let him use the van sometimes, when I don't need it, or for carting stuff around. But he has his own car.'

'And he didn't borrow the van last Saturday night?'

'No. I told you. It was at home, with me. Your witness must have it wrong. My van weren't in Chatswood Saturday night. I don't know what you're doin' here, wasting my time.'

'I'm investigating the kidnapping of a seven-teen-year-old girl, Mr Corelli,' Blaine said coolly. 'Could I please have a word with your son?'

* * *

The next few days were troubling ones for Beth. There was no news about Anna. Posters with her face on them and a bold heading in red – *'Have you seen Anna?'* – were plastered across the northern suburbs, but the media had been quiet. No body had been found.

Beth heard nothing further from the police, but Allan thought this was probably a good sign. He was certain they were busy following up the van and that any day now the case would break.

She hoped so, but the waiting was horrible. With each day it seemed less and less likely Anna would be found alive.

She also worried about what would happen when the whole business came out and it went to trial. She'd probably be called as a witness. Allan had said so. What would she do then? Stick to her story about sneaking out and risk being exposed, or tell them Allan had told her and drop him in it?

Her mind went round and round, searching for better stories ... other stories ... *any* story that would work. Every time she saw a police car she froze; when a runner interrupted a class with a message from the office, she automatically assumed it was for her; when the phone rang at home she jumped and found it difficult to breathe until she knew she was safe. The stress was becoming unbearable. At one point, certain Allan would be investigated just because he was her friend, she tried to talk him into running away. She was sure it would be better for him to get out while he still could, but he refused to leave her to face it on her own. She was grateful for that, she knew there was no way she could cope without him, but it left her taut whenever they were together in public.

Home was also a nightmare. She couldn't talk with her mother. They hadn't had a real conversation since the confrontation in the car on the way home from the police station. Her mother's stress levels seemed even higher than her own, which of course made Richard more prickly than usual as well. At least they didn't pressure her for explanations – but the resulting awkward silences were almost worse. Retreat was the only strategy she could tolerate, preferring to sit alone in her room rather than attempt any kind of 'family time'.

That at least gave her time to think – and one realisation especially burned: she'd *moved* in the picture. This was a significant change. She didn't know how she'd done it; it had happened so quickly without her even thinking about it – but it wasn't a one-off. *She'd done it again!*

Maybe now she could move whenever she wanted to, *where*ver she wanted to? That was tantalising. If she could … she'd be able to explore … go *inside* the castles … or around the corner at Machu Picchu … or even to see more of Nanna! Maybe she could go inside Nanna's house instead of waiting outside when they all went in?

Another little moment with Nanna …

It wasn't much, but she missed her terribly and anything was better than nothing. She only had the one picture of Nanna, only the one window into her life – but perhaps now she had a *door!*

Eagerly, she unhooked the picture from the wall.

* * *

March, 1964

'One more. Just in case,' yelled her grandfather.

'Oh, Cecil, that's enough,' said Nanna. 'I have to get that cake out of the oven.'

The boys raced off around the side of the house.

'Thank you, Edie. That'll do. Come on in for tea.'

Nanna walked back into the house as Edie walked past Beth and linked arms with Beth's grandfather. Her sandals clicked gaily against the wood of the verandah as the pair followed Nanna into the house.

The screen door banged shut.

Tentatively, Beth took a step. It *worked*. She took another.

Gaining confidence, forgetting that what she was doing had ever been impossible, she walked up onto the verandah to face the closed door.

Would she be able to open it? She'd never successfully touched anything before – let alone manipulated or moved it, but at that moment anything seemed possible. Holding her breath, she reached out and grasped the handle – and when she wasn't thrown out, she opened the screen door. Smiling, she stepped inside and the door banged shut behind her.

'I thought I shut that,' said Edie, looking around curiously in Beth's direction, not seeing her.

So, still invisible.

Edie was only a few feet away, standing with her grandfather, who was leaning against the wall in the hall.

'Probably just the wind,' said her grandfather in a

low voice.

Beth's eyes had now adjusted to the darkened interior, and she took in the unsettling expression on her grandfather's face. He was happy, but it wasn't the right kind of happiness. There was a hunger in his eyes as he looked at Edie.

As Beth tried to excuse away what she knew in her heart she was seeing, her grandfather obliterated any chance of that by sliding his hand around Edie's bottom and pulling her hips up tight against his. His other hand reached up to cup Edie's breast, and Edie lifted her face to his.

Beth gasped and immediately slapped her hand over her mouth, but they showed no sign of hearing her. Her grandfather leant in to kiss Edie, his hands roving.

Outraged, Beth edged past them and slipped through the dividing bead curtain into the kitchen.

The room was empty. Her pulse was racing. She had to find Nanna. She had to tell her ... warn her ... stop her from walking into the hall and seeing – but Nanna was not there.

Where was she?

Beth checked out the back door but couldn't see her. And then she heard the wardrobe door shut in Nanna's bedroom. She crossed to the open bedroom door and saw her grandmother standing by her bed.

'Nanna?' she cried, her voice thick with emotion; but Nanna didn't react.

'Nanna?' she tried again, a little louder.

Again she was ignored. Nanna didn't move at all. She remained still as a statue, staring down at her bed.

It was clear she couldn't hear her.

The disappointment bit sharp.

'Sorry, Nanna,' she whispered.

She was about to leave when Nanna moved. She'd been so deeply still, it was almost as though she'd abruptly come to life from some kind of frozen state. Beth watched fascinated as Nanna slowly laid her hand, palm flat, on the bed and shut her eyes in an intense concentration, a concentration Beth recognised; she couldn't look away.

But then Nanna let out an anguished moan and wrenched her hand back. She looked up and straight through Beth to the room beyond – confronting Beth with the raw depth of her pain.

And suddenly Beth understood.

Some things are better left unseen.

* * *

March 7, 2005

The next morning the police turned up at the house. Beth was packing her schoolbag when her mother appeared at her door.

'Honey, the detectives have come to talk with you. They're downstairs in the kitchen.'

It was the moment she'd dreaded. They'd finally come. She stepped into the kitchen, clutching her over-full school bag to her chest as though it might offer protection.

There were two of them: the one she'd seen before, Detective Sergeant Blaine, and a woman.

'Hello, Beth.' Blaine smiled. 'This is Detective Senior

Constable Frazer. We were wanting to have a few words with you.'

Her mother and Richard stood stiffly by the fridge.

'I have to get to school,' she said guardedly. 'I'll miss the bus.'

'This won't take long. Please sit down, Beth.'

Blaine said it politely, but it wasn't a request. Beth sat at the breakfast table. The detectives sat opposite. Her parents stayed by the fridge.

'We've traced the van you identified, Beth,' opened Blaine, his face unreadable, but clearly expecting some kind of response from her.

'That's good,' she answered cautiously.

'Yes ... but the owner of the vehicle is an older man with a solid alibi. He wasn't at Chatswood on the 26th, and he states that his van wasn't either. Are you absolutely certain you remembered the number plate accurately?'

Beth didn't hesitate. 'Yes.'

'It was dark ...'

'They were stopped under a light. I didn't make a mistake. That was the number plate.'

Blaine's eyes delved into hers. 'And you saw the men clearly?'

'Not really ... They pretty much had their backs to me the whole time.'

'You said you saw tattoos on one of them?'

Beth thought about it. 'Yes ... I saw them, but I wasn't that close. They were all down his arms, like sleeves, but I'm not sure about the pattern.'

She saw the arms again in her memory: dark, like snake skin.

'Scales!' she said suddenly. 'There were scales on his arm. Green. Like a snake.'

Frazer wrote it down as Blaine waited for more, but Beth couldn't remember anything else.

Maybe she should go back again?

'Nothing more?' asked Blaine.

She shook her head.

'Would you be willing to come to the station to have a look at a few different possibilities?'

'A line-up?'

'Just some photographs for now.'

'You haven't arrested anyone?'

'We're still pursuing investigations.'

Beth was disappointed. 'Was there anything in the van?'

Blaine showed surprise.

'Blood? Hair? Anything?' asked Beth. 'Did you do forensic tests?'

'I'm not at liberty—'

'You must have found something if you want me to ID someone, right?'

'Beth,' cut in Richard authoritatively.

'It's all right, Mr Fletcher,' said Blaine. 'Beth is just trying to decide if she needs to come to the station to help us or not. Am I right, Beth?'

Beth didn't dare to agree or disagree.

'Well,' continued Blaine, 'I can tell you honestly that your help could be very important to this case. You are the only witness, and your testimony is strongly contradicted. We need more if we are going to go further with this.'

Beth looked over at her mother, who stared back

at her in a silent, desperate plea. Now was the time to 'confess' that it was actually Allan who'd seen the crime … but Allan couldn't identify anyone.

She turned back to Blaine.

'OK,' she said. 'I'll come.'

Chapter 17

January 18, 1973

Gillian sat cross-legged on the sand, smiling at her cousins, letting their chatter wash over her and pretending she didn't care.

Jeff had been gone nearly an hour!

She'd saved him some fish and chips, but they'd gone all soggy and cold now and the family had just about finished lunch. Auntie Barbara and her mother were pouring tea from the thermos and cutting the cake.

With a sinking heart, Gillian folded the paper over the last of the fish and chips and put the package aside. She'd been so proud to introduce Jeff to the family. Having a steady boyfriend separated her from her younger cousins and established her firmly in the 'grown-up' camp, at least in her mind. All the older cousins had boyfriends or girlfriends. Her sister Gaby seemed to have a different boyfriend every week, all of them vastly different from each other – as though she was determined to try one of everything before settling on anything. This week's edition was a weedy-looking intellectual with serious eyes and greasy hair that hung limply around his face. Gaby described him as a revolutionary. He'd been a conscientious objector to the draft for the Vietnam War and was head of the student union. Gillian knew her parents weren't impressed with this one, especially since her cousin William had been such a hero in Vietnam, but that seemed to escalate his value in Gaby's estimation. She was a pacifist.

Gillian was certain Jeff made a better impression than Gaby's latest. Tall, with a lean, well-defined body, Jeff was a champion surfer and the best-looking boy she'd ever seen. He had a broad, warm face with deep-blue eyes, perfect skin and curly, honey-coloured hair. No one could fail to be impressed by him. She'd had her eyes on him since the very first time she'd met him, two years previously, but they'd only been going around together for six weeks. Today was the first time he'd met her family. An important milestone. She felt so grown-up announcing it and it went well, but she knew it looked rude that he'd gone off so soon.

She'd met Jeff at a youth group run by a local church. Gillian's parents weren't religious, but Gina had been raised a Catholic and she trusted the respectability of a church youth group, even if it wasn't Catholic. All of them made their first endeavours at social contact there. Single gender schools made those first contacts awkward and difficult to arrange. Gillian's brothers' friends were a lot older than she was, and other than the ritual pretence of ignoring cat calls from the boys hanging out of their school bus as it drove past, she didn't get the chance to interact with many boys her own age.

But there were *eleven* of them in the church youth group!

Lorraine'd had a boyfriend within the first month and was on her third now. Annette had someone too, and Babette was stringing two along. Gillian couldn't go past Jeff, but it was a while before he noticed her. All the girls were in love with him, and she didn't have Lorraine's vivacious personality or the De Veaux twins' ample boobs – hers had barely begun to develop. Then there was Veronica, the minister's daughter. Jeff's father was a deacon in the church and his mother taught Sunday school. His family socialised with the minister's family and Veronica and Jeff had known each other for a long time so he was usually paired with her for games. Everyone assumed they'd eventually get together.

But they hadn't. Jeff had chosen her!

His status had instantly raised hers. He had special privileges in the youth group. He knew where the keys were for the back rooms and came and went as he pleased. It was in one of those back rooms that Gillian first learnt how to French kiss. She smiled as she thought of it. It hadn't been that long ago, and she still wasn't used to it. She couldn't believe he was actually her boyfriend.

But where was he now?

Gillian searched the shops lining the road by the beach, but couldn't see him among the Saturday crowds. She scanned the surf again, shielding her eyes against the glare, but couldn't spot him there either.

'Where's your boyfriend gone, Gilly?' asked Mary,

Auntie Margaret's daughter, as she offered Gillian a piece of cake. Mary was seven, and annoying. Her pigtails were stiff with salt and the bright white stripe of zinc across her nose and cheeks made her look like an under-sized Amazonian warrior.

'He just went to get something,' said Gillian absentmindedly.

'What?'

'Nothing to do with you. He'll be back soon.'

Obviously not getting her cousin's 'rack off' vibes, Mary bounced closer. 'You wanna go for a swim?'

It was a hot day and the ocean was inviting. Gillian suspected Jeff had been tempted into the water and had lost track of time. The surf was perfect; it was a bit much to expect him to sit on the sand and watch it. That made her feel a little less rejected. She was tempted to go look for him, but not with Mary tagging along – and what if Jeff came back and she wasn't there?

'Nah, not just yet,' she said, mimicking her mother's not-now-dear voice. 'Let me finish my cake first.'

Mary initiated a determined whine, but just then Gillian caught sight of Jeff coming up the beach with his best friend, Derrick, and two girls Gillian didn't know. An uncomfortable pang of jealousy pricked at her heart, but Jeff smiled and waved. Gillian bounced up and ran to him.

'Sorry,' he said as she approached. 'I ran into Derrick.'

Derrick, a brawny seventeen-year-old, said hi and introduced the girls: Judy and Wendy.

'Hi,' they said in unison. They were older than Gillian, closer to Jeff and Derrick's age, and Gillian couldn't help feeling threatened.

'You missed lunch,' she said, attempting to establish her prior claim. 'I kept some for you, but it's cold now.'

Jeff was appropriately shame-faced. 'Yeah, sorry. I lost track of time.' He turned to Derrick. 'Give us a minute, will ya?'

Derrick nodded, and he and the girls headed up the beach towards the shops, snickering together as they went.

'Sorry. I forgot I told Derrick I'd meet up with him,' said Jeff with his most winning smile. 'Are your parents mad?'

Gillian was upset, and the comment about 'giving him a minute' was confusing her. But at least he'd come back. And he was staying with *her*. She looked over at her parents, deep in conversation with her aunts and uncles, relaxed and happy after several beers and oblivious to any of her interactions. 'No … Don't think so.'

'Listen,' began Jeff, but he was interrupted by a loud summons from Gillian's mother.

'Time for a photograph! Everybody, listen up! Come over here and sit down together!'

Everybody groaned, but Gina bullied them into a cooperative tableau in spite of protests. Gillian dragged Jeff over to stand beside her at the edge of the group. Gina, having cajoled a man under a neighbouring umbrella to take the photo for them, positioned herself front and centre between Gillian's father and Auntie Barbara and yelled, 'Smile, everyone!'

After two attempts and several agonising minutes of looking directly into the sun, the deed was done and a post-lunch swim suggested. While the group prepared for the water, Gillian brought the cold fish and chips to

Jeff, but he was looking uncomfortable.

'Listen, Gilly, I can't stay.'

She stared up at him speechless and he shrugged. 'I promised Derrick we'd hang out this afternoon.'

'But … you said you'd be here.'

'I know. I forgot. I'm sorry, but Derrick came all the way down here, and I have to drive him home. You've got all your cousins haven't you?'

'Well, yes … but—'

'Thanks Gilly. I knew you'd understand.' He gave her a quick kiss on the cheek, and then was gone.

Gillian stood there numb, watching his broad, brown back disappear up the beach to where Derrick and the girls waited. When he reached them, the dark-haired girl who'd been introduced as Judy linked her arm in his and the group disappeared behind the Surf Life Saving Club.

'Is everything all right, honey?'

It was Gina, looking concerned.

'Of course,' Gilly answered, a little too gaily. 'Jeff had to go home. He said to say sorry … and thanks.' She knew her lie hadn't fooled her mother, but the last thing she wanted was pity. 'I'm going for a swim.'

Forcing a smile, she headed for the surf and bounded into the waves. Lifting her knees high, she pushed through to where the full power of the waves could crash against her. She let them pummel her, holding herself rigid as her tears mixed into the foam.

Fortunately, she was left alone. No one came near her until her hurt was spent. But when she returned to shore, Mary skipped through the shallows to continue her pester. 'Wanna make a sand castle?'

'Later, Mary. I'm gunna sunbake now.'

As Gillian expected, Mary wasn't interested in that; she ran back into the surf. Gillian returned to her towel and retreated under her straw hat and tanning oil, pretending to take a nap. In the speckled darkness under her hat, her heart continued to break.

'Gillian?'

The voice was soft and low and Gillian didn't recognise it. She lifted a corner of her hat and squinted into the sun. Kneeling beside her was a woman dressed bizarrely in a long red coat. Gillian rolled over and sat up, grabbing her sunglasses to camouflage her swollen eyes. 'Yeah?' she said, not in the mood to talk to anyone, let alone this odd stranger, but unable to be rude.

The woman smiled. Her skin was pale like winter against her short black hair, a startling contrast in the glaring sun. 'It's all for the best,' she said. 'He's a pig.'

Gillian's stomach did a flip-flop. 'What?'

'He's not good enough for you. Forget about him.'

'What are you talking about?'

'Jeff. He doesn't care about you; he only cares about himself. You're well rid of him.'

Gillian's cheeks flared in indignation. 'I'm *not* rid of him!'

'You will be,' said the woman, and Gillian angrily pulled away.

'What do you know about Jeff and me? Who *are* you?'

'Don't you remember?'

The woman's dark eyes bored into Gillian's, thoroughly spooking her. She looked for her parents and saw her mother coming out of the surf.

The woman saw her too.

'Have a good life, Gillian,' she said with a mysterious smile. 'Remember. You can trust me. *Always.*'

With that, she stood up, brushed the sand from her jeans and walked away.

'Who was that, darling?' asked Gina, and Gillian turned to her, open mouthed.

'I've no idea.'

'What did she want?'

'Beats me.' She flopped back down on her towel, thumping her hat back over her face.

It was only then the penny dropped, there in the mottled safety under the straw.

The school photograph lady was back!

* * *

The hotel room crashed back around her. She was exhausted. That trip had taken far longer than she'd hoped; she hadn't counted on the swim.

It was strange to see her mother so young – so gawky and vulnerable. Oddly touching. Again she regretted how little she'd known her mother, how little she'd bothered to get to know her …

Flipping the pages of the album back to the high school photographs, she considered again making an appearance at those, but again she decided not to. Too much exposure was risky. What if she turned into a jittering paranoid? What if she never went to Europe?

No. Best leave it as it was.

Her head felt like it was trying to split in two. This was taking a lot out of her, and she was running out of stamina. She massaged her fingers deep into her temples, waiting for the tearing sensation to dull to a pulsing throb, fighting the strain. She was thirsty. It was almost dawn, and she needed to take a break. There was an old kettle in the room with a few tea bags, some instant coffee and milk sachets, but no biscuits. Her tummy rumbled. Her mobile phone, switched off but there in case she needed it, was lying on the sideboard. Allan was just a click way. He'd come if she called … they could go for breakfast. She could explain – and he'd try to stop her again.

Beth shook her head to clear the clinging doubts that cobwebbed through her mind. No. She was on her own in this. She placed the album aside, stood and stretched. Not much further now.

Grabbing her purse and the key, she set out for the street-side cafe below.

Chapter 18

March 7, 2005

Blaine sat opposite Frazer in interview room 2.

'She was doubtful about what she saw,' said Frazer. 'Even if she does ID him, defence will pull holes in it. She said she wasn't sure, and it was dark.'

'Tony Corelli knows something,' countered Blaine.

Frazer shook her head. 'His alibi checks out. He was with his mates, and they were definitely seen down at the Steyne.'

'*Before* ten.'

'Martinson says he was with Corelli around midnight.'

'Martinson wouldn't know *who* he was with at midnight,' snorted Blaine. 'No, there's something *wrong* about Corelli.'

'You can't build a case on "Spidey Sense",' Frazer

came back dryly. 'We still don't know what Beth is hiding, and she *is* hiding something.'

Blaine couldn't disagree.

Frazer fiddled with her pen. She was a large, awkward woman, but she was smart. Blaine trusted her instincts. 'I was thinking of the mother,' she said. 'She's worried about something, knows more than she's telling us. Maybe we should talk a little more with her?'

Blaine nodded thoughtfully. 'Maybe, but whatever is going on with those two, if Beth can identify anyone it will still give us something significant to work on.'

'And if she lies?'

'Even more so. Then we need to go in hard and find out why. Why she's dumping them in it, and what she's hiding. But first, let's see if she can pick out Corelli.'

Frazer nodded.

There was a knock on the door and Beth and Gillian were ushered in. The antagonism Blaine noticed between the two of them in their first interview was still apparent; if anything, it had intensified. Mrs Fletcher was uncomfortable and avoided his eyes, while the girl was tightly focused.

Blaine welcomed them and took charge, explaining the procedure to them before laying out several photographs on the table in front of Beth. They were pictures of tattooed arms from the side and from behind.

Beth examined each of them carefully, lingering over one that featured several rows of reptilian-like scales on the shoulder and down over the bicep. There was another that had scales of a similar colour, but they were more like armour and went further down the arm.

'It's *possible* it could be this one,' she said, separating the photograph and pushing it across the table to Blaine, 'but of course, I don't know how many other people are running around with the same sort of tattoo. It might be a "special" at the local tattoo parlour.'

Intelligent answer, thought Blaine. 'But it is the same tattoo you saw?'

'It might be.'

Blaine gathered up the photographs and placed another group in front of her. These were head shots: front and side. Beth stared down curiously. Again she lingered over one. The hard slope of the cheek and the curve of the earlobe matched the brief glimpse she'd had of the first man, but it had been a *brief* glimpse, and it was dark.

'This *could* be the first man,' she said. 'The tall one, not the one with the tattoos.'

Blaine and Frazer exchanged a glance. The man Beth singled out was one of Tony Corelli's mates, Don Crae. Like Corelli, his head was shaved, and he had several tattoos, but not sleeve tattoos, and none were visible in the head shot. 'He didn't have tattoos?' asked Blaine.

'Well, he might have,' said Beth, 'but not down his arms.'

'You're certain?'

'Absolutely. He was wearing a T-shirt.'

Gillian shifted in her seat. The movement wasn't lost on Blaine. 'Would you like to say something, Mrs Fletcher?'

She gave him a frightened glance. 'No. No, I don't have anything to say.'

But it was clear she did. Blaine turned his attention to Beth. She met his eyes unflinchingly.

'OK,' he said. 'Thank you very much for this.'

'Are you going to arrest them?' asked Beth as Blaine collected up the photographs.

'We will continue our investiga—'

'Is it their van?'

Blaine hesitated, surprised, and Beth felt compelled to explain. 'Well, if it's *their* van, then it was probably *them*.'

Blaine's gaze was steady. 'You're sure about the van?'

'Definitely.'

'And you're prepared to testify to that in court?'

She didn't hesitate. 'Yes.'

'And when the defence lawyer asks you why you were there, what you were doing there and how you got there – you'll be able to explain?' His question was cool and direct. Gillian's hand flew to her mouth – but Beth remained cool. 'Listen, Beth,' he said, softening a little, 'we appreciate your help here, but if it's going to do any good at all, you're going to have to be a little more open with us about what you were doing there.'

'I told you.'

'You told us *something*, but it wasn't the whole truth, was it?'

'Yes, it was! I told you. I was coming home from a party. I had some time before the bus came so I walked around a bit. When I got to the bus stop I saw Anna being attacked.'

'And you were alone?'

'Yes … I was alone.'

'Who did you go to the party with?'

'No one.'

'Whose party was it?' Blaine was relentless.

Beth coloured. 'I can't say.'

His eyebrows rose. 'Because …?'

'Because … it was a secret party … and there were drugs, and …'

'We're not the drug squad. We're investigating an abduction.'

Beth glared into his judgement, defiant. 'It was a secret. I promised.'

'Then why are you wasting our time?'

'To help Anna. Why does it matter *why* I was there? Isn't it enough I just *was*? I *saw* the van – and you found it, didn't you? A white van with that number plate number, SMI 121?'

'Yes, we did,' agreed Blaine.

'Well, I couldn't have made that up then, could I?'

'No,' said Blaine. 'You couldn't have.'

'Then what's the problem?'

'The *problem* is that you might have given us details of a van you just happened to notice in the street.'

Beth's mouth dropped open. 'Why would I do that?'

'Why indeed?'

'I saw it,' she repeated. 'I saw that van. I was there, and I *saw* it!'

Blaine was unfazed. 'The question is, *why* were you there? You weren't a friend of Anna's. Were you a friend of one of these two men? Did you come with them?'

'No!'

Gillian gasped

'Maybe it was a lark?' he continued. 'That went a little too far? Is that what happened, Beth?'

Gillian jumped in. 'No,' she said desperately. 'She wasn't there!'

'Mum!'

'Beth wasn't there. She wasn't! She's just covering for a friend. Tell them, Beth! *Tell them!* This has gone too far!'

'Mum. Stop it,' Beth hissed. '*Stop* it!'

But Gillian couldn't stop. 'Beth is a good girl,' she babbled, her cheeks flushed, her breathing bordering on hyperventilation. 'She was at home Saturday. *All night.* My husband and I were there; she didn't leave the house.' Tears began struggling through, but she fought to continue. 'She's a good girl! She's just too loyal. She's too young to understand the seriousness of this.'

Beth groaned and dropped her face into her hands.

'Mrs Fletcher,' interjected Detective Frazer gently. 'Please. Calm down.' She placed a box of tissues in front of Gillian, who reached out a shaky hand to take one. For a moment, the only sounds in the room were her attempts to control herself.

Blaine, flummoxed, leant back in his chair. It didn't happen often, but he was surprised. He'd been sure Beth had witnessed the events as she claimed. Her details were too sharp to be second-hand – or so he'd thought. Even more surprising, she wasn't contradicting her mother. She wasn't coming back with any more quick explanations. She just sat there, stiffly upright, staring resolutely at the table, a coiled spring ready to snap.

Changing gears, he cleared his throat. 'Beth?'

Beth cast an anxious glance at her mother and another at Frazer. 'What I told you was the truth … but you're not going to believe me if I tell you how I know.'

'Try me.'

Beth took a deep breath and let it slowly out. She

raised her chin. 'I'm psychic.'

Gillian moaned.

Blaine and Frazer stared.

'You're what?'

'Psychic. I *see* things. Things that other people can't see. I saw Anna getting pulled into that van in Chatswood.'

Blaine and Frazer exchanged another glance.

'See?' said Beth bitterly. 'I told you you wouldn't believe me.'

Blaine scratched the back of his head. *What was he supposed to do with this?* He looked over at Gillian, who was now a grim shade of off-white. 'Mrs Fletcher—'

'She … she … had some trouble before,' Gillian stammered, 'when she was little …'

This was too much for Beth. She reared in disgust – but Frazer reached out a firm, restraining hand. 'Let your mother speak please, Beth.'

'She doesn't know!' Beth snapped. 'She doesn't know *anything*. I didn't tell *her*.'

'Miss O'Malley!'

'It's not her fault,' apologised Gillian. 'Her father … died, when she was just a baby, and I … it's been … hard for her.'

'There's nothing wrong with me!'

Beth was livid. She pushed back her chair and stood, her face crimson with humiliation. 'I'm not *sick!* I've got a *gift*. And Nanna had it too!'

Frazer was instantly out of her chair, but Beth was beyond caring.

'Well, don't listen to me if you don't want to,' she shouted. 'Call me sick if you want to. I don't give a shit!

I gave you the van, and I told you what happened, and if you care anything about Anna you can follow that up and go find her! It's on your head if you don't.'

'Beth—' Blaine was on his feet now too, attempting to strengthen his authority with height, but Beth ignored him and ran from the room.

Frazer went after her, and Gillian got up to follow, but Blaine blocked her. 'Mrs Fletcher, just a few more minutes. Detective Senior Constable Frazer will take care of Beth. I'd like a few more words with you.'

* * *

Frazer caught up with Beth in the hall. She'd been detained by the beefy constable on duty at the front desk and was arguing volubly for the right to be allowed to leave, drawing curious stares from the few others waiting for police attention.

'Thank you, I'll take care of this,' said Frazer, and calmly steered Beth to the side. Head and shoulders above Beth and twice her weight, Frazer was a force not easily ignored. Beth complied without resistance. Once they were out of the way, Frazer leant in and forced attention.

'You're not helping Anna with this behaviour,' she admonished. 'If you want to be taken seriously, you need to control yourself.'

A woman who'd been waiting near the front desk stood anxiously.

Under Frazer's glare, Beth remained surly. 'You've got no right to hold me here. I told you everything I saw!'

'Psychically?'

'Is this about Anna?' butted in the woman, her eyes moist with frightened hope. She'd moved right up to the counter now. 'Have you found my daughter? Do you know where she is?'

Frazer ushered Beth around the corner as the constable hurried to placate Mrs Johnston.

'Keep your voice down,' ordered Frazer. 'You want respect? Behave respectfully!'

Beth lowered her eyes. 'You're not going to believe me anyway, so what's the point?'

'The *point* is getting to the truth of what happened to Anna!'

'I told you what happened to Anna. I told you what I know.'

'That you *saw* it by some kind of *psychic* ability?'

'Yes. I can't explain it, and I can't prove it, but it's the truth.'

Frazer waited for her to say more, but she didn't. Beth stood quietly, a serene, doomed expression on her face, leaving the next move for Frazer.

'Your mother—'

'—Doesn't believe me,' finished Beth. 'I tried to tell her once, and she sent me to a shrink. I haven't told anybody since. If I had, they'd just look at me like you're looking at me now.'

Frazer wiped the astonishment from her face and replaced it with her attentive, evaluative expression. 'It's not an easy one to sell, Beth. The courts—'

'Then don't "sell" it. Just use it. To find Anna. It's better than nothing, isn't it?'

'Perhaps,' said Frazer, and Beth's mouth curled into a sneer. She shook her head in frustrated disgust.

'Well, I'm sorry. I can't do any better than that. Can I go now?'

Slowly, Frazer nodded her assent. 'But wait for your mother here. I need to take care of Mrs Johnston. It's best you don't talk with her. It's not going to help to give her false hopes or expectations.'

Beth didn't argue. She leant against the wall submissively and Frazer walked back to the front office. Mrs Johnston stood as she entered.

'Was that about Anna?' she asked, her voice an almost terrified squeak. 'Did that girl know something? Does she know where Anna is?'

'Why don't you come with me, Mrs Johnston,' said Frazer kindly. 'Andy, could you organise a cup of tea?'

A young probationary constable got up from his desk to comply as Frazer led Mrs Johnston into a side room. Pale-faced, she took the seat offered her.

'Is she one of Anna's friends? I haven't seen her before. She looks—'

'No. She goes to Anna's school, but they're not friends. She's just helping us with inquiries.'

'Does she know anything?'

Frazer hated to dishearten her further. 'Nothing conclusive, I'm afraid, but we need to follow up everything, and we're doing that. We'll let you know immediately we have any news.'

'But, she saw something? You said she saw something?'

'Mrs Johnston—'

'And what did you mean, "psychically"? Is she psychic? Can she find Anna?'

'Mrs Johnston, please. There is nothing conclusive to

share with you.'

'But—'

'All kinds of people come in here, and they say all kinds of things. It's our job to filter through all of that and determine what is relevant, and that's what we are doing.'

'But is she psychic?'

'I'm afraid I'm not an expert on that, Mrs Johnston.'

'Yes, b—'

'But we will follow up every lead, no matter how improbable, and if anything comes of it, you and your husband will be the first to know.'

Frazer could see Mrs Johnston was far from satisfied, and she knew in her position she'd feel the same. Fortunately the constable arrived with the tea and Frazer diverted the conversation to a calmer reiteration of the facts and assurances that everything was being done that could be done. With nothing further to add, she offered to drive Mrs Johnston home. It wasn't required, but it was appreciated. With a reassuring smile, Frazer ushered Mrs Johnston out of the room.

Unfortunately it was just as Beth was leaving with her mother.

'Thank you, Mrs Fletcher. Beth,' said Blaine as he held the door open for them.

Frazer noted Mrs Johnston's hungry expression and felt her stomach sink.

Chapter 19

March 8, 2005

The next day at school, Beth could tell something had changed. Things were normal for the first few periods, but when she went to the canteen at lunch, eyes were instantly focused on her. Distain had somehow morphed into hostile curiosity overnight. Nobody said anything to her – in fact, the canteen went unnaturally quiet when she entered – but the message was clear. Something had happened, and she was in the centre of it.

Not daring to find out what, Beth gave up on lunch and went to find Allan. He was in the library. She slid into the chair next to him and reached for his hand.

'What's up?'

Her hand trembled in his. 'The police came to our house. I had to go to the police station. They wanted me to look at some photographs of tattoos and things, to see if I could identify any of those men I saw.'

Allen stiffened. 'Why didn't you tell them it was me who saw them?'

'Because you wouldn't have been able to identify anything. *I* had to do it.'

'But … but how did you … What did you …?'

Beth swallowed. 'I told them.'

'What?'

'I told them. I told them I was … psychic.'

'Oh, no,' Allan groaned.

'I didn't have a choice. I told them I was at a party, that it was secret and I couldn't say anything else – but then Mum jumped in and said I was at home and that I was covering for someone.'

'You should have said it was *me!*'

'They would've come after you.'

'I told you—'

'Allan, you couldn't have helped them. I was the only one that saw them. And I think I recognised the tattoo that was on one of the guys. And maybe another guy too. His face was familiar, the side of it anyway—'

'You told them you were *psychic?*'

Beth cringed. 'I thought it sounded better than saying I could travel into photographs …'

Allan wasn't so sure about that.

'What did they say?'

'Not much. It was pretty much a conversation stopper.'

'They can't get a psychic to testify in court.'

'Well … I wouldn't have been able to testify anyway, with Mum telling them I'm nuts and a liar.'

Allan's chin jutted out. 'I would've been able to.'

'Not if they found out about your mum, and how you're fooling everybody. You're practically a professional liar. Nobody'd believe you either if it came to testifying in court.'

'So you told them everything … for nothing?'

'It wasn't for nothing. Maybe they'll believe me now, and *do* something.'

'What?'

She sighed. 'I don't know. Arrest those guys! *Something!*' It all seemed so hopeless. Glumly, she stared out the window. 'At least I told them… What else could I do?'

'Not much, I guess.' He could see she felt awful and gave her fingers a squeeze. 'Least you tried.'

'Mum's booked me in to see the shrink.' Her lips twisted sourly. 'At least I know what to tell him now. He'll like the psychic thing. That'll give him something to analyse.'

'Don't overdo it,' he chuckled. 'He'll have you drugged to the eyeballs.'

Just then, three senior girls approached and sat down opposite: Evana Dainleigh, Tali Gatch and Melissa Halliwell. Beth recognised them as friends of Anna's.

Evana launched in without introduction: 'What do you know about what happened to Anna?' she demanded. She was the tallest of the three with an intimidating elegance, even in her school uniform, and her voice was cool and cutting. She was a prefect.

'Well?'

'What are you talking about?' stammered Beth.

'You were at the police station, giving a statement. What do you know? What have you got to do with this?'

Beth's mouth went dry. 'Nothing!'

'Bullshit!' spat Tali.

Broad shouldered and well-muscled, Tali represented the school in state swimming championships and wasn't someone to mess with. She was bigger than most of the boys and her eyes had an unmistakable glint of mean. 'What do the police want with you, then?' she pushed.

Allan jumped in. 'She doesn't know anything. They just thought she'd seen something. She hadn't.'

He had the confidence of a practised barrister, exuding integrity and truth. Beth eyed him gratefully, but the girls didn't buy it. Melissa, a shorter version of Evana, sneered.

'What's this about you being a psychic?' asked Evana.

Beth paled. 'A … what?'

'Rubbish!' Allan leapt to her rescue again. 'Where'd you get *that* from?'

'Anna's sister. Anna's mum was at the police station yesterday. She saw Beth there.'

'Did Mrs Johnston say the police said Beth is a *psychic?*'

Evana glared at Beth accusingly. 'She *heard* you. She heard you say you saw something, and that you're psychic.'

'I never—'

'Girls! Silence please. Remember where you are!' Mrs Simmons, the librarian, loomed over them, arms folded, face stern.

The senior girls looked up in irritation but quickly cowed. 'Sorry, Mrs Simmons.'

Satisfied, the librarian stalked away and Beth braced

for further attack, but it never came. Standing, Evana hissed, 'This isn't over! If you know anything, and you're not telling—'

'I don't. I swear I don't know where Anna is.'

'Then why did you say you did?'

'I didn't. Mrs Johnston must have misheard. I never said that.'

'Girls!' Mrs Simmons glared from her desk. Evana backed off and, much disgruntled, the girls abandoned their attack and left the library.

'I guess that explains why everyone was treating you weird in the canteen,' said Allan. 'They probably told the whole school.'

'I never said I knew where Anna was. I never said—'

'Chinese whispers. People hear what they want to hear.'

'But … what do I do now? How do I get them to leave me alone?'

Allan thought about it a moment. 'You gotta make yourself uninteresting. You gotta give them something, something to satisfy them, and then you gotta to make it clear you don't know anything else. You gotta to be boring. Invisible.'

'How?'

'Psychic won't work. If you go with that, they'll be all over you, and they'll never stop. They'll expect you to find Anna for one thing – if they believe you, that is.'

'I wish I *could* find her … but how can I?'

'That's just it. You can't. That's up to the police now.'

'I guess …'

Suddenly Allan beamed. 'I know! Tell 'em it was a dream!'

Beth didn't follow.

'Tell 'em you had a *dream* about Anna, and *that's* what you told the police. You know, say it was a really *vivid* dream, so you thought you should tell the police, just in case.'

'They'll think I'm nuts.'

'Exactly! And then they won't pay any attention to anything you say, and you're back to being invisible again!'

'They'll kill me,' she said bleakly.

'No, they won't. They'll tease you, sure, but they'll get sick of that after a while. Nothing they haven't done already, eh?'

That was true, but the prospect was not a thrilling one – hours, days, weeks of ragging …

'Maybe I should just get Mum to home-school me for the rest of the year.'

Allan laughed, attracting another glower from Mrs Simmons. Leaning in closer, he lowered his voice. 'It won't be so bad. They think you're nuts anyway. Who cares what they think?'

His confidence was infectious and finally Beth relaxed. They stayed huddled close for the rest of lunch, leaving for class several minutes after the bell to avoid more confrontations. It worked, and using that strategy, Beth got from class to class with no unpleasantness for the rest of the afternoon and when she and Allan eventually exited after their last class, the grounds were almost empty. They walked to the gate without incident – except for a few pointing fingers and stares from faces pressed up against the windows of the departing school buses. As they neared the crossing, however, Mrs Johnston jumped out of a parked car.

'Beth?'

Allan reached for Beth's hand.

'Yes?'

'I'm … Anna's mother.'

Drawn and tired, her hair unkempt, Mrs Johnston was wraith-like. Her eyes were deep pools of need.

'Mrs Johnston—'

'Please, I'm sorry to come here, to school. I know I shouldn't, and I don't mean to harass you, but I just had to know. The police won't tell me anything. If you know something, anything at all—'

'I'm so sorry, Mrs Johnston. I really can't say.'

'Because you're a psychic?'

'I—'

'It's all right. I heard the detective say you were, and it doesn't matter to me how you know. Psychics have helped with these things before. Please, I just want to know. *Anything.*'

'Mrs Johnston,' Allan cut in gently.

The woman turned her anxious eyes to him, but Beth interrupted. 'It's OK, Allan,' she said softly. 'Mrs Johnston, I really don't know anything for sure. I wasn't there or anything. I just … had … a dream, and—'

'A *psychic* dream?' Mrs Johnston prompted.

'I … I don't know … it was just a dream … but—'

'But, you felt it was important? That it meant something?'

'Well … yes.'

'You've had dreams … like this … before? That *came* true … or *were* true, I mean?'

'I … well …' It seemed wrong to lie to this desperate woman, but she was committed. 'Yes,' she answered slowly. 'A couple of times.'

Mrs Johnston bit into her lip. 'What did you dream?'

Beth glanced at Allan. 'I saw Anna … at Chatswood Station,' she said hesitantly. 'She was walking for the bus, and … two men … dragged her into a van …'

Mrs Johnston reacted as though Beth had physically hit her. 'They *dragged* her?'

Beth wished she could take it back. 'I … It was just a—'

'They *dragged* her into a van. They *took* her?'

The realisation crystallising in Mrs Johnston's eyes was a terrible thing to see. Beth nodded, hating to hurt her further. 'It was just a dream,' she said quickly. 'I … I wasn't there. I'm so sorry. I never meant—'

'No … No, I … appreciate you telling me—'

'I only told the police, because it was so vivid, and … but, it was only a dream.'

Tears were now streaming down Mrs Johnston's face. 'You did the right thing,' she managed, her face contorting with pain. 'Thank you.'

Overcome, she lurched back to her car.

Beth could only watch, rigid with shock.

'She believed me,' she whispered. 'She *believed* me! I did what you said … but she *still* believed me!'

* * *

March 9, 2005

It was in the newspapers the next morning: '*Psychic Schoolgirl Helps Police with Anna Johnston Disappearance*'.

Beth wasn't identified by name, but everyone at school would know it was her – if there were any questions of her involvement before, there wouldn't be now.

'Would you rather stay home today?' Gillian asked as she handed Beth a glass of orange juice.

Beth shook her head and pushed the newspaper away. 'Can't be any worse than yesterday.'

'Honey, I—'

'I'm late.' She downed her orange juice and grabbed her bag. 'I'm going to the library this afternoon, so I won't be home till dinner.'

Absorbed in her own personal black storm, Beth trudged to the bus stop and scared away the curious group gathered there with the fiercest of her scowls. None of them were in her year, they wouldn't have spoken to her anyway, but it made her feel she had at least a modicum of power to repel them in this small way. Perhaps that was how Nanna had felt? Perhaps that was why she accepted the label of 'witch'? It did seem the lesser of two evils.

When the bus arrived, they let her on first. She held her head high as she walked to the back, her face impassive, ignoring the whispers and stares.

It was the same when she entered her roll-call classroom. Ambrosia Mackleray swung back in her chair, eyes shining with malice, and announced in her grating voice, 'Watch out! Psycho schoolgirl alert! Guard your thoughts everyone.'

Stacey Adams collapsed in laughter, nearly falling off her desk, and most of the others hooted approval or called out similar mocking comments. Beth's face flamed as a wet lump of chewed-up paper, blown through the empty shaft of a pen, splatted against her forehead. She wiped it away as Rebecca Sweet leapt to her feet and swaggered across the room, taunting, 'What am I thinking, O'Malley? Come on, show us what you can do.'

Beth ignored her. She sat at her desk – but Rebecca was in full swing. Large and boisterous, she had a powerful presence in the classroom. She had the biggest breasts of any girl in year ten, making her an all-out favourite with the boys, and her forceful personality flattened most of the girls. She had the whole class's attention. 'Well, come on. What am I thinking?' she jeered.

Beth glared back at her. 'Piss off!'

Rebecca raised her arms triumphantly and spun to address the class. 'It's amazing! Yes! That's *exactly* what I was thinking! Well, actually I was thinking "Fuck you!" but close enough!'

Again, the laughter roared.

'What numbers are gunna win Lotto Saturday night?' yelled Alex Crabtree, the class thug, from the other side of the room. He was the biggest boy in the year; he played football with the year elevens. His endorsement of the bullying set off a cacophony of taunts that threatened to tip the class into total chaos. Beth fished her folder out of her bag and hunted for a pen, giving no one any more fuel to burn her with, until mercifully the teacher arrived and called the class to order.

It was the same for rest of the day. Beth's only respite was during actual lessons while the teachers were present.

Surely they'd get bored soon!

Allan was nowhere to be seen at break. Beth waited for him behind the toilet block but he never showed.

She didn't catch up with him until lunchtime in the library when he ambled in, his nose red and swollen and his shirt stained with blood.

Beth's eyes opened wide. 'What happened?'

Allan tried to shrug it off. 'Nothing. Crabtree needed sorting, that's all.'

'You picked a fight with Crabtree?' Beth was horrified; Allan against Alex wouldn't have been a 'fight', it would have been a massacre. 'Why did you do that?'

Allan didn't want to talk about it.

'Was it because of me?' She knew it was.

'Crabtree's a dickhead,' said Allan with unusual bitterness. 'Should've done it long ago.'

'What happened?'

Allan sighed. 'He was being an arsehole. So I decked him.'

Beth gasped, clearly impressed, and he broke into a lopsided grin. Shrugging, he pointed to his injured nose. 'And then, he …'

'I'm *so* sorry. Allan, I—'

''S OK. Like I said. He deserved it.'

'Yes, but *you* didn't. Did you get in trouble?'

'Nah.' Allan blushed. 'By the time the teacher got there, I was on the ground, blood all over the place, and he … uh … well, let's just say the damage I did to him was more … hidden. He said I *fell*, helped me up and dusted me off, and I … thought it best to leave it at that.' He grinned again. 'Keep my record clean.'

His smile warmed her, and his optimism erased the sting of her own battles, but the seriousness of the situation was not so easily shrugged away. He'd been hurt, defending her, because of her stupidity. Allan's smile faded as he noticed her returning angst. 'Beth, it's OK. Really. I'm fine. Looks worse than it is.' He reached for her hand. 'How did your morning go?'

She gave a sad little laugh. 'Pretty much as expected.'

Allan could imagine. 'They'll get over it and move on to something else,' he assured her. 'At least they didn't put your name in the paper.'

'They might as well have. Everyone knows it was me.' Suddenly she filled with sadness. 'I wonder if they'll ever find Anna ...' Her hopes trailed off into darkness. 'I wish I could do something ...'

'You've done enough,' said Allan.

He said it kindly, but Beth couldn't help taking it as a rebuke. Yes, she *had* done enough. She wasn't helping anybody with what she knew. Allan had even been beaten up! All she could do now was wait for everybody to forget about her, and try not to say or do anything else stupid in the meantime.

'I guess ...'

They remained sheltered in the library for the rest of lunch. The afternoon's classes went much the same as the morning ones, but Beth felt better knowing Allan was on her side. Nevertheless, when the last bell rang, she was relieved.

Allan had promised to meet her after school so she wouldn't have to brave the school grounds alone, so she lingered in her classroom over the packing of her bag. Her teacher, Ms Wainwright, the new English teacher, fresh out of university and full of idealistic zeal, also remained at her desk writing notes. Beth was grateful. When the last student left the room, Ms Wainwright casually commented, 'I'm headed for the staff room,

Beth, if you're walking that way.'

The English staff room was in the administration block near the front gate. Ms Wainwright was offering her safe passage.

Beth felt suddenly embarrassed. 'Allan will be here soon.'

On cue, he appeared at the door.

'Ah, the knight in shining armour!' smiled Ms Wainwright. 'Well, I'll be off then, but Beth, if this all gets too much, or if you'd like someone to talk to, I'm always available.'

Beth shrugged awkwardly and Ms Wainwright smiled and left.

'That was nice of her,' said Allan.

'Give her another year and she'll be like all the others.'

'Whoo hoo, cynic!' chided Allan, and gained his first real smile of the day from Beth. In a much lighter mood, they left the school and walked the few blocks to the municipal library: Allan's second home. On the way they stopped for hot chips at the local fish and chip shop and splurged on a couple of chocolate bars. After a few hours in the library, immersed in the banalities of homework, both of them were feeling better. Laughter bubbled up between them again. By home-time Beth was almost optimistic – until she saw the television crew harassing her mother on their doorstep.

Chapter 20

July, 2010

There was a gap in her mother's photo album after high school: no pictures at all until the European ones. Beth remembered her mother saying she'd cleared tables in a restaurant after school, spending little and saving obsessively for her big European trip. It took her a little over three years.

First stop had been Italy, and the first European photographs were of famous Italian sites like the Colosseum, the Trevi Fountain, the Palazzo Vecchio and the canals of Venice. Beth had visited them all. Venice was her favourite, but she adored Florence and found Pompeii fascinating. It was fun seeing these ancient places, and fun watching her mother explore them. Most interesting though, was discovering her mother's Italian boyfriend, Antonio. He was a surprise; her mother had never mentioned him, but she seemed so in love, so naively excited about him. At least, at first. Beth could see what attracted her mother to him – he was gorgeous, sophisticated, smooth and apparently wealthy – but he had a possessive manner that hardened as their relationship lengthened. The light of love gradually dimmed in her mother's eyes and was replaced by guarded caution.

Thank God she'd left him, thought Beth. Imagine having *him* as a father! And it was just as well he *wasn't* nice, she thought after that. How different her life would be if her mother had married in Italy. She'd be Italian! She would never have met Allan.

How odd that the progression of an entire relationship, the progression of an entire *life*, could be captured in a few photographs …

Beth traced her fingers over the fading photographs. Strange that these few scraps of her mother's life had become the centre of her own. She deeply regretted not having taken more of an interest while she'd had the chance. What a lost opportunity. Now all she had of her mother were these images … these moments … these crumbs. No more than what was left of her father, with so much hidden in the gaps.

There was no time for this now.

Turning a page, Beth found the photographs she'd been searching for: a series of shots taken at the Trevi Fountain in Rome on an overcast day in the winter of 1979. These were from early in her mother's relationship with Antonio. There was a lovely one of the two of them standing in each other's arms in front of the fountain. This was the first photograph Beth explored when she'd been given the album and it was perfect for what she needed now. There was plenty of space in front of the lens for her arrival and easy access to suitable places where she could safely materialise.

* * *

March 14, 2005

Beth tripped backwards against the wall in the toilet block, grazing her elbow.

'Take it!' demanded Evana, shoving the small, dangly earring in her face. 'Take it and tell me what you see!'

The earring belonged to Anna. She'd lent it to Evana at the party they'd attended the night Anna disappeared.

'I can't.'

'You mean you *won't*.' Evana's lip curled.

'No. I *can't*. I can't do that. I can't see things that way.'

'You're a psychic aren't you?' It wasn't a question, and it was clear Evana wasn't going to accept no – not after the full-page story in the paper that morning.

'Well, I … ah … sometimes I have … *dreams*, but—'

Evana sighed impatiently. 'Look, I don't believe in all this crap, but if you really are psychic you should be able to see something if you hold Anna's earring. That's how it works, isn't it? That's how psychics find bodies and things?'

'Bodies …?'

'Anna's dead.' Evana's tone was dull, her certainty chilling. 'I know she is. She wouldn't run away without telling me.'

'But, she could be—'

'She's dead. So, you *should* be able to see *something*.'

Beth shook her head. 'No, I … I can't. I'm not that *kind* of psychic. I don't see things … like that. I just … I just … sometimes … have dreams.'

For the first time, Evana's confidence wobbled. She flicked a look towards the door of the toilet block and then back at the junior girl cringing before her.

'Have you tried?'

'No, but—'

'Then try!' She thrust the earring towards her.

Beth flinched – and Evana, seeing her reaction, slowly withdrew her hand.

'Look, I don't care *what* it is you see. I don't expect it to be good, and I'm not going to blame you, whatever it is. I just want to know.' Her eyes searched Beth's. 'Anna was my friend. And if she's out there … lying somewhere …' Her voice went gravelly and she broke off and looked away. 'I know she's dead,' she said softly, 'but she deserves to be buried, properly … and if she's trying to tell us where she is … and you're the only one who can hear her … well then you *have* to help.'

Biting into her bottom lip, Beth stared miserably at the floor. 'I wish I *could*.' And she did. For Anna's sake, for her family and her friends – and for herself. But it might as well have been a request for her to fly. She wasn't Nanna.

'Please. Just *try*.'

The fragile piece of jewellery glistened in Evana's outstretched palm, caught in a single shard of light from the high windows of the toilet block.

Evana was probably right, thought Beth. Anna prob-ably *was* dead … lying hidden somewhere … waiting for the light to find her. But she didn't know where Anna was and she had no way of finding her.

Or did she?

Maybe ... just maybe ... Nanna's power *was* in her, and she just hadn't discovered it yet? Her abilities had been changing since she was a little girl – perhaps she was still growing into her full potential? She had to at least try.

Meekly, she reached for the earring. It felt cold against her skin as she closed her fingers around it. Bowing her head, she shut her eyes, just as she'd seen her grandmother do, and braced herself for revelation – but none came. She felt nothing. Saw nothing.

Undeterred, she tried again, this time running her fingers gently over it, trying somehow to charm it into revealing its secrets. She spread her senses out ... reaching ... seeking for traces of Anna – but all she encountered was a void. If Nanna's power was in her it hadn't developed yet.

But perhaps she was going about it the wrong way? She didn't enter pictures through touch; she did it through *sight*. Opening her fist, she looked down at the earring and tried to focus on it in the same way she focused on a photograph. She gave it her full concentration, staring at it as hard as she could, letting her eyes wander over every curve and surface, every silvery filament, begging it to pull her in – but she felt no drawing. Nothing happened.

Clearly, it only worked with pictures.

'Anything?' asked Evana eagerly.

Beth shook her head. 'I'm sorry. I really am.'

She saw the despondency in Evana's eyes and felt a

horrible guilt, as though *she'd* somehow caused it all. One thing was certain: she hadn't helped. Feeling completely inadequate, she gave the earring back. Evana slipped it tenderly into a little black velvet jewellery pouch. She pulled the strings to close it, put it back into her pocket and without another word turned and walked out.

Alone in the cool, semi-darkness, Beth waited a full five minutes before leaving.

* * *

February, 1980, Rome, Italy

The plaza was oddly comforting in its familiarity. She'd been there several times now, visiting and revisiting this moment, watching her mother and Antonio. The beauty of the Trevi Fountain never failed to thrill her. The sheer size of it was overwhelming, the exquisite detail in the stone, the strength of it. And this was an especially good day to view it – cool and blustery and definitely off-season. That meant a comparatively sparse crowd for such an iconic attraction and less competition for the surrounding cafes.

For Beth, it meant less potential for collision.

When she stepped into the photograph, her mother and Antonio were still posing; smiling radiantly as they waited for their volunteer photographer to signal she was done. Beth stepped out of the way and hurried invisibly across the plaza. Her destination was a bag shop with an elaborate display stand in front of it. Laden with dozens of beautifully crafted Italian leather bags it looked like a strange, multi-coloured Christmas tree. Its bulky mass would provide good cover. No one was inspecting the bags – not great for the shop owner, but perfect for her. She slipped in behind and, after making sure no one was watching, physicalised.

Peering through the bags she could see Antonio had turned away, scoping for potential cafes while Gillian retrieved her camera. Soon she'd take more photographs of the Trevi Fountain. Beth had watched her do this many times; she knew exactly how many she'd take and from which angles. There wasn't much time. Pulling the collar of her coat up around her face, she moved out from behind the bags, crossed the cobbled street and worked her way into the small crowd gathering around the fountain. At least she didn't need to worry about bumping into anyone now: her physical presence in this moment of time was fixed and she wouldn't leave until she chose to.

Keeping as close to the fountain as she could, with the bulk of the crowd shielding her from the view of anyone in the plaza – including her past invisible selves – she felt secure. Though she was wearing her brilliant red coat, it blended in with the other vibrant colours. It wouldn't stand out if someone wasn't looking for it. And *she* hadn't been looking for it on previous visits. She hadn't even owned the coat then.

She edged through a tour group, keeping her head down and her face angled towards the fountain until she estimated she stood within range of her mother's camera. Then, squirming through to the middle of the group and pulling her collar up even higher, she placed herself to be seen just as her mother raised her camera. She managed to stare directly down the lens when the shutter clicked.

So, now it was done.

Was it enough?

Would her mother notice her? Should she attract her attention and create another memory as well – or would that just freak her out?

Just then, Antonio wrapped his arm around Gillian. He planted a kiss on her forehead and presented her with options for lunch. Beth couldn't hear their conversation from where she stood, but she'd listened to it before. She knew what they were saying and what they'd decide. In a moment, they'd go to the trendy cafe on the far side of the plaza. Her mother would have spaghetti. Beth had followed them before – *was probably preparing to follow them now?*

An eerie thought.

Several invisible versions of herself were watching her mother and Antonio right now. They'd see her if she stepped into the open plaza. Best to avoid that. As her mother and Antonio walked off arm-in-arm, she nudged back into the crowd and pushed through in the opposite direction. When they entered the cafe, she dashed across the cobbles to a fashion shop. It was very chic. The displayed frocks and garments were beautifully elegant and – from the style of the decor, the groomed clientele, and the suspicious eye of the shop assistant – massively expensive. Beth straightened her shoulders, tossed her head and selected a garment from the rack. It was a cocktail dress of soft blush pink chiffon with delicate embroidery and light pink ribbons. She caught the assistant's eye, gestured towards the change room at the back and asked with a thick American accent – they had the money at this point in time after all – 'Can I try this on?'

The assistant brightened and nodded her assent, gliding to pull aside the curtain for Beth to enter.

She'll get a surprise when she comes to check on me, thought Beth with wry amusement as she hung up the dress on the hook.

And in another moment, the changing cubicle was empty.

* * *

April 13, 2005

Blaine replaced the phone in the cradle and stared thoughtfully out the window. He wasn't satisfied with Dr Martin's report.

Over a month had passed since Anna disappeared, and there was still no trace of her. No sightings. No messages. No body. Her young, confident face still smiled down from her position on his whiteboard, demanding action, and all he could do was wait … wait for her to return … wait for someone to come forward, or to slip up … wait for her to be found.

Experience told him that could be a very long time. Or never.

Beth remained his one and only source of information, and all logic insisted she shouldn't be taken seriously. But she was intelligent, and his gut instinct told him she was telling the truth, or at least what she *thought* was the truth. Her school counsellor warned that Beth was creative, over-sensitive and socially maladjusted, but she didn't agree with Dr Martin that Beth was 'a pathological liar' or 'delusional'. Blaine was inclined to go with the counsellor's assessment. Still, he conceded that Dr Martin's report, backed by his credentials, would carry more weight in court. Beth could never be a credible witness.

Yet, the certainty in her eyes remained with him. She knew something … somehow. He'd stake his career on that, and Frazer agreed.

But *how* did she know?

Easiest if she'd snuck out of the house without her parents knowing, as she'd initially claimed, but there was no way she could have climbed out her bedroom window; the drop was too high. And there was no way to get to the front or back door except through the living room. If Beth left the house, her parents would have known.

So, scratch that. For now.

He also couldn't quite swallow the theory that Beth's testimony was a second-hand account from a friend she was trying to protect. She'd picked out Corelli's arm and Crae's head shot! The two men had been together that night – and they'd had access to the van Beth described.

Just random luck?

Or did she know them?

He didn't think so. He'd found no connection between Beth and these men. In fact, he found no solid connections between Beth and *anybody*, except the Watson boy. There was a definite connection there. But the kid seemed even less likely than Beth to be involved in Anna's disappearance and he'd spent the night at his aunt's; she was prepared to swear to that.

That only left Beth's explanation: she was psychic.

Blaine walked back to his desk and scanned once more through her file: emotional … sensitive … secretive

... *What teenage girl wasn't?* Nothing about her being psychic, not in the counsellor's, or the psychiatrist's notes. Even her mother had seemed surprised about that.

Blaine knew of famous cases where psychics were purported to have helped with police investigations – also many more where they proved useless or even misleading. He'd never taken the stories seriously. He'd never even met a psychic—, until, perhaps, now. But as he turned the facts around to view them from that perspective, as uncomfortable as it was to admit it, several pieces slipped into place. In fact, if Beth *were* telling the truth about being a psychic, it would account for *all* the facts.

But where could he go with that?

Her testimony would still be useless in court, and they had nothing *but* her testimony. The van was clean and old man Corelli was sticking to his statement that it wasn't used that night. As for the son, he had no prior convictions and was holding firm. His mates were standing beside him. Without anything else, particularly without a body – and he was convinced it *was* a body they were waiting for – Blaine had nothing.

With a sigh, he shut the folder.

'I'm watching you, Corelli,' he said softly. 'You may have got away with this for now, but sooner or later you'll slip up, and when you do, I'll be there. Watching

Chapter 21

October, 2005

Weeks passed, and then months. A general acceptance accumulated that Anna wasn't coming home, but her absence left an indelible mark. Her friends maintained a brooding edge and the whole senior year adopted a more serious tone; the bounce had gone out of them. The junior school too, especially those in Anna's sister's class, remained jittery and unnaturally quiet.

For any who dared to forget, Mrs Johnston showed up at the school gate every afternoon to pick up her remaining daughter, progressively thinner, increasingly drawn and imparting an uncomfortable aura of accusation. But eventually even *she* showed signs of attempting to move on. Three months after Anna's disappearance, the family had held a special memorial service. All the school had been invited. The church was packed to overflowing and a mountain of flowers had been left in Chatswood Mall at the spot were Anna was last seen on the CCTV footage. Once again Anna's face had smiled from the front pages of newspapers and her story had dominated the current affairs programs, but only for a couple of days. After the memorial service, other stories reclaimed the front pages and at school attention slowly shifted back to football finals and gossip. Like earth falling softly into a grave, new concerns gradually covered the scars of the tragedy. Beth, who'd been keeping as low a profile as possible, slowly returned to being unseen and unmolested. Her peers lost interest in her. Even Rebecca and Ambrosia moved on to other targets. Stacey had done the unforgivable by going out with a boy Rebecca was interested in, so they were busy concentrating on ostracising her.

Beth was grateful for that, but Anna still haunted her dreams; she waited for her in unguarded moments and accused her through her mother's eyes. As the investigation into Anna's disappearance ground to a halt, Beth felt increasingly frustrated. She couldn't escape the conviction that the responsibility to find Anna was somehow hers. Allan said it wasn't, that there wasn't anything else she could do – but it wouldn't let her go. She'd considered going back, to see if she could see *anything* else, but Allan was dead against it. He argued it would only stir everything up again and she still wouldn't be able to prove anything, and neither would the police. Beth knew he was right – and it wouldn't help Anna. It wouldn't bring her back.

So finally, she let it go. Whispering an apology to Anna, she slipped the CCTV picture into the bottom drawer of her desk, burying it under layers of past home-work. She couldn't bring herself to throw it out, but she had to get on with her life. Just making that decision gave her some relief, even if she had left a back door open for later exploration. But soon thoughts of going back and fixing things for Anna became completely irrelevant, because a few weeks into the final term *all* her travelling came to an abrupt halt.

She'd been finding solace visiting photographs of British castles in a calendar she bought at a garage sale. They were moody, artistic views taken at dawn or dusk when the castles were pretty much deserted. Now she could walk away from the photographer and wander wherever she wanted, a new world had opened to her. Alone in her bedroom, she could disappear for a quiet walk anywhere she chose while her parents watched TV downstairs, completely unaware. They still had no idea – and there was no way Beth was going to enlighten them after their reactions to her claims of being psychic; Richard was still treating her as though she was conta-gious. This was her own private world – not shared with those she visited, as they had no idea she was there – or even with Allan. He was cautious about her travelling anywhere now. It was easier not to tell him. But shared or unshared, her retreats brought her balance … release. She rarely went more than a few days without a journey.

On this particular night – the night when everything changed – she finished her homework and threw a pillow on the floor so she could sit with her back against the door to prevent intrusion. She couldn't decide whether to go to one of the castles she'd already been to or to try a new one. There was only one photograph she hadn't yet visited. It featured Finlarig Castle in Scotland on an especially lovely summer evening.

She entered with restful expectations – but before she even got her bearings, a startled gasp jarred through her. It came from right behind her.

Spinning around, she almost collided with the photographer, who reared back in fright, utter astonishment on his face.

He could see her!

Immediately she exited.

She crashed clumsily back, bumping up against the bedroom door with a heavy thump. Pulling her knees to her chest, she braced against the door, heart thumping, as she waited to hear if she'd been heard. There was no sign of it. No one called out or came running. Downstairs, she could hear the television, still blaring, over-loud as usual.

No sign of disturbance.

Staring blindly at the room in front of her, she released her captured breath slowly.

He'd seen her!

She felt her world crumbling away.

How could she ever travel again if she was visible? Answer: she couldn't! She entered right in front of the lens, there was no way to hide. The photographer would see her – and she'd be in the picture!

Frantically, she checked the calendar – Finlarig Castle still graced July's page – but the shot was subtly altered: same angle, but the light was different and there were some clouds that weren't there before. The calendar had changed. He'd taken another photograph, and now that was in the calendar instead.

Her startled face was hardly calendar material, she

realised. His photograph would have been ruined. This one wasn't too different though, and the calendar still existed ... just a slightly altered version of it. She was safe ... this time – but what had the photographer thought?

Probably that he'd seen a ghost, her appearing like that in a misty Scottish castle ... She imagined him running to tell his wife and sharing the story around hushed dinner gatherings on Halloween, his moustache bristling with pride and his beady eyes glistening in the candle-light as he recounted his ghostly encounter. A wobbly kind of giggle rose from her belly. She'd probably done him a favour, given him a good story – but what if he'd published it? She guessed the photograph hadn't looked ghostly enough or he would have – but what if it had? *What if he had?*

Her stomach flipped. Was her face out there now in some magazine?

She had to be careful. This was too risky. If she could be seen, she couldn't travel.

How could she bear that? She'd only just figured out how to explore properly – and now she no longer could. The potential loss of it tore at her almost as much as losing Nanna. In a way, it was the same thing. She'd never be able to visit her again, or her father. It was like losing them twice!

But, *could* she really be seen?

The more she thought about it, the less sure she was of what she'd experienced. Perhaps the photographer had been surprised by something else? She'd exited so quickly, maybe he'd seen something *behind* her, *through* her?

It was her only hope and she couldn't bear to let it

go – but how could she confirm it?

The only way was to go back again … or to try another photograph and see if the same thing happened.

The second idea seemed safer – but which photograph? Which photograph could she dare to enter? Which one was least likely to cause a disturbance if a girl suddenly appeared in front of the lens? Certainly none of the calendar photographs. Maybe a crowded, chaotic place, where the photographer was too stressed to notice her? A war zone?

She remembered some pictures she'd seen from World War II, and thought she might be able to blend in to some of those without attracting too much attention, if she wore the right clothes. Since they'd been taken so long ago, even if she were accidentally caught in one, it would be difficult to connect it to her today. If anyone did notice a resemblance, they'd sooner believe she was a look-a-like than a time traveller. But what about bullets? Could they hurt her now? Would she still just bounce back to the present as she'd always done when she collided with something, or would bullets now hit her as they would any other physical body?

That was a frightening thought. What kind of body did she have there now? If it was visible, was it also physical? If it was damaged, would she bring the damage back with her?

Before she travelled again, she'd need to answer these questions. She had to know what her new boundaries were – but how could she safely find that out? What photograph could she enter to test this?

A natural disaster?

No, she'd face the same vulnerabilities as in a war

zone; she needed to go somewhere where she could be sure the disaster wasn't going to engulf her.

And then it came to her.

9/11.

The terrorist attack on New York City on September 11, 2001.

It was a well-photographed disaster, there were lots of photographs taken from far enough away to be safe, and the streets had been in a total chaos. No one would notice an extra person appearing from nowhere. All she needed to do was to find the best photograph.

'Can I use the computer?'

Richard took his eyes off the television. 'An assignment?'

'Yeah. It's due tomorrow.'

Richard could be a little precious about his home office and he looked like he wanted to object, but instead he let it go. 'OK, don't forget to turn it off when you're done,' he said, turning back to the TV.

It didn't take long to find a suitable photograph; there were so many on the net. She decided on one taken from the street near the base of the Twin Towers by Gulnara Samoilova, a Russian-born photographer. It caught the moment when the South Tower began to collapse, showing the top section of the building tilting wildly as it began to disappear into the smoky ring billowing at the point where the plane had ripped into the tower's side. The image was startling against the clear blue sky, frighteningly close, but a little research confirmed that Gulnara had survived. All she needed to do was stick close to her. And Gulnara's camera was aimed high, up towards the top of the tower, so she'd quickly drop out of sight. With such a back drop, even Gulnara probably wouldn't notice her, and likely neither would anyone else. They were all looking up.

After printing a copy of the famous photograph, Beth returned to her room. She was confident of her choice but still a little nervous. The events of 9/11 were not anything she'd ever been tempted to visit. After witnessing the Kennedy assassination, she was well aware that the horror of such events markedly increased when you witnessed them first-hand. And there was also a sacredness about such occasions. People had died. It seemed somehow wrong to invade or intrude, as though it was a tourist attraction. But she needed to know, and this seemed the safest way to find out.

Closing the door, she repositioned the pillow and sat. She leant back against the door and began to prepare – but then a tingle flushed over her scalp. If she was taking her body with her this time, what would be left behind? Probably nothing, she thought – which was disquieting. Rolling off the pillow, she wedged a chair under the door handle and moved her pillow to rest against the bed instead. It made her feel a little more secure, but still she hesitated, wondering if she should perhaps wait to do this with Allan. But she didn't want to wait. And she didn't need his worry. It was hard enough dealing with her own.

It didn't take long. Within seconds, she was gone.

* * *

September 11, 2001, New York
Instantly, she fell, but she was prepared for it and

crouched safely at Gulnara's feet just as the noise hit – a buffeting, crashing staccato of audible destruction. She looked up, as all around her were doing, and saw what Gulnara was capturing on film – the massive South Tower collapsing in on itself in full, three-dimensional horror. It took her breath away.

'Run!' screamed someone nearby.

Panic flooded into the crowd. They were gathered at the corner of Fulton and Church streets, trapped in the deep city canyons with over one hundred storeys of disintegrating office tower crashing down towards them. Terrified, they ran. Beth ran with them, fighting to keep up with Gulnara, knowing she had to stay close to her if she were to survive. Suddenly, with a mighty crash, the earth tossed beneath her, throwing her violently to the ground. She turned back, terrified, to see an enormous cloud of dust headed straight for them. Scrambling to her feet, just in time to see Gulnara diving behind a car for cover, she leapt after her, crashing to the ground behind the car just as the huge cloud hit. It slammed against them, rocking the car in a storm of debris, filling their eyes, noses, mouths and ears with suffocating dust. Instantly they were enveloped in thick, eerie silence.

In the choking dark, struggling to breathe, Beth wondered if she'd been separated from Gulnara. Was she sheltering behind the right car? Was she safe? Her heart began to pound as she clung to the bumper of the car, blind. Suddenly, out of the silence, an arm wrapped around her shaking shoulders and pulled her close – Gulnara's arm. It held her tight until the torrent passed over them, which seemed to take an eternity, but finally the buffeting stopped and sensations began slowly to return.

Hearing returned first. The sound of the fluttering of thousands of pieces of paper. A terrifying sound.

Beth remembered the pictures of the paper on the streets, scraps of people's lives, surviving beyond the hands that marked them. The image had burned into her. And now those desecrated scraps were raining down on her. She ached at the sadness of it.

Next, she heard the shuffling of feet, and finally voices came at her out of the dark, followed by vague, ghostly images limping out of the dust.

Gulnara squeezed her shoulder. 'Are you all right?'

Beth nodded, overwhelmed. She turned to face Gulnara, and the photographer smiled weakly. No words seemed adequate to the moment. Gulnara gave her shoulder a final squeeze and pulled herself up off the ground. Stepping out from behind the car, she began taking more photographs.

Beth felt awed and humbled by her strength. Her own legs felt like spaghetti. She wasn't sure she'd be able to even stand, let alone walk. They were opposite a beautiful ironwork fence which surrounded a small churchyard. Dusty ancient tombstones rose stubbornly out of a carpet of paper debris. Dust covered everything – grey dust … grey cars … grey people walking past in a daze.

They were dressed in what was left of their business clothes, some carrying purses, some barefoot, having obviously abandoned high heels, all of them caked in grey like walking corpses.

Looking back towards where the tower had been Beth could see nothing other than a few dark structural shadows in a wall of dust, but she knew there was one tower yet to fall. One tower, mortally wounded, dying in the fire and the dust.

It was time to leave.

And her question was answered. She *was* physically there, able to be seen, able to be felt, able to feel.

She had what she came for.

No one was watching her, they were all way too absorbed in the catastrophe around them to notice her go, but she stayed crouching low, hidden behind the dust-smothered car, as she reached back to 2005 and let go of 2001.

* * *

October, 2005

The returning was rough.

Violent nausea filled her. She landed on her knees in the same position she'd been in behind the car, and crawled desperately towards her wastepaper bin, only just making it in time to empty the contents of her stomach into it in a series of painful cramping retches.

When there was nothing left inside her, she sat there still, clinging to the clammy container, staring into the mess in a daze as a fine cloud of grey dust sifted down from her hair over her fingers, into the bin and onto the floor around her.

* * *

Beth reached into her schoolbag and pulled out a plastic bag. From that, she pulled out a T-shirt, caked in dust, and laid it on the library table between them.

Allan was confused.

'It's from 9/11,' she said. 'I went there last night.' She caught the instant betrayal in his eyes. 'I had to, Allan. Something's changed. I had to be sure.'

'What are you talking about?'

'Look!' She indicated the T-shirt. 'I was wearing that.'

Eventually, it sunk in. Beth watched as Allan's expression shifted from irritation through confusion to disbelief. He reached down and touched the T-shirt, and when he pulled his fingers away they were coated in grey dust. 'But … how?'

'I don't know … it just happened. I'm not invisible any more. They can see me, and what's more, they can *touch* me. Allan, I crouched behind a car with a woman photographer, and she put her arm around me! She *felt* me, and I felt her. I was *there!*'

'Are you crazy?' he whispered. 'You could have been killed! What the hell did you go there for?'

His anger surprised her and ruffled her feelings a little. 'I was OK. I knew the photographer made it out OK, so all I had to do was stay close to her.'

Allan was aghast. 'Two of the tallest buildings in the world were *collapsing!* Thousands of people were *killed!* And you—'

'Not *there*, not where I was. Not *then*. I researched it,' she snapped back. 'And anyway, I could have come back at any time.'

'Not if a steel girder fell on you.'

'I wasn't *that* close.'

'Where were you?' His eyes were daggers of accusation.

Beth blushed. 'Church Street and Fulton.'

'*Fuck!*'

'I had to know, Allan. I had to know if I really was visible or not – because I'd freaked this other photographer out – it might have been a fluke – but if it wasn't … Well, I had to know.' It all came out in a rush, and she realised she wasn't making sense. Taking a breath, she started again, as slowly as she could bear. 'I went to a castle last night, just to check it out, because it was peaceful and beautiful – and when I entered, the photographer kind of jumped. He could *see* me! I *saw* he could see me, Allan!'

Allan was incredulous. 'So, you went *back?*'

'Not there. I'm not stupid!'

'To *9/11?*'

Beth's cheeks reddened. 'I had to go somewhere nobody would notice someone suddenly appearing.'

Allan shook his head in disbelief. 'Oh, good choice. Yes, everyone would have been way too busy dodging collapsing skyscrapers to notice you.'

'We weren't *dodging* anything,' she shot back angrily. She slid the printout of the photograph she'd used towards him. 'The photographer had just taken this when the tower began to collapse. She was focused on the tower. Everyone was. No one saw me enter, and it was the same when I left. No one noticed. We were close to the towers, but there was plenty of time to run. I didn't take any stupid risks.'

Allan stared down at the photograph. 'And you did this … just to find out if you were visible or not?'

'I had to *know.*'

Allan sighed. 'Didn't it occur to you that if you were

visible, you might also be *physical?*'

The colour rose in her cheeks again. 'Yes, of course it did. That's why I picked—'

'A *terrorist attack?*'

'Where I'd be *safe!* And where I wouldn't be noticed!'

'And where you could be *killed!* Just like everyone else who was there. Beth, just because the photographer survived didn't mean you would. You weren't standing in the exact same spot she was. Something could have just missed her and hit you.'

'Well, maybe ... but—'

'And what if you couldn't get back?'

'What? Why shouldn't I—'

'Because more of you must be going now!' he said, exasperated. 'And things are changing. What if you got stuck?'

'I didn't—'

'But you could have! You didn't know that!'

'But I *didn't* get *stuck.*' Beth had never seen him so upset, but she just couldn't accept his fear. 'I came back from the Scottish castle. I could feel the pull, just like always. I *always* feel the pull. I have to concentrate to stay, and if I let go, I come back.'

'So far. What if next time there *is* no pull? How are you going to get back then?'

'Allan—'

'You can't say what's going to change next.'

'No one knows what's going to happen next. About *anything.* That doesn't mean you stop living. You have to take some risks. And I was careful!'

'You didn't have to take *that* risk.'

'Well, how else was I supposed to find out what I

can do and what I can't? Read it in a bloody text book?'

Her eyes were flashing, but Allan was incensed. 'Maybe you're not meant to find out. Maybe you just need to accept that.'

'Well maybe *you* need to accept I can't do that,' she humphed. 'I *have* to know. And if I do end up getting stuck somewhere, well maybe that's what's meant to be as well. Maybe whatever happens to me, eventually, has *already* happened ... and that's just how it is.'

Furiously, she grabbed her T-shirt and stuffed it back into her bag. From the front desk, Mrs Simmons coughed a warning. Allan let out an angry sigh and grabbed hold of her bag to keep her from leaving.

'I'm just trying to understand,' he pleaded. 'I just don't get it.'

Her first instinct was to rip the bag away and storm off, but the pain in his eyes stopped her. Now more than ever she needed his understanding. She had no one else. Letting go of the bag, she sat back down and looked at him sadly. 'I had to know, Allan. Because this – this changes everything. If this is how it is now ... I can't go ... wherever I want to any more. Because, I'm not ... hidden any more.' No more words would come. Loss crushed her vocal chords. But the news seemed to have the opposite effect on Allan. Relief gushed over his features. For her, it was a locked door, but for him, it was a *solution*.

'So ... that's it then?' he asked timidly, his eyes gentle and full of hope.

'I guess ...'

She struggled against the threatening tears and Allan reached out a reassuring hand. 'I know it's hard, but it's not safe, Beth, and you can see that, can't you? Especially now?'

She shrugged dismally.

'Well … promise me this at least,' he said. '*Please*. If you get any other ideas … about testing … or checking things out … don't leave me out of it.'

Her eyes darted up suspiciously, but his expression was tender.

'If you went off somewhere – somewhere dangerous – without telling me … and you never came back … I'd never know what happened to you. At least let me watch your back, Beth. At least give me the chance to *know* – if you ever get it into your head that you want to go travelling again.'

'So you can have a chance to talk me out of it?'

A fragile grin gentled the tension of his face. 'I guess. Or at least come after you – if you get stuck.'

Beth tilted her head to the side. 'How would you do that?'

He shrugged. 'If you don't go too far, and it doesn't kill you … maybe I can come and find you. Or you could come and find me.'

In spite of her looming sense of tragedy, she had to concede it was a very reasonable request. Seeing his hurt she regretted leaving him out. He was right, it wasn't fair.

'OK worrywart,' she said, 'I promise.'

Chapter 22

December, 2005

Beth kept her promise. It wasn't hard. All the pictures that attracted her were now impossible to enter. Defeated, she resigned herself to imprisonment in the present. She threw the little castle calendar away and tried to immerse herself in more normal concerns. At least she had final exams to prepare for. They provided an all-consuming distraction – but whenever her concentration lapsed, a lingering sense of loss leaked in through the cracks. No matter how hard she tried, she couldn't shrug it off, and now she had to carry that alone. Allan didn't understand. He didn't even notice anything was missing.

Once the exams were over she sank into a dull depression. She dragged through school days barely uttering a word and closed herself into her bedroom directly after dinner each night. She wasn't even interested in seeing Allan. There was no fight, no official break-up, but slowly she drifted away. Finally, she told him she needed time to herself.

Allan was shattered. He'd seen the distance increasing between them, but didn't know what to do about it. He wasn't the sort to force himself on someone – and Beth wasn't the sort to be forced. He tried to hope she just needed rest after the exams. They'd been gruelling, and even he was ready for a break – but not from Beth. It hurt and frightened him that she wanted a break from him.

But she did.

And he couldn't *not* give it to her.

Beth promised to be in touch, but as each day ground past without a word from her, his concern grew.

Gillian was concerned too. Things hadn't been good since Anna's disappearance. She knew Beth had been furious with her, but had hoped she'd get over it. Instead, she was becoming more and more withdrawn.

Richard believed that being firm and laying down clear boundaries was all that was required. He wasn't aware of any major problems and even thought things were improving. She'd been less combative than usual. But Gillian saw this as just one more worrying sign. It wasn't like Beth. Something had changed and her baby girl was slipping away. A terrible fear stole around her heart: if she didn't reach her daughter soon, she'd lose her.

It was eleven o'clock on Saturday morning, one week before school broke up for summer. Beth was still in bed. She'd taken to sleeping in and spending most of the weekend in her room. Gillian knocked on the door and let herself in.

Beth was dressed, lying on her bed, staring up at her poster of Machu Picchu. She turned dull eyes towards her mother.

'How would you like to come shopping with me?' Gillian asked cheerily. 'There'll be Christmas crowds, but I haven't had a chance to do any shopping yet, and I thought maybe you'd like some new clothes for Christmas? We could try some things on together.'

'The sales are better after Christmas,' said Beth without enthusiasm.

'Yes, I know, but it's nice to have something under the tree.'

'We haven't got a tree.'

'That's something else I need to do. Our old decorations are tired, half of them are broken. And we need new lights! I thought you might like to help me pick some out.'

She sparkled like an excited child and her warmth thawed Beth a little, but not enough to alter her sour expression. 'I'm tired,' she moaned. 'Can't Richard go with you?'

'He could … but I'd rather go with you. Girls' day out! Oh, come on, honey, I've hardly seen anything of you in weeks.'

That was true. She'd been avoiding her mother and had intended to go on avoiding her – but, in the face of this blatant attempt at seduction, her stored up resentments seemed suddenly petty. It wasn't her mum's fault she didn't understand; she'd never tried to explain. And what did it matter now anyway?

She pushed herself up from her bed, 'OK. But we have to have pizza for lunch.'

Gillian beamed, 'Of course!'

Six hours later they returned with a carload of Christmas decorations and presents: two new outfits and a new pair of shoes for Beth; chocolates, ties, books and socks for Richard; and assorted bits and pieces for various friends, associates and relatives.

Beth found perfume for her mother – her favourite kind – and managed to buy it without her seeing. She also bought a T-shirt from Billabong for Allan. The colour was perfect for his eyes. She hadn't spoken to him in over a week and they'd made no plans for Christmas, but the thought of him in the shirt made her suddenly ache to see him.

Gillian snuck in a surprise gift for Beth as well: an artist's painting set. An impulse buy, nothing Beth had requested but Gillian hoped some kind of creative expression would be cheering and she knew Beth had liked drawing as a child.

Both returned home pleased with their purchases. The afternoon and evening were spent putting up and decorating the new tree and wrapping Christmas presents. Richard made an appearance to praise the tree at the appropriate moment but other than that he stayed out of their way, retreating into a book on the back verandah. It reminded Beth of old times, before he came into their lives. She began to relax and lose herself in the simple pleasure of sparkly things. For the first time in weeks, she laughed. The misery of the past few months seemed lighter and she even began to get a little excited about Christmas.

Gillian, pleased at how enjoyable the evening was turning out, was happy just to follow Beth's lead and keep the conversation on comfortable trivialities, but as the night wore on she decided to risk it. She suggested cinnamon toast as a nightcap and they made their way to the kitchen. As they were happily buttering and sprinkling Gillian put the question out there.

'Are you OK, honey?'

Beth looked up from her toast. 'Why shouldn't I be?'

'No reason. It's just … you've seemed a little … sad, lately, and I've been a bit worried for you.'

Beth shrugged. 'Just exams and stuff. I'm tired, that's all.'

Gillian nodded, waiting for more, but nothing came. 'I … thought it might have been … Anna,' she said quietly.

Beth picked up her plate as though she would just walk away, but then she changed her mind. She met her mother's eyes with steely defiance. 'I'm not *sick*. There's nothing wrong with me.'

Gillian flinched at the attack, but was grateful for the honesty. 'Honey, I never meant—'

'You told the detectives I was mental!'

'No. No, I didn't. I only said—' It hit her and her face greyed. 'Oh, Beth … honey … I was only trying to protect you.'

Beth's mouth hardened into a thin line, and Gillian realised the futility of that defence. She scraped her hair away from her face and leant back against the counter.

'It's so hard sometimes,' she said slowly, 'as a mother … to know what to do … how to help. There's no manual. You just stumble around, trying to do what's best –

or what you think is best. But I … I never meant to hurt you, darling. It's just – I could see the way the detectives were looking at you, and … I … I could see where they were going. I was just trying to help.'

'I didn't need your help,' said Beth coldly. 'I just needed you to believe in me.'

'I did … I do—'

'You think I'm sick!'

'No, no I don't … but, honey, you had some … trouble … before … when you were young. And what you were saying to the detectives was …' She shook her head. 'This is all so difficult to understand. I'm trying to. Honestly, I am. But …' Her words trailed off.

Beth stared down at the table. What was the point of explaining it to her mother when travelling was lost to her anyway? She calmed a little, but the anger remained.

'I don't want to go to that *prick* of a doctor ever again.'

Relief rushed through Gillian. 'Of course. Never again. I promise.' Then, absurdly, she giggled. 'He was a bit of a prick, wasn't he?'

Surprised, Beth cracked a smile – and warmth seeped over the ridges of the chasm that separated them. 'A *major* prick!'

'I'm sorry, honey,' said Gillian, seeing an opening for grace and seizing it. 'I didn't mean to hurt you.'

Beth sighed. 'I know.'

The anger had softened from her face, but with it had gone the brief bubble of joy. She picked up her toast and moved back to the living room. Curled up in the corner of the couch, she licked at the oozing butter and stared into the pulsing lights of the tree.

Gillian followed and sat in one of the big easy chairs. She wanted to pretend the matter had been dealt with and retreat to easier topics, but she'd seen the defeat in her daughter's eyes and knew the wall between them would soon be rebuilt if she did. With a silent prayer, she searched for the right words. 'I do want to understand …' she tried. 'If you could just—'

'There's no point, Mum. It's all over now anyway. I won't be doing it any more.'

The hair rose on the back of Gillian's neck.

'Doing what?'

'The *psychic* stuff. That's all over. I'm not doing it any more. Allan doesn't want me to, and I … I've just decided … not to.'

Her tone was matter-of-fact, but leaden, and Gillian noticed a darkening at the mention of Allan's name.

'Is everything OK between you and Allan?'

Beth stiffened. 'Allan's fine.'

Gillian didn't trust herself to push into that. She picked up her toast and resigned herself to whatever Beth was willing to give. This seemed to be the right response because after a moment Beth relaxed and offered an unexpected question. 'Was Dad your first love?'

Gillian smiled. 'Well, no he wasn't. I had a few boy-friends before him. No *good* ones mind you, but I was besotted with all of them at the time just the same.'

'Who was your first?'

Gillian laughed. 'His name was Jeff, Jeff Everton, and he was a first-class arsehole!'

Beth snorted in delight and Gillian grinned. 'I've got a picture of him, if you'd like to see it?'

Beth perked up with curiosity. 'Where?'

'In my old album. Come on.'

She led the way upstairs to her bedroom, dragged a chair to the wardrobe, climbed up and fished out an old photograph album from the top shelf. Sitting with it on the bed, she patted the space beside her in invitation. They sat side-by-side as Gillian flipped through the pages. There were old black and white pictures of Gillian as a child, even one or two of her as an infant, and several school portraits. She flipped through those until she came to the colour photographs and searched until she found a family portrait taken on a beach. To the side of the grouping stood a gangly fifteen-year-old Gillian, clinging proudly to the hand of a tall, good-looking youth.

'That's him,' said Gillian. 'It was taken the day he dumped me. I'd have cut him out of the picture, but then I thought, why should I let him ruin a perfectly good photograph?'

Jeff stared cockily at the camera: good-looking, but obviously too aware of it. It wasn't difficult for Beth to detect the arsehole within.

'I think you did well to get rid of him,' she said.

'Yes, definitely, but it broke my heart at the time. He was my first love.'

Beth nodded, and Gillian flipped the pages to another photograph of a dark-haired man playing guitar and singing to a crowd in a European setting. He was slender, with olive skin, full sensuous lips and smoky dark eyes. 'Francoise,' said Gillian. 'One of the better ones. He was French. A musician. He had a beautiful voice.'

'Beautiful eyes, too. Is that France?'

'No, Spain. We went busking in Spain.'

'*You* went busking?' Gillian was tone deaf.

'Well, I helped to gather the crowd and watched the hat. We did pretty well. Survived the whole summer on it and ate in restaurants every night. Played in a few of them too. Got some great crowds.' She smiled as Beth peered down at the photograph.

'He looks drunk …'

'Artistic temperament,' said Gillian, and quickly flipped a few more pages to find one of Beth's father from before their marriage. He was young and scruffy, sitting on a bench in a park, his arm wrapped affectionately around her mother's shoulders. Both were flushed with the excitement of new love.

'I haven't seen that one before.'

'No? I'll make a copy for you if you like.'

It was un-enterable, just another reminder of what she'd lost.

'That's OK. Where was it taken?'

'London, Hyde Park, on New Year's Day, 1982.' A different kind of smile lit her face. 'It was the morning we met …'

She reached a finger to trace over the image, and her smile faded, but she didn't linger there. Brightening again, she flipped on through the pages, sharing comments and memories as they were inspired.

'What's that one?' Beth pointed to a picture of a beach at sunset. There were no people in it and it was a little dark. It seemed like a strange photograph to keep.

'That was across from our flat in Manly. We lived right on the beach, back when you were little. Not the best photograph … but it was the last one your father ever took.'

'The day we were all at the park?'

Her mother had told her about the day her father died, about their last morning in the park. She had a photograph of her and her mother playing in the lagoon in the album her mother had given her. She'd thought *that* was the last photograph he'd taken.

Gillian only nodded, lost in remembrance, and Beth began to feel bad for raking up hurt; but then her mother's face softened. 'Your father was a very special man. I loved him from the first moment I saw him, and I'll always love him.'

It was the first time her mother had admitted this longed-for truth – that her father was the *one* – that she loved him still and always would. Beth understood it was a secret; Richard didn't need to know he was 'second best'. For a moment she even felt sorry for him.

'That's how it is with Allan and me,' she said.

The seriousness of her tone surprised Gillian and it drew her back from her reflection. Beth was so young for such a declaration, it gave her an anxious niggle. But she wasn't going to risk pushing her away again.

'It's a beautiful thing to find that kind of love, darling. Treasure it.'

'I do,' said Beth thoughtfully. 'I do.'

* * *

January, 2006

The night was hot and sticky. Business had been slow. Jade was uncomfortably damp, her skimpy dress was sticking to her skin and her hair had gone to rat-tails.

Not a good look. She was considering giving up for the night when the white van pulled up beside her.

Briefly, primitive instinct bristled a warning – though even logic told her two to one was risky. But she needed the money, and the men were offering double her normal fee. An hour's work, and she'd end the night with all financial needs met. Jade slipped her fee into her purse and climbed into the van.

Further down the street, another car pulled up and another young woman climbed out. She watched with some annoyance as Jade disappeared into the white van.

For her, it had been a slow night as well.

Chapter 23

December 31, 1981, London

New Year's Eve – and she was in London.

The sprawling, ancient city thrilled Gillian. She'd spent the last few years travelling around Europe – almost eighteen months in Italy; a couple of months in Paris; a summer busking in Spain; and the obligatory 'seven countries in ten days' Contiki tour and subsequent backpacking expedition with newfound friends – but England was different. It felt like home. Even though she had more family in Italy, she'd been born and raised in Australia and had never been part of the Italian community. Perhaps her Italian mother had been trying a little too hard to adopt her new homeland's culture?

First stop in the UK had been Ireland, where she and some Swedish backpacking friends went on an extended walking tour-cum-pub crawl. The laid-back Swedes were a breath of sanity after Spain. Francoise was talented, but life with a charismatic alcoholic was not for her. When the Swedes returned home, Gillian caught a ferry to Scotland and travelled slowly down to London, where she found a small but comfortable room in a share flat in Hackney. She had been just in time for the wedding of Prince Charles and Lady Diana Spencer. What an amazing time to be in such an amazing place! The streets were alive with the colours of the Union Jack. Everything from tea cups to T-shirts was adorned with the royal couple's faces. It was like one massive, extended street party. She spent the entire summer discovering all the iconic treasures of that real-life Monopoly board and when summer was over she determined to stay. With her funds running low she began job hunting and was taken on in a busy pub in Soho. Lousy pay, but the tips brought in enough for her to survive quite comfortably. By Christmas, she was feeling like a local.

And now it was New Year's Eve.

She got an early shift – crazy busy, but it gave her the most important part of the evening off – and after work she and two girlfriends set out for Trafalgar Square to see in the New Year. Most of London seemed to have had the same idea. By the time they reached the square and pushed through to as near Nelson's Column as possible, the crowds were packed in so tight the girls could lift their feet off the ground without falling over! Human sardines squashed into a tin. Lifting her face to the clear night sky, Gillian laughed in delight. High above her, perched on his column, Nelson looked down sternly. What an astonishing tangle of humanity. So many people, pushing, shoving, whistling and laughing as they waited for the magical moment. But as still more attempted to cram into the square, the crush intensified and it became difficult to breathe; there was literally no space for the girls to expand their chests. Getting nervous, they fought their way to the steps of the National Gallery, where it was a little less congested. It took them nearly twenty minutes. Within moments of getting there, the cry went up: a large shout of celebration. Enthusiastically, the girls joined in, leaping up and down and yelling until their ears rang – and when a frenzy of kissing-everyone-in-reach began, they threw themselves into that with equal abandon. Everyone was drunk with excitement. No one took advantage. Goodwill reigned.

Somewhere, some fireworks went off, sparkling in the night sky like an air-borne orgasm. Gillian craned her neck to watch, and as she did a few attempts at Auld Lang Syne rose briefly above the din.

The New Year had arrived.

The girls toppled together, weak with the thrill of it all, and threw their arms around each other. The spectacle had surpassed expectations. They lingered in the joy of it a moment more before tossing around ideas for the rest of the night and getting out of the square was decided on as first priority. The clamour was bewildering. But when they left the safety of the steps, there was another massive crush. Everyone else was also trying to leave. Almost immediately Gillian's friend's hand was ripped from her grasp. The girl was swallowed by the mass, leaving Gillian cut off and alone in the throng. She struggled to remain upright, knowing that if she fell she could be crushed to death, but the sheer mass of humanity was suffocating. Sinking, she grabbed frantically at the man pressed up against her chest, unable even to ask for help as the last of the air was squashed out of her lungs. Instantly, his arm forced its way around her. With his other arm he shoved the man behind her far enough back to allow her to take in a breath.

'I've got you,' he said into her ear. 'I won't let you fall. Breathe!'

An Australian!

Gasping gratefully, Gillian met her rescuer's eyes. They were kind, and he was grinning, clearly having the time of his life. 'Hang on,' he said. Holding her securely in his arms, he used his body as a shield and kept her upright as they were dragged along with the crowd. It was slow going, but once they passed the boundaries of the square, they spurted out into a feeder street like water gushing from a breaking dam.

Exhilarating!

Resting back against the window of a shop, out of the main push of pedestrian traffic, they laughed until they could laugh no more. Only then did Gillian's rescuer hold out his hand. 'Mike O'Malley,' he said, his eyes dancing in the pale neon light.

Gillian had never seen a more perfectly beautiful man. His dark hair, thick and wild like a salt-soaked surfer's, set off his amazing eyes in a breathtaking way. His face was alive with fun and his body lean and strong like a cowboy.

'You're Australian,' said Gillian, dumbstruck and forgetting her manners.

'New South Wales, west of Lithgow.' He smiled. 'You?'

'Oh, sorry. Gillian Crawford. Sydney.' She grasped

his offered hand and gave it a formal shake. 'Thank you. You saved my life.'

'Well, it would have been messy if you were squashed all over my feet.' His face was serious, but it melted into an easy laugh as Gillian's expression transitioned from confusion to delight. 'You here alone?'

'No. I was with some friends, but we got separated.' She searched the crowds doubtfully. 'Don't s'pose I'll ever find them in this …'

'Did you make plans to meet up somewhere later?'

'No, we didn't get to that, but they'll probably head for the Rock Garden at Covent Garden,' she said, brightening a little. 'What about you? Are you with anyone?'

Mike shook his head. 'First night in London. I was just out getting the lay of the land.'

'Seriously?'

He nodded, unable to mask his awe as he watched the river of hyped-up humanity still flowing out of the square. 'Pretty intense place!'

'Well, it *is* New Year's Eve.'

'Yeah, I guess.' He stared at a rowdy bunch of teenage girls in leather and tights with spiky pink hair and gaudy make-up. They whistled and yowled as they passed. Gillian smiled at his naivety. It was fun to be the experienced woman-of-the-world.

'Where you staying?' she asked.

'Earl's Court. Youth Hostel. Bit of a dump, but I won't be there long. Just the first couple of nights till I sort out what I'm doing.'

'I'm in Hackney,' she declared proudly. 'A share flat. It's not bad.'

Mike appeared appropriately impressed. 'So, what

do you wanna do then? You going to head for Covent Garden to see if you can meet up with your friends?'

'I guess so ...' Impulsively, she took a gamble. 'You wanna come too? Or – no, of course not. You're probably exhausted. Twenty-six-hour flight?'

'Forty-eight all up, door to door. But I couldn't sleep if I wanted to. What is it?' He checked his watch. 'It's not even lunch time back home.' He treated her again to his jaunty grin. 'So what's this Rock Garden? A restaurant?'

'A disco. You'll love it!'

They partied at the Rock Garden until about three a.m. Gillian's girlfriends never showed up but that gave her and Mike more time together, which suited them both. When they tired of the noise, they returned to the streets, spending the rest of the night wandering aimlessly, waiting for the tubes to start up again at seven. Gillian was smitten. But she also needed a shower and a change of clothes before starting work that afternoon. So as the grey dawn crept out to reclaim the streets they parted company at Monument tube station with plans to meet up at Hyde Park for a picnic brunch a few hours later.

The first day of the New Year turned out to be cloudy, but that didn't bother them. They picked up fish and chips and entered the park. With most of London's inhabitants still sleeping off the night before, it was almost empty; peaceful and quiet and entirely beautiful. They claimed a bench, wiped it down, and set out their lunch between them – and were immediately sniffed out by the local squirrel population. These strange little Disney creatures were much more appealing to the colonials than seagulls. Mike and Gillian were happy to share their lunch. Gillian felt like Snow White as the squirrels accepted food right out of her hand, and Mike jumped up to capture the moment. He spent the next several minutes snapping off what he hoped would be interesting squirrel-feeding shots and was delighted when a passing girl offered to take a picture of the two of them together. Eagerly, he handed over his camera and scooted back to the bench. Squeezing in close to Gillian, his face expanded into a silly smile as the girl laughed and snapped the shot.

Accepting their thanks and returning the camera, the girl pulled her red coat close against the chill. 'No problem,' she said. 'Enjoy your chips.'

Oblivious, Mike and Gillian carried on with their brunch, as their as-yet-unborn daughter walked down the path towards the Serpentine Lake.

* * *

Cover was hard to find. The trees were bare, as it was winter, and there were no buildings in sight. All she could do was keep on walking … searching … hoping … as the minutes passed and the ache behind her left ear worked its way across the whole back of her head. It felt like the top of her skull was being slowly torn off. She struggled to hold on to the contents of her stomach, forcing herself to walk slowly, trying not to draw attention to herself, knowing she couldn't do it for much longer.

Fortunately, there were few people about.

Berating herself for not working this out *before* entry, she pushed on, until finally she spotted a bush. She ran for it, without even checking for witnesses, as her remaining seconds of consciousness sped away.

She just made it in time.

* * *

On the other side, she crashed face-first onto the hotel room carpet as the retching hit. It was several minutes before the painful convulsions had run their course. Shaky and breathless, splattered and reeking with her own sick, she stared at the mess around her.

Shit!

This wasn't going to work.

* * *

Allan was getting panicky. Beth had never done this before – leaving without even a note!

Where was she?

Was she all right?

His heart crumbled inside his chest; she clearly didn't *want* him in on this, which could only mean one thing ...

But, where would she go?

A hotel?

That seemed the most likely. She'd want somewhere private, safe – but he couldn't check every hotel in Sydney. And knowing Beth, it would be the last one he'd think to check. She could be anywhere!

Why hadn't she waited to talk with him about it?

Why hadn't she listened?

Beth and her *bloody* obsessions were tearing their lives apart; and there was *nothing* he could do to stop her.

Dumping his coffee in the sink, he kicked the cupboard door underneath with all the violence he could release. It felt good, really good, but it changed nothing. His anger was merely replaced by depression; his rage merely dampened into gloom.

There was no way to find her. She could be lying somewhere, alone, sick, unable to call for help, and there was nothing he could do about it.

How much of it could she even stand?

She was already sick, and she was going back for more! She didn't seem to care if it killed her.

Allan yelled his frustration at the empty flat – but only silence echoed back.

Chapter 24

January, 2007

Art was a solace for Beth. She began experimenting when she received her new paint set but it wasn't until she came under the inspiration of a particularly brilliant teacher in year eleven that she really discovered her passion for it. At last, she'd found something capable of consuming her creative energy, and capturing and expressing the world as *she* experienced it fascinated her. The darkness seemed to flow out of her onto the canvas, leaving her cleansed. It was a joy.

And she was good at it!

Her major work for her Higher School Certificate was a haunting canvas of merging photographs and oils. In the bottom right-hand quadrant, Kennedy drove along a Dallas street, waving at the crowds. Behind him a swirling crimson cloud exploded across the canvas and melted into fiery yellows at the base of Apollo 11 as it launched. In the bloodied flames, barely noticeable in the billowing colour, was a self-portrait: herself as a witness, seen from behind, a muddied fistful of photographs at her feet, discarded.

Mr Mountmark, her art teacher, considered it 'a savage political statement, sensitively executed with exceptional ability'. Her classmates liked it as well. Allan – the only one who actually understood it – was her biggest fan.

For the first time, Beth was content at school. Art classes became the highlight of her week and she was usually found in the art room in spare periods working on her major work or other projects. The smell of paint and the placing, creating and controlling of images brought her peace.

This was a relief to Gillian. She was delighted her impulsive gift had opened a new talent for Beth. It pleased her to see her daughter regaining her sparkle and settling down, becoming genuinely happy and achieving something. Something *normal*.

And in most ways, Beth's last two years of school *were* normal. She concentrated on her studies, spent time with Allan, participated in school activities – and didn't invade time through photographs. It pulled at her sometimes, especially when she worked on a collage and the images lay raw and undiscovered at her fingertips, begging entry, but mostly she had no desire to travel. There was no point if she was visible, and she preferred to spend time with Allan anyway. As she shrugged off the last of her childhood, he became interesting in a whole new way. Their explorations together were far more exciting than anything she'd found in a photograph – and it was a journey they could make together. She could follow *his* lead, to unexpected destinations, or take him along with her. He became her centre, where she found release or rested content. And in the nakedness, as the barriers shuddered open, she could believe she wasn't alone.

It was the same for Allan. Beth was all he needed. Their secrets still kept them apart from the herd, but he had no desire to integrate. He preferred to keep a safe distance. Even when he became old enough to live independently and a foster home was no longer a threat, he didn't want to unsettle the life he'd set up for himself. After graduation though, with the assurance of a scholarship to study science at Sydney University, he thought it was time to sort out his status. He moved out of his mother's flat and into a converted garage closer to the university. He then handed in the keys of the flat and told the Department of Family and Community Services his mother had taken off without telling him where she was going.

There'd been no difficulty setting up his independent-student financial support after that. For the first time in nearly seven years he was put on the books, in his own name. It felt good. With the scholarship and government support, he had more than enough to live on and now, *finally*, he and Beth could live together. She'd been accepted into the same university to study art.

They were both excited at the new life opening up for them, caught up in the flurry of change. Gillian, however, had reservations. Her little girl was leaving her childhood home, moving in with a man she loved and beginning a new independent life, without ceremony or celebration, without even an announcement. To Beth and Allan it was a matter of course – their lives having melded long before – but for Gillian the day was momentous, as wrenching as Beth's first day at school and as life-changing as the day of her birth. As she helped unload and arrange Beth's things, she couldn't quite climb over her angst. Her baby girl had grown up and was leaving her. *Was she ready? Would she be safe? Happy? Well cared for?*

She knew the answers. She'd grown to love Allan and had no doubt he was a good choice for Beth. And it wasn't as though this move was a surprise. Allan was already part of the family; Beth spent more time at his home than her own. No, not a surprise – but sooner than she was prepared for. Beth was still her little girl, and surely *way* too young to be going to university!

And yet she was.

And the university *was* too far away for an easy commute. Moving closer and sharing accommodation made sense. Sydney housing was ridiculously expensive; few people could afford to live alone, and Gillian wouldn't have wanted her to live alone either. It comforted her to know Allan would be there for Beth. Her daughter was fiercely independent, with ramrod resolve, but such rigidity left her fragile, open to fracture, and sometimes her judgement was erratic. Allan's steady conservatism offered hope of some boundaries.

In many ways it was a relief to hand over Beth's care to someone else – someone who loved her as fiercely as she did – and it was logical and practical that this transition should come at this point. Even Richard supported the idea, although that didn't mean much. He was happy just to reclaim his home as a teen-free zone; which was fair. Richard was fifteen years older than her and he liked things peaceful and quiet. He'd been very patient. The demands of helping to rear a difficult child, one not even his own, had been stressful. She understood his longing for a return to a fully adult space. But she was grieving. A part of her was being wrenched away. As she lifted the last box out of the back of her car and carried it into her daughter's new home she already felt the emptiness that would be left behind.

'Are you sure you'll be all right here?' she asked, running a critical eye over the small bare room. 'What about laundry? What will you—?'

'We can use theirs,' said Beth. 'It's just across the yard. They've got a dryer, and there's the clothesline.'

Gillian nodded and wandered to the rear of the apartment to inspect the bathroom. It was barely big enough to turn around in, but it had the basics and was clean. Next, she turned a disparaging eye on the 'kitchenette'. It was little more than a sink, a counter and a couple of cupboards, with a microwave oven and bar fridge added almost as an afterthought.

Beth followed her mother's critical gaze and sighed. 'We'll be fine, Mum. Stop worrying.'

'I'll take care of her,' chipped in Allan as confidently as he could. 'It's really quite comfortable. The bus goes from just out front and the train station is a few blocks away. It only takes half an hour to get to uni.'

Gillian smiled and tried to look positive, although now the uninsulated walls caught her attention. They weren't going to provide much comfort in winter. They'd freeze! She made a mental note to buy them a heater and sort out extra quilts. At least they had a separate bedroom, and even though it only fit the bed, it did have a nice window onto the yard.

'Would you like a cup of tea, Mum?' asked Beth, playing hostess for the first time in her life.

'Good idea!'

Allan unloaded a chair for her to sit on as Beth hunted for cups. Soon three cups of steaming tea warmed their fingers and they began excitedly discussing the prospect of getting a couch from Vinnies. The big question was *where* to put it.

The young couple's joyous resilience in the face of insurmountable decorating challenges brought back memories of Gillian's first home with Mike. This garage wasn't all that different from their London flat. They'd had a one room apartment in Mile End, a run-down area, grimy and decrepit. The noise of traffic boomed at all hours. There'd been barely enough room to circumnavigate the bed when it was folded out and the kitchen facilities had been no more extensive than Beth and Allan's. There wasn't even an internal bathroom – just a shared one down the hall. But she and Mike had considered it heaven.

Gillian's eyes wandered to the bare walls of the garage. 'I could get your poster framed for you,' she offered. 'If you like. It would look very cheery here.'

Beth had deliberately left her poster of Machu Picchu behind. It filled her with pain, knowing she could never step into it again. But she didn't have the heart to reject her mother's first attempt at showing acceptance of her new home.

'Thanks, Mum.' She smiled.

And so it was sorted.

* * *

May, 2008

Ambrosia Mackleray's car was in for repairs. Distracted by her phone, she'd rear-ended a Volkswagen at some traffic lights on her way home from university. She barely scratched the Volkswagen but her car was completely caved in at the front, leaving her without transport for three whole weeks and no alternative but public transport and the charity of friends.

Tonight, it was the bus. She was a little nervous about taking public transport late at night, but she'd overspent on a new pair of shoes and a taxi was out of the question. She'd been having drinks with friends in Manly and was expecting to come home with her best friend Rebecca, but Rebecca and her boyfriend were invited to a party in Palm Beach and she hadn't wanted to go with them; leaving her to make her own way home. She could have pressed Rebecca to take her, but it would have been an imposition since she basically needed to go in the opposite direction and Rebecca's boyfriend was stressing about the time. At least it was possible to get a bus home from Manly, even though there would be a walk on the other end.

After saying goodbye to her friends, Ambrosia left the pub for the bus stop. She pulled her coat tighter for protection from the autumn chill and regretted not bringing a warmer one, or wearing more sensible shoes; her toes went quickly numb. Grumbling as she hobbled down the Corso, she tried to cover the distance as quickly as possible. It was still fairly busy and there were police about so she felt safe enough. But when she reached the bus stop, no one else was waiting. The street was deserted. It unsettled her until she checked the timetable and saw she'd just missed a bus. The next one wouldn't be along for twenty minutes. She was in for a chilly wait.

Frustrated, she reconsidered a taxi as the wind whipped in from the harbour and bit into the backs of her unprotected legs. She made mental calculations as to how she could afford the fare and had just resigned herself to asking her parents for another loan when her mechanic and his friends pulled up beside her in a white van and offered her a lift.

Relieved, she gratefully accepted.

Chapter 25

June, 2008

It was a glorious Monday morning. Sun was streaming in through the window. It danced through Beth's collection of Nanna's fairies that dangled in the frame, and filled their bedroom with at least the appearance of warmth. Actual warmth was yet to be achieved. There was little chance of that without several more hours of sunshine or a steady blast from their little electric heater. But underneath their thick quilt it was toasty.

Beth curled against Allan's body, luxuriating in their weekly lie-in. She wasn't yet ready to abandon the comfort of their bed, even for a much wanted cup of tea, but she was building up to it. Neither of them had classes on Monday and Beth wasn't due at the cafe she worked at until eleven. Monday morning was their time for catching up on each other, a sacrosanct time reserved exclusively for them when they could sleep in and share a lazy breakfast. But she was done with sleeping now and breakfast was calling. Her tummy was rumbling. She nudged Allan.

'Aren't you hungry?'

He groaned and snuggled in closer. Bed time always won out over food as far as he was concerned.

'Eggs?' suggested Beth 'Or just tea and toast?'

Allan refused to be inspired. Beth's stomach expressed another gurgling protest. 'Lazy bastard,' she chided. Giving in, she climbed out of bed and shivered into the kitchen. She didn't really mind. She was usually the first up in the morning anyway unless Allan had an early class. He was more active in the evenings.

After putting on the kettle, she jumped into the shower and manipulated it to its maximum warmth. The water heater was a little temperamental. This morning though, she got it just right. A gush of hot water cascaded over her, chasing away the chill and steaming up the bathroom in seconds. Blindly, she reached for the shampoo and was halfway through rinsing it out when Allan knocked on the door.

'Someone here to see you. A detective. "Blade" … or something.'

'What?' She shook the water from her ears.

Allan held out her bathrobe. 'There's a detective here, and he wants to talk to you. Did you forget to pay your Student Union Fees?'

Beth stared back at him, shampoo running into her eyes. 'Where is he?'

'Outside. I told him to wait there while you get dressed.'

Beth was relieved – she had to walk through the living room to get to the bedroom – but she was also confused. She wasn't in any trouble that she knew of. Quickly, she rinsed out the rest of the shampoo, donned the robe, scurried to the bedroom and struggled into her jeans and a thick woollen jumper, wondering what he could want. With no time to blow dry, she gave her hair a rub down with the sodden towel and then a vigorous shake. The result was a wild shag, but it would have to do. Her curiosity was building.

It wasn't until she saw Detective Blaine standing in the yard that she realised he was the detective who'd interviewed her about Anna's disappearance.

'Hello, Beth,' he said politely. 'I was hoping you would spare a moment to talk with me.'

Beth was inclined to decline if the choice was really hers, but before she could, Allan appeared behind her shoulder. 'Like a cup of tea?' he offered cheerily.

Blaine smiled and accepted. Before Beth processed what was happening, she and Blaine were seated opposite each other in the breakfast nook and Allan was making tea. Feeling cornered, she remained silent, waiting for Blaine to explain himself, and eventually, pleasantries done with, his expression settled to a more serious cast.

'I ... uh, suppose you've heard about Ambrosia Mackleray?' he began cautiously.

That gained him a blank stare.

'I understand she was in your class in high school?' He tried again. 'It's been in all the papers, and on the news ...'

Beth and Allan didn't get a paper and they didn't have a TV.

'What happened?' asked Beth, showing little sign of interest.

Blaine tried to deliver it as gently as possible. 'She went missing, two weeks ago.' He allowed a moment for that to sink in before continuing. 'She met some friends in a pub in Manly, left the pub alone about midnight to head home, and then just … disappeared. Her friends said she'd intended to get a bus. But whether she did or not, she never arrived home, and she hasn't been seen or heard from since.'

'Scheisse,' said Allan, placing a hot cup of tea in front of them both.

'What's that got to do with me?' Beth asked guardedly.

It surprised Blaine a little. He'd been prepared for shock … tears … concern … or at least curiosity – but then, Beth's responses were never what he'd call typical. He was grateful though that she'd got straight to the point, and so should he. 'It seems there might be a connection between this case and Anna Johnston's disappearance. The men you pointed out from the photographs were in the area the night Ambrosia disappeared, and they knew her. They were her mechanics. There's nothing to tie them to Ambrosia on that night, nobody saw them with her, but they *were* in Manly.'

'It was dark,' said Beth quickly. 'I couldn't really be sure about those men. I told you that when you showed me the photographs. I didn't see them properly. It was the van I was sure of.'

'Yes, yes, I know,' he assured her. 'But those men you identified are connected to the van. It belongs to the father of one of them.'

'And still you didn't arrest them?'

'We needed more, Beth … and we haven't yet been able to find anything.'

Beth rolled her eyes in disgust, and Blaine's jaw tightened. 'A case like this depends on hard evidence. Evidence that can be presented in court. It's not enough to *know* who did it, or to *think* you know. You have to be able to prove it.'

'Well, that's your job, isn't it?' said Beth. 'Finding evidence?'

Blaine coloured. 'Many cases go out the window for lack of evidence. You'd be surprised how many. We followed up your leads, Beth. The men all had alibis, the owner of the van was prepared to swear in court that it never left his property that night, and the van was clean! All we had was—'

'The word of a *psychic?*'

'The word of an under-aged girl,' he countered, 'with no connection to the missing person, or to the men she was accusing. A girl whose mother claimed she was at home on the night in question and whose psychiatrist labelled her as delusional.'

It was harsh, but instinct told Blaine that truth would carry more weight with Beth than a sugar-coated petition.

She didn't look away. 'So, why are you here? What do you want?'

'I was hoping you might be able to … help.'

Her face darkened. 'How do you think I could do that?'

'Well,' said Blaine, stumbling for a way to put it. 'We thought that, maybe … since Ambrosia is a friend of yours—'

'She's not a friend of mine.'

That stopped him in his tracks. 'Well … OK … uh … Beth, we're at a stalemate with this investigation. And we hoped maybe you could help confirm … a connection, for us.'

'A connection? How?'

'Well, if you maybe used your … *skills*—'

Beth snorted. 'You want me to do my "psychic" thing again?'

Allan's hand moved to her shoulder. Blaine felt even more ridiculous than he'd anticipated, but he'd determined to pursue this and he wouldn't be swayed. Relaxing his posture as much as possible, he tried again. 'Beth, I can understand you might feel a little burnt.'

'That's an understatement,' said Allan bitterly.

'Yes. Yes, I suppose it is,' admitted Blaine. 'I'm sorry about that. I really am.'

'So why is the word of a "delusional" girl suddenly worth something? You couldn't do anything with it before – so why do you want it now?'

'Because we've nothing else to go on,' he said simply. 'I must admit, this whole thing seemed a little crazy to me before – but … well, I can't deny that what you told us does seem to have … credibility. And it did help. We may not have been able to use it to bring about any arrests, but it *was* helpful.'

He wasn't sure whether she was accepting, or even listening to his apology. Her expression gave nothing away – but she wasn't throwing him out either. He continued. 'The truth is, we suspect Ambrosia isn't the only one. Two other girls have gone missing in the area in the past two years, in similar circumstances, just disappearing off the streets. And we think these cases could be related. A guess really. A hunch. But we think we may have a serial killer, or killers, here … and we need to stop them.'

He waited for some sign of understanding, but Beth's face remained impassive.

'Beth,' he said gently. 'You were able to help before. I know it was tough on you, and it must be difficult to have a … a *gift* … like that … and I'm sorry for the way everything turned out with Anna, but I think that what you … uh … *do* … might be helpful to our investigation again. If you could just … uh … think on it … and see if you can … *see* … anything that might confirm we're going in the right direction … well, that could be really helpful.'

At that, Beth let out a deep sigh. 'You don't understand. It's not like that. I can't just *think* about something and then *see* things. That's not what I do.'

Blaine's lips parted in confusion. 'Oh, but … uh … I—' His knowledge of psychic phenomena was limited. 'Do you need something … uh … of Ambrosia's to—?'

'No!' Allan moved in closer, protectively, warningly. 'She's not that kind of psychic.'

Blaine felt like Alice diving into the rabbit hole.

'Then … what kind of psychic is she? What does she need?'

Allan's eyes flashed. 'She doesn't *need* anything. She can't help you.'

'I'm sorry,' Beth interrupted. 'I'd help you if I could … but I can't.'

Blaine knew he had no right to argue it further. He

was feeling like a fool for ever agreeing to try to get her to help. Frazer had convinced him to do it. They'd hit nothing but dead ends. Beth's information remained the only viable lead they had. Frazer argued they had to at least try; they had so little else to go on. The disappearances were random. The girls had no apparent connection to each other or to Corelli and his mates – except that Jade was seen getting into a white van and Ambrosia's car had been in for repairs at Corelli's garage. Nothing solid though. Nothing to build a case on. He'd brought Corelli's van in twice now for a full forensic examination with no success. But he and Frazer were convinced these girls hadn't just run away. They'd been abducted. They had to chase any lead they were offered.

But now he was confounded. Beth either couldn't, or wouldn't, help.

He leant back from the table, preparing to take his leave. 'Well, I'm sorry to hear that … but thank you, for listening.'

'Do you think Ambrosia might still be alive?' Beth asked suddenly. 'After two weeks?'

Blaine hesitated. 'Well, the likelihood of that lessens every day. As I said, we believe we're dealing with serial killers here.'

'So … you think she's dead?'

'Well, not necessarily. It's possible they may be keeping her somewhere … but, I think what we need to focus on now is stopping them, protecting other girls, even if we may be too late to help Ambrosia.'

Beth paled. 'But, she *might* be alive?'

It was a gruesome possibility. What would she be enduring? What would they be doing to her, and for how long, if no help came? The idea made her shiver; even though it was Ambrosia. She remembered the beady malice of her eyes, always on the attack. She'd been like a hyena, running with the pack, hungry for the destruction of the weak.

But she didn't deserve this.

No one deserved this.

'She could be,' Blaine agreed.

Beth felt a flood of sadness, and at the same time, a heavy burden of responsibility.

'Was there any CCTV footage?' she asked, her voice barely above a whisper. She felt Allan stiffen and raised a hand to cover his in reassurance.

'No. There wasn't.' Blaine answered. 'No one was sure which direction she went. There are a few cameras in the area, but none of them picked anything up. Why?'

'Because that's how I do it. I go in through pictures. For Anna, I went in through the CCTV pictures.'

Blaine stared at her, speechless.

Allan let his breath out slowly. Reeking disapproval, he pulled out a chair and sat down beside Beth.

'Not what you were expecting?' asked Beth, a certain grim satisfaction in her tone.

Blaine could only shake his head. 'No … I, uh … can't say I really understand any of this …'

Beth wrapped her hands around her mug of tea, stealing comfort from its warmth. 'I used to just … look at a picture … and then, kind of … enter it. Invisibly. So, when they put that picture of Anna from the CCTV camera in the papers, I entered it, and saw what I told you I saw.' She searched Blaine's face for judgement, but saw only astonishment. 'Is that harder to believe than seeing psychic images?'

Somehow, it was, but Blaine was too stunned to voice that.

'But … I can't do it invisibly any more,' Beth continued. 'Something changed. Now, if I go in, I go in physically. If I went in now, the camera would pick me up, and if there were people there they'd see me.'

'Oh,' said Blaine, aware that some response was required, but unable to give any more.

'You're a bit late with this,' said Beth, her tone dry, 'but, I still might have been able to do it, if you had a photograph.'

Blaine swallowed, still struggling to take it in. 'You mean, you can … *physically* … enter a *photograph*?'

'Yes, she can,' said Allan. 'But she doesn't, because it's not safe. She doesn't do that any more.'

'Allan.' Beth reached for his hand again. 'It's all right, there aren't any pictures anyway, but if I'd been able to help, and if he promised to wipe the film—'

'How can he promise that?' Allan's eyes flashed. 'You can't risk it, Beth. Remember what happened last time!'

'Wait, wait,' interjected Blaine. 'Are you saying that if I could get a picture—'

'She's not saying anything!'

'Allan!'

'If I could get a photograph of Ambrosia,' Blaine persisted doggedly, 'you could … actually—'

'Not just any photograph. It'd have to be from that night, close to where she disappeared and safe for me to enter.'

Blaine couldn't believe he was having this

conversation.

'*Safe?*'

'I enter in front of the lens,' she explained. 'So there needs to be space. No good getting a selfie, or one taken across a table on a mobile phone. I'd land on the table. Or any regular pictures really because I wouldn't be able to hide. If there was some CCTV footage, that might work because there's no one behind the camera and you could wipe it before someone decided to check it for evidence. But if you don't have that and you don't even know which way she went …'

Blaine was in a daze. He stared at Beth, who was now calm and composed. She'd dropped her defensiveness and was giving every appearance of being completely genuine and rational. He had to agree with Frazer that her conviction was compelling, but even more compelling was Allan. *He* believed in her, and he wasn't stupid, nor presumably gullible, even if he was besotted with her. Against all logic, Blaine opened up to believing her too. An eagerness rose inside him – but there were no 'safe' photographs.

'All the CCTV footage from that night would have been wiped by now,' he said, unable to keep the disappointment from his voice. 'They don't keep it without a reason.'

'Are you sure?' asked Beth.

'I'm afraid so. There might be some incidental photos, from the pub, but as you say—'

'That wouldn't work,' said Allan, finishing the sentence for him.

Blaine shrugged, dissatisfied.

Allan relaxed, but Beth seemed to share Blaine's

regret.

'I'm sorry,' she said, and Blaine saw she meant it.

'Me too.'

A collective despondency sank over them as each retreated to their own thoughts.

'What about Anna?' Beth asked. 'Can't you work on that? I mean if you think they're connected?'

Blaine shook his head. 'Without some new information, there's not much we can do.'

'New information?'

'A body,' said Blaine bluntly. 'Or a confession.'

Beth considered his words. 'What if I made a definite identification?'

Allan bristled. 'No way!'

But Beth was fired. 'I still have the picture from the night Anna disappeared. I could go back again.'

'They'd see you!'

'Yes. So I could get their attention. I could get them to turn around so I could see their faces!'

'*What?*'

'Maybe I could even scare them off! Maybe I could stop them and save Anna!'

'Or get yourself *killed!*' Now Allan was furious. 'You heard what he said. These guys are probably serial killers! And you want to confront them? Late at night? Alone!'

That got her back up a little. 'I can leave any time I want to.'

'You *think* you can. You *hope* so. That's if they don't knock you out and drag you into the van and kill you first!'

'I'm not stupid. I wouldn't let them get close. If they came at me, I'd leave, and I'd still get to see their faces.'

The exchange was so fast and so bizarre that Blaine was lost for a response. Clearly he couldn't allow Beth to put her life at risk trying to get new information this way – but was that even what was at stake here? *She could leave? At will? Could it be safe?*

'Would it help?' She demanded fiercely.

Nonplussed, Blaine's mouth dropped open. 'I … don't want you to—'

'Would it help if I could identify them, or not?'

Still he hesitated. In the end, he decided on the only course his conscience would accept: he shook his head. 'No. Not really. I mean, it would confirm things, and we might … but, I'm sorry, Beth, I didn't realise that your … abilities … worked like … *that*. I thought you might just … *see* something … or *sense* it – but I can't ask you to put yourself at risk. Allan's right. Whoever is hurting those girls is dangerous, and there's nothing you can do to stop them, or to help Anna. We'll just have to work with what we have. Sooner or later, they'll slip up.'

It wasn't enough. They all knew it wasn't enough – for Ambrosia, or for any potential future victims – but it was all there was.

Blaine was disappointed, but also in a way relieved. It pushed things back into familiar territory for him. He felt bad about having disturbed Beth, but he'd done what he'd come to do. And now it was best to leave. Apologising again, he thanked them both and stood. 'I'll show myself out.'

With a heavy spirit Beth followed him to the door.

'At least he believes you now,' Allan said cheerily as she returned. 'That's something.'

'It won't help Ambrosia.'

They sat in the breakfast nook. 'I agree with Blaine,' he said gently. 'It's probably too late for her.'

'He never said that! He sai—'

'He said they're *serial killers* Beth. Serial killers *kill*.'

'Yes, but—'

'You have to let it go. There's nothing you can do.'

Instantly, her eyes ignited. 'Yes, there is. I can go back. To Anna. They're cowards, picking on a schoolgirl all alone on the streets at night. All I have to do is run up and yell.'

'They're *psychopaths*, Beth! Anna yelled, didn't she? It didn't help her. There was no one there to hear her! No one except you, and you weren't even there, not then, not when it *really* happened. You were *way* too late. A *week* too late. And now it's three years too late! Whatever happened to Anna has *already* happened, and you can't change that.'

'Why not?'

'Because it'd change everything else!' he snapped, losing all patience with her.

Beth stared at him, stung and confused, and he sighed. 'I'm sorry, but what if you *do* save Anna? What then? She'd go home? And none of this would have happened? What about the last three years? Everything would change, Beth. *Everything.* We'd be in some kind of alternate universe. How would that work?'

Fear crept into her eyes. 'I don't know … nobody knows that.'

'No. Nobody knows, because nobody's been able to do what you can do, and maybe nobody *should*.'

He saw her resolve shake. 'Maybe not …' she admitted, 'but I can't just not do anything. Don't I have a responsibility to help?'

'*How*? How the *hell* can you help without changing the past?'

'Well … what about the future? What about Ambrosia … if she's still alive? What about the next girl they take?'

'You can't stop that.'

'Yes I can. If I can give Blaine a proper identification, he can arrest them. That might mean he can save Ambrosia. And even if he can't, he could at least stop them getting anyone else.'

Allan was about to object, but Beth barrelled on. 'No. Listen! I don't have to get their attention – they don't even have to see me. I just need to see them. I don't need to change anything in the past, I just need to get a better look at their faces!'

'But Blaine said it wouldn't make any difference if you identified them.'

'He *said* I could help confirm who they are! He just didn't want me to risk it, but I won't be risking anything, I—'

Allan shook his head stubbornly. 'No. He said he needs a *body!* And you can't give him that!'

'Maybe not, but I *can* get an ID, and that's something. It might be enough.'

'How? You've already tried that. Twice. You didn't see anything.'

'But it was all so quick, and I couldn't look everywhere at once. I was concentrating on getting the number plate and I missed the second guy getting out of the van. If I went back again, I'd see him at least.'

'But he'd be able to see you too!'

'No, he wouldn't. There's a shop front there with an alcove. It's all dark. I can hide there. No one would see me. I wouldn't be changing anything in the past.'

'What about the camera, in the mall? How are you going to avoid that? Don't you think it will raise questions if you're seen running down the mall after Anna?'

'Blaine'll wipe it.'

'He'll be wiping it three years too late if he does!'

Beth opened her mouth to answer, but stopped. Allan was right. It was too late to wipe the tape. She would have already been seen. Three years ago. And that would have changed everything. Blaine would have recognised her when she came into his office that first time. She would have been a prime suspect. There would have been no explaining it away as a psychic phenomenon, no way of explaining it at all.

'Then … I'll just have to make sure I don't get on that tape,' she said slowly. 'I could smash the camera!'

Allan was horrified.

'It's only a camera. They can fix it, and if it saves lives—'

'If you smash the camera you won't have a photo to enter through!'

'Oh … Well, then, I'll spray the lens with paint or something, *after* I enter. That won't damage my entry shot. They'll still have the footage of Anna but they won't see me.'

Allan had had enough. He pushed back his chair and walked to the window, turning his back on her. She saw the tension in his stance.

'Allan, Detective Blaine needs *more*. He came to *me* for more, and he must have been pretty desperate to do that, you've got to admit that.' She got up and went to him. Wrapping her arms around him from behind. 'I *need* to do this, Allan. Please. I couldn't live with myself if I did nothing and more girls went missing. I'll come up with something for the tape, and I'll be careful. I promise. If it looks dangerous, I'll leave.'

Slowly the muscles in his back softened and she turned him around. Taking his face between her hands, she gently kissed him. He tasted of pain. 'I love you,' she said. 'It'll be all right. I promise.'

He drew her close and buried his face in her hair. 'I'd die if anything happened to you,' he whispered. 'You know that, don't you?'

His words echoed through her.

She'd won – but at what cost, and for what gain?

Chapter 26

July, 2010

Showered and dry, Beth felt better, but far from stable. At least there were little bottles of shampoo and conditioner in the hotel bathroom; the smell of vomit was overpowering. She regretted not bringing extra clothes with her. She'd sponged off most of the sick, and the pungently sweet perfume of the hotel soap helped to mask the smell, but she didn't have time to wash them properly. A spot clean would have to do. The carpet was harder to deal with, but she'd scraped most of it up and mopped it with a towel. It would just have to stay wet; that was better than reeking.

One thing was clear, she'd only just made it back from London; she'd barely handled the trip. Travelling seemed to have a cumulative effect. With each successive visit she became sicker, and she became sick *sooner.*

She needed time to recover between visits if she was going to continue, or some kind of anti-nausea drug at least. And she *had* to continue.

It didn't take long on her phone to find what she needed: Maxolon. It seemed the best choice for nausea – at least according to the internet – not too dangerous provided she kept to the instructions and didn't take too many. She hoped this would stop her vomiting long enough to do what she had to do. The drawback was that Maxolon was a prescription-only drug. She toyed with the idea of approaching a chemist, letting them see how sick she was and hoping the law would be overlooked in a case of clear need – but they'd probably still tell her to go to a hospital.

Finally, it came to her.

Opening her Facebook page, she found a photograph she'd posted of the Pisco markets in Peru. Anything could be bought there. And prescriptions weren't required in Peru!

* * *

June, 2008

Allan insisted she wait for him. He made her promise not to go without him watching her back. It wasn't as though he could go with her or be of any protection for her where she was going, but he argued it was dangerous to leave her body unattended; and he had a point. Anyone could walk in. Or what if there was a fire?

They set the time for when she got home from work. Her shift ended at six p.m. Allan, determined that if she was going to do this, she'd do it at full strength, had dinner ready when she arrived. Considering the sickness she'd experienced after her last attempt at physical travelling, she wasn't sure eating was such a good idea, but after a long shift on her feet she was hungry and grateful for Allan's chicken rice and the care that went into providing it for her.

She wasn't really worried. A quick in and out. That's all it was. Results were pretty much guaranteed if she got to the alcove in time. She'd have to run, and run fast, and she'd have to be careful she wasn't seen, but she was confident she could manage that.

The first challenge was to keep hidden from her previous selves; she hadn't seen herself on her previous visits, and it should stay that way. On her first visit, she'd merely popped in and out, but on her second visit, she'd stood in front of the camera watching Anna until she disappeared around the corner at the end of the mall. So for this next visit, she'd have to stay hidden until then. But that didn't seem too hard. She hadn't looked behind her on the previous visits – her attention had been straight ahead, down the mall, on Anna – so, if she jumped back quickly after entry and kept quiet, she should escape detection. The fact she *wasn't* seen before was encouraging. She hoped it was a confirmation her strategy had worked.

The next challenge was to take out the camera – but she was prepared for that as well.

After dinner, Beth showered and dressed in runners, a pair of skinny-fit black jeans and a long-sleeved black skivvy. She grabbed a towel and the CCTV photograph, and sat down on the couch. Draping the towel around her neck, she smiled at Allan, who sat nervously on the chair opposite.

'Well, here goes.'

'No heroics,' he warned sternly.

'In and out!' she promised.

It didn't seem to calm him, but he nodded his acceptance. Beth smoothed the photograph over her knees.

* * *

11.07pm., February 26, 2005

Finding the way in, she was once more immersed in the disturbing fog. Her heart pounded as she waited for it to clear, hating the fibrous glugginess. Gradually sounds filtered through – traffic noises and the wail of a siren – and finally Anna's form clarified … lone and vulnerable … walking steadily towards the corner, and her doom.

Beth leapt backwards, pressing herself up against the wall.

The strategy seemed to work. She couldn't see her past selves, but neither did she remember having noticed a black-clad form behind her on her past visits – so she must have got out of the way in time.

Holding her breath, she waited, still and silent, underneath and out of range of the camera that was mounted on the wall above her. The seconds stretched like eternities, but finally the van passed the end of the mall. After a moment more, figuring her past selves were now all safely out of the way, Beth hurled the towel up into the air and smiled as it landed on the camera, covering the lens.

Her practice sessions had paid off.

Safe from being recorded, she started to run, and reaching the corner she slipped into the alcove just seconds before the man with the snake sleeve tattoos jumped from the van. As the back door of the van crashed open she saw his face clearly in the blue-white wash of the streetlights. It was dark with hatred. His eyes were black like death. In an instant, his features were burned indelibly into her mind.

She *had* him! She would never forget that face!

In and out!

But the man was now on Anna – his fist was smashing into her skull with a horrible, sick thud – and Beth stood paralysed, frozen, as the men dragged Anna to the van and forced her in.

It was instinctive. As the van moved off, all Beth's resolutions dissolved. She couldn't let this happen! She wouldn't! Without thinking, she charged after the van and leapt for the handle of the back door. Catching it, she pulled down with all her strength and yanked the door open, screaming at the top of her voice as she grabbed for any part of Anna she could get a hold of and caught her ankle.

'Fight Anna, fight!' she yelled, desperately trying to haul her out of the van.

Stunned, the men in the back of the van didn't react at first – but the driver slammed on the brakes and Beth was thrown painfully up against the bumper. Hands then came at her, hard and fierce, and dragged her into the van.

She fought back, ramming her elbow into the crotch

of one man – and she nearly got free – but with a explosion of hot pain, everything went black.

* * *

June, 2008

Allan stared at the empty couch.

The photograph, abandoned when Beth had vanished, lay like a gravestone on the floor where her feet had been.

Oh God, she was really gone!

There was *nothing* of her left behind … nothing to hold on to … nothing to pull her back with.

What could he do now?

He scrambled across the carpet, knelt in front of the couch and numbly ran his fingers over the fabric. He could still feel her warmth. A few seconds … she'd only been gone a few seconds. He checked the clock – twenty past seven.

'Come on, Beth. In and out. You promised. Come on!'

* * *

11.07p.m., February 26, 2005

Her cheek was cold … her head, hot with pain.

Her face was resting against a thick plastic sheet that covered a hard metal surface …

Suddenly a scream ripped through her, shocking her eyes open as the cry strangled into a muffled, choking sound. It was dark, but she could see Anna beside her, thrashing in a terrified panic as the man on top of her forced a wad of shimmery material into her mouth – her halter top. Anna's chest was bare. At her feet, the other man was wrestling down her jeans.

'Shut the fuck up, bitch!' yelled the man on top; the man with the snake skin tattoos. He slapped her face, hard, and the force of it sent Anna's head crashing to the side. For a second her eyes, full of pain and horror, caught Beth's.

Snake-man caught the connection.

'Get her!' he yelled, and in an instant, the other man, the tall one, was on top of Beth, crushing her back against the side of the van.

She hadn't even realised she'd thrown herself at snake-man in a frenzied retaliation. Now she went for the tall man's eyes – but he was way too big and way too strong for her. His fist crashed into her chest, winding her, and then smashed into her face. Pain exploded through her head, blinding her with its intensity. Dazed and struggling for breath, she put up no more fight as he flipped her onto her stomach and sat on her.

'What the fuck's going on back there?' yelled a voice from the front of the van.

'The other one's awake,' grunted the man on top of Beth. 'The bitch is mental, and there's no room back here.'

'Go to the oval!' ordered snake-man. 'They can scream as loud as they like there.'

The oval?

Beth heard Anna whimpering as the van rocked into a hard turn. At least she was still conscious. But where were they headed? *Which* oval?

A tense calm hovered in the back of the van. The tall man's weight crushed into Beth's ribs. He leant on her, pinning her flat to the floor of the van, and worse, the hardness in his groin dug obscenely into her backside. Her face was throbbing. She felt blood trickling down over her lip and already her nose was so blocked she couldn't breathe through it.

Suddenly the van turned and a sharp pain shot through her leg. She couldn't even remember when that injury had happened. Tentatively, she squirmed to relieve it, and was flattened with a heavy shove to her back. It knocked the breath out of her but angered more than frightened her. He had no real power over her. She could leave whenever she wanted. And how would he feel then? How would he react when she suddenly disappeared?

Imagining his surprise brought a pained smile to her face, but then she remembered Anna.

How would it affect her?

Would they take it out on her?

Or would they perhaps freak out enough to let her go?

Hope ignited – but then immediately extinguished. She knew they'd never let Anna go. These men were intent on murder. Anna was doomed, and there was nothing she could do to save her.

It was time to remember what she'd come to do. *In and out*. She'd seen the tall man's face now, properly and up close. She'd never forget it. And snake-man's cruel, hard face was also etched in her memory. She hadn't seen the driver, but the identity of the other two would be enough. She'd done what she'd come to do, and it was time to leave. All she had to offer Anna now was justice, retribution for what was about to happen.

With a sinking resignation, she shut her eyes – but then ice-cold fingers gripped her wrist. Anna's fingers. Twisting awkwardly, she faced her. The movement earned her a cuff to the back of the head, but her new position was accepted. Her face was now only a hand's width away from Anna's. She could feel Anna's breath fluttering against her cheek in little erratic pants as her wide frightened eyes locked on hers.

'I'm so sorry,' Beth mouthed, and Anna's eyes filled with tears. They were so hungry for comfort. Beth shifted her arm to take hold of Anna's hand. She squeezed it gently, trying to impart some kind of strength to her, or to at least take away some of the chill. The gratitude she saw in Anna's eyes brought tears to her own. *The bastards!* She wanted to *kill* them!

'There! Over there!' barked snake-man.

Wherever they were, they'd arrived. She should go, she knew it, but as Anna's frightened fingers dug into her own, Beth couldn't bear the thought of abandoning her.

Could they fight them? Together? Could they beat them?

Anna was sobbing now, lost in a low desperate wail.

She wouldn't be any help.

The van veered to the right and Beth heard a crunching under the tyres as they left the road. They didn't drive far. Soon the vehicle stopped and the driver jumped out. Moments later the back door opened.

'Get this one outside,' yelled the tall man, crawling off Beth's back.

Someone grabbed her ankles. She didn't resist as she was yanked violently towards the door. Instead, she gave all her attention to Anna, trying to leave her one last moment of comfort before her hand was ripped away. But as her hips reached the edge of the van her moment came. Anna screamed, and the van rocked as one of the men fell back against the side of the van. The driver, distracted, and in the midst of changing his grip to haul Beth out of the van, let go of her ankles for just a second and she took her chance. She twisted her body, reared back and kicked him full force in the face. He howled and fell back, and Beth jumped out – out of the van, and out of 2005.

* * *

June, 2008

Allan fell backwards as Beth suddenly reappeared on the couch she'd left nearly an hour before. He stared at her, stunned. Her nose was swollen and bloodied, her lip was split and her eyes were already showing signs of blackening. Blood caked into her hair and her clothes were completely dishevelled. She'd even lost one of her shoes.

Beth stared back at him, her face a sickly shade, and then she began to heave, vomiting up chicken rice all over her knees.

It was another hour before Allan got a coherent sentence out of her. He helped her out of her ruined clothes and into the shower and she didn't come out until she'd used up all the hot water. Wrapped in her dressing gown, sitting on the couch, cradling a cup of tea, she was still trembling two hours later.

Allan was angry. Even after her explanation he couldn't understand why she hadn't come back straight away.

'She was all alone, Allan,' said Beth tiredly. 'I couldn't leave her.'

'You could have ended up like her!'

'But, I didn't, did I?'

'Look at you! They beat the shit out of you!'

She raked her fingers back through her damp hair. 'It was just a couple of punches ...'

'They could have killed you!'

She wanted to argue further, but she didn't have the strength. She needed to be in his arms, soaking up his warmth – and to forget. 'I'm sorry, Allan. You're right. It was dangerous. I won't go back again. I promise.'

For a long moment, he stared at her, his hazel eyes hard and disbelieving, but then he stood and walked to the table. Without a word, he picked up the newspaper photograph and carried it back to Beth.

'Do you mean it?' he asked, and she knew what he wanted. Solemnly, she took the clipping from his hand and tore it into pieces, letting the pieces fall disregarded at her feet.

Allan bit into his lip and nodded his approval. He offered her his hand, helped her up and led her to the bedroom.

Chapter 27

The next day, Beth called Detective Blaine. He'd given her his direct line.

'Can I come in and see those pictures again?' she opened without preamble. 'I can identify them now.'

Caught in the middle of something else, it was a moment before Blaine placed her voice.

'Beth?'

'I may also know where they buried her,' she said, her voice dull and flat.

'Beth, you didn't—'

'Can I come in now? I have a class this afternoon.'

Blaine agreed and sent a constable to pick her up. She arrived an hour later. Blaine and Frazer were waiting for her at the front desk, eager to hear what she had to say, but also a little anxious. When they saw her swollen and bruised face they were horrified.

'Have you seen a doctor?' Blaine asked tightly as he

led her into the interview room.

'I'm fine.'

'What happened?'

Beth sighed as she sat at the same table she'd sat at three years before. 'They overpowered me and pulled me into the van with Anna. They drove us to an oval. I got a good look at two of them, but not so much the third one.'

'They overpowered you?'

Beth was instantly irritated. 'Look, do you want me to identify them or not?'

Blaine's jaw dropped, torn between the merits of lecturing her further and his curiosity, but when Beth got up to leave, he caved.

'Wait. OK.'

She stared at him coolly. 'OK, what?'

'Please, I'd like you to take a look at the photographs.'

Calming, Beth sat back down, and Blaine signalled Frazer to lay the photographs out on the table. Beth had no difficulty identifying Tony Corelli as the snake-man with the sleeve tattoos and Don Crae, Corelli's friend, as the tall man. She was less sure about the driver, but selected another man as a possibility: Marco Ponti, another of Corelli's friends.

Blaine and Frazer already had Ponti in their sights. It was gratifying to have their suspicions confirmed, but as Frazer gathered up the photographs, Blaine looked over at Beth, and any sense of triumph fizzled. Her face was rudely raw in the stark morning light.

'They did *that* to you?' he asked, his jaw tensing in anger.

Beth bristled – Allan hadn't completely forgiven her

either – but she couldn't regret it. 'Yes,' she answered, lifting her chin defiantly.

'Why did you—?'

'Because it was the only way to know for sure who they were. And because I *could*.'

She was ready to take him on, but Blaine dropped his attack and Beth finally registered that his anger was not aimed at her, but at the men, on her behalf. Mollified, she dropped her antagonism a level.

'I only meant to get a good look at them,' she said in a more conciliatory tone. 'But I … when they hit Anna, and dragged her into the van … I couldn't help myself. I had to do something. I almost had her out, but the driver slammed on the brakes, and—' She winced. 'He must have hit me, from behind. I don't remember, but I … just woke up in the back of the van. With Anna, and those two guys.'

Blaine waited, but Beth's throat thickened as lewd images of hate-filled faces smeared across her memory, trapping all her words inside. *Fists smashing … the weight of his body on hers; his dick, hard against her bottom; Anna's eyes pleading … terrified; Anna's hand, ripping out of hers as she was torn into oblivion; hands grabbing at her ankles … pulling at her jeans …*

'Beth?'

It was Frazer, softly nudging for attention. 'Beth, are you all right?'

Beth blinked and was surprised by the tears trickling down her cheeks. She wiped them away, annoyed, refusing to acknowledge or give in to them.

'I'm not sure where they took us,' she said, her throat still thick, 'but it was an oval … and there were trees …

and a sand bank.'

'A sand bank?' asked Frazer. 'The beach?'

'No. Definitely not the beach. It was just a wall of sand in the side of a hill. In a park of some kind I think, next to the oval. I only saw it for a few seconds. The driver came round the back and opened the doors, and I ... I had hold of Anna's hand, but the driver pulled me out of the van ... and, just as I came out, I saw the trees, and the sand ... just for a second ... and then he let go, and I kicked him in the face and jumped.'

'Jumped?'

'Back,' she said quietly. 'Back here.'

It was what she'd been told to do ... what she'd agreed to. *In and out.* But still Anna's scream echoed through her and she felt sick with guilt for leaving her to face that horror alone.

Blaine and Frazer were staring at her with dazed expressions. Suddenly exhausted, Beth gave up. 'Well, you can take it or leave it, but that's what happened.'

She moved to leave again, but Blaine stopped her. 'How long were you driving for?'

Beth's deep brown eyes met his. 'I'm not sure. We were driving when I came to and I don't know how long I was unconscious. But maybe not long ... because they were fighting with Anna when I woke up; trying to ... get her jeans off, so I don't think it could have been too long. And then they ... they decided to take us to an oval. I heard them say that. They turned ... and it was only a few minutes away after that ... five ... or ten ... I'm not really sure, but it wasn't long.'

Beth blushed at her inability to give them more, but Blaine was energised. He turned to Frazer. 'Ovals?'

'There's a few near Chatswood Station,' she said. 'Should I bring a map up on the computer?'

'Good idea.'

Frazer left the room and Blaine stood. 'Would you mind looking at a map, see if we can find anything that might fit?'

Beth was glad to break her thoughts away from what had happened inside the van. Blaine led her into a back office where Frazer had brought up the area on Google Maps in satellite view on a computer. It was easy to identify the ovals. They focused on those in the Chatswood area: the ones near parks with higher levels of isolation and access by road. After about an hour they'd narrowed their attention to several possibilities.

Her class long forgotten, Beth agreed to go with the detectives to see if she could recognise anything. The closest was Chatswood High School oval. There was a car park next to it and it was surrounded and screened by a strip of trees. They drove there first, but there was no trace of sand, or anything that might have looked like sand in the moonlight.

'It's all right, Beth,' said Frazer. 'We've got several more to check out.'

Beth's heart sank. The Google map had shown just how many possible sites there were. With no real idea how long they'd driven, and such a brief glimpse of the area, in the dark, she wasn't at all sure she'd recognise *anything*. But back in the car, as Blaine keyed the next option into the GPS, Frazer had a thought.

'Hang on. The sand wall ... could it have been a bunker?'

Beth was confused. 'What's a bunker?'

'It's a hazard on a golf course. A pit filled with sand to trap the balls. Look here.' She leant over the seat with an open map book and pointed to another oval a little further away on the other side of Chatswood near the Garigal National park. 'Roseville Chase Oval. It's only a few kilometres from the station. It's surrounded by bushland. It's completely isolated from any through roads or residential areas – and it's right next to a golf course.'

Blaine was immediately fired by the idea. 'Let's go.' He keyed it in and they drove off.

Several minutes later, Beth's heart pattered nervously as they wound up the bush-lined road that led to the oval. The isolation was eerie, even in day time. She began to hope – but as they turned into the parking lot next to the oval, nothing was familiar. In front of them was a clubhouse and beyond that, the oval. She hadn't seen any buildings that night.

At the far end of the parking lot was the golf course. Blaine drove to the fence that ringed it and parked. He turned to Beth, who was staring fixedly out the window, her eyes wide. In front of them, to the left, was a small hill with a large gash-like sand bunker carved into the side of it.

* * *

December, 2009, Peru

Beth slipped behind a piece of woven fabric that hung in display beside a market stall. She almost trod on a small girl seated on the ground, nestled among the folds, guarding her mother's wares. Spread out in front of her on a large sheet of blue plastic was a patchwork of brilliantly coloured fabrics.

'Lo siento,' whispered Beth, materialising only an instant before the child raised her face.

'No pasa nada!' the child responded shyly, staring up in open curiosity.

Beth smiled and peered out from behind the fabric. Less than a metre away, her past-self was slipping her camera back into her woven bag and, without looking back, walked over to the vegetable man's stall to select produce for the evening meal.

Beth remembered that occasion. She remembered taking the photograph and even remembered thinking at the time that she might re-visit it at some later date. Now here she was, as predicted, invading her own photograph. The thought tingled in her stomach.

She had to hurry.

At least she knew where to go. She went in the opposite direction to her past-self and wove through the market crowd to the ATM on the other side of the square. It didn't take long to get local currency; she had the same visa card now as she'd had then. Pocketing the notes, she hurried to 'the drug man'. The queasy feeling had already returned by the time she stepped into his little shop and a fine sweat had broken out on her forehead. She'd forgotten how hot it was in Pisco. But even though the impact of the desert heat was intensified by the sudden contrast to Sydney winter, it wasn't the heat that caused the sweat.

The room was empty and barely more than a metre square. It was stuffy and claustrophobic and she was grateful the chemist appeared quickly at the glass divider.

He had large ears and a haircut resembling a medieval monk's and showed no sign of recognising her even though she'd had multiple dealings with him. It was his way. He didn't want anyone presuming on familiarity.

'Vómitos,' she explained, placing a hand on her stomach. 'Maxolon?'

The little man nodded, disappeared and returned with a single sheet of pills, which he passed to her over the glass in exchange for the required amount of cash. 'Agua,' he said, miming drinking.

'Gracias. Sí, lo sé,' replied Beth, and exited the shop in search of water and a private place to leave from. She found both a few streets over in a small cafe. The pungent smell of spices hit her as she walked in the door, resurrecting memories of fireside feasts and food poisoning. Her stomach heaved as she sat at a spindly laminated aluminium table.

'¡Hola!,' said a large, round girl with a calm, welcoming smile. She had thick, dark hair braided into a two long plaits that snaked down her back.

'Agua sin gas por favor,' ordered Beth with as much of a smile as she could manage and the girl waddled to the fridge in the corner of the room and returned with a bottle of water.

'Gracias. ¿Dónde está el baño, por favor?'

The girl pointed to a curtained doorway at the back of the restaurant. Peruvian toilets weren't for the weak-stomached, but Beth had no choice. She left money for the water and a generous tip and made her way to the toilet.

Chapter 28

June, 2008

A thick strip of bush surrounded Roseville Chase Oval and the golf course, separating them from the nearest residential pocket. It led all the way to a steep gully down to Middle Harbour, a tide-dominated estuary of Sydney's harbour. Dense and tangled, with only a few straggly tracks, it was an obvious place to hide a body, difficulties of access notwithstanding.

Blaine figured the men wouldn't have wanted to go far carrying a body so he concentrated the initial search on the narrower strip of bushland next to the car park. Success was almost immediate. Within the first few hours they found a shoe; a simple cloth running shoe. Inexpensive, badly stained and even rotted through in places – it had clearly lain undisturbed for quite a while. And it fitted the description of Beth's missing shoe exactly. Goosebumps prickled down his neck when she produced the partner of the shoe: clean, fresh and barely worn.

'It does match,' said Frazer as they headed back to the station. 'Same make, size and colour.'

'It's half disintegrated!' He just couldn't get his head around it.

'Well, it's been lying in the reserve for three years.'

'Three years since two days ago!'

It seemed ridiculous, but Frazer wasn't bothered. Facts had precedence over logic as far as she was concerned; and if there was a disparity, it was logic that needed adjusting, not facts.

'Well, I guess DNA will settle it,' he said, slowing down for a red light.

Frazer gave him a sideways glance. 'You sure you wanna put that shoe in for DNA?'

He stared back at her, surprised. 'There's still a chance it might not be Beth's. It's a common, cheap shoe. If it belongs to someone else—'

'It's Beth's.'

'It's still evidence. We can't *not* enter it. And if it's not Beth's, it could be vital.'

'And if it *is* Beth's?'

Frazer's accusing glare gave him pause.

'Her DNA's not on file. It'll just come up unknown,' he hedged. 'But … even if we enter her DNA, and it comes up a match, she has an alibi for that night. She could have lost it any time. It would just confirm things for us.'

'You need that?'

It wasn't a *need*, but it was definitely a want. There

were unanswered questions here. They dragged at him. And as long as they remained unanswered, he would never let go. But he understood that the risks outweighed the benefits in this instance; especially when there was no chance of Beth testifying.

'The shoe goes in, but we leave Beth's DNA out,' he conceded grumpily.

Placated, Frazer placed the plastic evidence bag at her feet.

'It must have been weird for them – her vanishing like that,' she said after a moment's silence.

'It was dark, and she kicked him in the face. He didn't see her go, and the others were in the van. They probably thought she just ran into the bush.'

Frazer nodded thoughtfully. 'I don't think we're going to find Anna in that reserve. If they thought Beth had escaped, they'd want to get out of there. Quick. They probably just tossed the shoe and left.'

'We'd better hope that's not the case,' said Blaine. They had little else to go on. Beth's shoe meant nothing unless she stood behind it as a witness and that could never happen. It seemed ghoulish to hope for the body of a teen, but if Anna hadn't survived the attack, then that was exactly what they needed. It was a depressing thought.

Frazer let her breath out slowly and rested back against the seat.

'We're not done yet,' said Blaine. 'Something may turn up at the reserve, and we've still got Ponti.'

* * *

Beth washed the Maxolon down and waited for her queasiness to settle. It didn't take long. She wasn't sure how long the effects of the drug would last, but it was good to feel her head clearing and her stomach becoming a little more stable. Soon, she felt up to attempting another trip.

Thank God she didn't have too many more to make.

After pulling on her red coat, she sat on the bed and opened her mother's album to the wedding pictures. These weren't taken by the official photographer and hadn't been included in the wedding album – they were Auntie Gaby's. There were only a few, and most were un-enterable, taken during the ceremony from the midst of the crowd, but there was one of her parents kissing that had a little space in the foreground. Beth hadn't been interested in these photographs before because the wedding album had far better shots and she'd seen the ceremony dozens of times, but she didn't have the wedding album with her now so this would have to do.

She was preparing to enter when she noticed the edge of another photograph peeping out from behind one of Auntie Gaby's.

Intrigued, she fished it out.

It was one of the official wedding photographs, but not one she'd seen before. The photographer had taken pictures during the ceremony and then organised several formal group portraits before finishing with random shots of the wedding party and guests enjoying the reception. This was one of the random shots. It was taken on the lawn with the hotel in the background. In the centre of the frame was a group of women in their thirties, Auntie Gaby included, smiling at the camera with their glasses raised in an exuberant toast. At the far left edge of the frame were two elderly men, talking animatedly. Beth vaguely remembered that one of them, a huge walrus of a man, had been pointed out to her at one time or another as 'Uncle Bill', but the other was a complete unknown. In the far right corner of the photograph, striding towards the women, was a large, middle-aged woman in a bright blue frock with massive shoulder pads.

Why was this photo hidden? It wasn't a bad one. Had she run out of room, or was she keeping it aside for something? Regardless, it would work perfectly for what she needed now. She wouldn't draw attention if she stood on the hotel verandah when this shot was taken, even in a winter coat. If anyone looked in that direction they'd think she was a patron of the hotel.

The only problem was finding an earlier entry photograph. Auntie Gaby's was taken almost an *hour* before – but would the Maxolon hold her that long?

It was a risk, but there was no other choice. It would *have* to do.

* * *

Saturday afternoon, January 18, 1986

Thankfully, it was an easy entry. Auntie Gaby nearly bowled her over as she raced forwards to hug the happy couple, but other than that there were no problems.

Beth didn't stay to watch. She wove invisibly between the unsuspecting guests and climbed the gentle slope to the hotel. There was a thick planting of bushes to the side of it that was promising, and when she reached it she saw it offered more privacy than anticipated. Intended as a barrier to the road, the foliage was dense. A service path led around it, but the entry to the garden for guests was through the hotel. No one would be likely to walk behind the bushes. She'd be undisturbed. Choosing a soft grassy shallow behind the lushest bush, she sat down to wait, deciding to hold off on materialising and stay invisible for as long as possible to minimise strain on her body.

All around her, the laughter and music of the wedding reverberated. Through the bushes, she caught glimpses of the guests positioning for photographs, her parents at the centre of it all, their faces glowing. The poignancy of their innocent expectations stung: they thought they'd have a lifetime together instead of a few years.

Beth distracted herself by attempting to remember people's names, but the process wore on and the tension in her head transitioned into an ache and then a throb. She shut her eyes and listened to the music instead. It was soothing, and she was grateful her stomach was holding.

She wasn't aware she'd dozed, but suddenly a loud snort from Auntie Gaby jarred her awake. Through the bush she saw that the group photographs were done and waitresses were carrying around large trays of drinks and finger food.

Had she been there an hour already?

A little giddy, she tried to shake clarity into her head and looked over at the verandah. The mood in front of it was relaxed and happy. Little clusters of guests were forming. Gaby and her friends had gravitated together and were gleefully helping themselves to the goodies on a waitress's tray. The Walrus and his companion were walking up from the lower gardens – but the bright blue dress was nowhere to be seen.

Beth materialised and looked for the photographer. She spotted him working his way towards Gaby. He would reach the women soon. Then she saw her – the woman in the blue dress, at the far end of the garden, striding purposefully in their direction.

Taking that as her cue, Beth stepped out from behind the bushes and hurried up onto the verandah. She reached a central, heavily shadowed spot just as blue dress puffed past, and positioned herself just in time.

Done!

* * *

June, 2008

Beth and Allan's flat was icy cold after the warmth of the patrol car. Blaine was chilled to the bone. Frazer, rugged up in her thick winter jacket, seemed oblivious to the temperature, but that didn't stop her actively radiating icy hostility at him. Ignoring her silent reprimand, Blaine doubled his attempt to exude easy confidence to Beth and Allan, who sat rugged up in thick woollen jumpers and Ugg boots on the couch opposite.

'We don't think Ponti's the leader of this group,' he said, leaning back in his chair. 'He has a rock-solid alibi for the night Ambrosia went missing, so he wasn't involved in that. Maybe he was only there for the assault on Anna. He might want out of this whole mess. We think there's a good chance he'll cave and put his mates in it.'

'Well, that's good,' said Beth, relieved and pleased they were making progress, but she caught Blaine's hesitation. Clearly there was more he wasn't telling her. She looked to Frazer, but Frazer avoided her eyes.

'But …?' she asked. 'There's something else? What is it?'

Blaine shifted uncomfortably. 'Well, actually … it would help if we had something to pressure him with.' His eyes flicked to Frazer, but she was offering him no support. 'I was wondering if you wouldn't mind coming in and—'

'Oh, no,' said Allan. 'Beth's not going to be any more involved in this.'

'Not in court, no,' Blaine agreed quickly. 'Not officially.'

If possible, Frazer was now even more embarrassed, but Beth's expression remained neutral. 'What then?' she asked.

Blaine didn't hedge further. 'Ponti's weak, but he's scared. He thinks if he stays quiet he'll be safe, and he's clinging to that. We told him we had a witness, and that rattled him, but we need to follow that up. We need to produce something concrete. His lawyer's asking—'

'No way!' said Allan firmly.

'We're not asking you to testify in court, Beth,' said Blaine, keeping his tone calm. 'But if you could just come in to identify Ponti—'

'In a line-up?'

'Well, yes … you wouldn't have to face him. He'd be behind glass. He wouldn't be able to see you.'

'But, I can't testify. If it's all hanging on my

identification—'

'It wouldn't be. And, you're right, it can't, but I don't think it will have to. Once Ponti knows we have him, or thinks we do, he'll cave. It'll be *his* testimony the case hangs on, not yours. He'll lead us to the evidence, and then your identification will be irrelevant. I'll drop your statement as unreliable.'

'Unreliable?' Allan's eyebrows rose in disbelief. He was about to launch into another burst of protest, but Beth slipped her hand over his.

'And if he doesn't cave?' she asked.

Blaine had no plan B. 'Then … we try something else.'

Frazer spoke up. 'You don't have to do this, Beth. It's your decision.'

'Yes, of course,' said Blaine, 'but we have to face the fact that this might be the only way to break him. Beth, I won't bring you in if I can avoid it. I'm thinking the threat of an ID parade might be enough. But I have to know if I can follow through on that threat or not.'

'If she identifies him, it will go down in the records, won't it?' asked Allan, getting angrier by the second. 'They'd know who she was.'

'Well … yes … but if he confesses—'

'They'd come after her!'

'Allan, they could do that anyway,' cut in Beth calmly. 'They know I was there that night, and that I could testify against them. They probably thought they were safe because I wasn't coming forward, but now I'm a threat. I'm not going to be any safer staying out of this. The safest thing for me is to get them put away, for good.'

Allan was on the edge of the couch. 'But they don't know who you are. They don't have your name. If the police go telling them you'll testify—'

'We won't do that,' assured Frazer, flashing a defiant look at Blaine. 'We'll keep your identity anonymous and record the results as inconclusive, whether Ponti confesses or not.'

Blaine nodded his agreement.

'I'll come in,' said Beth. 'If I have to. If you really think it will help.'

This elicited another deep, frustrated sigh from Allan, but he bit back on his comments and sank into a scowl instead. Blaine realised he'd made headway. He relaxed and thanked Beth, assuring her he'd endeavour to keep her out of it.

And he certainly intended to do that. Beth had given him the key to open up the case and he was confident it would help. But he was also starkly aware that the only real power of this particular key lay in *not* actually using it.

* * *

The giddiness she'd experienced at the wedding came back with her. She didn't vomit, but she knew she needed to rest. The Maxolon had carried her through, but she couldn't risk another trip just yet.

Trembling, she lay back on the bed. A heavy thickness crawled through her, but a satisfied smile crept to her face; she was almost there!

Exhausted, she tried to focus on the next step, but her thoughts wouldn't come together. Instead they fractured rebelliously out of grasp. She drew a breath deeply into her lungs and she let them go. Within seconds she was asleep.

As the afternoon slipped away, Beth lay encased in a dreamless sleep, oblivious to the retreating sun, the maid who accidentally walked in on her and quickly exited, and the messages steadily building up on her mobile phone.

Chapter 29

August, 2008

It was easier than either Blaine or Frazer thought it would be. Ponti caved almost immediately.

'He was only trying to shut her up,' he said wretchedly, his face draining to the colour of a muddied puddle. 'She just kept screaming … she wouldn't stop.'

'So, Corelli strangled her?' Blaine didn't blunt his accusation.

Ponti's left eyelid began to twitch. 'We never set out to kill anyone. If that other girl hadn't shown up, none of this would've happened. It was too much with the both of 'em in the back – and when she run off – and I went after her – Corelli lost it.' His shoulders sank in frustrated despair. The events of that night had grown in him like a cancer. 'It was an accident.'

'Oh, right.' Blaine nodded. 'You only meant to *rape*

them.'

Scarlet blotches blazed through Ponti's mottled complexion. 'We only ever picked up girls from the pub before – drunk girls. They were up for it. Most of 'em probably never even remembered it they were so pissed. We never hurt 'em.'

Blaine raised an eyebrow, his disbelief apparent, and Ponti shrugged awkwardly. 'Not much … Corelli liked it when they squealed …'

A sour expression twisted Frazer's lips. 'And you thought Anna Johnston was "up for it"?'

'That was Corelli and Crae. They wanted to try something new. They were sick of drunk sluts.'

Blaine jumped in on that one before Frazer could react to it. 'And you were happy enough to go along?'

A mixture of emotions swam across Ponti's face, but he offered no rebuttal.

'And when the girl was dead, you went along with burying her as well?'

'What were we supposed to do? We couldn't leave her there. We had to put her somewhere she wouldn't be found – the other girl was still out there and she could go to the cops.'

Ku-Ring-Gai National Park, on the northern boundaries of Sydney, had been a good place for hiding a body. It was wild and remote, and there was road access that wasn't closed off at night. The men had driven to an isolated spot in the park, carried Anna a few hundred metres from the road and buried her in a shallow grave underneath a mess of low bushes.

Ponti cringed as he remembered it. Terrified of snakes, his attention fixed on his feet, he'd walked face-first into a massive spider's web, freaking him out even more than he already was. But Corelli and Crae had only laughed and pushed on. They thought the dense scrub would be a perfect deterrent for casual bushwalkers – and it had been. Anna was left in peace – until the next girl joined her – and then the girls after that …

'Best just to help them cover it up then?' Blaine sneered.

'What else could I do? She was dead!' He met Blaine's glare. 'I *had* to go along with it. It was *them* against *me.*'

'So, you stayed silent, protecting your own miserable arse, while Corelli and Crae murdered five more girls?'

'I didn't know about that. I told you, I wanted nothin' more to do with 'em after that. I didn't know about those other girls until you dug 'em up.'

'Oh yeah. That's right. You're a real hero, aren't you? We'll be sure to let Ambrosia's mother know, won't we, Frazer?'

Frazer shook her shoulders, as though to shake off a lingering filth, and left the room without further comment.

Corelli and Crae confirmed Ponti's testimony. There was enough evidence to convict them anyway, but they made no attempt to deny it. They showed no remorse and even seemed to get enjoyment out of confession. The whole experience had given them a massive adrenaline high. They'd entered a new realm, done something few others had done – and it excited them. Excited them in a way nothing else could.

At the lonely spot in the national park, the bodies of six women were found, including Anna and Ambrosia.

And so it was over.

The killers were brought to justice. Blaine was satisfied, and relieved he didn't have to involve Beth or record her statement. As far as the records went, the mystery second girl remained a mystery, an anonymous source who'd chosen not to give a statement.

It was, thought Blaine, a very satisfactory conclusion.

But for Beth, it was the beginning of a whole new horror.

* * *

February, 2009

Allan found her on the floor of their bathroom. Blaine, seeing Beth run from the courtroom and making the connection as to why, had called him. She was huddled in a corner, hugging her knees to her chest and staring at the floor in front of her feet. She gave no sign of noticing he'd entered or any response when he knelt beside her and gathered her into his arms.

After a moment, she spoke, her voice small and shaken.

'I went to court.'

'I know. Blaine told me.'

'I heard Ponti's testimony …'

She waited for his response, but Allan only nodded.

Pushing herself out of his arms, she turned to face him. 'It was all because of me. Anna died because of *me* … because I was *there*. If I hadn't gone, they probably would've just raped her and then dumped her, but because *I* showed up, it all got out of control.'

'They were killers, Beth,' Allan said gently. 'It was

only a matter of time. You didn't force them to kill.'

Her eyes searched his with fraught desperation. 'Anna's death was an accident, Allan. And she was their first killing. If they hadn't killed her, those monsters might never have discovered they liked it. I *blooded* them. I gave them a taste for it. Don't you see? *None* of those other girls would've been killed if I hadn't gone there. It was *my* fault, my fault that *all* of those girls died.'

'That's a little dramatic—'

'No, it's not. I intervened. I went in, and things changed. And there were consequences.'

Allan couldn't deny that. 'Yes, you did, and there *were* consequences, but you didn't turn them into murderers. It was in them from the start, and it was going to come out sooner or later. They were getting more and more violent in their attacks. There is nothing to say that Anna wouldn't have freaked out anyway and that they wouldn't have killed her anyway.'

'But, I—'

'No! Listen, Beth,' he said, shifting his body to face her more directly. 'You wouldn't listen to me before, well, listen to me now! What's done is done. You can't undo it. You've got to let it go.'

How could she let it go? Her thoughts spiralled. It was her fault. She was cursed. Her gift brought only trouble, and now it had killed. She'd killed.

Allan shuffled closer. 'Beth … you heard about the other girls, didn't you? The ones they attacked before Anna?'

She nodded miserably and Allan tenderly lifted a stray lock of hair off her face and tucked it behind her ear. 'Any one of those girls could have died, Beth. It was only luck they didn't.'

'I know … but it was still me who flipped the switch that turned those bastards from rapists into murderers.'

'And you who got them locked up before they killed any number of other girls. Beth, if you hadn't jumped into this, something else would've flipped that switch, for sure, and there would've been nobody to stop them.'

She looked up at him wonderingly, daring to hope there might be some truth in what he was saying. He smiled. 'Let's close the chapter on that one, eh? They're going to jail. It's over. OK?'

There was no point in objecting further. Nothing could be undone. There was nothing she could do except learn to live with it. And learn from it. *No more travelling,* she swore to herself. *No more interfering. Ever!*

'Come on, let's go out for dinner, to Romano's,' said Allan. 'We should celebrate.'

'Celebrate?'

'Those bastards are going to jail. You're alive. Detective Blaine thinks you're amazing. He's stoked that the case is closed. We won!'

He reached for her hand and Beth allowed him to help her up. She'd run out of fight. She wanted desperately to buy into his optimism, to shrug off the guilt, to forget. Leaning against him, she burrowed into his warmth. 'No more travelling,' she promised softly. 'No more!'

Allan smiled and traced his fingers down her back. Beth wriggled in closer, feeling her own warmth rising as she released her tension into his strength.

Chapter 30

October, 2009

It came to her in a kind of urgency while she was out for her morning walk: Call Beth.

Ideas often came to Gillian at that time, when her mind was open and uncluttered. It was the best time of day – before the sun reached full ferocity and before everyday concerns crowded in. Usually, she let her mind wander wherever it wanted: sometimes she'd plan a fantasy garden or design a dream house; other times she'd just enjoy the neighbourhood. Today, Beth was on her mind. She hadn't seen her since Easter. It was time for a proper catch-up. They usually kept in touch by phone calls and emails but for the past few months it had been text messages only – which Gillian didn't rate as communication. She could hardly believe it had been six months since they'd spoken properly. Where had that time gone? It was nearly Christmas! Not that she expected anything to be wrong; she would have heard if there was. She knew it was just because they were busy – and it was precious to have that certainty. She felt blessed. But it was still time for a catch-up.

Since the court case, Beth had been a lot better. It seemed as though she'd finally found her stride. Her marks were good, her art works exceptional, and she had a healthy glow to her complexion. For the first time in her daughter's young life, Gillian felt released from worrying about her. Such a good feeling! She even felt free to hope she might have the common things of a happy life. That brought a smile to her face as she rounded the corner into the prettiest street in their suburb, where massive oak trees overhung the road like a bridal arch. Gillian's ponderings catapulted into wedding dreams. Joyfully, they danced from dresses to venues to menus to honeymoon possibilities to grandchildren.

She needed to organise that catch-up!

A dinner perhaps? Or maybe she could take them out to lunch at the uni, save them the trip? Somewhere nice. She glowed with possibilities and plans as she turned towards home, determining to call Beth and discuss it with her as soon as she got back.

But she didn't.

There was an urgent message from work waiting for her, asking her to come in. She'd had to rearrange her appointments and race to get dressed and out the door. Banking and a visit to the post office devoured lunchtime and then she had to squeeze shopping in on her way home, making dinner late. By the time she relaxed into the couch after dinner and remembered her resolution to call Beth, she was too tired. First thing tomorrow, she promised herself as she sank into the nightly television ritual. There was nothing on, but it was relaxing. She had no energy for anything else, and Richard enjoyed it too. He usually fell asleep within moments of stretching out on his recliner chair. Peaceful, if a little dull.

And so, another evening passed.

As Gillian removed her make-up and readied for bed she had no premonition this was anything other than a normal evening. Looking at her tired and slightly worn face in the mirror she had no expectation she wouldn't be staring at it for many years to come, watching it sag and age. It was just a night like so many others.

'Did you get that form off today?' Richard called from the bedroom. After a nap on the couch he'd hit his second wind and was propped up in bed with his book.

'Yes,' answered Gillian from the ensuite. 'I sent it by express post.'

'Thanks. That's good.'

Gillian slipped into bed beside him. She wore her 'not-tonight-darling-I'm-tired' nightie, but Richard was too involved in his book to notice either way. He patted her hip affectionately as she snuggled her backside up against him and curled into her sleep position.

'Night, honey,' she mumbled. 'Love you.'

'Love you too,' replied Richard.

As Gillian drifted off to sleep for the last time in her life, she never suspected she'd spoken the last words she would ever speak. Nor did she yet regret she hadn't followed through on her inner prompting to call her daughter. Three hours later, at 1.47 a.m., Gillian Crawford/O'Malley/Fletcher died of a massive stroke at the age of fifty-two.

* * *

'You can't *not* go.'

'Why not? *Mum* won't care.'

'No ... but you will. Maybe not now, but later. It's an important part of saying goodbye, respecting the person who died, making a public statement to show their life mattered and they're missed.'

Beth's face contorted into a defensive growl – but Allan persevered: 'Beth, I never got to go to my mum's funeral, and I regret it. I don't want that for you.'

Beth struggled. 'Maybe we can do some kind of private thing later? When you get back? For both our mums.'

'Yeah, we could do that. That's a great idea. We'll do that ... but, you should still go to this one. She's your mum. Everyone will be expecting you and it will look bad if you don't go. And Richard needs you there. It's not fair to make him go through that alone.'

She could still hear Richard's voice over the phone, cracking, oddly thick as he delivered the news that split her in two. She'd known what she was expected to say ... but she couldn't say it. She couldn't give him absolution. Instead, she wanted to scream at him – *Why did you let this happen? Why didn't you see? Why didn't you take care of her?*

Allan took out his phone.

'What are you doing?'

'I'm gunna change my flight.'

'What? Why?'

'Because you shouldn't have to go through this alone either. I'll go next week.'

Allan had won a scholarship for a summer science program in Tokyo and was hugely excited about it. It meant she'd be spending the uni holidays alone, but they couldn't afford for her to go too and he'd be busy in any case. She had art projects she could work on.

He was due to fly out the day before the funeral.

'You can't miss the program introduction.'

'They'll understand. They always do for things like this.'

'No. You worked so hard. I don't want you to miss it. That will make me feel *worse.*'

And it was true. It would have. And she couldn't deal with that just now.

'A few days won't matter.'

'They *will*.' She let out a frustrated sigh. 'Look, I'll be fine. I'll go to the funeral, I'll do all the things I'm supposed to and make everyone happy, and then I'll deal with it my own way. Alone.'

'Beth—'

'I'm fine, Allan.' She'd made up her mind. 'I just need some time to myself. I *want* you to go. At least I'll know you're OK and I'm not dragging you down.'

Allan decided to accept that. To go against her would only stress her further, and maybe a little time by herself would help. Still, it was with some misgivings that he left for Tokyo. He called from the airport and again as soon as he'd landed and then when he was settled into his lodgings. His descriptions of the trip seemed to cheer her a little. He tried to call her one last time before the funeral, but her phone was turned off.

* * *

The funeral had a bizarre edge of unreality for Beth; it was so very … *Richard*. She sat in the church, hearing nothing. Numb. She couldn't even cry. The only emotion she felt was a panicked need to run – but there was nowhere to run to, not even into a picture. She was incarcerated. She hated being pinned to one spot … one place … one moment in time. Even though it had been her decision to stay away from picture-travelling, it was a forced decision, the kind you make with a gun to your head. And Allan, in his disapproval and his sensibility, had become her jailer.

After the funeral, Richard had organised tea and cakes. Beth was surprised at how many showed up, and grateful. It made it easier to slip away. Richard couldn't hide his disappointment, but he let her go. She allowed him a stiff parting hug before turning to leave.

'Wait,' he said, reaching inside his jacket and taking out an envelope, which he handed to her. 'Something from your mother, some money she put aside for you. I meant to give it to you later, but …'

'Thanks.'

'I was going to give you a lift home. Do you need money for a taxi?'

'No. I want to walk for a bit. I need some air.' Shoving her fists deep into the pockets of the black jacket she'd bought for the occasion, she strode briskly out of the churchyard and around the corner towards the main road.

It felt better to be surrounded by a mass of unknown, uncaring suburban shoppers. Much easier than well-meaning mourners. Their blind gazes made her feel almost as invisible, which was just what she wanted. She let her eyes linger over the expensive window displays, losing herself in distraction – until a large poster of Machu Picchu almost leapt out and slapped her in the face. A travel agency.

A sign?

Beth felt for the envelope.

Chapter 31

November, 2009

The fog had not yet cleared; the valley hid in the clouds. But Beth could hear its depth; distant, invisible birds called to each other across the vast chasm that gaped in front of her.

Somewhere, far, far, below, a river rushed – the sacred River Urubamba. Unseen, it twisted along the valley floor, brown against the lush tropical green of the valley. She didn't need to see it to know it was there. She knew every detail of that landscape from her many previous visits, but it was strange to experience the mist. She'd only ever visited Machu Picchu in perfectly clear conditions. Today the weather was damp and cold with a light drizzly rain and the air lay thick and heavy around her like a shroud.

Physically, she felt entirely different as well. This

was the first time she'd borne the full impact of the altitude. It made her struggle for breath as she climbed the many steps to the peak and now, as she rested, she was ridiculously tired. Altitude sickness. At least that's what she assumed it was, she was nearly twenty-five hundred metres above sea level after all. She hadn't had to deal with that before, even though she'd been to Machu Picchu many times. She'd only ever popped in and out, never staying long enough to feel the effects of the height.

How strange to be *fully* there – by *conventional* means!

It hadn't changed, at least not that she could tell, and sitting on the cold stone, her legs hanging over the edge, watching the mist slowly thin, the same familiar peace flooded her.

Was that enough to justify what she'd done?

She hoped so. She hoped *Allan* would think so … It had been an impulsive decision, but she had the money, and it wasn't as if she were leaving him alone. She'd been meaning to paint over the holidays, but all creativity had left with her mother. She couldn't face her easel. And without painting, without travelling, without Allan, the sucking hole in her heart was unbearable. The garage was unbearable. She had to get away.

She'd been in Peru nearly a week now, leaving the day after the funeral and flying into Lima and then up to Cusco where she organised to be on the first available trip to Machu Picchu. That involved two buses and a train and a horribly early pre-dawn start – but the journey into the sunrise had taken her breath away – and seeing Machu Picchu, in context, was worth every bit of it. She'd gaped in awe at her first sight: ghostly stone structures struggling out of the early-morning mist! They begged exploration – but first she'd wanted to find 'her spot'. It was near the Inca Bridge and reached by a precarious mountain path, a tiny ribbon of stone draped around the mountain's edge. She'd hurried on past the main structure, her heart clenching tighter with each step, overwhelmed by the actuality of finally getting there and a little anxious that this 'regular' visit might somehow be less than her private stolen moments – but finally, finding and taking her usual place, dangling her feet into the abyss, breathing in the familiar damp scents, she'd been filled with the same still, sweet euphoria. It stole into her lonely hurting places, the hidden places that not even Allan could reach, and she sighed in pleasure. Tranquil, she sat and watched the valley floor slowly melting through the mist as the sun breached the overhanging clouds.

Allan should have been with her. She missed him more than ever now – but he didn't even know where she was…

She'd meant to email him when she got here … but she hadn't. She could have, every hostel had a computer and internet connection, but every time she thought of it she reared away. She wondered why… Was it just the enormity of what she'd done? She was certainly nervous about telling him, and every day she put it off made it worse – but in her heart she knew he'd support her.

And, perhaps that was it.

She didn't *want* support just now. She didn't want concern or restrictions or demands for explanations or demands for *anything*.

Suddenly, she felt desperately alone.

She'd hoped that by being there, *really* being there, in *present*-tense, she'd be able to reclaim the peace she could no longer reach through her poster – and she had, in a way – but somehow it didn't satisfy. She was still alone. Her mother was gone ... and Nanna ... and her father – she couldn't even visit them through pictures any more. She had no one now, except Allan. And she'd excluded him.

Hurt swelled inside her.

Tonight, she determined, she'd write to him.

Feeling a little better, she stirred from her reverie as a group of tourists rounded the mountain, their faces shining and their voices excited at the sight of the Inca Bridge. It was an amazing place, quite apart from its special relationship with her. She couldn't help but smile at their enthusiasm and when they moved on she thought she'd go exploring as well.

But first, there was one thing she needed to do.

Moving back against the rock wall, she dug out her camera and aimed it at her spot. She took a photo and then swiftly turned away.

With her back turned, she paused.

Am I there, she wondered?

She listened a moment, but heard nothing. If a future version of herself was using the photograph, she couldn't hear her.

What a bizarre thought!

She felt an almost irresistible urge to turn around, but she didn't. Somehow the thought of seeing her future was a little scary. What if she didn't like what she saw? Instead, she walked straight ahead, away from the bridge.

She had at least one safe way back to her favourite spot now, a photograph where not even the photographer would observe her entry. She supposed it could only be used once, now she was entering physically, but once was better than nothing. If she tried twice, there'd be *two* of her, in the *same spot*, at the *same* time – and that didn't seem possible. Would one of her two selves just bounce out – or what if they *melded* into each other?

A frightening thought …

At least she had one safe entry shot, and she had all day to find others. That lifted her spirits. She felt as though she were winning something over fate.

When she reached the open plateau the sun was dazzling, lighting up the ruins below. Rows of roofless stone buildings shone in the sun. Tourists gathered in the open spaces and trickled through the lanes like bubbling streams. Way too many people for any useful photographs, but still a stunning sight that deserved recording, even if only to show Allan.

Briefly she considered joining a tour, but instead decided to explore on her own. She descended the worn stone steps to the ancient complex and wandered through at whim, stopping only to catch her breath or take in detail. The stonework was so perfectly cut that not even the blade of a thin knife could be fitted in between. It fascinated her. The whole place fascinated her! And the best thing was that nothing could bump her out or pull her away. There were advantages to present-tense living after all!

Towards the end of the day, she climbed to the Inti-huatana Stone at the summit of the Sacred Pyramid. It was quite a hike, but the view at the top was worth it.

If possible, it was even more awe-inspiring than the one from the Inca Bridge. She sat down on a low stone wall to appreciate it, taking a few swigs from her water bottle. In front of her, dominating the platform, was the sacred stone, the 'Hitching Post of the Sun'. It was formed out of a single piece of rock with a vertical structure jutting up out of a larger base. The guidebook said it pointed directly at the sun during the winter solstice and could, according to legend, hold the sun in place at the time of the two equinoxes. It was interesting, but more impressive to Beth was the view. And now, late in the day, with the temperature cooling and most of the tourists retreating to queue for the buses, she could appreciate it alone. She reached for her camera, determining to create an entry shot, but was interrupted by a sharp-featured man with a worn hippy look, complete with dreadlocks, who barrelled up the stairs. Ignoring her, he went straight to the sacred stone and placed his hands on it – long, thin, sensitive hands. Then he laid his forehead gently against the stone – and he remained like that, still and silent, with no movement at all, for over a minute.

In spite of herself, Beth was intrigued. She couldn't draw her eyes away and wasn't quite quick enough to avoid his glance when he rose. Catching her stare, he beamed.

'This is a magical stone,' he said, in a soft, dreamy voice. 'A very sacred object. There used to be many of them, but most were destroyed by the Spaniards.' His smile grew even broader, exposing broad, plank-like, yellowed teeth. 'They didn't find this one.'

Beth nodded politely. He took it as encouragement.

'If you're sensitive, and you touch your forehead to

the stone, it can open up your vision to the spirit world. We're lucky it's not roped off. I read they don't always have the ropes up this late in the day, so I waited until now on the off chance.'

Beth couldn't help herself. 'Did you see anything, when you touched it?'

'No. Not this time.' The hippy showed no sign of disenchantment. 'Not yet. It doesn't always happen. But I've seen things before.' His chin jutted out with pride. 'I've *travelled*.'

The hair at the back of Beth's neck rose. 'Travelled?'

'*Astral* travelling.' He almost whispered the word. 'The Incas did it all the time. They travelled through sacred stones, like this one,' he caressed the stone reverently. 'These stones are portals, doors to the sacred realms.'

A shiver ran down her spine. *There were others who could travel? By touch?* 'You've done it?'

'Not through the stones. But with ayahuasca. I've travelled with ayahuasca.'

Beth stared at him blankly.

'Aya-wa-sca,' he clarified hopefully. 'It's a sacred brew of jungle vines and leaves. The Incas made it. It's dangerous, you have to make it right or it'll kill you, but when it is done right and you drink it, it opens your mind to the spirit world. It lets you travel to the astral planes, through time and space to the sacred realms. It's amazing!'

Her stomach sank. 'Drugs?'

'Just to help you let go, so you can connect to what's natural. It's in all of us. We can all do it. We're spiritual beings, connected to the spiritual world. This flesh is just a temporary home.' He slapped his chest enthusiastically. 'We go beyond this, and ayahuasca helps us get there.'

The hippy broke into a jaunty grin and Beth suspected the man's chemical explorations might have left him a little mentally compromised. But still she was drawn. If the drugs were only to help people tap into what was *natural* – and natural was 'travelling' – then she *had* to know more. *Were there others travelling like her? Were they able to do it safely?*

'Can you take my picture?' The hippy asked, suddenly pushing his camera into her hands and hurrying back to arrange himself in front of the stone.

She obliged.

'Where do you get it, this ayahuasca?' she asked.

'Oh, you can't do it alone. You need a guide. A shaman. I met mine in Pisco. I was working at the aid organisation there and others said they were going to a cactus party, so I went too. There's lots of shamans in Peru. You can find them everywhere, especially around here. You just have to be careful to find a good one.'

'How do you know if they are "good"?'

'Ask around. Get one that's recommended. Mine was good.'

She opened her mouth to ask another question, but the hippy was checking his watch.

'Last bus to Agua Calientes leaves in fifteen minutes,' he said fretfully. 'I can't miss it or I'll miss the train back to Cusco.' He regarded her with friendly eyes. 'You headed down?'

They sat together on the bus, and on the train and then the final bus back to Cusco. By the time they parted company, Beth had heard his entire life story, including multiple, detailed accounts of his experiences with his shaman and ayahuasca, and all of his best tips on how to get the most out of Peru. He offered to continue the discussion at his hostel but Beth, full to the brim with information and the overwhelming resonance of Machu Picchu, begged off. As they said their goodbyes, he wrote down the contact information of the aid organisation in Pisco for her and reiterated detailed instructions on how to contact his shaman.

That night, Beth slept a deep, dreamless sleep and in the morning she woke with her mind already made up.

She *had* to know more. She had to know if there were others like herself, and if they could help her.

After breakfast, she called the aid organisation in Pisco and arranged to stay there to do volunteer aid work and then booked a flight to Lima. After that, she wrote an email to Allan. There were several messages from him – at first informative, about his trip, but later increasingly anxious as to why she wasn't answering his emails and why he couldn't reach her on the phone. She'd left it at home. She felt bad about worrying him, but didn't think he'd be reassured if she told him what she was planning. She wrote him a brief note explaining she was in Peru taking some time to sort her head out and promising to write again when she could. Better to fill him in later when she had a greater clarity about what she was seeking, and hopefully about what she'd found.

She left for Lima on an early-morning flight and took a taxi from the airport to the bus station. The chaos of the traffic was assaulting after the simplicity of Cusco but the drop in altitude returned her energy instantly and kept her buoyant. Air flooded easily into her lungs and her backpack seemed to have halved its weight. She felt like she had super-strength, but the three and a half hour bus trip through the coastal desert strip to Pisco soon sapped that sensation. By the time she arrived, she was bathed in sweat and completely enervated.

Pisco was also a rude awakening. Decimated by an earthquake in 2007, where hundreds were killed and nearly eighty per cent of the buildings were damaged, it was still a mess. International disaster relief organisations had hurried in to help, but funding ran out and three years on, many of the structures were still unrepaired. Piles of rubble lay on the broken, dusty streets, and in many places sheets of blue plastic, or even cardboard, did for walls.

With more than a few misgivings, Beth hauled her backpack off the bus. It was too late to go back to Lima. She accepted the hassling of one of the many taxi drivers that gathered near the bus and allowed herself to be herded into the back seat of a tuk-tuk. She hung on tightly as it lurched between potholes, debris and other vehicles – road rules seemed an optional extra. More than once she squeezed her eyes shut, expecting collision, but eventually, still in one piece, she was deposited wide-eyed in the dust outside a ramshackle building at the far end of town near the ocean. A hand-painted sign confirmed the building as the right address.

Watching the taxi drive off, and not really having anywhere else to go, Beth knocked on the battered wooden door. After a moment, a middle-aged woman in ragged shorts and a bright blue T-shirt opened it. She looked more like the survivor of a summer camp than the office administrator of an aid organisation, but her no-nonsense manner was comforting. With a welcoming smile, she introduced herself as Deborah and ushered Beth into a side room where a collage of smiling faces, presumably of previous volunteers, greeted her. They covered almost all the wall space and, in spite of the worn furnishings and the piles of clutter suffocating every level surface, they made the office a cheerful space. Feeling a little eased, Beth offered Deborah a tentative smile as a chair was cleared for her. It didn't take long for details to be exchanged and basic information to be imparted.

That done, Beth was given an official tour. It was a one-storey brick building consisting mainly of dormitory-style bedrooms. They opened onto a large covered deck and an enclosed yard. An odd assortment of couches and chairs – most looking as though they'd been rescued from the rubble of the quake or constructed from scrap – were scattered around the deck to form cosy clusters. A television and sound system were balanced on some rough-hewn shelving along with piles of books, magazines, DVDs and board games. The volunteers, Deborah explained, were all out working at this time of day.

Beth was shown to a bed in a three-bunk room labelled *The Slums*. There was no door, just a piece of hanging fabric, and the mattresses were made of hay – hard and lumpy and scratchy – but the alternative was a spot on the roof, reached by a home-made ladder. Beth considered herself lucky. At least hers was a 'girls only' room, and the price was cheap. Volunteers paid less than fifty dollars a week for room and board.

Hefting her backpack onto an empty upper-bunk, Beth followed Deborah out for the rest of the tour. She listened as the mysteries of the bathroom were explained and made note of the warnings not to touch the drain in the shower as it was sometimes electrified by the dubious water heating system. She signed up to help with dinner preparation and was given a briefing of the running of the place: breakfast was at eight; group meeting at nine, (where the daily assignments would be handed out); work ended at five; dinner at six. All meals except lunch were included in her board. She'd be driven to her work assignment in one of the organisation's trucks and there were several assignments to choose from. Most of them involved some kind of basic construction work, for which she was assured she needed no previous experience or particular skills, just an openness to learn and a desire to work hard.

Overall, Beth was impressed, in spite of the primitive accommodations. She expected it would be an interesting and worthwhile stay, regardless of what she discovered about the shaman.

Deborah then led her down the road to a separate building where the kitchen and dining area were. She was introduced to the cook – a burly twenty-year-old named Simon, who was also from Australia – and put to work peeling potatoes. The kitchen was barely bigger than Beth's kitchenette in Australia, with makeshift benches and an ancient cooker, but even so, they put together a tasty meal of chicken and potatoes for the seventy or so volunteers who rumbled in later that evening. Hungry and full of satisfaction with their day's work, they were a happy, high-spirited group. Beth liked them straight away. After serving, she joined them around the benches to share the meal, with no sense of being the awkward 'newbie'. There was no floor, just the dust beneath their feet, and no roof over their heads (it never rained), but Beth felt encased in plenty.

* * *

Allan was working on an assignment in his dorm at the Tokyo University of Foreign Studies when his phone rang. It was two a.m.

'Allan?'

Her voice sounded a world away; it wasn't the best of connections.

'Beth! Are you OK? Why haven't you answered my emails? I've been worried sick. Where *are* you?'

'I'm fine. I … just haven't had access to a computer. How are you? Are you—'

'Where are you?' he barked.

She could hear his irritation but tried not to let it annoy her. 'I told you. I'm in Peru. Didn't you get my email?'

'What are you doing in *Peru?*'

'I'm working with an aid organisation in Pisco, Pisco Sin—'

'What? *Why?* Beth, what's going on? What are you doing *there?*'

Pink flushed to Beth's cheeks.

'Well, you're in Japan,' she snapped back. 'It's the holidays. Why shouldn't I go somewhere too?'

'I'm here for study!' he said indignantly. 'I got a scholarship!'

'And I got some money from my *mother!* I didn't take anything out of the bank!'

Allan swallowed his fight. He was upset and angry, but he could hear she was too, and she'd used the 'm' word – mother. He still felt guilty about leaving her to go to her mother's funeral alone. He tried to compose himself. At least she hadn't hung up, but he couldn't think what to say next. Fortunately, he didn't have to.

'I'm sorry,' said Beth, her tone conciliatory, 'I should have told you … but it was all so sudden. I … had to get away. It was so empty there, without you. And then Richard gave me some money from Mum. She left it for me. It wasn't much, just enough for this. I didn't think you'd mind—'

'No.' He sighed. 'No, of course not. I don't. I never wanted to leave you there alone. But, *Peru?*' Allan couldn't keep the astonishment out of his voice. 'Why didn't you come here? I could have got us a room nearby.'

'You're busy.'

'Only during the day.' He was warming to the idea. 'There's lots you could see. At night we could go out or just be together.'

An uncomfortable silence followed.

'What's wrong?'

'Nothing,' she said, a little too quickly. 'I … just wanted to come *here*. I wanted to go to Machu Picchu. And I can't get there through my poster any more.'

She heard him sigh on the other end of the phone.

'I just thought I'd feel peaceful there,' she tried to explain, 'and I did. Allan, it's even more amazing when you come here normally. Everybody feels it. It just gets into you. You have to come here too. You'll love it.'

'But … you're not at Machu Picchu now?'

She hedged. 'No … I came down to Pisco, to work

with an aid organisation. I'm doing some volunteer reconstruction work, helping to build houses and stuff. There was a massive earthquake here a couple of years ago and people are still living in temporary shacks. Today I helped lay a concrete floor! It was for a family, and they helped us build it, and they were so grateful. The mother was crying, and she gave us all a hug.'

She waited a moment for his approval, but he wasn't ready to give it. A prickle of irritation dampened her enthusiasm for sharing further and there was another awkward pause.

'How long are you intending to stay there?' Allan finally asked. 'Will you be back for uni?'

He meant it provocatively, but was nevertheless chilled when Beth replied: 'I'm not sure … I need to work some stuff out …'

Apprehension shot through him. 'What stuff?'

'Just … stuff.'

'Beth—'

'Look, I have to go. Calls are expensive. I'll write.'

'Wait—'

'Bye.'

Abruptly, the line went dead.

It was Christmas Eve, but seasonal greetings had been left unsaid.

Chapter 32

January 27, 2010

Nearly three weeks passed. Beth was quite acclimatised as February approached. She and Allan, unable to stay disjointed, had negotiated an uneasy truce and maintained their relationship through Skype calls and emails, sharing their experiences and discoveries. But the topic of return was carefully avoided. There was still a month before she needed to be back for uni and Allan didn't want to push it. Beth didn't either. But there were plenty of other things to talk about. Allan's summer program was going well and Beth was learning the ins and outs of concreting, mural painting, cooking for large numbers on a budget and basic Spanish. She was proud of the skills she was acquiring, and Allan was proud of her, and happy she was happy. She was too. After the first few weeks of blisters, aching muscles and desensitisation to the constant filth, she was enjoying her stay. Her only frustration was that she still hadn't been able to meet up with the shaman. He'd been away in the jungle with another group, and then the Christmas celebrations had overtaken everything. Christmas was big in Catholic Peru.

Her search for a shaman was, however, not a topic she discussed with Allan. He was having enough difficulty worrying about all the normal advertised risks of a place like Peru, and Pisco was an especially raw town, even by Peruvian standards. But Beth wasn't afraid. She had a strong, experienced group around her and the locals did their best to guide and protect them. She felt safe and content, even if she was a little impatient to meet the shaman.

Every evening after dinner they'd retreat to the roof to sit under the stars and relax. The cool desert evenings were deliciously refreshing and the company was good. From her chair she could lookout through the spider-web of electricity wires to the sea. All around her on neighbouring rooftops, life bubbled joyously.

Their rooftop was a simple flat concrete-slab, like most of the surrounding rooftops. And like the other rooftops, it was covered in dust and cluttered with building debris, and it didn't even have a rail to prevent people from falling off. Beth learnt this was a deliberate strategy. There were tax deductions for those attempting reconstruction work, so everyone made sure their buildings looked like works-in-progress. It didn't stop them being functional though: the aid organisation's roof provided a second lounge and bedroom area. In among the piles of scrap were a collection of chairs and couches as well as several mattresses and even a two-man tent – for those preferring a little more space and air than the dorms afforded.

Beth's first impression of 'The Roof' wasn't positive but the atmosphere there was always relaxed and accepting and it soon became one of her favourite places. It symbolised the spirit of the whole place: simple, free and without limit. In Pisco, a cluttered, half-built rooftop space was better than no space; a sheet of cardboard was better than no wall; and half a building was better than none. Here there was no need for meeting any kind of standard; anything and anyone was acceptable. A volunteer was appreciated no matter what they looked like, where they came from or how skilful they were – because they were better than nothing. Here, Beth didn't feel judged. She didn't even feel particularly freakish, considering those she worked alongside. They were an interesting collection, mainly back packers and wanderers but also a generous sprinkling of misfits, idealists and eccentrics. Compared to some of them, she came over as relatively conservative.

Contented, she rested back in her favourite chair. She'd spent the day helping Simon in the kitchen and buying food in the local market. He'd become her closest friend in Peru. A few months younger than she was, Simon was an old soul. Even though he was Australian, his parents were from Sweden and he seemed to have retained something of the Viking spirit in his love for the rough adventure of Pisco. For him, the ever-present threat of robbery, kidnap and murder made life exciting. He refused to be contained or confined to what was considered 'safe'. He looked like a Viking too: massive and blond with pale, ice-blue eyes. Beth found him refreshing. She even enjoyed his bizarre sense of humour, although it didn't always go down well with the others. Shannon, one of the longer-term volunteers, had nearly knocked him out with a lump of wood when he let off a firecracker near her as a 'joke'.

Shannon was a Canadian naturalist. She had an explosive temper and was one of the oddest people Beth had ever met.

Shannon and Simon didn't get on very well, but generally Simon was well liked. He was the provider of all things yummy, after all. He gave them ever-varying feasts and longed-for treats in place of the endless unimaginative rice and beans his predecessor had dished up. And he maintained a light, fun atmosphere in his kitchen – quite a feat considering the challenges of feeding up to a hundred volunteers with differing tastes and diets on virtually no budget. Beth liked him, and she enjoyed helping out in the kitchen.

Today, Simon had taken her to the market. It was an experience; an assault of exotic sounds and smells and confronting sights. He delighted in taking the new recruits there. He loved watching their horrified reactions and he laughed out loud when Beth gasped at the sight of a mangy dog nibbling at the meat-man's hanging carcasses on her first visit there. But today's expedition was to chase down some special ingredients. He wanted to make Szechuan soup for Dieter. Dieter was a German backpacker who'd wandered in for a cheap place to stay for a couple of nights and ended up staying six months. He was now a fixture around the place. He had plumbing skills! But it was finally his last night, so a farewell celebration meal had been planned – and Dieter *loved* Chinese food.

Procurement wasn't easy, but Simon was up to the challenge and found everything he needed. He even located fortune cookies. It was fun, and as a 'special treat', he introduced Beth to her first 'frog smoothie' – a drink literally made of frogs, taken fresh from a tank and blended in a blender with a dash of rum. He was happy she was satisfyingly revolted by the idea, but also impressed that she dared to drink it. It tasted like caramel. Beth was looking forward to telling Allan about that.

Dinner was a great success. Bloated, but completely satisfied, Beth surveyed the little group that shared the roof with her. That night, there were Frank and Dave – two students on a gap year from the UK; a young couple from California, Tom and Katie, who were serial volunteers who came down for all their holidays to improve their Spanish and 'give something back'; Camilla, a sixty-year-old from Florida who was working through her mid-life crisis; Dieter; Shannon; Simon; and Beth. Dieter had bought beer for everyone, which was much appreciated. After the first couple of bottles the conversation mellowed and drifted from Dieter's future plans to well wishes for Beth's appointment with a shaman, which had finally been organised. Although the hippy's shaman was still out of town, another shaman, a woman, was visiting Pisco on the weekend. She was based in the jungle but her cousin's American-born grandson lived in Pisco and his wife had just given birth to their first son. The shaman was coming to bless them. The grandson – a connection of Simon's – had arranged a personal consultation for Beth.

To Beth, this seemed like a much better idea than hiking off into the jungle. This shaman wasn't as well known among the volunteers – she didn't hold ayahuasca 'parties' and her 'cleansing ceremonies' were generally more involved and required a deeper level of commitment and preparation – but Simon said she was good. Beth was intrigued.

'You're going to have an amazing experience,' said Shannon in her typically sleepy drawl. 'I'd come along, but I have my own shaman in Iquitos, and I think you should stick with one.'

Beth was relieved to hear that. She didn't want company, especially not Shannon's. Shannon could be awkward at the best of times and would always take things over to revolve around herself. Beth found her a little disturbing; she was always doing strangely radical things. Today's dramatic gesture had been to shave half her head and get *Fucking Buena!* tattooed across her scalp.

'Thanks, Shannon. I'll be fine.'

'I think you should be careful,' warned Katie timidly. 'Ayahuasca is a hallucinogenic drug. People have died.'

Katie was very petite and very pretty – a heath nut with a delicate physique and a conservative background. She'd spent her first week at the aid organisation sick in bed with food poisoning.

'Oh, that's scare mongering,' chided Camilla. 'It's perfectly safe. Anything is dangerous if you use it abusively, even water!' Camilla had been on many 'cleansings'. She was an expert. She was also an expert on most recreational drugs, having been brought up in a Californian commune. 'Ayahuasca has been used here for centuries for spiritual and physical healing. I knew a woman who was healed of cancer! It opens up your eyes and connects you with all life.' Camilla's face almost glowed. 'I had some amazing visions. My shaman said I was especially sensitive. My spirit guide is a snake, and I rode through the jungle on his back. I became part of him, and of the jungle. All life is one.'

'I'm sure it's really cosmic,' said Katie dubiously, 'but we had a friend who went to one of those parties and he said the only thing that happened to him was that he was violently sick. Isn't that right, Tom?'

Tom nodded grimly. 'Yep. Lots of people have had complete psychotic breakdowns over it.'

'Nonsense!' Camilla scoffed.

'No, it's true.' Katie nodded earnestly. 'Tom researched it.'

Camilla was having none of that. 'That's an exaggeration. It can happen, yes, but only if you're working with a charlatan.' She turned her attention back to Beth. 'Who are you seeing, Beth?'

Unsure, Beth looked to Simon, who replied dramatically, 'Mamma Rosa.'

'Are you sure she's OK?' asked Katie.

'She's fine,' said Simon confidently. 'Mamma Rosa has been doing it for years. She hasn't killed anyone yet.'

He turned to Beth with a grin. 'I guess you could be the first though, Beth. Are you covered for astral journeys with your travel insurance?'

The British students launched into a high-pitched giggle and Shannon snorted into her beer. 'It does taste *vile*,' she agreed, her eyes lighting up mischievously. 'And it does make you throw up. That's part of it. It's supposed to *cleanse* your body, get all the toxins out.'

'Sounds like a good idea for you, Shannon.' Simon laughed.

'It makes you sick?' asked Beth, getting concerned.

'Yes, but that won't hurt you,' said Camilla with all the weight of her accumulated experience. 'Shannon's right. It is part of the cleansing, and it's not dangerous if you prepare for it properly.'

That didn't really alleviate Beth's doubts.

'Why'd ya wanna do it for anyway?' asked Dave, sucking deep on his reefer. 'This stuff is cheaper, and safer. And you don't need a guide.'

'I'm just interested,' answered Beth. 'It seems pretty amazing, to travel to … other realms.'

She blushed in the darkness as Simon's eyes fixed on her, feeling uncomfortably exposed, but it wasn't as though she was the first to be curious about ayahuasca. She lifted her chin defiantly and Simon chuckled.

The conversation moved on to other topics, but the night had developed a taint for Beth. A little knot of anxiety began to twist in her belly. *Was it dangerous?* She'd feel safer if she could meet the shaman first … but the possibility of discovering something new about herself, even if the method was a little frightening, was too intriguing to be abandoned. She was compelled to try it. If the ancient Incas and these modern-day shamans were doing the same thing she was doing – *travelling* – then she *had* to find out more.

Beth took the day of her appointment off work and headed for the house she'd been told the shaman was visiting. It wasn't that far away, just down the road near the beach. She was able to walk, though all the volunteers were warned never to go in that area alone and never, under any circumstances, to go to the beach. The beach was where murders happened and bodies were dumped. As Beth rounded the corner of the street she'd been directed to, a man ran out of his house, waving his arms and miming the slitting of his throat as he ranted excitedly in Spanish.

She was wearing the aid group's distinctive bright blue T-shirt and he was clearly trying to protect her.

'¡Señora, no pase por allá! ¡No vaya! ¡Es malo! Es peligroso!'

Smiling, she tried to explain in her completely inadequate Spanish that she was only going to visit the shaman a few houses down, but if he understood her it didn't ease his anxiety. He continued to lecture her, with energised and increasingly graphic gestures of violent death, as he followed her down the street. When she reached the house though, he backed off and returned to his own doorstep to maintain watch.

Well, I guess he'll notice if I don't come out, she thought as she walked up to the door and raised her hand to knock.

The door swung open before her knuckles reached the wood, and a small girl peeped out of the inner darkness.

'¡Hola!' said Beth, with what she hoped was a warm smile.

The child smiled shyly and opened the door wider, beckoning Beth inside before shutting the door softly behind her. It was a moment before her eyes adjusted. If there were windows, they were well covered. The room was murky dark and over-warm. Beth halted by the door, nervous to take a step in case she stepped on or collided with something.

'Come in,' said a deep male voice with an American accent. Beth thought he must be the grand-nephew.

'I can't see anything,' she replied. 'It's so dark in here.'

An older female voice spoke in Spanish. Her voice was light and scratchy, but with an odd undertone of confident authority. The nephew spoke again. 'Mamma Rosa says that without the light, she can see you better. Come. There is nothing in your way.'

Cautiously Beth inched forwards and lowered herself to the floor in front of them. By now, she could make out the shapes of their bodies in the dark.

'Mamma Rosa asks why you are here.'

Beth had the uncomfortable notion that somehow the shaman already knew. 'I ... heard you do ceremonies ... with ayahuasca ... where people can travel to other realms ...' she said, and waited as her words were translated, responded to, and then translated back to her.

'The cleansing ritual is not a game,' said the American in cool, clipped tones. 'It is a key to a doorway to yourself and to other dimensions. It will help you move beyond your defence mechanisms into the depths of your unconscious mind where healing can take place, but you must be aware that the unconscious mind holds many things you don't want to look at: repressed emotions, destructive beliefs, suppressed traumatic events. You must be willing to face your demons.' He paused dramatically. 'Are you strong enough for that?'

In spite of the cloying heat of the room, Beth shivered. 'I don't know,' she answered honestly, and the old woman laughed and muttered something.

'Reach out your hands,' the young man said. 'She wants to touch you.'

Feeling as though she was stepping over a line from which retreat would no longer be possible, Beth shuffled forwards on her knees to the edge of a thick rug. There were a number of dark objects on it, but she couldn't make out what they were. Timidly, she reached out her hands and they were encased in the old woman's cool, rough palms. Her grasp was light and gentle, knowing.

Beth relaxed a little – but then the woman began to make a low moaning sound – a single-noted, word-less song that petered out at the end of each breath to a strange pulsing whisper, like the beating of a vocal drum. A most unearthly sound. It tickled at the hairs at the nape of her neck and snaked tendrils of anxiety into her belly. She wriggled uneasily, but the shaman remained absorbed in her slow song, choosing different notes and sliding eerily between them. Eventually she lapsed into a penetrative silence.

Beth wasn't sure which was more disconcerting: the singing or the silence. The singing created an atmosphere of timelessness, making Beth feel she'd been there for hours when she knew it was only minutes – but the silence had a finality about it, the hush of a pronounce-ment about to be made. She had an urge to run.

But then the shaman spoke, her voice quiet and low, almost hypnotic, and her companion translated. 'Mamma Rosa says there is much darkness in you. She says you are lost. Divided.'

Beth felt as though she'd been stripped naked in front of them. Her face flushed hot in the darkness.

'You are in pain,' the man continued. 'There is loss in your life. Much loss.'

Thoughts of her mother tried to force past the wall she'd constructed in her mind to lock them in, and her heart began to pound. The shaman moaned and started her strange crooning again. It unsettled, but also lulled, leaving Beth somehow paralysed between her yearning to know more and her instinct to flee.

Presently the woman stopped and softly murmured.

'I see a spider,' the man translated softly, 'spinning a web over your soul … feeding on your spirit … holding you fast.'

The hair at the back of Beth's neck prickled again.

'The spider weaves a web of fate between the past and the future, between the physical and the spirit, but she can also catch you in her web. She can weave poison into your soul. We must break her web to set you free.'

Spooked, Beth pulled her hands away. 'What are you talking about?'

The crone's ancient eyes opened. 'Do you want to be free?' she asked through the translator.

'I … want to know about astral travelling. I want to know what it is … what it feels like … and if …'

'You can do it?' The translation was almost simultaneous.

Beth swallowed. 'I'm just curious. I want to know more about it.'

The old woman nodded and the man spoke.

'There is a cost to knowing.'

Beth could now see his eyes. They glittered in the dim light. Hope and fear lurched together inside her. 'I have money.'

'Not in money, in your soul,' he said smoothly. 'It will take time, and much pain. You will have to face the darkness in yourself. Can you do that?'

The old woman was watching her intently with a mixture of warmth and curiosity. Her strange seductive presence washed over Beth's fear.

'I ... I don't know.'

Again the old woman chuckled. She said something to her nephew and watched Beth shrewdly as he translated her words.

'She says you are right. You don't know. There is much to gain, but also much to lose.'

Beth didn't like the sound of that. She glanced nervously at the door, but before she could turn her impulse into action, the shaman grasped her hands, and this time her grip was firm. She raised her chin and resumed her song, and in spite of her discomfort, Beth felt again that strange pull to the oddly vibrating tones. In the heat of the stuffy room, she began to feel sleepy; her hold on staying alert loosened. The song slithered into her heart and invaded her mind. Soon, she no longer resisted, and her thoughts ran loose—

Allan ... holding her close; her mother... running away from her down a darkened street; the tilt of Nanna's chin; Kennedy's head exploding; Anna's eyes, frightened and imploring; blood ... blood pooling in the street ...

Abruptly the old woman stopped her singing and let go of her hands.

Disoriented, Beth opened her eyes, unaware they'd been closed. The shaman was staring at her with razor-edged perception.

'Spirit Walker,' she pronounced through her translator. *It was a naming. A classification.*

Beth squirmed.

'You have travelled to many realms, but without a guide. Alone. Without protection. And now you are lost.'

Beth's heart raced. 'I'm not lost. I'm just trying to—'

'Find out who you are?'

This was not a translation, these were the man's own words. A smile smeared his lips and Beth felt belittled. Softly, the shaman spoke and the nephew bowed his head and resumed his role.

'You like to hide, Spirit Walker,' he said, 'but with ayahuasca no one can hide.'

Beth shifted uneasily, irritated and defensive but unable to let it go. 'I'm not trying to hide. And I don't do it with just my "spirit". I take my *body* with me. I go to *real* places … other times. Not "realms".'

The old woman showed no surprise. 'Time is an illusion. It is never linear but exists simultaneously on many planes at the same time.'

'OK … whatever … but I *go* there. I take my body with me. It doesn't stay here.' She searched the old woman's wrinkled face. 'Is that what you do? Do you travel *physically?*'

There was a pause as her words were translated. The old woman was silent a moment before replying. 'No. That is not how it is for me … but every journey is different.'

Beth's stomach sank in disappointment. 'Does *anyone* do it the way that I do, besides me?'

'We are all individuals, and yet, we are all one. You shouldn't expect to be the same as anyone else. It is not helpful to compare yourself with others.'

'I just don't see how you can guide me if you haven't been there yourself. I thought you were doing something like me, and that's why I came here. I thought you might be able to help me … but it doesn't look like—'

'Your power is unique. It belongs only to you. We are all unique.'

Beth sighed. 'I see.'

'But I can help you. You have keys to open many doors, but you don't know how to use them. It is the way with everyone. We must learn who we are and how to use the power we have.'

'You can help with that?'

The old woman's face relaxed into an enigmatic smile. 'A child is mastered by his own potential, but an adult must learn to control it.'

Beth was losing patience with the riddles. 'Yeah … well …'

The shaman shut her eyes and began rocking back and forth, humming softly. This time Beth felt excluded. As strongly as the song had seduced before, it now repelled. She straightened, readying to leave, but the old woman's eyes snapped open.

'He is lost to you,' she said through her nephew. 'You must let him go.'

'Who?'

'You *saw* the blood. You must let him go.'

Her words chilled the space between them. They threw Beth completely off balance. *Had the shaman seen the visions inside her head?*

'Whose blood?' she demanded. 'Who am I supposed to let go? My boyfriend? Was it his blood?'

The shaman raised her hands as Beth's panicked

words were translated to her. 'It is your soul I am speaking of. Your soul is tangled with his. You must let him go. The spider is spinning her webs over you, and you must break free.'

'I don't want to be "free" from my boyfriend!'

'You do not see things as they are. You must be set free if you want to find yourself.'

'Well, maybe I'm not ready to *find* myself yet,' she said, pushing herself up off the floor.

The shaman's face relaxed into a gentle smile. 'That is as it should be. One day, you will want to be free. When that day comes, when you are ready and not before, come back to me and I will help you.'

'Well, I'm not so sure about that,' said Beth as she pulled some Peruvian soles out of her pocket – the price for the consultation – and placed them on the mat in front of the old woman. 'But, thank you anyway.'

Her eyes were now fully adjusted to the dark. She had no difficulty finding the door and was hugely relieved as she exited into the sunshine. Across the street, the man who'd tried to warn her was still maintaining his watch. He smiled as she approached but her head was too full to make sense of anything he said, or to respond with anything other than goodbye and thank you.

Lowering her head, she hurried on towards the town, but as she did, the vision of the pooling blood splashed across her mind and rushed into her chest.

Whose blood was it?

Not Anna's ... not Kennedy's ...

She'd never seen it before – it wasn't a memory. But it *was* connected to her, something that had not *yet* happened, but *would* happen – something that had not *yet* been seen, but *would* be seen. By *her.* She knew it.

Her heart raced.

Allan!

She set off in a run towards the internet cafe. By the time she reached it, she was bathed in sweat and so wound up she could barely count her coins out to pay for her session. She huddled over the computer and keyed in her details in a shaky rush – but he wasn't online and she couldn't reach him by Skype either.

It was the middle of the night in Japan. He was probably asleep – *but what if he wasn't? What if he was lying somewhere … on the road … hurt … bleeding …*

A tear of frustration slid down her cheek as she sent off a brief email, telling him to call her as soon as he woke.

She arrived back at the aid organisation headquarters in a less than happy state.

'What got up your arse?' greeted Simon as she passed him on the way to her room.

He was bunkered down playing Xbox on the deck. Beth wasn't sure she wanted company, but there was nothing she could do about Allan until he called and she owed Simon something. He'd manoeuvred the introduction to the shaman after all. She dropped down into a seat next to him.

'Didn't go well then? With the shaman?'

Beth tried to let her tension go. 'She was OK … but she was a bit *freaky.*'

His eyes sparkled in anticipation. 'Yeah, she's pretty heavy.'

'That's an understatement.' Beth grimaced at the remembrance of the murky room, but it was good to talk about it, and to have her impressions acknowledged. 'She was in this dark room, with her translator. I could hardly see them, and it was so hot I could barely think ... and then she grabbed my hands, and did this weird singing thing.'

Simon chuckled. 'Yeah, they make a good show of it.'

'I guess ... But, then, I actually ... *saw* some stuff. Just in my head – but really vivid. Memories, and images ... and stuff.'

She felt silly telling him, and even worse when the humour in his eyes transitioned into appraisal.

'Did you drink the jungle juice?'

'No. It was just the singing, but, it was weird. I saw ... blood. A pool of blood on the ground. In my vision, I mean. And the shaman seemed to see it too – *through* me! I don't know whose blood it was, but the shaman said that person was *lost* to me – like he must have died – like she *knew* it – like she saw it *too!*'

She was shaking now and embarrassed at her lack of control, but if Simon noticed, he didn't show it. 'I thought she meant my boyfriend, because he was in my vision too, and there isn't anyone else other than him. So I tried to call him, but it's the middle of the night in Japan and he didn't answer.' The panic began to rise again and she fought it down. 'He's probably just asleep ... but I can't ... I can't help worrying. I mean, is this shit for real? Could she *see* stuff like that? Could *I*? I mean, if he *was* ... hurt? Could she *make* me see it?'

Leaning back in his chair, Simon put down his game control. 'Who knows what they can really do, and what's for show? But they're not fortune-tellers. They don't usually run around predicting stuff. What did she say?'

Beth scowled. 'She said she was just talking about my "soul".'

'Well there you go then. That's more what they're into. That and connecting to the spirit world.'

'Load of crap!' said Beth, and Simon laughed.

'Probably. Some people get a lot out of it, but usually they're the ones looking for that kind of stuff in the first place, and they can always make whatever the shaman says fit with what's in their head and what they want to hear.'

Beth nodded, but she wasn't satisfied.

'I wouldn't worry about it,' said Simon. 'Your boyfriend's probably asleep. He'll call when he wakes up.'

Beth glared out over the backyard. 'She said I was all tangled up with him, and that I should break up with him – kept saying she saw spiders … spinning webs!'

'Well, she's not talking about *real* stuff then, is she?'

Seeing Simon's relaxed smile, Beth felt eased. 'I guess not.' It did sound ridiculous when she said it out loud, outside of that hot, stuffy, darkened room. But the shaman's piercing eyes remained with her.

'So … not what you were expecting?' asked Simon.

Beth thought about it a moment. 'I'm not really sure what I was expecting. I just heard they could … travel … to other places, through stones … and things … And I thought that was … interesting.'

Simon gave her another curious look, but didn't twist her discomfort into a joke as he would have with Shannon. Instead, he nodded in a surprisingly understanding manner and said nothing. Somehow that was harder for Beth to shut off from than ridicule. She felt impelled to explain.

'It's just … well, she said I could do her cleansing thing, but it sounded pretty heavy. All about facing your "inner darkness" and setting you "free" and stuff like that – and that's not what I wanted. I wasn't after some kind of drug-induced psychoanalysis thing.' She shrugged. 'I was just curious …'

'Fair enough.'

Beth glared at him suspiciously, but his expression was amused and not at all judgemental. Somehow she knew it would take a lot to unnerve him. 'Have you ever done it?' she asked. 'Have you tried ayahuasca?'

'Nah, I don't need drugs and a night of throwing up in the jungle to face my "inner darkness".'

'What do you mean?'

'Well, it's *my* darkness, isn't it? I'm the only one that can face it. If I *want* to do any facing, that is.' She raised an eyebrow at that, and he grinned. 'I don't want anyone else fucking around in my head. Not that they'd want to. It's a scary place in there.'

Beth couldn't help giggling. Suddenly, everything seemed lighter.

'Beth?' called a voice from the office, 'phone!'

With a gush of relief, Beth jumped up and ran to the office.

It was Allan.

'Thank God you're all right!'

'Of course I'm all right. What did you expect?'

Beth felt instantly foolish. Simon was right, it was all a big performance to suck the tourists in. 'Nothing.' She smiled. 'I just met a shaman here, and she was going on about some man being hurt, and I got worried about you, that's all.'

'A *shaman?*'

'It's nothing. It's just a tourist thing, just a show – but she freaked me out when she spoke about a man being hurt and I just wanted to check you were all right.'

'I'm fine,' said Allan, still confused. 'Why were you going to a shaman?'

'I told you. I was just curious.'

'About what?'

Allan always had a way of going after every bit of information – which was fine, if she was happy for him to have it. Something told her he wouldn't be thrilled about this.

'Well, I heard they claim they can … travel, to astral realms, through stones and things … and I—'

'Travel?'

'It's just a spiritual thing,' she said dismissively, 'but when I first heard about it, it sounded a bit like what I – Hang on.'

Deborah was staring up at her goggle-eyed, not even bothering to pretend not to be listening. Annoyed, Beth shifted out into the corridor, carrying the phone with her as far as the cord would stretch. She turned her back and spoke as quietly as possible. 'Sorry, no privacy in this place! I was just saying, what these shamans say they can do sounded a bit like what I do, so I had to check it out.'

She heard the sigh on the other end of the telephone line.

'I was just curious,' she said, her defensiveness mounting, 'and it turns out they don't do it anyway, it's just a spiritual thing for them.'

'I thought you were leaving that alone.'

He said it softly, but that didn't eliminate the bite of it. The fact that a huge part of who she was should be described as a 'that' that should be 'left alone' was grating.

'I am,' she said, her colour rising, 'but that doesn't mean I don't want to understand it. And anyway, why shouldn't I? It's part of who I am. I can't ignore it.'

'It doesn't help to dwell on it,' Allan snipped bitterly.

'Oh? Because it's not "acceptable"?' Her voice was getting louder, but she no longer cared who overheard. 'You think I should chop off half of myself because you don't *like* it? I don't tell you what you're allowed to think and what you're not!'

Allan, still only half awake, was startled by her venom. 'Beth, calm down. I only meant—'

'Never mind,' she said abruptly. 'I'm glad you're all right.'

With that, she slammed the receiver down, cutting him off. Hurt and enraged, she returned the phone to the office, ignoring Deborah's eager face, and stormed back to her room – but before she'd reached it, she heard the phone ringing again.

Cursing, she grabbed her bag and made for the front door.

Simon couldn't repress a chuckle. 'So, he's all right then?' he yelled after her, laughing as she responded with an angry yell before slamming the front door.

Chapter 33

It was difficult to find a peaceful place to be alone with her thoughts; isolated places weren't safe, and the town was buzzing with its usual activity. In the end she chose the internet cafe. At least there she'd be left to herself, if she paid for internet time. Not the most congenial of atmospheres but satisfactorily nonintrusive.

Fortunately, she got a computer in the far corner. Her back was to the wall, giving her a measure of online privacy, but she inserted her memory stick and brought up a photograph of Machu Picchu to have something standard on her screen in case anybody wandered over. She glanced around at the intense faces that surrounded her; most were writing emails or uploading photographs; all were lost in their own thoughts. They probably hadn't even noticed she'd entered the room.

Good.

She slumped back in her chair and stared at Machu

Picchu. It was time to re-think her plans. The visit to the shaman was done. She had her answer: the shaman wasn't travelling like her – and probably no one was.

She was alone.

So, what now?

She still had a few weeks before uni, but her excitement for Peru had blunted. Her excitement for *everything* had blunted. On the screen, Machu Picchu shone in the sun. So beautiful – but it didn't quiet her soul, not on this side of the photograph. In fact, it only irritated her resentment about not being able to go there. She did have a few safe pictures now, but only a few, and that was somehow worse than none. They were just a reminder that she could use them only *once*.

As she stared at her now inaccessible refuge, her desire for it burned to a compulsion. It stood for everything that blocked her, every restriction on her life. She felt as though she were bound by a thick, scratchy rope, tethered to a single ring in a small walled-in yard, with all of life, unexplored and beckoning, just on the other side of the wall, out of sight and out of reach.

And this was what Allan wanted for her.

The thought rankled. Why couldn't he accept her as she was? It hurt. He was the only one she'd let into her world – and now all he wanted was to drag her out of it and for her to abandon that part of herself. Well, she'd tried, and she couldn't. The more she stayed away, the stronger it pulled. And the effort of holding back was turning something inside her rancid.

But that didn't change the facts. It wasn't safe to travel now that she was visible. She could no longer go into pictures without frightening photographers or altering history. She'd lost that key; and the doors were locked.

Or ... *were* they?

Abruptly a new possibility emerged. Why shouldn't she be able to change this? She'd been invisible once, so why shouldn't she be able to be invisible again? It must be biologically possible for her since she'd already done it. Perhaps it was only a matter of figuring out how – like the shaman said, maybe she only needed to learn how to use the power she already had?

A spark of excitement ignited inside her.

But where should she start?

She hadn't *tried* to be visible; it just happened. She'd done nothing differently. She hadn't even realised she *was* visible at the time ... so how could she control that?

It was daunting.

But then she realised she *had* made some things change: she'd learnt how to stay inside a photograph longer for one thing. She couldn't remember discovering any special method to do that, she'd only *wanted* to stay longer and gradually she'd been able to. Then there was the walking. It was unexpected, but she might have just been ready for it when it happened, after years of slow improvements. Maybe she could have walked sooner if she'd tried?

Perhaps becoming visible was just another part of her natural development?

If so ... then what she needed was to *un-develop* it, go back to the stage before – unless she could figure out a way to do *both!* Being visible and physical had its advantages: she could interact and she didn't get bumped out. It was only really a problem with entry. If she could *enter* invisibly and *then* become physical – once she was out of sight of the photographer and others – she'd have the best of both states. She'd be able to enter any picture safely, multiple times instead of just once, and also to explore safely once she was in! That would solve everything! Perhaps that was meant to be her next stage of development?

But, how to get there?

The shaman had offered to help – but the thought of the old woman with her skewering eyes chilled Beth. No. She'd do it alone. She'd worked through all the other changes alone. If travelling was a skill that needed developing, then surely all she needed to do was travel; the way to develop skills was to use them. So all she needed were safe shots to enter, and a private place to practice.

Re-energised, Beth logged off. First on her new agenda was to get some appropriate photographs.

* * *

February 2, 2010

The sky was clear and the night was bright with a full moon. Most of the group were in town to see one of the local celebrations; the mummified body of a saint was being paraded around the main plaza in a garlanded coffin. The building was pretty much empty with just a few parade-jaded volunteers staying behind to watch a movie. Beth was both nervous and excited as she climbed the rickety ladder to the roof.

There was no one up there. She had the space to herself.

Off in the distance she could hear a party – music and laughter – and down in the yard the movie soundtrack pulsed out its adrenaline-inducing action theme.

She stepped into the clearest stretch of rooftop space – off to the side near the tent – aimed her camera back towards the lounge area and depressed the shutter.

Almost immediately, she came face to face with *herself*. Standing directly in front of her, with a determined expression on her face, was a future version of herself. Gasping as their eyes locked, Beth's heart fluttered. *She was seeing the future!* She was watching herself already experimenting with the photographs she'd only just taken.

She thought to speak, but before she could, her future-self was gone, vanishing as instantly as she'd appeared, leaving behind a curious stillness. Cautiously, on full alert, Beth waited – but no further selves appeared; no invisible selves materialised. If she'd entered invisibly on a second attempt, she wasn't revealing herself.

She must have failed.

But then it occurred to her – the physicalised entry might have blocked the photograph – not just for other *physical* entries, but for *invisible* entries as well. She'd always been cast out if she collided with a physical object when travelling invisibly, so even if she *had* figured out how to enter invisibly she might not be able to get through. That made sense – except she'd entered Anna's photo physically *and* invisibly, and she hadn't been bumped out ...

Or *had* she?

Perhaps she hadn't been physical when she'd entered Anna's photograph that last time?

A shiver crawled over her scalp.

Had she already done it? Had she entered Anna's photo invisibly, without knowing it – and then become visible by the time she reached the van? If so, then she *could* do it, and all she needed to do was discover *how* she'd done it – and how to do it again!

She aimed the camera far enough away from her first shot to avoid any kind of collision – it was a different moment in time but she figured extra space wouldn't hurt – and depressed the shutter.

Again, instantly, her future-self appeared, and just as quickly left.

So, she'd been right. The entry shot must have been blocked by the physicalised entry. But her future-self clearly still hadn't found the key to entering invisibly; the look on her face was enough to communicate that.

Undaunted, Beth carried on. She took shot after shot, each time hoping desperately she wouldn't see herself, but each time she did. Her optimism began to fade – but her future-self remained fixedly focused. She must know, Beth realised. She's already *seen* that this works and she's just working her way through the photographs to get to the one where I figure it out! Surely, she wouldn't keep going if she knew it wasn't going to work, so I must have succeeded.

One more time Beth raised her camera, and again the result was frustratingly the same – but the next time, when she glanced over the lens, her future-self did not appear.

She let out a squeal of triumph.

'What are you doing up here?' asked Shannon, teetering on the top of the ladder.

Beth jumped. How long had Shannon been there? How much had she seen? But Shannon wore her typical myopic expression. Clearly whatever she'd seen hadn't struck her as unusual. Beth swallowed and forced a smile to her face.

'Just getting some pictures. It's so pretty up here.'

'At night?'

'Well, that's when we're usually up here, isn't it?'

That seemed to satisfy Shannon. 'Yeah, I guess.' Her face brightened. 'Hey listen, I found a dead seal on the beach this afternoon and I want to skin it. Do you have a knife?'

Beth's mouth dropped open. 'Why do you want to skin a dead seal?'

Shannon gave a sagely nod. 'You shouldn't waste things. I never do. I use everything.'

'Aren't you afraid of disease?'

'Oh, no. It's all natural. So, do you have a knife?'

'Ah … no.'

Shannon's face fell. 'Oh. OK then. Thanks.'

She disappeared back down the ladder.

Beth giggled, deliciously euphoric. *She'd done it!* Somehow, her future-self had figured it out!

Chapter 34

February 5, 2010

It was three whole nights before Beth had the chance to be alone again. The group was working hard to finish several projects and most didn't have the energy to go out again after their long hot days so they gathered for companionable evenings on the roof. On Friday night though, they had a big celebration dinner. Several of the long-timers were heading home. Simon dug a barbeque pit in the middle of the earth floor of their eating area and prepared a party.

Beth excused herself early, claiming she wasn't well – all too common considering the working and sanitation conditions – and returned to the dorms and then up to the roof with her camera.

She'd never tried entering through anything as small as a camera screen, which made her a little nervous, but she didn't have a computer and borrowing one would raise questions. She was also apprehensive that someone might come back unexpectedly and interrupt her. It was certainly a risk, and if she was inside a photograph she wouldn't even hear them – but she couldn't hold off any longer. She could only hope Simon's feast would keep everyone's attention a good while longer, which wasn't an unreasonable expectation. He had plenty of food, all of it deliciously prepared, and there was cake.

Choosing one of the more stable chairs, Beth sat and listened for sounds below. There were none, so she switched on the camera and flipped through the photographs. There were twenty-three of them. She was tempted just to go to the last one – as that was the one that had worked – but she realised she'd need to enter all of them. She'd seen herself do that after all. Presumably she'd discovered whatever she eventually learnt through the process. So she brought up the first of roof shots and focused her concentration.

Entry was swift. Events ensued as she'd seen. She stepped in, made eye contact with her past-self and slipped out.

Disturbingly, it gave her no clue. Whatever allowed her to enter Anna's photograph invisibly didn't seem to work any more, and she'd no idea what to do to make it happen again.

She brought up the next shot and tried again, this time begging silently she wouldn't be visible, even though she knew she would be; she'd already seen this attempt wouldn't work. And it didn't. By the fourth attempt, she was queasy and heavy in her head. By the seventh attempt, she'd developed a thumping migraine and felt depressingly defeated, and after the nineteenth attempt she had to stop and race down to the bathroom to throw up.

'Beth? Are you all right?'

It was Katie. She'd come back to get a long-sleeved top to ward off mosquitoes. At least that provides evidence for my claims of not being well, thought Beth, as she climbed up from the floor where she'd been kneeling in front of the toilet.

'Yeah, I'm fine. I'll sleep it off.'

'You're sure?'

'Yep. I'm sure. Thanks.'

'Well, OK …' said Katie doubtfully. 'Make sure you drink plenty of water.'

'I will.'

Beth waited for the front door to open and close again, her hands trembling as she clung to the sink for support. She felt terrible. She wasn't sure how much more she could take, but she was *so* close. She couldn't stop now with only four more photographs to go – but then a horrible thought struck her. Maybe the reason she hadn't appeared after the twenty-third photograph was because she hadn't been able to enter it? Maybe she'd collapsed – or maybe this had even killed her?

Fear trickled over her.

There was only one way to find out.

Resolutely, she walked back through the common area and climbed the ladder. She stepped up onto the roof, re-set her camera and took another photograph.

Her future-self didn't appear.

Well, thought Beth, I guess that means I'm either dead … or I figured it out.

Which?

Shakily, she stared down at her camera. Was it worth her life to continue with this? She wasn't getting any closer to controlling it … the only thing she'd achieved so far was to make herself violently ill. Perhaps she'd really reached the end of her travelling and she should give it up – accept it as childhood left behind – make Allan happy.

'We figured it out!'

Beth nearly jumped out of her skin. With a startled yelp, she spun around. There, a metre away, was her future-self, grinning like a Cheshire cat.

'Stop now,' she said. 'Get some rest and check into the hostel tomorrow. Try again there.'

And then she was gone.

It was a moment or two before Beth remembered to breathe, but when she did, the same grin was glowing all over her face.

She'd done it!

Chapter 35

February 6, 2010

The hostel was smelly and noisy.

It was only a block from the aid organisation's headquarters and the volunteers were its main patrons because it was cheap and close. Volunteers often checked in for a night or two to take advantage of the hot water – the rooms had ensuites – and couples preferred the private rooms over the dormitories. The only downside was the mess. The tiled floors were constantly flooded and muddy from the dust tracked in from the streets, and the toilets stank. It didn't help that toilet paper couldn't be flushed. The used fragments remained in a basket by the toilet until the staff removed them.

Beth would have preferred not to share her sleeping space with what amounted to an open sewer, but the room was private. She wouldn't be disturbed. And if things progressed in a similar fashion to the night before she might need a bathroom close and accessible.

She made her first attempt that afternoon. She'd checked in to the hostel in the morning but had taken her future-self's advice to rest. At this time of day, the hostel was nice and quiet; most of the guests were out and the staff were taking a siesta. Conditions were optimal. But as she sat to ready her camera, she hesitated.

How was she supposed to do this?

What could she possibly do differently? Was there a trick – or was it only a matter of repetition?

Bringing up the picture – roof vista number twenty – she tried again to think of anything she'd done differently when she'd entered Anna's photograph that last time; and came up blank. She'd only thought of getting there, of helping those girls; she hadn't *tried* to be invisible. She hadn't known she could be.

And maybe she wasn't …

Maybe it was just the grainy photograph that gave her a few seconds to get out of the way. Perhaps she hadn't entered invisibly at all.

Her confidence crumbled.

Rest.

Her future-self had instructed her to rest!

And she had – but enough? She still felt tense. Perhaps all she needed was to relax a little? Taking a deep, slow breath, she shut her eyes and wiggled her shoulders to ease some of the tension. Anxiety twisted stubbornly inside her, squirming to other parts of her body to escape attention, but she fought it, and finally she managed to breathe in a tenuous calm.

She opened her eyes and stared at the little lit-up

frame on her camera. She hadn't been able to enter this photograph invisibly – it was only number twenty – but perhaps this more relaxed state would help to reveal a new clue?

Trying to hold onto the calm, she entered.

It didn't work. She learnt nothing.

Twenty-one didn't go any better, but she hadn't expected it to. And neither, logically, should twenty-two. She already knew she failed there. She jumped in and out to get it over with.

Could this be a part of it? Belief? Faith?

Perhaps she wasn't succeeding because she *knew* she wasn't going to?

If this was the case, then she had all she needed, because there was only one photograph to go and she already knew it was going to work – *but was that really the key?* She hadn't *believed* she could be visible when she went to the castle. She hadn't even known she was …

Was there anything else?

She thought of her last entry into Anna's photograph. She remembered waiting for the fog to clear … waiting to see Anna before jumping back—

Jumping back?

Could that be it? Had the act of *physically* jumping back … out of the way … out of sight, been enough to transform her into an invisible state?

Her entire focus had been on escaping detection … she'd *willed* to be unseen. Perhaps the desire, combined with the physical action, had been the key?

The only way to know was to try it. It seemed a little odd, but it was worth a go – only not with roof vista number twenty-three. Better to test it on something else first in case she was wrong or in case it needed a few goes to get it right.

She scrolled back through the pictures she'd taken since arriving in Peru and stopped at the first one she'd taken at Machu Picchu: her special spot. It was a precious photograph, but if she figured this out she'd be able to go back any time she liked. Perhaps the magic of Machu Picchu would help her?

Taking a moment to shake out her tension, she told herself this was going to work, and then focused.

* * *

December, 2009

In an instant, she was there.

She turned to see her past-self from only weeks before, standing in front of her, her back turned, listening.

Holding her breath, she kept perfectly still.

She remembered taking this photograph; standing there, trying to sense if some future version of herself had entered it … and now there she was.

Visible or invisible?

She had no idea – and she didn't want to test it on her past-self – so she made not a sound until past-Beth had moved on. When she'd rounded the bend, Beth slowly let out her breath – but she knew she didn't have long. She could hear voices at the Inca Bridge. Wasting no more time, she focused on the moment of her entry into Anna's photograph, imagining herself standing in the dark, waiting for the clearing of the fog – and as the memory became sharper, the feelings of that moment returned. Urgency flooded her. She leapt backwards – out of the way – out of sight – into the covering darkness.

For a fraction of a second she felt its *thickness* – the thickness of the darkness – and she *clung* to it.

Certainty replaced urgency. She held herself still and let it fill her, but when she opened her eyes her certainty vanished.

Had it worked? Was she invisible?

She didn't feel any different – *or did she?* As she spooled through her senses, there *was* something different … something *else* … something she'd forgotten. There was a variance in the pull, the force that drew her back. It wasn't a significant difference, she hadn't even noticed it at first, but it was there nonetheless. The pull she felt now was different from the pull she'd felt when she entered. She tried to place the difference, to identify it and hold on to it – but suddenly, a group of tourists exploded up from the bridge.

She held her breath. *Did they see her?*

They didn't appear to, they didn't make eye contact – but she probably wouldn't have made eye contact with her in these circumstances either. She must look like a nut case.

Time to find out.

Setting her chin, she stepped out in front of them, right into their path—

—and was thrown back into the hostel room.

* * *

February 6, 2010

Splayed back flat across the bed, gasping with exertion, a grin spread over her face.

She'd done it!

She let out a triumphant whoop of victory, not caring who heard, and burst out in happy laughter. For the first time in her life she'd taken control! She'd gone after a key and she'd found it!

Well ... almost.

She still needed to confirm *how* she'd done it. She was fairly certain it wasn't because she'd jumped back or because she'd evoked the emotions and sensations she'd experienced in Anna's photo. She didn't think it had much to do with being more confident and relaxed either – though that probably helped. She suspected the subtle variation in the pull was the real key. But she had to be sure. She had to test it. She had to see if she could find that pull again and use it to make herself visible *or* invisible.

She chose another Machu Picchu photograph and entered again.

* * *

December, 2009

This time, while waiting for past-Beth to move on, she calmed herself and searched inside for the pull. It was there. She felt it. And this time the difference was more obvious to her. It wasn't quite like the pull she'd felt when invisible, so she suspected she was visible.

She had to test it.

A young couple rounded the corner, their faces

bright with wonder and oxygen deprivation. She smiled a greeting – and they smiled back.

'Amazing up here, isn't it?' said Beth, and the young couple gushed an agreement before continuing on.

Visibility established and once more alone, Beth shut her eyes and drew in a deep breath. She had only seconds before the next group of tourists would come her way. She calmed and concentrated on the pull. She didn't think of Anna or Chatswood Mall; she sought only the memory of the pull she'd felt when invisible. And it was there, hidden in her heart – only a memory, but as she sank herself into it, it clarified. She locked on to it – felt an inner alignment – and her heart began to pound.

Opening her eyes, she saw the next group approaching and, a little light-headed, she walked directly at them. They made no adjustment to let her pass. Clearly, they couldn't see her.

Exhilarated, she exited just before collision.

* * *

February 6, 2010

Back in the hostel, Beth was too excited to notice the strain. All that remained was to see if she could *enter* invisibly. She'd achieved nothing if she couldn't do that. She skipped photograph twenty-three because she remembered that Shannon had interrupted after she'd taken that one and went straight to the final shot.

Loosening her shoulders, she centred on the memory of the 'invisible' pull and willed herself into the photograph.

* * *

February 2, 2010

The rooftop materialised around her.

She was facing out towards the sea.

Turning swiftly, she saw yesterday's Beth peering through the lens of her camera. She waited for her to look up, and when she did, a jolt of elation shot through her; past-Beth's gaze went straight through her.

Chapter 36

Allan shut down his computer and raked his fingers through his hair.

She hadn't come.

He'd posted the photograph on Facebook anyway, with a comment: 'This one is safe!' It seemed a little pointless – since she hadn't turned up, she never would; she always appeared at the moment the photo was taken. But he reasoned she couldn't enter it if he didn't post it. He might *need* to post it, to complete his part of the transaction. And so he did.

But nothing changed.

He felt gutted. He couldn't imagine life without Beth; couldn't believe he'd messed things up so badly – but then soft arms wrapped around him from behind.

He spun to face her; and she greeted him with a kiss, a deep, wanting, promising kiss. The sweetness of it made him gasp. He climbed into her embrace, wrapping himself around her, hungry to strip away any separation between them and lock back into place; his place; *their* place. They fit so perfectly together. He could feel the warmth rising in her body as it was in his own and they fell onto his bed in a tangle of trembling flesh and half-discarded clothing; racing for release.

He almost yelled when he came, moments after her – didn't care if he woke up the whole floor, and Beth laughed happily as he collapsed on top of her.

'So, you missed me, huh?'

He nodded into the crock of her neck, moaning contentedly as she played her fingers through his hair. He wanted just to stay there, luxuriating in the silky smoothness of her skin flush against his, and she didn't seem in a hurry to separate either – but he knew he had to be crushing her. She was tiny beneath him; he was nearly half her weight again now he was finally fully grown.

Rolling off, he propped himself up on his elbow and smiled. She looked relaxed and happy and so, *so* beautiful. Her thick dark hair was tousled around her face, framing her extraordinary eyes, and a satisfied flush tinted her cheeks. His heart swelled with love.

'I didn't mean to hurt you,' she said softly, rolling onto her side and mirroring his position. Her body was taut, stronger than when he'd last seen her, brown from working in the sun. Allan felt himself rising again and ran his hand playfully over her flank.

'I just had to figure it out.'

'That's OK,' he said stupidly, sensible only of the softness of her skin under his fingers.

'And I did.'

'Huh?'

'I figured it out. I can enter invisibly now, and turn myself visible once I'm there.'

He still didn't understand, and she pulled herself up to sit cross-legged.

'I came here just after you took the photo, like I always do, but I came invisibly. I waited until you posted your picture on Facebook and then became visible.' Seeing understanding dawning on his face, she beamed. 'You see what this means? I can travel safely now. I can enter invisibly, and not disturb anything at all – or I can physicalise.' She raised an eyebrow provocatively. 'If there's a good reason to …'

He laughed. 'So, we can have sex every night, and all I need to do is post a photograph?'

'Well, I guess we could do that before, couldn't we?'

'Hey, yeah,' said Allan, suddenly realising. 'Why didn't we think of that?'

'Because travelling is supposed to be evil, remember?'

His face crumpled. 'Beth, I only wanted—'

'I know.' She smiled, but then her eyes shadowed. 'So … you're not mad at me any more?'

Allan pushed himself up to face her. 'Beth, I love you more than I ever knew it was possible to love anyone. I can never stay mad at you. I just want you safe.'

'I *can* be safe now. And I'll be sensible. No more butting in on murders. Promise. I love you too. More than ever.' She took his face gently between her hands and kissed him, softly and searchingly. The taste of his mouth was intoxicating and she felt herself swelling again, but at the same time the familiar headache was beginning its steady beat at the base of her skull. Time to leave. It galled her she could only stay for such a short time, but there was no sense ruining her visit by letting him see her sick. 'I have to go.'

She climbed off the bed and tugged on her clothes.

'Why?'

'Just to be safe. Someone might come in.'

'Oh. Of course. You mean in Peru. You are still in Peru aren't you?'

'Yes. But I'm coming home. I'll be there when you get back.'

Allan beamed.

She gave him one last kiss and smiled. 'Bye.'

Instantly, she was gone.

Allan fell back on the bed and laughed with happiness.

Chapter 37

February 19, 2010

Simon prepared a special feast in honour of her departure: his signature chicken curry with fresh baked naan bread. The night was full of laughter and fun. She was going to miss them, but she was also excited to be going home. Everything felt freer now. She wasn't locked into one place or one time, and she could visit this special place as often as she liked.

After dinner, they gathered as usual in their open-air rooftop lounge for drinks. The conversation meandered through memories of the past months and they laughed again at the funny moments, basked in the satisfaction of the rewarding ones and cringed at the gross ones. There were plenty in all categories. Then future plans began to dominate and finally contact details and promises to keep in touch were exchanged before the group slowly broke up and most headed down to the dorms. Beth chose to linger. The rooftop was almost sacred to her now. She wanted to savour her last evening.

'Looking forward to getting back?' asked Simon lazily, smiling over his beer.

They were the only two left on the roof now; Shannon had just tottered off after presenting her with a piece of dried seal skin as a parting gift.

'Yeah. Be nice to see Allan again.'

'What's he gunna say about your hair?'

Beth blushed. 'He'll cope.'

Simon chuckled, but Beth quickly recaptured her composure. She'd been insecure about her new haircut at first, but everyone said it suited her, and she liked it too. She'd kept her hair much the same length since she started high school. It was time for a change. The new short, shaggy cut was easier in the desert heat, and, according to Shannon, it gave a dramatic flair to her appearance.

'Course he will.' Simon laughed. 'You're gorgeous, as always. And if he doesn't like it, you can come back here.'

For a moment, Beth saw something deeper beneath Simon's mocking eyes. *An invitation?* She liked Simon … but he wasn't Allan.

'Thanks.' She smiled, trying to sweeten her rejection with warm affection.

Simon wasn't fooled. He took another swig of his beer. 'So … did you find what you were looking for?'

His expression, warmly lit by the haphazard lighting on the roof, was mischievous. The vulnerability she'd seen before had scurried out of sight and been replaced by challenge.

She hadn't told him about the travelling, about her struggles or her success, so she wasn't sure what he was referring to. It could have been just a normal, polite parting phrase. The kind everybody used – everyone who came here, to work in a place like this, was looking for something after all – but Simon always gave the impression of meanings layered behind his meanings.

'Yeah, I guess so,' she said, deciding it was safest to go with the polite, parting phrase interpretation.

Recklessly, she wanted to tell him. *Everything.* Somehow she believed he'd take it in his stride, but caution intervened. It wasn't that she didn't trust him; she did. She suspected he might even have heard part of her phone conversation with Allan and probably already had a few odd ideas about her – but ideas were different to revelations. What if the unravelling of the mystery of herself changed her place in his estimation from misfit equal to separated other?

This was a risk she didn't need to take.

'This is an amazing place,' she said, shutting him out with a smile. 'I love it here. I'll miss it.'

Simon raised his glass in a solemn salute. 'Well, wherever you travel, Beth O'Malley, live the journey! You only get to take it once.'

His words landed before her like tossed dice, daring her to play. She froze in indecision, but when he broke into a grin she let it go and raised her glass in return.

'Thank you, I will. You too,' she said. 'And if you ever go home, look us up.'

For the first time in her life she meant it, even hoped he'd take her up on it, though she doubted his restless spirit would ever lead him home.

'Same to you,' he said, finishing his beer and opening another. 'So, how are you going to get that hunk of dead seal meat through customs?'

* * *

March, 2010

It was easier to slip back into routine than Beth had anticipated. The first few weeks of semester were always all-consuming: new texts to be bought, new timetables to be negotiated, work commitments to be re-scheduled. It kept her busy. But her free time was easier as well. She and Allan wanted nothing more than to be together and catch up on time missed. Thoughts of travelling slipped down a notch in importance. Now she could go wherever she wanted, whenever she wanted, she was happy to put it aside until she needed a change of pace. She was totally content in the present. But three weeks into the new semester, the past came to her.

She was at home alone when there was a knock on the door. Opening it, she saw Richard standing on the threshold, holding a large cardboard box. He looked ten years older. His hair had greyed, the bags under his eyes were heavy and more pronounced, and his shoulders held a stooped, defeated look.

'Hello, Beth,' he offered tentatively. 'I've been trying to contact you, but ...'

'I've been away.' Her hand fluttered aimlessly to her throat. 'Sorry ... come in.'

Richard shuffled past and turned to face her. 'I ...

uh, brought this over for you,' he said, holding the box out towards her. 'Some of your mother's things. I … uh … thought she'd want you to have them.'

Beth stared at the box as though it might bite her.

'I'll … uh … put this on the table, shall I?' Richard asked, looking around for an appropriate surface.

Beth finally jolted into action and reached to take it from him. 'Thanks. You didn't have to. I could have come and picked it up.'

Richard smiled, but it was a smile soaked in pain: it spread across his face like a wilting flower. 'It's no bother, Beth. There's not much there, just some personal things. I have her clothes, boxed up, in the garage … if you'd like to come over some time and—'

'Thanks,' said Beth, shutting off that conversation before it had a chance to take hold.

Richard shifted awkwardly. 'So, ah … you've been away?'

'Yes. To South America. With that money you gave me. Thanks again for that.'

'It was from your mother. She'd kept it aside for you. She … loved you very much, you know.' Instantly, his eyes filled.

Beth turned away and put the box on the table. 'Would you like a cup of tea or something? I might have some instant coffee …'

'No. No thanks. I have to get going. I only just dropped by on the off chance … But, ah … thank you, anyway.'

Beth could only nod.

'Well, I'll be off then,' said Richard, but as he reached for the door he hesitated and turned. 'I'd … uh … love to have you and Allan over to dinner some time ... when you can make it.' His cheeks flushed a little. 'You know, I'll always be here for you, Beth. I want you to know that. I know we haven't always hit it off ... but we're family. You're the only daughter I've got ... and ... your mother would want ...' Again the tears came, and he bit into his lip. 'Well, so long as you know,' he managed. 'Anything you need ... I'm here for you.'

This was the first and only declaration of connection Beth could remember coming from him and she could see he was in great agonies trying to express it, but also that he was sincere. Even if he was only offering her support for her mother's sake, even if love for her mother was the only thing they had in common, she couldn't deny that he *did* love her. His crushed pain, so uncomfortably threatening to release her own, roused her pity.

'Thank you, Richard. I appreciate that. She loved you too ... and you were good for her.' It was as close as she could get to absolution.

Richard nodded briefly and pushed outside with only a backward wave to express the parting words he couldn't release.

For a full minute, Beth stood there, staring at the closed door. An uncomfortable regret nagged at her conscience. It was almost as though her mother were there in the room, still pushing for acceptance of the man she loved.

Ironic if she should achieve that only now, after her death ...

Beth's eyes wandered to her mother's box. It was loosely shut. She was tempted just to tape it up and put it away under the bed – but she knew she'd have to face it some time.

She flipped it open.

As Richard said, there wasn't much: some hand-printed silk scarves; her mother's jewellery box; a cashmere cardigan; a few bottles of perfume and some letters and papers. Nestled in the bottom of the box were two photograph albums: her parent's wedding album and the older album of her mother's with all her photographs from before her marriage to Richard.

Chapter 38

6 p.m., Tuesday evening, January 14, 1992

Beth's father stood opposite her on the other side of the road, but he didn't see her as he gazed at the spectacular sunset he'd just captured on film – the last photograph he'd ever take. Behind Beth, the waves rumbled against the beach: rhythmically, peacefully, yet unstoppably powerful.

Directly behind her father was an old brick cottage. She assumed it was her parents' house as her mother told her this photograph had been taken across the road from their home. It was in a prime position – right on North Steyne Beach – and was painted a sunny yellow, but it had seen better days; one of the few original cottages, it was surrounded by a ring of steadily encroaching up-market apartment blocks and looked like it was being left to slowly rot. Money didn't appear to be going into anything other than basic upkeep.

Through the slats of the venetian blinds in the front window, Beth could just make out her mother working with something on a table.

When her father went back inside, Beth darted across the road and entered the yard. She picked her way across the broken concrete to the window and watched her mother preparing for her night out. She looked almost un-reachably beautiful, her tummy ripe and round, her face was glowing with happiness.

Beth's chest began to tighten.

How long? How long would it be before her happiness was shattered?

She didn't know when her father's heart attack had hit. Her mother had never said.

Poor Mum.

She was so close. If the window hadn't been there, she could've reached out and touched her – if she phys-icalised – which, of course, she could never do. What would be the point? She wasn't really the daughter of the woman in front of her; *her* daughter was only two years old. And this woman wasn't really her mother either. Not really. Not yet. She was only a memory, and there could be no new interaction with a memory; she'd never be able to touch or talk with her mother again.

'I'm so sorry, Mum,' she whispered.

The words bounced back unheard, uselessly late.

* * *

April, 2010

The cold emptiness of their kitchen clenched back

around her.

It was getting dark. Allan would be home soon.

Time to put the album away.

She ran her fingers tenderly over the ageing cover. Already, it was showing signs of degradation; it was only a cheap album. She'd need to think of a better way to preserve these photographs if she wanted them to last, and she did want them to last. They hurt, but not as much as it would hurt if she didn't have them. They were the most precious things her mother left her. They opened the door for a hundred one-way conversations, a hundred new insights into her mother's life. Even if they couldn't give her the opportunity to say goodbye, they kept her close. And *close* was all she had now.

She'd been delving into the album obsessively ever since Richard had given it to her, working her way through, observing every moment, absorbing every detail. She couldn't stay away. There were only a few photographs she hadn't yet visited – all from the last outing in the park, the day her father had died. Her mother had given her a photograph of the two of them playing in the lagoon before – and she'd visited that many times back when she was in school – but these were new to her. They showed her and her mother building a sandcastle in a sandpit. One was exceptionally lovely; their faces were almost nose-to-nose and bursting with happiness.

Beth figured she had time for one more.

* * *

9.35 a.m., Tuesday morning, January 14, 1992

She saw the sandpit first: a large lake of sand shaded by towering pines. Scattered across it were young children and their parents, scooping and building – and about a metre in front of her, looking like a large, happy beach-ball in her sundress, was her mother, playfully encouraging her toddler-self with the construction of a sand fortress.

Slipping quickly out of the way, Beth turned her attention to her father. A faint smile lit his face and she wondered what he was thinking of. It was lovely to see his enjoyment ... even though it would be fleeting. She watched, deeply moved, as he put the camera in the bag at the back of the stroller and looked up.

'Beautiful, darling! That's an excellent castle.'

Beth followed his gaze – but just at that moment, her mother lifted her head – *and their eyes met.*

Startled, Beth leapt back behind a tree, scrambling for balance.

She was *visible!*

And she was trapped! She couldn't de-materialise in public!

Heart pounding, she sprinted out of the park and headed for the beach. Reaching the surf lifesaving clubhouse, she bolted into the public toilets. There was a queue – but she jumped it.

She only just reached the toilet in time.

* * *

April, 2010

'She recognised me!'

Beth was sure of it and she couldn't let it go.

Allan handed her a beer and sat down on the lounge.

'How could she?' he asked reasonably.

'I don't know, but … the way she looked at me … she was almost *scared*.'

'Scared?'

'Well, not quite that. Shocked. Like she *knew* me!'

Allan just shrugged. There was no arguing with Beth when she was set on something.

'Why could she see you all of a sudden? I thought you'd figured that out.'

Beth's face fell. 'So did I. I don't know what happened. I entered invisibly. I know they didn't see me when I came in. So it must have happened while I was standing there watching them. I didn't feel any different, I didn't even know until she looked at me. Lucky I was out of the way or they'd have seen me become visible.'

'Maybe they did. Maybe that's why she was shocked.'

'No way. It wasn't *that* kind of shocked. She didn't scream or anything.'

'Whatever,' said Allan, getting a little tired of the debate.

Beth halted at the sourness of his tone. 'What's the matter?'

Again he shrugged, not really wanting to drag up an argument, but at the same time a little peeved. 'You just seem to be fixating on this a bit, Beth.'

That brought a flush to her face. '*Fixating?*'

'You get stuck on stuff,' he said with a sigh, 'and you just can't let it go.'

'But, if she recognised me—'

'For God's sake, Beth, she didn't recognise you. She

saw this crazy girl, perving on her and her kid in the sandpit! *Stalking* her! You don't look like a parent; you look like a psycho-stalker. How's she supposed to react?'

Beth's mouth fell open. 'I wasn't stalking her!'

'You were. You *are!* That's *all* you do lately! You and those *bloody* pictures! You spend more time in them than out of them.'

Beth's eyes flashed. 'My mother is dead, Allan. And I never got to say goodbye. I just want to spend some time with her.'

'You've been "spending time with her" for the last three weeks!'

So he knew.

Beth thought she'd managed to keep the amount of time she'd been spending on this from him. She felt suddenly exposed and shamed; which only fired her defensiveness further. 'There were all those new photos in her album. Come on, if you were able to go back into some of your mother's photos, you would!'

'Yes; maybe. A couple of times – but not over and over again, *all* day, *every* day.' Allan's cheeks burned to an angry red. 'It's past, Beth. Gone. You've got to live your life in the *present*. You're hardly ever in this space now; you're always off chasing what's gone!' He dragged in a tense breath and forced his tone down a bit. 'I know you haven't been to classes. Zinea called me, wondering if you were all right. It's too much, Beth. You've got to get some balance here.'

'Zinea called?'

'I told her you had the flu.'

Beth bit into her lip and stared out the window. Seeing she was thinking it through, Allan nursed his beer and waited for her response.

Eventually, she let out a sigh, 'Sorry.'

Allan shook his head. 'You're worse than a bloody heroin addict, Beth.'

Tears welled in her eyes. 'I just wanted to ... see ... her again ...'

Now it was Allan's turn to sigh. 'I know.'

She saw her own sadness mirrored in his eyes. He knew exactly how she felt. She regretted rubbing his face in the fact that he couldn't visit his mum. And he was right, she *had* got a little out of balance. She *had* put her whole life on hold these past few weeks; *their* lives. If she didn't pull up, she was in danger of failing her classes this semester, and her boss was also losing patience – but how to stop? Even though visiting her parents in their photographs was a poor substitute for the precious present-time contact she craved, it was all she had – and it was completely addictive in its insufficiency.

'It's just so hard to stop.' she said in a small voice.

Allan heard her defeat.

'But ... I guess I've seen everything there is to see in those pictures now. You're right. I might be a bit out of balance.' She knew it was the truth. She had to face it. 'Maybe that's why I couldn't stay invisible ... I'll slow down.'

Allan flicked her a glance, and Beth raised her hands in surrender. 'All right, I'll stop. I'll put the album away. OK? I'll give it a break. Next time I want a study break, I'm off to Machu Picchu. Promise!'

'Oh, God!' groaned Allan, but he was unmistakeably relieved and so was Beth. It *was* time to move on. She crawled on to his lap.

'Wish I could take you with me,' she said, her deep brown eyes softening as she gazed into his.

'We'll book a trip.' He said gently. 'Soon as we can – and you can show me everything. The conventional way.'

Beth smiled at that, and Allan drew her close. She melted into his arms, but even though her heart was now beating calmly against his chest and he could feel the trusting love in her embrace, he couldn't dispel the sense of separation. Something had slithered in between them, and he had no idea how to fix it.

Chapter 39

June, 2010

The next few months were fortunately busy ones. It helped Beth to re-focus. She had work to catch up on, and her course was also shifting to final projects. She started on a new major work, a series of paintings inspired by her trip to Peru. The idea was ambitious and it brought back many happy memories. She threw her energy into research: revisiting her Peruvian photographs and finding others; searching out colours, textures and fabrics; deciding on faces and places, and making sketches. It fired an enthusiasm for all things South American and she extended her foraging into neighbouring countries, seeking out the colours of the Carnival in Rio, exploring exotically painted buildings in Chile and roaming stunning landscapes in Patagonia. There was so much to see, and now she had no difficulty entering invisibly, staying invisible or switching to visible and back, her travelling options were unlimited. She felt free, unfettered.

Allan loved the new subject she was working on: beautiful, warm Peruvian women and children in exotically lush, or dusty dry landscapes. The scenes were so grounded and contented. He also loved that Beth was absorbing some of the positive energy of her subjects as she worked on them. At last, she was benefiting from her travel instead of being consumed by it. She was happy and at peace, and therefore, so was he.

South American travel brought other benefits as well. Beth became passionate about trying out new recipes and began creating Spanish feasts for them with spices and ideas collected from all over the continent. She even got inspired to decorate their home, returning with cheap, colourful rugs and fabrics from the markets and bright, handcrafted ceramics from tucked-away villages. She turned their drab converted garage into a South American enclave. Their landlord was so impressed he offered to pay for paint to spruce up the flat. For a few weeks she happily hummed along to loud South American music as their home was transformed.

It was when she began on their bedroom that she found it again: her mother's box. Buoyed by her mood, she decided it was time to tackle it. The cashmere cardigan, she put on immediately as the afternoon chill was already setting in. Its softness enveloped her. Next, she tried on a few pieces of her mother's jewellery, but none of it was her style. She slipped the little jewellery box into her underwear drawer along with the perfume and the scarves. She wasn't quite sure what to do with the personal papers and documents. Opening a passport, she smiled at the photograph of her father and glanced through the various passport stamps. He'd travelled around Europe too. Unfortunately there were no photographs of these trips. She placed the passport into a smaller decorative box with her own passport and decided to put the rest of the papers aside to sort through later, but as she lifted them from the box, a newspaper clipping slipped out and fell to the floor. It was from the *Sydney Morning Herald*, dated Wednesday, January 15, 1992 and featured a picture of her father in his ambulance officer's uniform, smiling proudly.

The bold headline thrust out like a knife.

YOUNG FATHER SLAIN AT CITY ATM

She read the article in a daze.

> *Michael O'Malley, a 34-year old probationary ambulance officer from Manly, was stabbed to death while attempting to make a transaction at an ATM on Sussex Street last night at approximately 9pm.*
>
> *This is the third such incident in the area in less than six weeks. Andrew Moffatt, a businessman from Perth, was robbed at knifepoint on December 28 and on January 5, 19-year-old student Greg Platts was assaulted and robbed while using an ATM on George Street. Police believe that the attacks are gang related.*
>
> *Mr O'Malley leaves behind a wife and daughter. The couple were expecting a second child in a matter of weeks and were celebrating*

their anniversary at the popular Ming Cha Restaurant. Police have requested that anyone with information pertaining to this incident should contact them.

Stabbed?
The room swayed.
Her father had been *stabbed?*
Murdered?
He didn't die of a heart attack?
There had to be some kind of mistake ... this couldn't be right.
But ... the article appeared *genuine* ... why would anyone make something like that up?
And why would her mother keep it if they had?
There was another photograph, underneath the article, showing police and forensic officers in a taped-off area in front of an ATM on a city street.
She didn't think about it; it was pure instinct. She smoothed out the photograph and entered.

* * *

12.57 a.m., Wednesday morning, January 15, 1992

She was just inside the cordoned-off area.
Bright lights blazed the night into an unnatural day, creating an illuminated cocoon for the forensic officers to work in. They were hunched over their tasks, quietly concentrating. Others rushed in and out ... uniformed ... focused ... urgent. Their faces flickered blue, white and red in the lights of their vehicles, giving the whole

scene a surreal aspect, emphasising the seriousness of the situation.

Suddenly, the flash from a camera lit up a shallow puddle on the ground near the ATM. It was dark and viscous, muddied with grit.

Blood.

'Yeah, an ambulance officer,' said a gruff voice behind her, jolting Beth to awareness of those around her. 'Off duty.'

The owner of the voice was an overweight police officer, near to retirement age. He was positioned just on the other side of the tape next to the photographer who'd taken the picture she'd entered through. A gaggle of journalists surrounded him. Beth lurched back as a camera thrust out in her direction and a flash went off in her face.

'What about the wife?'

Blinded, Beth couldn't see who was asking the question.

'She wasn't with him,' answered the officer.

'I heard she was in Royal North Shore Hospital? Something about a baby? She was pregnant, wasn't she?' called out another voice.

'That's all. Contact Media.' Turning his back, the policeman stepped over the tape and headed straight for Beth.

Too dazed to avoid him, she jumped out.

* * *

June, 2010

Shaking with shock, one hand against the wall to steady herself, the dreadful reality sank in. Her father had been *murdered!* He hadn't died of a heart attack; he'd been *stabbed to death!* What a pointless, wasteful thing! The paper wasn't wrong. It *was* her father who'd been killed. It was *his* blood she'd seen on the street—

She'd seen that blood before in the room with the shaman …

The gruesome, chant-induced vision clicked into context. Not *Allan's* blood – her father's! She'd seen her *father's* blood in that vision; seen what happened to *him.* She'd seen *his* past – her *future …*

The contents of her stomach heaved to her mouth, bitter and burning – she felt again the cloying heat of the darkened room; heard the strange pulsing tone of the old woman's voice; saw *her mother running away from her down a darkened street … Kennedy's head exploding … Anna's eyes, frightened and imploring … blood.*

Real.

All real!

She reached once more for the steadying wall, but it couldn't steady the riot in her head.

Why hadn't her mother told her?

Why did she lie?

In a fit of repulsion, she threw the clipping away from her – but it merely fluttered and landed by the bed, face-up, glaring at her like a cobra.

Had Nanna known?

Richard?

Why didn't they tell her? Didn't she deserve the truth?

And what about her father? Didn't he deserve it too

– didn't he deserve to have his story told? *Why* did they hide it? It wouldn't have made any difference, dead was dead, but—

And yet, it wasn't.

The manner of dying made a *big* difference. This new knowledge filled her with pain: thoughts of her father dying alone, violently, uselessly, desecrated her carefully gathered memories of his gentle joy. It was *much* easier to accept him going naturally and without fear.

A tear trickled over her chin and ran down her neck. She hadn't even realised she was crying, but now she couldn't stop. Grief ached through her chest: suffocating, crushing grief. When she opened her mouth it escaped in thick, heaving sobs that dragged at her throat and gave no relief – the hurt seemed only to deepen. It clawed at her heart and thrashed at the doors that held back her loss, threatening to release an unstoppable ocean that could never be emptied. And all she could do was fight for control. If she lost, she would drown.

Clenching her teeth, she tried to breathe the pain out … deep, panting breaths … and eventually … she succeeded – not to breathe it out, but to force it in.

She had no idea how long it took. The room was now dusky dark. Damp sweat covered her chest and her clothing plastered cool against her skin. Depleted, she leant back against the wall, waiting for strength, for the claggy slowness in her head to clear – but even in the vacuum that now filled her, a new resolve was hardening.

This wasn't right.

Chapter 40

Blaine was in a meeting when she called. He phoned as soon as he was free. He hadn't heard from Beth in over a year but he still felt uneasy about what he'd asked her to do, and what it had cost her. He often thought about her strange ability, and more than once considered the potential advantage he might gain in a case by capitalising on it, but he'd never once moved on the thought. The shattered look on her face as she'd run from the courtroom had been enough to stop that, and if it hadn't been, Frazer's sharp dressing downs, and Allan's cutting accusations and protective hedging, would have been.

But this time she was contacting him.

'Beth, how are you?' he opened brightly. He was walking across the street to the local cafe to get a coffee.

She cut, as always, straight to the point. 'Do you know anything about my father's murder?'

Blaine stopped short. 'What do you want to know?'

'Did you catch them? Are they in jail?'

Blaine had looked into the case when he'd first met Beth and her mother: basic background research. He had no difficulty recalling the details. 'No. Sorry. We never did. The investigation went on for some time, but there were few leads.'

There was a pause on the other end of the line. 'Can I see the files?'

Blaine was instantly wary.

'Well, there's not much there, Beth. There were no witnesses—'

'The paper said it was a gang.'

'Yes, well, that's just the papers. There was some trouble in that area at that time, but no one was apprehended. We didn't have anything, Beth. Just your mother's statement really, and some corroborating evidence from some of the staff and a couple of patrons of the restaurant your parents were eating at ... but no one saw anything.'

Again there was silence on the line.

'Have you spoken to your mother about—'

'She's dead.'

Dead?

'She died last year.' Beth's tone softened a little. 'Stroke. Can I see her statement?'

'Well, I ...'

'Are there any pictures?'

'Beth, you're not thinking—'

'I don't know what I'm thinking. I only just found out about this, through an old newspaper clipping, which you're telling me is inaccurate. I just want to know what happened.'

'It was a simple mugging. Your father was trying to

get some money out of an ATM and he was attacked and killed. A simple mugging, Beth.'

'Which ATM?'

'There's no CCTV footage.'

'I just want to know what happened!'

Blaine sighed. 'I'm not sure which one. Somewhere on Sussex Street. I'd have to check the files. The ATM might not even be there any more. And there are only forensic photographs, all after-the-fact, of your father, and the scene.'

'I've been to the scene. And I don't want to see … the other … Just the statements, then. Can I have a copy of the statements?'

Blaine heard the hurt behind her words, but her voice was calm and determined. 'Beth—'

'Please.'

He let out another long sigh. 'OK. I'll track it down. I'll text you when I have it and we'll set up a meeting.'

'Thank you,' she said, and cut off without further conversation.

Shaking his head, Blaine pocketed his phone and stepped into the cafe. He was troubled. He suspected that giving Beth that kind of information wouldn't bring anything good, but he couldn't refuse her either.

* * *

Allan cuddled up next to her on the couch and handed her a glass of wine.

'I can understand why your mum might not have wanted to tell you,' he said gently. 'It wouldn't have been a nice thing for a kid to know.'

'No, I guess not. I'm not a kid now though.'

Allan only nodded.

'I know she just didn't want to hurt me,' Beth conceded, 'and it wouldn't have made him any less dead. Nicer to think of him going naturally ...'

'I'm sorry, babe,' said Allan, pulling her close. 'It's shit, any way you look at it.'

'Yeah, I guess.'

Laying her head against his shoulder she settled into a thick silence. Never a good sign, as far as Allan was concerned. He glanced at her sideways. 'What?'

'Nothing.'

'Come on, what is it?'

'It's just, well ... they never caught them.'

'Oh, Beth!'

'Well, they didn't.'

Allan pulled away. 'You're not thinking—'

'It's not going to hurt anything if I can get some more information.'

'Like you did with Anna?'

That brought a flash to her eyes. 'They killed my father!'

'It was twenty years ago, Beth.'

'That doesn't mean they should get away with it! They're killers. Who knows what they've done since, what they're doing now?'

'They could be *dead*. Maybe they're married, with kids? Maybe they found Jesus and are running a Salvation Army mission somewhere!'

Beth's eyes hardened to an almost steely black. 'They still should pay for it!'

'Beth—'

'Look, I can do a lot more now than when I tried to

help Anna. I can do it invisibly. I won't be in any danger. I just have to see if I can get anything to help Blaine. If I can, that's good, and if I—'

'If you *can't*, you'll just walk away?' He was angry now.

'I have to try.'

Her chin set firm. It was clear she'd made up her mind.

Huffing, Allan got up from the couch and walked to the window. Arms crossed, he glowered at her. 'How are you even going to do it? You said there were no pictures.'

'I'll just have to find some then. There's got to be something out there, somewhere.'

'Right. You do that then,' said Allan, shaking his head. 'I'm going to bed.'

Turning his back, he walked into their bedroom. It was a severe statement from him; they never went to sleep without connection. Beth knew she was supposed to follow him and resolve it – but if resolve meant giving up before she'd even tried, she couldn't do it.

Staring down into her wine, she let him leave.

* * *

July, 2010

Ming Cha Restaurant capitalised on its long, successful years of business. Elaborate Chinese tapestries imported from the founding family's restaurant in China adorned the walls; the original carved wooden counter from the first Australian establishment graced the foyer; and they'd retained their signature lantern lighting fix-tures. Decorating the wall behind the reception counter were photographs of famous faces who'd eaten there over the years. There was also an old photograph of the original family restaurant in China, taken in the early 1950s, and another of the opening of the Sussex Street restaurant in 1981. These were the only two photographs that were dated.

Sitting at a small table near the door, Beth was disheartened. When she'd discovered the restaurant was still in business she thought it would be worth a visit, but although it gave some idea of what it was like when her parents ate there in 1992, it offered no other clues. She stared dismally into her short soup. She'd found nothing in her internet searches either, and after a frustrating afternoon trawling through the newspaper archives at the State Library all she'd come up with was the original article reporting her father's murder. She knew she'd only just scraped the surface and that there were many other publications to search through, but it was a daunting task. Overwhelmed, she abandoned her soup and went to the counter to pay. The famous faces seemed to leer at her failure, mocking her. Actors and actresses, TV stars, politicians, musicians. Most of them meant nothing to her, but she recognised a few faces. The present leader of the Liberal Party had pride of place, and in the second row was a picture of Alexander Reilly, a moderately famous Hollywood actor who'd been making movies since the mid-80s.

'I see Alexander Reilly came here,' said Beth as the waiter arrived. He lit up in a smile.

'Yes, many famous people come here. You see Narelle Adams there?'

Beth nodded politely. 'Oh, yes. Fun! Did you meet them?'

'No. Before my time.'

He handed her the bill and she paid in cash and waited for the change. Putting it away in her purse, she tried to sound casual. 'I heard there was a murder near here too.'

The waiter looked confused.

'Just down the street, at an ATM? One of the diners from this restaurant? He was getting money from the ATM.'

The waiter's confusion didn't clear.

'Back in 1992,' Beth prompted. 'It happened in 1992, just down the street. Were you here then?'

At last the man's face showed understanding.

'Oh, yes! No! Not here then. Before my time.'

A little depressed, Beth thanked him and left.

* * *

Narelle Adams was a theatre actor, a local Sydney girl. The photograph of her could have been taken at any time between the mid-80s and 90s. It would be hard to pin down her visit to an exact date. But Alexander Reilly was an American film star. According to an internet movie database he'd only made one film in Australia: 'Wild Ride'. It was released in 1993 but filming was in late 1991. A little early – and the only photographs of him taken in Australia that she could find were publicity shots from October 1991.

At least one thing was obvious: the internet was the repository of millions of photographs, possibly billions, and each of them represented a potential doorway to somewhere, sometime. But how to find the *right* doorway – the one that led back to January 14, 1992?

She'd just have to be more specific in her searches.

Switching to date and location, she almost immediately came up with some pictures of a live performance by Kurt Cobain at the Phoenician Club in Ultimo. It was an old cinema, converted into a live entertainment venue, and it wasn't far from the Ming Cha – but the date of the performance was January 24, 1992, more than a week too late.

Doggedly she continued, searching for other possible shows or concerts, other events, other venues, but all her leads trailed into nothing. There were pictures from a charity event at Government House held on the fourteenth, but in the afternoon, way too early for entry. And there were pictures of a birthday party that someone had posted on Facebook years later to celebrate an anniversary. They were closer to the right time, but in Palm Beach, the other side of the city. There were write-ups of events in the city centre that night, but no photographs.

Hours of searching turned into days. She became increasingly irritable and frustrated, but couldn't let it go.

A week after she'd contacted Blaine, he got back to her. It was nine in the morning and she was walking into class. He said he had the file and they set up an appointment to meet, but when they did, it was as he'd said. The file contained little of any use, nothing about any suspects, no photographs and no information about the gangs. No further information could be wheeled out of him either. The only possible lead Beth gained was the exact location of the ATM on Sussex Street. It wasn't much, but at least if she could find a way in she'd know where to go.

Her mother's statement didn't give her much either, other than details of her parents' last evening together: how they'd eaten at the Ming Cha and how her father had gone to the ATM to get some cash while her mother waited for him. It was hard to read. She appreciated that Blaine left her alone with a cup of tea in the interview room to read it, but nothing could make it easier. Her mother's transcribed words were so vivid and so stark. She could almost hear her saying them. The statement had been taken the evening after her father's murder, at the hospital, just hours after Beth's sister had been born.

So, her mother had lost two people in almost the same breath.

They'd never spoken much of her sister. It wasn't a topic her mother liked, and Beth suspected she might not have told her at all if she hadn't been so obviously pregnant in the lagoon photograph. But only basic information had been offered: she'd had a sister, but it had been a still birth; there'd been something wrong with the baby.

She'd never been told it happened so close to her father's death.

A flood of pity filled her for her mother, and also a new respect. What a strong woman she must have been to rebuild her life after that.

'I'm sorry, Beth,' Blaine said kindly. He was standing in the doorway. Taking the seat opposite, he gave her a moment to say something, and when she didn't, he ventured into the gap. 'You know, there are counsellors for this kind of thing … to help … with situations like this …'

'They can solve twenty-year-old murder cases, can they? Bring back two lives?'

'You're not the only one who's lost someone, Beth.'

It wasn't a rebuke and she didn't take it that way. She could see his compassion.

'I know that life is very different for you … and no one is ever really going to understand how it is for you … but losing a loved one, traumatically, like this … well, there are people trained to help with things like that, good people.'

She didn't want this.

'Thanks, but I—'

'You've got too much to carry, Beth,' he persisted. 'We all need a little help sometimes.'

'I've got Allan.'

'Does he know what you're doing?'

A blush flushed to Beth's cheeks. 'I need to get some peace on this, just for me. I need to *know.*'

'And if you find out? If you discover who murdered your father?'

'I'll bring it to you, and you can find a way to lock them up.'

Blaine let out a deep sigh. 'For God's sake, be careful, Beth. After what happened last time—'

'I will.' She cut him off, the edge in her voice clearly designating the conversation as over. She put the file down on the table and left the room without another word.

* * *

The next day she found it.

She'd left early for university, telling Allan she had research to do for her assignments – which was true, her university work was slipping worryingly behind, though she had no intention of rectifying that yet.

She searched out a quiet spot in the library, logged on to the internet and set to work. For the first hour, she hit nothing but dry leads, but then another photograph of Alexander Reilly turned up. It was taken in 1992, but later, in June. The interesting thing was that it was taken by a fan and was published on a fan site. On this site were links to other fan sites, other galleries of 'Alexander photographs'. There were many such sites on the net, and many of them featured amateur shots and obscure articles that weren't published anywhere else. Alexander apparently liked to party and didn't mind posing for fans; and his fans were almost rabid about sharing. After another four hours of jumping from site to site and trawling through countless galleries, Beth discovered a scanned article from an obscure American magazine about a sighting of Alex in Australia. He was reported exiting a bar, disguised with a fake moustache – *and there was a photograph!*

More than that, there was an address and a date: the Civic Hotel on Pitt Street, Tuesday night, January 14, 1992.

No time was mentioned, but the writer of the article said it was 'early in the evening'.

Chapter 41

She had it! Assuming the photograph was taken at a usable time, she had a way in – but to do what? What could she achieve? Even if she got a good look at the gang members, would it help? Pointing out someone's face in a twenty-year-old mug shot, without any evidence, wasn't likely to be enough. And Allan could be right. They might all be dead or in prison already. What good would it do?

Could she even *do* it – stand by and do nothing while her father was murdered, just to identify his murderers? It was hard enough just coming to terms with what had happened, but to witness the actual act?

No. Not possible.

But neither could she walk away. How could it be right to know something evil was going to happen and do nothing to stop it? If it was possible to stop it – even if only for her – then shouldn't it be done? Surely, the fact she *could* do it made it part of the natural order of things? Her choice might be unique, but the very fact she *had* a choice must mean she had a right to use it; maybe even a responsibility. And hadn't the shaman said that doors were only closed to her because she didn't know how to use the keys? Well, now she knew! Now she *could* walk through those doors – so surely she was supposed to.

But walk through to do what?

How could she stop this?

The best thing would be to keep her father away from the ATM and the gang altogether. How? Would he listen to her? Would she be able to convince him?

When it all came down to it, there was only one way to resolve this, only one way to find out. She'd have to go there and try!

* * *

7.45 p.m., Tuesday evening, January 14, 1992

She stepped into pandemonium. The photographer

was about a metre from his prey. Alexander was surrounded by a group of hangers-on who were swinging haphazardly in all directions.

Instinctively, she dropped to her knees and materialised before anyone could bump into her. Almost immediately one of the hangers-on – a skeletally thin but exceptionally beautiful girl of about Beth's age – tripped over her. Fortunately, she was also exceptionally drunk, as were most of her companions, and no one seemed to think it out of place that Beth was crouched on the ground in their path. She was helped up, apologised to and quickly ignored.

But not before she managed to get the time; it was 7.49 p.m.

A little early, but not too late.

She realised she might need to wait up to an hour before she could make contact with her father but, pumped with adrenaline, she didn't doubt she could do it. She was determined to.

After gaining her bearings, she headed for the restaurant. She'd memorised the route and had no difficulty finding it. Most of the buildings looked the same, though the Market City Complex hadn't been built yet. The original Paddy's Market facade stood empty, poised between excavation and construction.

Withdrawing to a dark entryway, Beth resigned herself to waiting. There was some time to go. Positioned on the other side of the street – a little further up from the restaurant, towards the intersection of Sussex and Hay streets where the ATM was – she had a good view of the Ming Cha and was satisfied she wouldn't miss anything. As the minutes dragged on, she distracted herself from her gathering migraine by shifting her weight from foot to foot and gently stamping on the hard pavement. It helped a little, and eventually her father appeared and headed her way. As soon as he'd passed her spot, she stepped out of the shadows.

'Excuse me … Excuse me!'

He turned to face her, surprised. 'Are you talking to me?'

Nanna's eyes stared back at her.

'Yes,' she puffed, faking breathlessness as her heart pounded wildly. 'There's a gang, up on Hay Street. I've just come from there. They're drunk. They beat this guy up. Don't go up there. They're crazy!'

He looked at her without comprehension. 'A gang?'

'Yes. Up there. We have to call the police!'

Now his look turned doubtful. He took a half step back. 'Someone got beaten up? Did you—'

'Yes! We need to call the police!' She looked around wildly and gestured to the Ming Cha. 'They'll have a phone, we can call there.' She reached for him – but he raised his hands.

'OK … you do that. Call 000. Tell them to send an ambulance. I'll go and see if I can do anything.'

'*No! Don't go up there!*' She grabbed his arm. 'There's too many of them!'

'Take it easy, I'm just going to take a look. I'm an ambulance offic—'

'They'll *kill* you!' She was almost frantic. 'They have a *knife! I saw* it!' She felt him stiffen – but couldn't let go; every second she held him back was a second he wasn't walking to his doom. Irritation flashed in his eyes – but then he switched tactics. He stopped resisting, calmed his features and adopted a manner a professional might use when addressing a frightened child – or a psych case.

'Go and call 000,' he said patiently, gently but firmly reaching for her clinging hand. 'Get them to send an ambulance. I'll just take a look and come straight back. OK?'

She let go, wilting under his pity, and he turned and walked on.

Standing alone, her head pounding, bile burning her throat, she could only watch as he approached the intersection of Sussex and Hay.

* * *

7.45 p.m., Tuesday evening, January 14, 1992

This time, Beth stayed invisible and dived out of the way of the skeletally thin girl; managing to scurry to the side without connecting with any of them.

It wasn't easy with the sledgehammer.

Crouching against the wall, she watched as her previous self departed for Sussex Street. She followed invisibly as far as Hay Street, where she found refuge in a darkened alcove opposite the ATM. Resting against the cool of the brick wall, she took a moment to recoup before materialising. Edging to the boundary of the shadows, she peered out at the street. Fortunately, it was empty. She didn't want witnesses.

With thudding heart she adjusted her grip on the sledgehammer, launched herself out into the light and bound across the street. The following moments passed in a blur. Rage exploded out of her and smashed into the machine; rage at what the machine had cost her; at what she had lost. She thought of nothing but destroying it – completely – oblivious even to her own screams of exertion and mindless to the fact that her goal had been achieved at the first explosion of metal on metal. Only when her fury had lost the strength to drive her did she stop and step back, her chest heaving and her arms struggling with the weight of the sledge hammer. She glared up, triumphant – and saw a man watching her. In an almost manic impulse of 'fuck you', she considered dematerialising in front of him; instead, she turned and walked around the corner and out of sight.

Chapter 42

It was mid-afternoon when Allan got home from university. He heard her being sick as he opened the front door and was well aware what that probably meant. Walking into the bathroom, he found her on the floor with her face hovering over the toilet.

'Hi honey, I'm home,' he quipped, making no attempt to dampen the sarcasm in his tone. 'I see you've had a busy day.'

Beth merely panted, still recovering from what had obviously been a violent spasm of vomiting.

The room reeked.

Unable to offer sympathy, Allan went to make himself a cup of tea. Freshened up but still decidedly pale, Beth joined him a few minutes later. She stood in the doorway, hesitating as though trying to decide what to say, and then walked to the table where she picked up the printed-out article with the photograph and held it up to show him.

Allan couldn't read it from where he was standing, but he understood what it was. 'You found a picture,' he said heavily.

She nodded. 'An hour earlier, and a few blocks away, but it works.'

'Congratulations.'

'Don't be a dick,' she snapped. She put the article back on the table and reached for the newspaper clipping.

Instantly, her face fell.

'It hasn't changed,' she said in disbelief. 'It still says he was killed.'

Now Allan was worried. 'What were you expecting?'

Beth ignored him, continuing to read through the article.

'Beth? What did you do?'

'I went back. I tried to stop him but he wouldn't listen, so I went back again and destroyed the ATM.'

Allan's eyes shot wide. 'You did *what?*'

'I smashed the fucking ATM. With a sledge hammer.'

Allan was speechless. Shaking his head, he walked past her and flopped down on the couch.

'Well, he couldn't use it if it was broken, could he,' argued Beth, 'and those thugs wouldn't be hanging around it looking for a victim either, so I thought he'd be safe.'

'Safe?' Allan was flabbergasted. 'I thought you were going to stay out of meddling with the past? *That* would be safe! I thought you were just trying to get evidence for Blaine, to get the guys who did it, not—'

'I couldn't do it!' She rounded on him. 'Would you be able to watch your mother dying and do nothing?'

Allan dropped his head in his hands. 'God! I don't believe this!'

'It didn't work, anyway. The clipping says they still killed him at the ATM. But, how could they? How could that happen? I got rid of the ATM!'

'I've no idea, Beth.' His voice was dull and flat.

'Wait a minute …' she said, her cheeks flushing. 'The picture's different! That's not where it happened – oh wait … *George Street?*' She looked up, confused. 'It says he was stabbed at an ATM on *George* Street – not *Sussex* Street!'

Allan's expression remained blank, but hers transitioned into awe. 'It *did* change. Allan, it used to be *Sussex* Street!'

'What are you talking about?'

'Look.' She thrust the clipping at him. 'It says *George* Street, but he wasn't on George Street, he was on *Sussex* Street, at the corner of Sussex and Hay. And I smashed that ATM—'

A further realisation hit.

'He must have gone to another ATM!'

She ran back to the table and exchanged the clipping for a printout of a Sydney Street map she'd used to find the restaurant. Just around the corner from Sussex Street, intersecting Hay, was George Street. A narrow block separated them, just one building wide. The two streets met Hay like a bended elbow.

'He went around the corner …He went around the corner, to *another* ATM!'

Chapter 43

It was a miserable afternoon for Allan, the cap to a miserable week, and the evening was no better. He was grateful Beth had at least come home – after storming out of the flat and ignoring his texts for hours – but nothing was resolved. At least, not for him. He still couldn't believe she'd actually destroyed an ATM!

She'd said she was *sorry*, but not for what she'd done, only because he wanted her to stop and she couldn't. *He* was her only regret; she didn't want to hurt him – which he appreciated, but it wasn't enough to hold her back. She was like a missile, already launched, with no abort button. And there was only one end for missiles.

He'd made her supper, hoping that after she'd finished in the bathroom she might be willing to talk, but she didn't even want to eat. She'd begged off tired and retreated to bed. Abandoned, his heart sank at the emptiness she'd brought home with her. It washed up against the walls of their flat like a rising tide, seeping into the soles of his naked feet with a desolate chill as he lingered in the living room. Craving her warmth, he followed her into the bedroom – but when he pulled up the covers to join her, she curled onto her side, facing away. Not hostile, but not approachable either. Aching against the space between them, he lay in the dark, waiting for sleep to take him, hoping the morning would make it better.

There was no sleep for Beth either. She didn't want to cut him off, but there was no point in fighting about it. Allan was *wrong*. The past *wasn't* unchangeable; she'd already changed it. Sussex Street had become George Street. So it *was* possible. And the world hadn't ended: in fact, remarkably little seemed to have altered. Allan hadn't even noticed the difference. But it *had* changed – and if she could change things in a small way, then she must be able to change them in bigger ways. She only needed to figure out how to make the changes go the way she wanted them to.

Restlessly, deep into the night, she pulled at the tangled threads of possibility as Allan's breathing gradually succumbed to its slower sleep pattern. She was relieved for him, and for her; it left her free to think. But she wasn't making much progress. She kept coming back to the same place: she needed to keep her father from going to the ATM, but couldn't think of a way to stop him.

One thing was certain – she couldn't confront him again. She'd burnt her bridges there. A second appearance would be even *more* threatening and freakish. The only way to stop him now would be to get someone *else* to do it: someone he'd respect; an authority figure, or someone he knew.

Her mother was the obvious choice. He'd listen to her. But it would be just as hard to get her to cooperate. She wouldn't like a stranger coming at her out of the blue either.

Time was the real problem. It put a lot of pressure on things when a response was required straight away and there was no time to build up credibility.

Then she realised – time was something she had! She wasn't limited to visiting her mother just *once*; she could visit her as many times as needed to get her trust, or at least to spark her curiosity. She could take time to build a relationship, so that when she approached her on that final night she'd at least recognise her and, hopefully, be ready to listen.

But what should she say?

Claiming to have seen a gang hadn't worked with her father and probably wouldn't with her mother either. But what else was there?

Psychic knowledge?

That could explain how she knew her father was in danger, and her mother *had* eventually accepted psychic ability as an explanation for what she'd known about Anna ... but it had taken a *long* time ... and she hadn't accepted it easily ...

Perhaps it would be simplest and quickest to just present herself as paranormal from the start? She could say she was a guardian angel, watching over her. That wouldn't be hard to make her believe, all she'd have to do would be to make appearances throughout her mother's life, always looking the same, never ageing. That would make it clear she was beyond time if nothing else. And if she was beyond time, she'd obviously know what was going to happen. Her warning would carry the weight of angelic fore-knowledge, and *that* wouldn't be so easy to dismiss.

This was a plan that could work!

She'd have to be careful, of course, she couldn't let her mother know who she *really* was as that would affect their whole lives together – and she'd need to make sure she didn't spook her too much when she visited her throughout her life as that could also change things in the wrong direction. She had to be seen and remembered – but not *too* seen, not *too* remembered. The best thing would be if her mother didn't put it all together, didn't even notice she was being regularly visited, until that final moment when she had to be persuaded to stop her father from going to the ATM. Quite a task – but with a whole lifetime of moments in her mother's photograph album, it shouldn't be too hard. She only needed to pick and space her visits to make them less obvious.

The plan buzzed through her. She couldn't wait until morning; and she didn't want to lie to Allan, not to his face – so, as silently as possible, she slipped out of bed, struggled into her jeans and a T-shirt, tugged on her shoes, retrieved her mother's album from under the bed, grabbed her bag and coat, and crept out of the bedroom and out of the flat.

Chapter 44

This was the last one. Just one more appearance: one final reminder before she confronted her mother at the restaurant. For her mother, this would be the second time she'd see her that day, including the accidental appearance in the park. Beth figured that two appearances in one day would get attention – and now was the time for her mother to start putting it all together. Beth was pretty sure she hadn't made any full connections yet, but she was close.

It was her previous visit (a month before in her mother's time, ten minutes in hers), that really got the ball rolling. Her mother had taken her to have her photograph taken on Santa's knee at the local shopping mall, resulting in an adorable picture of her toddler-self sitting bright eyed on a pleasantly fat Santa's lap. Not the easiest of photographs to enter through – it was tight dodging the professional photographer, and an over-excited child had actually seen her physicalise behind Santa's sleigh – but it was a good opportunity for a random appearance, and the child's squalling alerts were easily dismissed. For once, her red coat worked as camouflage; she looked like part of the show.

Exiting the glittering cardboard enclosure and separating from the crowd, Beth had waited for her mother, and when she wheeled the pram out of the crowd, distracted with her purse, she'd stepped directly into her path.

Gillian had pulled up short and graciously apologised. Beth had smiled and moved out of her way.

The interaction was unremarkable – but Beth had seen the resonation in her eyes.

Her mother was remembering, or beginning to. A lifetime of visitations were connecting, clicking into place. It took a moment – her mother hadn't seen her for nearly ten years, not since London, and on that occasion she'd only been interested in Mike – but it was coming back.

And now, a month later, her recognition was no longer hesitant – but also not fully connected. One more appearance should do, thought Beth. Something a little more obvious, a little more dramatic.

5.45 p.m., Tuesday evening, January 14, 1992

Invisible, she watched from the footpath in front of her parents' home in Manly.

She was waiting for herself to leave.

She couldn't see her previous self, but she knew she was there. When she judged she'd left, she walked through the gap in the low brick wall and approached the window.

Her mother was still by the table, distracted with toddler Lili.

A perfect opportunity.

She took it, physicalising quickly.

The sudden transformation – matter materialising out of nothing – caught her mother's peripheral attention. She looked up, and for a second their eyes met.

Beth saw her startled look and wanted to say something to her, to reassure her – but instead she reached out her hand and slowly placed it, palm flat, against the glass.

Chapter 45

8.35 p.m., Tuesday evening, January 14, 1992

Gillian couldn't let it go. She was glad Mike had insisted they still go out for dinner, it at least gave them a chance to talk, but it was hardly the relaxed night out they'd anticipated. She barely tasted her food and she couldn't be distracted from endlessly rehashing the possible intentions and identity of their stalker – for that was what she clearly was. A stalker!

Mike wasn't sure what to think. He couldn't, logically, see any danger in the girl but her harassment was a nuisance and she was worrying Gillian. This level of stress wasn't good for her and the cyclic conversation was draining him.

'What if she's after Lili?' Gillian reached for his hand. 'She's clearly unbalanced. She obviously wants *something*. Why not Lili?'

He placed his other hand over hers, encasing it. 'Lili's

safe with your mum. It's a secure block. She'd never get in.'

'We should call her. Warn her.'

'That'd just put her into a panic.'

'We have to do something!'

It was a plaintive cry – and the evening was ruined in any case. 'Fine. We'll go home.'

'And call the police?'

He let out a tired sigh. 'OK. First thing tomorrow. All right?'

Slowly she nodded and then relaxed. 'I have to go to the loo.'

'Then I'll go pay.' He smiled, but the smile didn't quite reach his eyes. Gillian felt a stab of guilt.

'Sorry.'

'It's OK, honey. I don't think the police will do anything, but telling them won't hurt. And if it makes you feel better—'

'It does.' She offered him a much-recovered smile and picked up her purse to head for the toilet. Her bladder was dangerously full. Fortunately, the restroom was empty. She squeezed into the single booth and relaxed into the task at hand. It was nice to sit in the quiet. After a moment, someone else entered, so she finished up as quickly as she could and exited, a smile ready – and froze. Standing in front of her was the girl in the red coat.

She almost cried out – but the girl quickly raised her hands. 'Don't ... I'm not going to hurt you.'

'Who are you?' Gillian was so frightened she could barely speak. Her tongue was thick and dry. 'What do you want? Why are you *stalking* me?'

'I'm not stalking you. I'm here to warn you. Your

husband … he's in danger. Don't let him go to the ATM.'

'What are you talking about? Who *are* you?'

'Someone who cares. Someone who cares very much. Listen, there's a gang out there, attacking people on the streets. Don't let your husband go to the ATM.'

'*What ATM?*'

Gillian's panic was escalating. Beth could see pushing her further wasn't going to work. She had to hope she'd said enough. With one last pleading look, she turned and fled.

Gillian stared as the door thudded shut, but then quickly flared to the attack. She hauled the door open and raced after Beth, running heavily down the narrow passage back into the restaurant, her high heels clicking aggressively against the tiles – but there was no sign of her: no red coat at the door or beyond on the street; no red coat at any of the tables. No sign of *any* girl with wild dark hair and striking brown eyes.

Behind her was the kitchen, open to the restaurant. The girl was not there either, and the kitchen staff, tautly focused, showed none of the ripples of disturbance that a stranger fleeing through their sanctum would have caused.

Mike was at the counter, putting his credit card back in his wallet, equally unflustered. Gillian hurried over to him, bouncing between the tables like a pinball through the gates, almost knocking an elderly man out of his chair with her over-large stomach.

'They can't take credit cards. The machine's broken,' said Mike in greeting. 'I need to go to an ATM.'

Gillian's heart lurched in her chest.

'It's not a problem,' he smiled, 'there's one just down

the street. I won't be a minute. You wait here, or go to the car if you like. I can meet you there.'

'No!' She grabbed his arm, finding her voice. 'The girl – the girl in the red coat – she was in the restroom. She *spoke* to me!'

Mike was caught off guard. He ushered her gently outside to give them some privacy.

Her eyes were wide with fright as the words spilled out. 'She came into the toilet – the girl – and she was standing there – waiting for me. She told me to stop you from going.'

'What? Wait, slow down. What are you—?'

'How did she know you were going to an ATM? *I* didn't!'

'Gilly—'

'It was *her!*'

They were blocking the threshold of the restaurant; the cashier was eying them disapprovingly through the window. Mike gently led her aside and lowered his tone.

'Where is she? Where's the girl?'

'Didn't she go out past you?'

'No. And I was right by the door the whole time.'

The information seemed to stab at her. She drew back, confused. Mike laid a hand gently on her shoulder. 'Honey, you were the only one who went back to the restrooms, and no one else came out. I would have seen.'

'I … I don't understand…'

Mike's concern was deepening. 'Sweetheart, you're tired, you've been under a lot of strain. You know the doctor told you to rest, this is too much. Go back to the car. I won't be a minute, and then we'll go home.'

'What? No – I—' but before she could say anything

else, Mike leant down to kiss her on the forehead and headed off.

'Gillian!'

Gillian spun to face the voice behind her. It was Beth, standing in the recessed entrance of the neighbouring shop.

Gillian advanced on her. 'Who the hell *are* you?' she demanded. 'What are you doing? What is going on here?'

Over her mother's shoulder, Beth could see her previous self waiting to approach her father. She eased deeper into the alcove; out of sight from her previous self; out of sight from her father, should he turn around – and Gillian pursued. 'What do you want?'

Beth had never seen her mother this angry. 'I told you … I just wanted to warn—'

'How did you know about the ATM?'

Her mother's voice was rising dangerously, her eyes flashing wildly. Beth jettisoned all thoughts of claiming to be an angel. 'I'm … from the future!' It came out on an impulse – but it got her mother's attention. Whatever her mother had been expecting, it wasn't that. Her mouth dropped open in a stunned gape. Beth took a deep breath and continued as evenly as she could. 'I came back in time, to warn you. I've been visiting you all your life … the school photographs … the beach … The Trevi Fountain … London … just so you'd know me, so you'd listen. I didn't want to frighten you, but I didn't know how else to reach you, and I had to get you to listen – because if you don't stop Mike going to that ATM, he's going to be killed! You're going to be a widow!'

'The future …?' Gillian's eyes glazed over. 'How …? Why …? Why are you—'

'Because ... I'm your granddaughter! I'm Lili's daughter.'

How else could she explain it? She couldn't say she was Lili, because that would colour their entire relationship, it would change *everything*. But her mother wouldn't live long enough to taint any relationship with future grandchildren. And she had to say something! Her previous self would be gone by now. Her father would be discovering the smashed ATM. Soon he'd head up to George Street. *She was running out of time!*

Right or wrong, she was committed now. 'I love him too,' she said, her voice quavering. 'And if you don't save him, we *all* lose him. Lili will never have a dad! *Please*,' she begged. 'Please, just trust me! Run after him and stop him. *Quick!*'

The last word was almost a shout. It jolted through Gillian like an electric current, jarring her into function. Turning, she saw Mike rounding the corner. Without a further word, she kicked off her high heels, picked them up, and ran up the street after him.

Beth ran after her.

The gang was already circling Mike when they reached the corner; their arrival went unnoticed. Mike was backed against the ATM, his hands raised in defence. They were jabbing his chest, spitting out aggressive demands. His voice was lost in the din.

A knife glinted.

'Nooooo!'

It happened so fast. Gillian threw herself in front of her husband, swinging her shoes as a weapon. She caught one of them a vicious blow to the cheek before he lunged back at her and knocked the shoes out of her hands.

Beth froze in surprise, but Mike reacted instantly. He elbowed the man in the face and pulled his wife out of the way. The thug yelled and fell to the ground; but the others then dived at him – punching – kicking – stabbing.

Beth jumped into the fray, yelling and pounding her fists into the kidneys of the nearest thug. There were satisfying *thwumps*, but it didn't stop him. His elbow swung back at her, hitting her in the chest, winding her. She was knocked to the ground – but as she went down she heard the man grunt with pain as her father's boot connected with his groin. He caved away – and she scrambled up to stand by her father, gasping for breath, braced for further attack – but it never came. A shout rang out from further down the street; someone was running towards them, and the gang scattered – rats skittering into the darkness.

They were left alone.

Safe.

It was over.

Beth turned to her father, exulted. *He was alive!* His face was a little bloodied, his nose battered, but nothing that looked life threatening.

She'd done it!

Tears rushed to her eyes – but then her father dropped to the ground, a look of utter horror on his face.

At his feet, curled awkwardly, with her mouth open in wordless shock, her mother lay on the pavement … blood pulsing steadily out of a deep slice in her arm pit.

Chapter 46

The returning was like no other she'd experienced. Memories flooded in like a rabid dream – half remembered, charged with emotion, carrying icebergs of connection that sank into murky depths. Swirling … overtaking … swamping.

Beth fell to her hands and knees, retching acid bile over her shaking fingers as the torrent washed over her like a tsunami – sweeping away all that was established and leaving a new landscape in its wake, crushed and raw, on the desecration of the old.

Straining to drag air into her lungs, she stared unseeing at the mess on the carpet, fighting the violent shuddering that threatened to overwhelm her.

She remembered *two* realities: one – growing up with her mother and Richard – and another – parallel and intertwined – growing up with her father and stepmother, Julie.

Birthdays, Christmases, school parent nights … all doubled, blended, merged: *cuddling up to her father as a child being read to … making pancakes with her mother … meeting Richard for the first time … being a bridesmaid with her step-sister at her father's wedding—*

He was alive!

Her father was *alive!*

Barely able to keep herself from crumbling into a heap, Beth crawled to the sideboard and grabbed her phone. She opened the contacts and scrolled down. Alarm spiralled at the unfamiliar names – yet they didn't *stay* unfamiliar. As each name reached her mind, associative memories clicked into place.

Again her stomach heaved.

What had she done?

And then, there it was – *'Dad'.*

Her heart leapt with joy – then clenched in fright.

Allan!

Terrified, she scrolled back; but she already knew. *Allan's name was not on her contact list.*

* * *

'Dad?'

'Beth! Where are you?'

His voice sounded tense, strained … and achingly familiar. Tears flooded her eyes. Talking to him was so *right*, so part of her life, part of everything she knew – and yet, so wrong!

'I … I … don't know …' she shivered, looking around the room properly for the first time. It wasn't the same hotel room she checked into yesterday … yester*life*. The walls were a rich, clean cream in the warm afternoon sun; the bedspread was trimmed with gold.

'I don't know where I am … I don't know what happened … I … What did I *do?*'

There was a moment's silence on the other end of the line.

'Honey, listen to me, it's OK. You're OK. Just, take a deep breath …'

'Where am I? … Dad, what did I do?'

'Are you hurt?'

She had to think a moment. 'My head … is splitting.' She reached a hand up, trying to push out the pain. 'I need … something … for my head.'

A wave of dizziness hit her and her stomach gripped treacherously.

'Beth … darling … where are you?'

The unfamiliarity of the room assaulted her.

She was now shaking so hard she could barely hold the phone. Swapping it to her other hand, she felt the slip of her skin against the plastic. Sweat mixed with blood; on her clothes as well as her hand.

Not *her* blood.

'There's blood …'

Her voice was tiny, thin, and the room disappeared in a melee of images: *her mother … lying on the ground … blood pumping from her arm … puddling in the gutter …*

There was no strength left in her to scream, though screaming was what instinct called for.

What had she done?

'Beth? *Beth!*'

She tried to block him out. *He shouldn't be there …*

'Honey! Honey, please, talk to me. I need to know

where you are, so I can come and get you. Do you understand?'

Beth had heard those exact words before ... many times ... *other* times. He'd rescued her before.

He knew! She'd *told* him – told *others* ... but none of them believed her: not her father, and not the others.

Holding her down ... needles stabbing into her ... electrodes on her temples ...

'Beth? Are you listening to me, honey?'

White walls ... locked doors ... questions ... tests ...

'Beth!'

Worried despondency on her father's face ... fear and hatred on Julie's ... memories blurred ... disjointed ... not all there ...

She was *insane!*

The realisation hit her with a sudden certainty. *He* thought she was insane; they *all* did. He wanted to come and get her to take her back to where she could get treatment!

'Honey?'

She hung up.

Allan. Where was he? She couldn't lose him. He must be alive, somewhere. If he wasn't in her contacts list on her phone, then *this* Beth probably just hadn't met him yet – but that didn't mean she *couldn't* meet him. He had to be out there somewhere. She just had to find him.

She scrambled up from the floor and lurched to the window. It was a city hotel. Still Sydney. *Thank God for that!*

But what was she doing in a hotel?

Why had she come here?

Another memory clicked into place – *to save her mum.* In this alternate reality, where she'd grown up with her father, it was her *mother* she'd been trying to save.

And she'd failed.

Her mother's eyes staring … blood pooling around her arm …

On the bed lay a yellowed newspaper clipping:

YOUNG MOTHER SLAIN AT CITY ATM

Beth stared at the headline as the implications reverberated.

What else had changed?

Memories of both realities shuffled together. It was hard to tell them apart. Which was from before … and which was now?

But then, some began to solidify, dominate – and others began to *fade.*

That hadn't happened before.

She'd always remembered, even when Allan had forgotten. When things changed, she remembered *both* realities, perfectly. When her father had gone to the George Street ATM, she remembered he'd first gone to Sussex Street. She'd remembered *everything.*

Hadn't she?

Frighteningly, her mind went blank.

What was it she'd remembered?

Gone.

… and other things were going!

Panicked, she grabbed a sheet of complimentary hotel paper and a pen from the sideboard and wrote as fast as she could: *Dad was killed at ATM. Not Mum. I live with Allan.*

It was fading.

Allan. Allan Watson! He knows everything. He loves me. I love him. We go to uni together. He studies science. I study art. We live at … at …

It had slipped away.

We live … at … in a … a …

Fuck!

She raced for something more concrete – his face – and saw it!

Quickly she sketched every detail she could capture onto her notepaper, even as it faded. *Red hair?* No, blond. Eyes – hazel, flecked with gold, warm with love.

Tears spilled down her cheeks as she held the memory close, etching it deep into her new reality as she drew – and it held – like an image remembered from a dream that is examined on waking. It left the dream and became part of the waking.

Frantically she sketched everything she could grab on to: a room, small and cosy, with a poster of Machu Picchu on the wall; a delicate silver bracelet; her mother, mature and serene; Richard, sad and hurting. She added them all to her haphazard collage, every image she could rescue, everything that didn't fit with the new firming reality, until there were no more.

Putting the pen down, she looked up at the room.

Her dad would be upset. He loved her. He was only looking out for her. He'd be worried.

She should call him back.

Reluctantly, she reached for her phone – and noticed again the dried blood on her hand.

Shower first! Explanations later.

It was a nice bathroom; nice room. Luxurious. Julie would be upset when she saw the credit card bill but she knew her father wouldn't want her in a cheap and nasty hotel. She shed her clothes, stepped into the shower and let the gush of hot water envelop her. Thrumming against her chilled skin, washing away the blood and the pain, it soothed some of her agitation. She opened her mouth to let the water flow in to rinse out the sour taste.

Had she been sick?

Vomiting onto the floor ... vomiting into a toilet in a constricted bathroom ...

Where was that?

She pushed the memory aside.

There were small bottles of shower gel, shampoo and conditioner lined up on a narrow marble shelf. She used them all – pouring, scrubbing, rubbing, rinsing and pouring again until the little bottles were empty. As she let the water cascade over her, reaching its heat into her, easing the knots in her muscles, she thought only of the warmth and the sweet smell of 'clean'.

When she'd finally had enough, she stepped out and scrubbed herself dry with the soft, white, hotel towels. Next, she brushed her teeth with the complimentary toothbrush and small tube of toothpaste before blow-drying her hair.

Refreshed and feeling much more stable, she walked back into the bedroom and hefted her overnight bag up onto the bed to get some clean underwear—

She hadn't brought a bag ... she hadn't brought any clean clothes ... not the first time.

The *first* time?

Memories peeped at her like the dim shapes of

strangers in another room.

There were *other* times?

The shapes began to clarify – voices whispered out of the darkness – faces began to form –

Allan!

She remembered him. Crisp and clear. And even though he was separated from her into a no-longer-existent past, unreachable except in her head, little details of her life with him filtered back to her and she clung to them. Other details too ... her Mum ... her *other* childhood ... Richard.

But mostly Allan. Her heart ached for him.

Did he remember too?

How could he? The Allan in this world would *only* know *this* world. He hadn't lived any other reality. She was alone, the only witness in the middle of a vortex, the only one who would remember that reality had ever been different.

A disturbing thought.

But, perhaps it made things easier? At least this way no one could judge the consequences of her actions except *her* – and what consequences there had been! Her mother was dead!

And Allan was lost to her.

Or was he?

He was her soul mate, surely that hadn't changed. The river was still there; it had only taken a different course.

She had to find him!

Naked, she searched for her phone. It was on the sideboard; and next to it, on several sheets of hotel stationery, was a sketched collage of images. She couldn't remember drawing them, but she knew they had to be hers; she recognised her style. Some of the images were of things and people she remembered – others were completely foreign.

That was frightening. In *this* transition, part of her seemed to have fallen into a void – some of her memories recovered, others not. Would they ever be retrieved? She hoped so, gaps were disturbing – but at least some memories of Allan remained intact.

Allan!

With trembling fingers, she keyed in his mobile number.

'Brooke speaking,' said a cheerful voice.

Horrified, Beth hung up.

No longer his number?

What else had changed? How would she find him?

She didn't have much to go on; without her, his life would be completely different, obviously had been. But she couldn't imagine he wouldn't still be good at science; university was still probable, and likely the same university. Maybe even the same address? Why not?

Facebook!

It didn't take long. His warm, intelligent face was soon grinning at her from his profile picture – but he was 'in a relationship'. Draped over his shoulders, laughing, with her arm extended for a selfie, was a redheaded girl with almond-shaped green eyes and a nose ring.

Beth's blood ran cold.

Her mind filled with images: *Allan's arms around her … his touch … his kiss … the scent of his skin … the sad love in his eyes …*

No more.

He wasn't hers any more. This was a *different* reality, an *alternate* reality. Now he belonged to that girl. *Facebook* girl. Half of her had been torn away – *his* half.

But not her memories of him – not her memories of their life together. Those remained to taunt her.

How could she live without him?

Despairing, she clicked on her own name. Her profile picture was a self-portrait she'd painted – abstract and fractured in rough, rude colours. The eyes were black – enormous and tortured. They took up the entire face. There was no mouth.

Underneath was a photograph of her father raising a glass in celebration at a recent birthday dinner. She was in that one too, in the background, but she barely recognised herself – her face looked different. Her eyes were heavily outlined in black and her lips were a garish red. It made her look wan. And there was a puffiness about her face, her cheeks were rounder.

Shocked, Beth raised her hands to her cheeks and stared at her reflection in the darkened window. She looked familiar now – but she didn't like what she saw – realised she'd never liked what she saw. She didn't look well.

Grimacing, she returned to the Facebook page.

She was wearing a tight black leather skirt with a skimpy top and looked defeated and bored – a signature look for her, but she *had* been bored that night. She remembered it well. She'd dressed like that mainly to annoy Julie, and it had succeeded – but she regretted the disappointment in her father's eyes.

She should call him.

But – Julie would know. She'd rail about the medication – force her to take it – make her father call the doctor …

Sour resentment swilled. She couldn't live with that woman any more. She shouldn't *have* to. This was not her real life: this was an *alternate* life! All of this life, every bit of it, was never meant to be. She was never supposed to have grown up with her father; it should never have happened—

… and it was all her fault.

The facts were unavoidable. It was *her* interference that had gotten her mother killed. It had changed all of time. *Everything! She'd* created this wreck of a life she'd been thrust into. She'd exchanged her mother's life for her father's … she'd *killed* her!

That realisation sent her spiralling into depression – a dangerous place to be in *this* new life. If she didn't hide it they'd lock her up for sure – but, then she thought, if I *made* this happen, I should also be able to *un*-make it; if I undid my father's death, I can undo my mother's!

A plan.

A calling.

She saw she really had no other choice – she'd initiated this change, so she had to *complete* it. She had to make it right.

And, there was only one way to do that now. If she couldn't stop her parents from going to the ATM, she'd have to stop their murderers!

Chapter 47

The gun hadn't been difficult. Beth had simply Googled semi-automatic rifles. It hadn't taken long to find a YouTube video featuring an elderly American lady firing one. She seemed to have been selected to demonstrate how easy this particular gun was to shoot. A good sign, because Beth had never even held a gun before, let alone fired one, and she didn't have time to learn. This YouTube clip was doubly useful because it was meant to be instructional as well as inspirational. There was a lot of footage demonstrating how to load and use the rifle, which was very helpful.

Beth watched it through a couple of times until she was confident she knew how to handle the gun and then saved a screenshot of a point that appeared safe to enter. She didn't anticipate it would be difficult to do what she needed to do, and it wasn't.

November, 2009, Huntington, Texas

She jumped quickly out of the way of the camera-man. He was weaving energetically around his subject – the old lady – keeping her in the frame of his hand-held camera as he danced for the best angles.

Invisibly, Beth moved over to the side to wait and watch.

There were only three people involved in the filming and it seemed a remote spot. They were in a field adjoining a small farmhouse surrounded by dense woods. The air had a crisp bite to it.

A few metres away a campsite had been set up under a magnificent oak, just a couple of brightly patterned foldable chairs, a picnic basket and some equipment. Two cars were parked close by, marking a territorial boundary like the circling of wagons. At the other end of the field was a target. The old lady was now taking pot shots at it under the instruction of a squared-jawed man in a checked flannel shirt. The cameraman, a younger copy of the 'director', orbited closer for detail shots of the gun.

Only the old lady held a weapon, but Beth could see other guns and ammunition by the oak. Unattended, they were an easy steal. Without wasting time, Beth walked behind the tree, materialised, grabbed a gun and a case of ammunition, and exited.

* * *

She'd taken the extra ammunition for practice, but quickly dropped that idea. It would be too time-consuming and she didn't have enough strength left to travel through a photograph to a safe place to practice. She needed what strength she had left for this last mission. Her body was already telling her she should rest, take time to recover, a couple of days at least – but she had no time to waste; her father would be looking for her. She had to get on with it.

At least her thinking was less scattered. Memories continued to shuffle, out of sequence and sometimes mixed together so that she still couldn't quite discern which life they came from, but that was no worry because she didn't intend to keep this reality long anyway. Soon she'd construct another. She was as ready as she could be and as ready as she needed to be. She could load and fire the gun and she didn't need to be accurate in firing it. She only needed to scare the gang away; she didn't plan on hitting any of them. No gang – no murders. *Both* her parents would be safe.

She brought up the map again on her phone and went over her route one last time, making sure she had it committed to memory. At least she could remember the details of her previous journeys, particularly the entries. That was important.

Nothing else to do – she put down the phone, picked up the gun and reached for the photograph of Alexander Reilly leaving the nightclub.

7.45 p.m., Tuesday evening, January 14, 1992

Without materialising, she weaved off to the side, dodging the thin girl as before.

Turning back, she saw her previous self being tripped

over. She didn't wait to see anything more. Holding the gun close to her chest, she sprinted off towards George Street. It was heavy, and she was disturbingly light-headed, little spots flickered annoyingly in front of her eyes, but still she made good time. She was certain she got there well before her previous selves.

The intersection of George and Hay was busier and better lit than further down at Sussex – George Street was a major artery during business hours – but at this time on a Tuesday night, things were still fairly slow. Cars only passed in fits and starts. There was an open pub on the corner but it was quiet and contained and all the shops in the vicinity were closed. It seemed fairly safe, but there was no place to hide. The only coverage was a couple of ornate wooden posts belonging to the verandah that stretched along the length of the street. They were thick and would shield her from the street, but not from anyone exiting the pub.

It wouldn't do to be caught lingering outside a pub with a semi-automatic rifle.

Beth decided to remain invisible for the wait. She'd need to materialise before firing the gun, but she had a clear view down Hay Street and up and down George Street and, while she hadn't seen where the gang came from last time, she knew they had to have come from one of those streets. She'd see them coming. She'd just need to be ready – and she'd need to be *quick*.

Hopefully, she'd be able to scare them away even before her parents left the restaurant.

Hopefully, that wouldn't be long, the lurking nausea wasn't lifting.

Nervously, she stroked the trigger of the gun. The

muscles across her shoulders were burning and her pulse was racing. Her senses were ramped to hyper-alert. But the streets in front of her remained deserted – until a black shadow streaked across Hay Street towards the Sussex Street ATM. She couldn't see the ATM from where she was positioned, but she recognised the sound of shattering metal and remembered obliterating the machine.

The memory chaffed. It was so soaked in failure. As distant as childhood, it still pierced like a nail, hammering deeper and deeper with each resonating blow. She tightened, wishing it to end, and eventually it did, as abruptly as it had begun.

Silence rushed into the vacuum.

There was now one less version of her in this moment of time. The Sussex Street ATM was gone.

Gulping at the air, she realised she'd been holding her breath and tried once more to relax.

It was all happening now – down on Sussex Street, she'd be waiting to approach her father, and in the Ming Cha she'd be standing invisibly in the corner watching her parents finish their last meal – or maybe she was already in the toilet? Was she already speaking with her mother, trying to convince her?

It was difficult to mark the passage of time …

She moved to stand behind the nearest post and braced for action.

It wouldn't be long.

Soon they'd come. They were already out there, somewhere in the vicinity. Soon, they'd reach the intersection – and then shortly after that, her father would arrive.

That was her window of opportunity. *She'd have to be quick!*

Again, unbidden, gory images assaulted her, rushing in to remind her of the consequences should she fail, memories that didn't belong in this life, that she hoped wouldn't belong in the next. Shaking her head, she tried to flick them away. She forced her focus back to the present, back to the streets in front of her.

Still empty.

Her head now felt like it was being slowly pierced, squeezed between two giant pincers. A sharp pain pulsed from the back of her head to somewhere deep behind her right ear and nausea swilled treacherously. She wasn't sure, but she couldn't remember it ever being this bad before, not when she was invisible …

Something was wrong.

But it was too late to worry about that. She stamped her feet to dispel the dizziness and ignored the tremble that crept into her fingers – and suddenly she heard them – heard them before she saw them – a shout – the smashing of a bottle.

She looked down Hay Street and saw them – five of them – faceless in the night – moving up out of Thomas Street at the junction of Sussex and Hay. They loitered by the corner opposite the Sussex Street ATM … and then all at once became alert.

Her father must have reached the ATM.

Physicalising, she raised the gun and aimed it in the gang's direction, just above their heads – but then they broke into a run, loping off across the street – and Beth saw her father, rounding the corner and heading her way.

She swung back to the gang, and as she did so, the

gun went off. She hadn't pulled the trigger, not intentionally, but the effect was as desired in any case. The gang halted, alarmed. Fury possessed her. She aimed the semi-automatic over their heads and fired again – three – four – five times – and they scattered, melting into the surrounding streets as her shots chased after them. She squealed in giddy triumph. She'd routed them! She'd *won!* She'd chased them away – back into the darkness where they belonged – rats, back into the sewer – and the horrible tragedy in her past, her *original* past, had finally been erased. Now there'd be a *new* past, a *better* past – and a new future! She could hardly wait to discover it.

But – somewhere … someone … was screaming. A ripping, agonised cry.

Beth looked back; vaguely irritated that the screamer was unaware she'd just rescued them from danger.

Until she saw it was her mother.

Until she saw the cause of her distress.

On the ground, his head torn open like a shattered melon, lay her father in a pool of blood.

Chapter 48

'Fuck!' Allan screamed, kicking the bed as hard as he could. It helped a little, released a little of his wretchedness, but he'd have to kick down the whole building to get rid of it all. And that would solve nothing. He gritted his teeth and roared – and nearly had a heart attack when an urgent knocking started up at the door.

Had he been that loud?

Whoever it was, he didn't want to deal with them now – but the knocking persisted.

'All right! All right! I'm coming!' he yelled and stormed to the door. Yanking it open, ready to throw his frustration at whoever it was forcing their way in on him, his aggression fizzled when he saw Detective Blaine standing there.

'Is Beth available?' Blaine asked politely, giving no indication of having heard the angry outburst. Allan's chin rose.

'No. And I don't know where she is or when she'll be back. You can try her mobile if you like, but she's not answering.'

Worry creased across Blaine's broad forehead – and Allan had calmed enough to read it. 'Why do you want to talk to her?' he asked apprehensively.

Blaine hesitated. 'Can I come in?'

'I guess …' Allan's mind raced to catastrophe as he stood aside. 'What is it? Why do you want Beth?'

Blaine turned around. 'I just want to talk to her. I wouldn't normally have considered this, because it's … But, well considering what Beth can…'

'What?' Allan was impatient now.

Blaine sighed. 'Can we sit?'

Reluctantly, Allan gestured towards the couch. Blaine sat and waited for Allan to take the chair opposite. 'Beth came to me last week,' he said soberly, meeting Allan's eyes with an uncharacteristic openness. 'She was asking for the files on her father's murder. She said she just wanted to know what happened, and I thought she had a right to know. There were no photographs. I gathered she was going to try to find one, but that didn't seem likely and—'

'She did. She found one.' Allan spat it out in accusation, but regretted it as he saw his confirmation clicking into place behind Blaine's eyes.

'Allan … I need to ask. Does Beth have access to a gun? Specifically, an assault rifle?'

'What? No! Of course not. She's never even fired a gun. We've never done anything like that.'

Blaine's grey eyes bored into his. 'An M16A2 semi-automatic rifle was found at the scene of her father's murder: the murder weapon. It raised a few questions at the time because the serial number didn't exist. Investigators assumed it was a counterfeit, but … after I spoke with Beth … I took another look. The gun wasn't a counterfeit, Allan. It was stolen from a privately registered owner in Huntington, Texas. In November 2009.'

Allan's mouth gaped.

'Where is she, Allan?' Blaine asked gently. 'Tell me this isn't her.'

But Allan could only shake his head stupidly.

'Allan—'

'No!' Allan struggled to his feet and backed away. 'No … she wouldn't do that … there must be some mistake.'

Blaine stood too, but he kept his stance calm. 'There's no mistake, Allan.'

'There has to be! She wouldn't! Why would she?'

'That's what I was hoping she could tell me. Allan, I'm just wanting to talk to her, to find out what happened—'

'She was trying to save him! She was trying to stop it!'

'With a gun?'

'No! I told you, she doesn't know anything about guns.'

'But she *was* going back – trying to change things?'

'It didn't work! She went back, and smashed the ATM – with a *sledgehammer*, not a gun. So her father couldn't use it. But then he went around the corner to another ATM and they killed him anyway. *They* killed him. Not *her. She* didn't kill anyone.'

'She told you that?'

'Yes!'

'And then she went back again?'

'She didn't *kill* him! Why would she? That's crazy!'

Blaine raised his hands. 'I'm just trying to find out what happened. Maybe it was accidental, or maybe the gang got hold of the gun – but whatever happened, if Beth took that gun back there I need to know.'

Allan turned away.

'Listen, Allan, this is a cold case. I only looked into it because Beth asked me to – but it wasn't hard for me to find the stolen weapons' report, and if she keeps stirring this up, others could find it too. I *need* to talk with her.'

Allan reached his hands up to clasp them behind the back of his head, bringing his elbows forwards to hide his face, as though attempting to prevent reality from penetrating further.

'I should have stopped her,' he said brokenly. 'I tried – but she wouldn't listen. Oh, God! Oh, God!' Tears sprang into his eyes. He looked like he might shatter.

'I'm not going to arrest her, Allan,' Blaine said gently. 'I just want to talk to her. I'm trying to *protect* her. Where *is* she?'

'I don't know – honestly, I don't. She left last night after I was asleep. She won't answer her phone. I tried the hospitals …'

Blaine felt a cold flush. 'She hasn't come back?'

Allan shook his head miserably, then stiffened. 'You … don't think …'

'Does it normally take this long? When she … goes into a picture?'

'No … but I … I don't know what she's doing … she had her mother's photograph album with her – she might have just been wanting to see her.'

Blaine had the horrible premonition he'd be searching for Beth among the unidentified bodies found in
1992. 'Let's just concentrate on finding her for now,' he
said. 'Haven't you got any idea where she might have
gone?'

'No … no … she—'

'Money? Does she have cash with her?'

'She has her card – but no transactions are listed yet.
I checked.'

He was shaking and Blaine gave his shoulder a gentle
squeeze. 'Let me try.'

Allan nodded. He went into the bedroom, came out
with Beth's computer and set it up on the kitchen table.
With a few clicks, he brought up Beth's account.

This time, a new transaction was there. The hotel
had processed their accounts.

* * *

The door slammed open on a dreadful scene. Beth
was lying on the floor, face-down in a pool of vomit, still.

Blaine leapt to her, flipping her over as he yelled for
the hotel manager to call an ambulance.

Allan stood dazed by the doorway – watching –
impotent – as Blaine checked to make sure Beth was
breathing and dragged the cover from the bed to wipe
her unconscious face clean. She began to cough, and he
rolled her onto her side, offering soft encouragements.

None of what he said registered with Allan.

When the paramedics arrived, Allan was pushed
aside as they rushed to Beth, and ignored when they

bundled her on to a trolley and wheeled her out.

Blaine might have spoken to him ... he couldn't be sure – but somehow he ended up in Blaine's car again – and then at the hospital.

Hours passed. Allan barely noticed. He was surprised when he saw it was 9.36 p.m. – but his legs were stiff and his mouth was dry and there were no more thoughts to think, no more scenarios to hypothesise over, no more fears to feel – so he knew the clock must be accurate. His eyes rested tiredly on the coffee machine in the corner of the small lounge he'd been left in to wait. He was thirsty, but he didn't want tea or coffee. They'd told him where the cafeteria was, but he didn't dare leave, not even for a moment. What if they came for him?

His eyes wandered again to the clock on the wall.

Had they forgotten he was there?

He hadn't seen any hospital staff since he'd arrived. Blaine had been in at some stage, but he hadn't been forthcoming and hadn't stayed long, and that was a while ago. The room had been starkly empty ever since. Exhausted, Allan dropped his head into his hands. Sleep was threatening to take him, but worry refused to let him go.

'You can see her now.'

A nurse was standing in the doorway. She was young but crisply competent and her smile was sympathetic.

'Is she OK?'

'She will be. Down the corridor and first on the right. Go straight in – they're expecting you.'

Blood tingled into Allan's stagnant limbs as he followed her instructions. It felt good to be on his feet, to be walking. Good to be included, to be able to see her at last. *Good to know she was going to be OK!*

He had no difficulty finding the ward. Pushing open the door, he stood in the entrance and scanned the room, searching for Beth. The room was quietly busy. Nurses in soft-soled shoes padded efficiently between the beds, adjusting and monitoring. On the bed nearest Allan, a middle-aged man with sallow complexion and sweat-soaked hair breathed heavily through a slackly gaping mouth, wheezing slightly on the exhale; and next to him, a distressed elderly woman was being tended to by two nurses. Her fragile moans spilled over the mattress and spattered to the floor as she thrashed weakly against their care. Allan had never been in a hospital before. He found it unsettling.

'Allan?'

The query came from an older nurse behind the desk at the nurses' station. Her face was coarse-featured with a reassuring wholesomeness; her eyes were authoritative but welcoming. He nodded and she smiled and indicated the corner bed where Beth lay. Relieved, and yet at the same time petrified, Allan girded himself and wobbled down the aisle between the beds towards her.

She was chalky pale against the white linen and so tiny in the high metal bed. Tubes snaked into her arm and electronic equipment glowed announcements of her vital statistics. The technology frightened him. The whole room seemed full of threat. It reeked of powerlessness and death. Hushed into silence, he stood uncertain, wondering if he should wake her – or if he even could. She was as still as death. He could barely detect a breath. Her eyes were closed, her long dark lashes rested limp against the ghostly white of her cheek – but as he hesitated, her eyes fluttered open. They were dull at first, but when she registered it was him, life flickered into them.

Holding out her arms, her chin began to wobble. 'Allan!'

Her voice was barely audible. She looked shattered – broken – terrified.

Allan dragged a chair to the side of her bed and reached through the tubes to comfort her as best he could. Her fingers caught his and pulled them weakly to her chest, holding his hand close, as tears began to trickle down her cheeks. With his free hand, he tenderly wiped them away. 'Oh, Beth …'

'When did we meet?' she whispered hoarsely, the effort clearly taxing her.

Allan's mind went blank.

Her fingers tightened around his urgently. 'When?' she insisted. 'How long have we known each other, Allan?'

He had no idea where this was headed. 'We met in high school. We've known each other forever.'

'And you lived in your mother's flat? Alone?'

'… Yes.'

'And I went to the moon launch for us?'

'Yes. Beth, what is this—?'

'Is my mother … did she die of a stroke?'

'Yes. Eight months ago. Beth, why—?'

'And my father, he died when I was a baby? Stabbed?'

Allan was getting scared. 'He was shot, Beth. You know that.'

Frantically, she dug under her pillow, twisting painfully in a desperate search.

The nurse glanced up from her station.

'Beth, what are you doing? Don't hurt yourself.' Allan tried gently to distract her, but she persisted until she managed to pull out some scraps of paper and thrust a crumpled copy of a newspaper article into his hands. Only then did she lie back, drained and wan.

With a nervous glance at the nurse, Allan folded out the paper to stare uncomprehendingly at the stark headline.

YOUNG MOTHER SLAIN AT CITY ATM

'Mother?' He looked at her wonderingly.

'I brought it with me,' she said. 'If I hadn't, it would have changed, like the other newspaper articles. But, because it was with me, it didn't.'

He looked even more confused.

'You don't remember, do you?' She said sadly.

It wasn't a question, and Allan had no answer. He only gaped at her. She was the only one who knew about the alternate histories; the only one who'd *lived* through *all* of them.

It had to stop. This new Allan – so like the *first* Allan except that in his memory her father had been shot; not stabbed – would have to be the *last* Allan. She couldn't risk losing him again. The past must *stay* as it was *now*. Forever. No more going back; no more trying to change it. *This* history must be her *only* history from now on; *this* Allan, her *only* Allan.

But this Allan needed to know.

He needed to know *everything*.

'I went back.' She hesitated. 'I tried to save my dad … but then Mum got killed instead – and when I got back, the whole of everything had changed. I'd been brought up by Dad, and his horrible new wife – and we weren't together; you didn't even know me. We hadn't met.' She searched his eyes. 'But I remembered. I remembered when we were together – and I drew what I could remember so I wouldn't forget.' She pushed another piece of paper into his hands, the piece of paper with her sketches of Allan, their bedroom, her silver bracelet, her mother and Richard.

'That's our home, isn't it?' Fear and hope clung together in her words. 'That's where we live … isn't it?'

Allan stared down at the delicate illustrations, recognising all of them, and nodded.

'Then it's all back the same.' She let out a feeble sigh. 'Except for Dad being shot …'

The gun!

Allan straightened in the chair and took her hands in his. 'Beth, Blaine is here … he was asking about a gun that was left at the scene of your father's murder. Beth … you didn't …?'

Pain splashed across her face. '*I did.*'

Her voice was small, almost inaudible. She shrank back into the sheets. 'I went back again. I couldn't let Mum die … I stole a gun – so I could scare off those bastards and save *both* of them. I only wanted to scare them … but I missed.' Her tears began to flow again. 'I *shot* him, Allan. *I* shot *Dad!* I *killed* him. It was *me*. If I hadn't—'

'Shhh …' Allan's response was instinctive. He drew in as close as the tubes would allow, terrified of hurting her, unable to let her suffer alone. And gently he wiped her tears away and lifted her face to show her the love in his own. 'It's all right. You gotta let it go now.' His voice was cracking. 'You gotta let it go, Beth.' With her, there had never been any choice for him. Whatever she'd done, whatever she *would* do, there was nowhere else he belonged. Tears stung into his eyes, long held back. They joined with hers as he laid his cheek carefully against hers, resting into her pain, letting go of his own as she wrapped her arms around him.

* * *

Blaine watched from the nurses' station, his expression deep and thoughtful. He'd never covered up a homicide before, but how could you prosecute someone for a killing that happened twenty years before they'd committed it? And no one had been falsely convicted; there was no wrong to right. It was an accident – and Beth had surely paid for it; would continue to pay for it …

Blaine felt a surge of pity for her.

But she was dangerous too. She'd proved it. Foreboding coloured his thoughts as he watched the young couple clinging desperately to each other at the far end of the ward. All he could do was hope she'd learnt her lesson.

Shaking his head, Blaine turned and walked away.

* * *

Acknowledgements

This book would not be here without the support and contributions of many special people, for which I am very grateful.

First and foremost, my patient and loving husband whose belief in me and constant encouragement kept me inching forward.

Special thanks also to my family and friends who endured early read-throughs and offered generous feedback; to Sue Bonaretti, Ruth Carter, Susan Korrel, Abigail Nathan and Kate O'Donnell who all contributed editing input; Kylie Castor, for many coffee catch-ups that gave me clarity and kept me buoyant; to my children who allowed me to borrow from their experience; to my nephew, Jason Loewenthal, who helped with the Spanish and my niece, Lia Loewenthal who photographed the cover.

Special thanks also to Gulnara Samoilova, whose amazing photographs inspired me, and whose encouragement was much appreciated.

Many thanks!

About the author

Born in Canada, Jini Liljeqvist was educated in Sydney, Australia and has spent many years working in theatre in the USA, Canada, the UK, Europe and Australia.

A produced playwright and screenwriter, Jini has also published a number of short stories as well as educational articles. She now lives with her husband in the Tweed Valley, NSW, where she writes, gardens, sculpts, enjoys yoga and manages an educational publishing company.

Fantasy has always fascinated Jini. She delights in the 'what ifs' and is always seeking to go beyond what can be seen. Above all, she loves a good mystery.

She'd love to hear from you. You can contact her at:

www.jinililjeqvist.com
jini@jinililjeqvist.com